from
ASHES
to
FLAMES

USA Today Bestselling Author

A.M. HARGROVE

First Edition

Cover design by Letitia @ *RBA Designs* | *Romantic Book Affairs*

Editing by *Gray Ink*

Proofreading by *Petra Gleason*

"Angry people are not always wise."

— Jane Austen, Pride and Prejudice

Stalk A.M. Hargrove

If you would like to hear more about what's going on in my world, please subscribe to my mailing list on my website at http://bit.ly/29j74CX

You can also join my private group—Hargrove's Hangout— on Facebook if you're up to some crazy shenanigans!

Please stalk me. I'll love you forever if you do. Seriously.

www.amhargrove.com

Twitter @amhargrove1

www.facebook.com/amhargroveauthor

www.facebook.com/anne.m.hargrove

www.goodreads.com/amhargrove1

Instagram: amhargroveauthor

Pinterest: amhargrove1

annie@amhargrove.com

For Other Books by A.M. Hargrove visit www.amhargrove.com

For The Love of English

For The Love of My Sexy Geek (The Vault)

A Special Obsession

Chasing Vivi

Craving Midnight

I'll Be Waiting (The Vault)

From Ashes to Flames

From Ice to Flames (summer 2018)

From Smoke to Flames (fall 2018)

Cruel and Beautiful

A Mess of a Man

One Wrong Choice

A Beautiful Sin

The Wilde Players Dirty Romance Series:

Sidelined

Fastball

Hooked

Worth Every Risk

The Edge Series:

Edge of Disaster

Shattered Edge

Kissing Fire

The Tragic Duet:

Tragically Flawed, Tragic 1

Tragic Desires, Tragic 2

The Hart Brothers Series:

Freeing Her, Book 1

Freeing Him, Book 2

Kestrel, Book 3

The Fall and Rise of Kade Hart

Sabin, A Seven Novel

The Guardians of Vesturon Series

Chapter One

GREYDON

SUSANNAH SHOVED the crying baby into my arms as our son protested the absence of his mother's embrace. Gently cradling him, I kissed his head and rubbed my cheek against the downy fuzz on top. I loved the softness of it and couldn't help but notice the contrast between the two of us—my scruffy beard and slightly calloused hands and his soft, velvety skin. Inhaling his scent, I smiled, loving his baby scent.

"You sure you want to go? I mean isn't this trip going to be tough on you."

A soft chuckle came from the closet, where she'd disappeared. "You're the one who's going to have it tough."

She was probably right. I'd be here with a four-month-old and our six-year-old daughter. It was a good thing my mother was coming to help. I was used to handling it with my daughter, but adding our four-month-old son would create a new spin on things.

"True, but traveling so soon after maternity leave. I mean that's quite a bit to take on."

She rushed out of the closet with her packed rolling bag and laughed. "Might as well get used to it. I did it after Kinsley. There's no reason to think I can't do it with Aaron too."

"No, that's not what I meant."

She paused and gave me that look, the one with only one brow raised. I'd always wondered how she managed that. "Well?"

"I was only thinking that you're jumping in too fast."

"Come on, Grey. You know me better than that. I was off for twelve weeks and have been back for a month now. This is the first trip I'll be taking. I usually travel once a week."

She was right. "Yeah, I know. I guess I've gotten used to having you around."

She walked up to me, grabbed my face, and planted a chaste kiss on my cheek. "I hope you didn't get spoiled. You know staying home was never part of my plans."

"True." I was far from spoiled, but I didn't mention that. Her career was important to her and one of the things that attracted me to her in the first place. Susannah exuded confidence in everything she did. She worked for one of the big hotel chains and had risen up the ranks. The problem was the rise brought a shit load of travel, which I wasn't fond of. It took her away from the kids, even though I loved handling the home front. But I wanted to see her succeed and didn't say a thing about it when it started happening. "It just seems like you can't wait to get out of here. If I didn't know any better, I'd think you were rushing off to meet someone." I was joking, of course. I trusted her explicitly.

Her eyes avoided me as she let out a cackle and said,

"Guess I'll have to make it up to you when I get back." She slid a manicured nail down my arm. Susannah was great at avoiding my comments.

"Hey, I'm holding you to that."

Walking to the small desk in the corner of our expansive room, she quickly stuffed her laptop into a messenger bag and grabbed the charger putting it into the bag as well.

"You have your phone charger and mobile battery?" I asked.

"Yep, and I think that's everything. I'll text you when I land."

I juggled Aaron in one arm and hugged her with the other. "I'll miss you every minute you're gone."

"Same here, Grey. Love you." She gave me a quick peck on the cheek, which was surprising, considering she'd be gone all week. I handed Aaron to her and carried her bag down to the waiting car that would take her to the airport. The car sped off as Aaron and I watched it go. Dawn hadn't broken yet, but I would soon have to wake Kinsley up for school.

———

THE MORNING WAS HECTIC, but I managed to make it to work on time for my first appointment.

As I walked into the back entrance of the building, my nurse asked, "Morning, Dr. West. How was your weekend?"

"Great Nicole. I hope yours was too." I kept moving until I got to my private office. I donned my starched lab coat and checked my emails. Nothing urgent in there, so I quickly checked my investments when Nicole informed me what the day ahead held. Then I scanned the office computer to see the charts of my patients.

"Mr. Parton went to the ER last night. Chest pain. They admitted him. Dr. Goldsmith saw him since he was on call and they cathed him. He has another blockage. Looks like he's going to need CABG." CABG—coronary artery bypass graft—was a big surgery for someone with Mr. Parton's debilitating health issues, which concerned me.

"Did Goldsmith call in this morning?" I asked.

"Yes, sir. He wants to talk to you ASAP."

"He's not coming in?" John Goldsmith was one of the partners in our cardiology practice.

"Not until around noon."

"Okay, thanks, Nicole."

I jumped on a call with Goldsmith. "John. What happened with Parton?"

"Oh, man. His LAD is ninety percent blocked. Not to mention he has restenosis with the stent he has. Five of his arteries are greater than sixty. He's a train wreck."

"Right, but he's not a candidate for CABG. Have you looked at his total picture? I don't think he'd survive the surgery."

John began, "He's older but ..."

"Failing kidneys, post-stroke, and that's only the beginning. If they graft him, they'll never stabilize him afterward. He may survive the surgery, but the post-surgical arrhythmias would probably kill him."

"Fuck, Grey, why wasn't any of that charted?"

"It is. I'm looking at it on the computer now."

"I didn't see it and I combed through everything last night."

"When you get to the office, check his chart. I'm not sure what's being transferred via electronic medical records to the hospital, but it should all be in there."

"Yeah, okay."

"Are you still at the hospital?" I asked.

"No. I'm home. Why?"

"He needs to have stents. We can't risk him having an MI." A myocardial infarction spelled certain death for Mr. Parton.

"You're right. How's your patient load this morning?"

"Heavy. Let me see who's on call to do it. Thanks, man."

Electronic medical records were supposed to solve all the problems of missing medical information. It sure did miss the mark on Mr. Parton.

All morning I was swamped but finally broke away for a fifteen-minute lunch. I checked my emails while I scarfed down a sandwich. One was from an Allie Gordon, but I ignored it because I didn't really have time. I was back in the saddle until three, when George called. He was the other partner on call.

"Update on Parton for you. We've got him stabilized after the stents. That LAD was dicey, man. He's stable now but there's no guarantee with it. You know what I'm saying?"

"I do. He's lucky though. With that kind of blockage, he could've had the big one."

John agreed. "They don't call it the widow maker for nothing."

I was finally winding down the day, dismissing my last patient, when Nicole, met me in the hall.

Grabbing my arm, she tugged me to the side and said, "Uh, there's a woman in the waiting room. She says it's urgent and needs to see you. She looks really upset. Says it's a personal matter. Linda tried to turn her away, but she started crying."

Linda was the front desk receptionist and was great at handling people. If this woman was still here, Linda must've thought it was important enough for her to see me.

"Did she leave a name?"

"Yes. Allie Gordon."

"Okay. Send her to my office. I'll be there in a second."

After a quick bathroom break, I headed to my office. A woman close to my age sat there. Her eyes were red and swollen making it obvious she'd been crying.

"Can I help you?"

"Hi, I'm Allie Gordon."

"Grey West."

"Yes, we've met. Our spouses work together."

As soon as those words left her mouth, she sobbed. Shit, what the hell was going on?

"Mrs. Gordon, are you okay? Can I get you some water?"

She shook her head. "I didn't know what else to do, but I knew you ought to know the truth. Here." She handed me a large, thick manila envelope. I stared at it, unclear as to what it was. "You should probably open it. It will make more sense when you do."

I tore it open to solve the mystery. The first thing I saw was a letter. It was from Allie to me. So I read it.

DEAR DR. WEST:

For months I suspected my husband was having an affair. After many unanswered questions, I decided to hire a private investigator. He uncovered much more than I ever imagined. Since our spouses work together and after learning what I did, I thought it was only fair you should know too. I hired him a year ago. He uncovered things from over two years ago. Evidently, this has been going on for quite some time.

I am deeply sorry.

Allie Gordon

INSIDE WERE PICTURES, lots of them, and a thumb drive. I was not prepared in the least for what I was about to see. The pictures were damning. Susannah and Allie's husband were embracing, kissing, doing things that punched me straight in the sternum, stomping the air out of me. My hands shook as I held the stack of them. They would've brought me to my knees if I hadn't been sitting.

I cleared my throat, forcing the bile back down into my gut. "You said over two years?" I hardly recognized my voice.

"Yes."

My tone was dead, lifeless as I asked, "Does your husband travel?"

"He left this morning for the week. I assume your wife did too." She dabbed her eyes with a tissue.

I nodded, numb with pain. A blade of fire ripped through my heart, but it didn't stop there. It was gutting me wide open, leaving me to bleed all over the damn place.

And then I stopped. "We have a four-month-old." The words rasped through my lips like desert air. I dropped my head in mortification. *Oh shit. Oh fuck, fuck, fuck. Aaron could be his son.*

"I know." I raised my head and gazed into watery eyes filled with pity.

Two hands fisted my hair. I stifled the urge to scream in fury … and frustration.

Mrs. Gordon asked if I was okay.

"Fuck no, I'm not okay," I moaned.

Her mouth briefly hung open before it slammed shut. Then she asked, "Is there anything I can do? I know exactly how you feel."

She was trying to help, to be kind, but I was lost in another dimension. I only shook my head in response. My emotions were an amalgamation of disgust, hurt, mortification, and fury. How could Susannah possibly have done this to our family ... our *children*? Hadn't she stopped to consider the ramifications it would have on them? I already knew the answer to that.

Gathering all the evidence on my desk, I tore off my lab coat and without another word to Mrs. Gordon, I stormed out and headed for home. I needed to speak to my attorney and fast. Plans had to be made. Drastic ones. My cheating wife was going to learn what it felt like to be financially ruined. By the time she returned home on Friday, the locks would be changed on the house, and our bank accounts would be emptied. She fucked over the wrong guy.

Only that's not what happened. Little did I know those plans wouldn't be necessary.

Later that night I received a phone call that changed everything. Susannah and her co-worker, her lover, never made it to their final destination. Karma is a cruel bitch. Their plane crashed somewhere over the Pacific on its final approach into Seattle. There were no survivors. I never got the chance to vent my anger ... to tell her the affair she'd been having for over two years had been exposed. I never had the opportunity to question why she had done such a terrible thing to our family and marriage. And I never had the chance see her expression when I asked her whether or not Aaron was my son.

Chapter Two

GREYDON

RESENTMENT ... outrage and utter misery filled every pore as I listened in stony silence to the minister eulogize my wife. He sang her praises about how she was a star in the community, always willing to lend a hand to those in need. The bitter part of me thought how she lent not one, but both of them, along with her mouth and the rest of her body, to her co-worker. Those thoughts swirled around exactly what those hands did and I ground my teeth even more. Would I ever get past this when the object of my anger was no longer walking the earth? But then the good times we had, the family we created came to mind, and grief nearly slammed me to my knees. I was gut punched from the inside out, repeatedly. When would the pain cease? Mom squeezed one arm as my daughter clung to the opposite hand. I hired a babysitter to watch over Aaron. The day was overwhelming enough, but with him here, I probably would've lost it.

The church was packed with my colleagues as well as Susannah's. My mother-in-law sobbed non-stop, and at times I wanted to shake her, to tell her the truth about her daughter, but I wasn't that big of a dick. She'd been through enough already, losing her husband to cancer a few years ago. And now this. Thank God she'd moved to California to be with her sister and other daughter.

It was a miracle I made it through the service, all things considered. Kinsley kept asking when her mommy was coming home. Explaining death to a six-year-old was next to impossible.

"Remember how I told you Mommy went to live with the angels?"

Her pigtails swung as she bobbed her head.

"Well, sweetie, I'm afraid that means she won't be coming back here to live with us."

"But who's gonna rub my tummy when it hurts?" Oh, God, this was brutal. It was monumentally painful to see your daughter look at you with tears in her eyes, wondering why her mommy left. Why did this happen? I would take Susannah back, affair and all, just to allow my little girl to have her mother back.

Grabbing her hands, I said, "I will, polka dot. I'll always be here for you. You're my little marshmallow— soft, sweet, and good enough to eat." And I kissed her chubby cheek and damned my wife again. My heart punched through my ribs, aching like hell for my sweet little girl as she stared at me through eyes exactly like Susannah's. They were the first things I noticed about Susannah— hazel rimmed in gold— and I hit on her trying to be cool. I wasn't and she called me on it. It was during my medical school days, so I threw some ophthalmology bullshit at her, but she was far too astute to buy it.

"Come on, Slick, you can do better than that," she said.

Seriously! *"Then how's this? I've been lusting after you from across the room and it's taken me all night to work up the nerve just to speak to you."*

The gold in her eyes sparkled as her mouth curved up. "Much better. I'll take an honest man any day."

We were married a year and a half later and I figured it would be the two of us forever. Guess I figured wrong. And how the hell could I have been *that* wrong? How did I miss the signs? Where had it all gone south? Was I that naive or was I so involved with work that I just buried my head in the sand? But thinking back, I was the one who was more engaged at home, and I worked at *not* being that workaholic husband. I handled most of the things for the kids. In fact, she was the one who spent more hours working than I did. She had the best of everything—jewelry, clothing, cars, because I was the one who bought it all for her. I went out of my way to make sure flowers waited for her in her hotel room when she traveled, which really pissed me off now. She probably got a huge kick out of that as she fucked her little boyfriend while my flowers sat in the room staring at the two of them. Shit. I rubbed my face, still trying to compute the shambles of our lives. And that honesty line she threw at me back then. What utter bullshit.

The funeral service ended and we filed out of the church. Since Susannah was being cremated, there was no graveside service, thank God. We were receiving guests at my parents' home afterward. I couldn't deal with doing it at my place, so Mom handled everything. I wasn't sure of a single thing I said that day. All I saw were those fucking pictures and videos on the flash drive that replayed through my brain.

How long had that affair been going on? Susannah worked with him for years but the PI only had evidence going back a couple of years. That doesn't mean they weren't together before then. Kinsley was definitely my daughter. Other than the eyes, she was a dead ringer for me—hair, nose, she even had my long fingers. We always said she was going to be tall like her daddy. But Aaron is a different story. What was she thinking? Did he wear a condom every time? Looking at Aaron, it was difficult to tell. He looked a lot like Susannah—soft curly hair and that nose of his. What if he wasn't mine? What would I do? *Fuck.*

"Grey, I think you need to take a month off." It was John, one of my partners, talking.

"Uh, I don't think so."

"You need to spend some time with your kids and process this."

How would I even begin to do that? "Maybe."

"All of us at the practice have talked and we can bring in a locum tenens to take your place for a while. It's why we took out that insurance policy— in case something like this ever happened."

"Yeah but getting back to work might do me good too."

He grabbed my shoulder. "Listen, you don't want to get in there and fuck up a procedure."

He made a good point. "Let me think about it and let you know."

Later, after everyone left, Mom suggested she come and help me every day. "You'll need a hand with Aaron and even more so when you go back to work." Jesus, it plowed into me that I'd be on my own on a permanent basis now.

Both of my brothers were there. My youngest one, Pearson, said, "She's right, Grey. Let Mom help. It won't be easy doing this on your own."

The middle one, Hudson, said, "Listen to them, man. Accept the help when it's offered. Raising kids alone is hard."

"You would know, wouldn't you?" Hudson was a single dad too. His ex walked out on him, leaving him to raise his son alone.

"Yeah, I would. Take it from me, man. Besides, Mom loves being around the kids," Hudson said.

"Let me give it some thought, Mom."

"Maybe you should hire an au pair. That's what I have," Hudson said.

Groaning, I asked, "Dammit, would you all just give me a little time to wrap my head around this shit?"

Pearson came to my rescue. "He's right everyone. This is all so new to him, he hasn't had a chance to process. Give him some time."

Mom pressed a fist to her lips. I immediately regretted my outburst. "Grey, I'm only trying to help," she said.

"I know, Mom, but like Pearson said, I need some time. Please," I snapped. I felt bad for the way I reacted, but my brain was swimming with so much shit right now. Susannah's company had contacted me to discuss some things—something about accidental death and dismemberment since she died on a business trip. I would be meeting them tomorrow.

"I have to meet Susannah's HR rep to discuss the terms of her accidental death policy."

Pearson spoke up again. "If you need a hand, let me know." He was an attorney so his services might come in handy.

"I will. Thanks, man."

After thanking and hugging everyone, Kinsley and I left for home.

When we walked in, Aaron was screaming bloody

murder. The babysitter was on her cell phone, completely ignoring him while he sat in his swing. It pissed me off something fierce.

"Are you deaf?" I yelled. Her head jerked toward me. She hadn't heard me walk in. How the hell could she with Aaron screaming like that? "Were you going to just leave him in there all night?"

"No. He wouldn't stop."

I picked him up and he was so shaken up it was difficult for him to catch his breath.

"You should never let a baby scream like this. Something could be wrong with him. At least try to soothe him. He may have a fever or an upset stomach!" I wanted to knock her across the room. Kinsley sensed how upset I was and she started crying.

She tugged on my leg, whining, "I want Mommy to come home. I don't want her to stay with the angels."

Oh, for fuck's sake. This was not what I needed.

Grabbing my wallet out of my pocket, I pulled out some bills and pretty much threw them at the sitter. "I won't be needing you anymore. You can go."

She gathered up the money, asking, "But what about tomorrow?"

"I can't trust you with my kids. There won't be any tomorrow."

She gawked at me like I was nuts. Maybe I was. But if she couldn't pick up Aaron when he was screaming his head off, I could never leave my kids with her again.

In a curt tone so there was no misunderstanding, I reiterated, "I said you can go. I won't be needing you anymore."

"But, I need this job."

"Then you should've thought of that before your

phone conversation became more important than my son. Please leave."

She finally collected her belongings and left.

Aaron settled down, but Kinsley still whimpered. I had a baby to feed and a small child to comfort. Which one did I start with?

Patting my daughter's back, I said, "Kinsley, honey, I need to feed Aaron. You wanna help?"

She nodded, but her sad eyes told me more than I wanted to know.

Even though I knew where everything was, I asked, "Do you know where his bibs are?"

She chipped in and in no time a small smile peeked across her tiny mouth as she helped me. We both took turns feeding the baby and then I made a frozen pizza for dinner. I was used to daddy duties, but this was the first time I'd done it with two kids alone.

A long, drawn out sigh wheezed out of me.

"Are you sleepy, Daddy?"

"I sure am, polka dot."

"Me too. Can I go to bed?"

I tugged one of her pigtails and said, "Sure thing." Aaron's eyes were droopy too. After that crying jag, I'm surprised he was still awake. He never cried like that. It made me wonder if she pinched him or something.

"Polka dot, did you like that babysitter?"

Her shoulders bunched up around her ears as she said, "I dunno."

"Is she fun?"

"She doesn't play with us. She talks on the phone a lot."

"Okay. Well, she won't be coming around anymore."

We marched up the steps and I went into Aaron's room first. After I changed him and put him in a clean onesie, I laid him down in his crib. Then we went into Kinsley's room. Once her PJs were on, we went into her bathroom to brush her teeth.

"Daddy?" she asked. "Why doesn't Aaron brush his teeth?"

For the first time that day I chuckled. "He only has one tooth to brush, polka dot."

A bubbling giggle broke out of her. "Oh, yeah."

She climbed into bed and said, "Who's gonna read to me now that Mommy moved in with the angels?"

I usually told her stories as opposed to reading from a book. "Guess it's going to be me from now on."

Large hazel eyes gazed at me in wonder. Then she asked in amazement, "Daddy, you know how to read?"

I sure had my work cut out for me.

Chapter Three

MARIN

TALK ABOUT A SHITTY MONTH. No better make that a shitty year.

It had started out with a bang. I was hired as one of the contributing writers for *Newsworthy Magazine,* one of the best news sources in the country. I couldn't believe my luck. Mom said it wasn't luck at all. I'd always been a writer from the time I was a little kid doodling creative notes on paper everywhere. When I graduated with my coveted degree in journalism, she and Dad could not have been any prouder. Even though Dad would rather have seen me go on to law school, it wasn't in the stars for me. I had no more interest sitting in a courtroom arguing a divorce case than I had sitting in a dental chair getting a root canal. No thank you. Give me a juicy story to chase. That was what perked me up.

Everything was perfect until the day my news director sent me off on a mission. He wanted me to poke my nose into a possible story on what was happening in a chain of popular daycare centers. Someone leaked a story of potential abuse and neglect. When I returned empty-handed, he threatened to give the story to someone else.

"What story? There is no story," I said, challenging him. That was the day I learned how things worked at this publication.

"When I say there's a story, there's a story."

One of the things I prided myself on was my investigational abilities. So, I caved and went back to the drawing board. As I sat in my tiny cubby, scratching my head, trying to figure out where to go on this, another colleague approached.

"Who pissed in your coffee?"

"Pete, I'm stumped."

"What's up?"

Pete wasn't my favorite reporter. He did some things that I wasn't particularly fond of, like stretching the truth a bit. But I needed an ear, so I spilled. He laughed.

"Welcome to reality journalism. Tell me what you've got."

I shared my notes with him. His eyes were on fire. "You have enough here to write the most damning exposé ever."

"What do you mean?"

He pointed to a quote. "Look. This right here, for instance, where this one caregiver says, 'At times we watched an extra child, which meant leaving one or two unattended in a play area, for a minute or so.' Take that out of context saying they were unattended for an undetermined length of time."

I insisted, "But that's lying."

He patted my arm. "That's journalism, sweetheart."

"But the play area was penned off with nothing in it but a couple of toys. It was a virtual playpen."

"Who's to know the difference?"

I was dumbfounded.

The conversation left a sour taste in my mouth that lingered all day. My conscience could not ... would not ... accept that. Instead, I returned to the daycare center and went for another interview. After asking them countless probing questions, I determined there was no neglect or abuse going on there. Maybe they didn't change a diaper immediately after the child soiled it, but who did?

Returning to the office, I told my director once again what I found.

"Either you write an exposé, or else."

"Or else?" Was he going to fire me?

"There is one other option." He got up from behind his desk and walked around to where I stood. When he got in front of me, his beady eyes raked my body from head to toe. Was he really asking for sexual favors in exchange for my job?

"What exactly is the other option?" I wanted him to spell it out for me.

"I doubt I need to explain that to you. You're a relatively bright woman."

Relatively bright woman? I wanted to punch his smug face. "If you're suggesting what I think you are, that would be considered sexual harassment."

In a sickly sweet voice, he hit back with, "Well, Marin, I haven't suggested anything at all. So that would be difficult to prove, wouldn't it?"

My jaw sagged open. What a fucking bastard. He was right. It would be his word against mine.

"But getting back to your assignment, I believe you have a job to do. If you feel you're not up to the task, unfortunately, it looks like we may have to let you go."

"You know what? I'll save you the trouble. I quit. You'll

have my resignation on your desk by the end of the day." I spun on my heel and got the hell out of there. My next stop was that daycare center. They needed to be warned. It was a good thing all my notes had been handwritten and not copied into the computer. Those fucking assholes would've ruined that place.

My fingers frantically typed out my resignation letter and I left it with his admin as I walked out of the building, carrying a banker's box filled with my things. I made sure it was done after I downloaded all my files onto a thumb drive. Then I hurried over to the day care center to warn them.

They were numb.

"I'm sorry. I was sent to uncover abuse or whatever," I explained. "When there was none, my director basically told me to manufacture something in not so many words. The reason I'm here is to tell you not to grant a single person an interview."

The woman I spoke to rubbed her eyes. "This is a total nightmare. We're being targeted because of one mother who didn't approve of our standards. When she hired us, we explained the way we did things and she even signed an agreement. But then her child came down with strep. It happens. When one gets it, it sweeps through like wildfire. And that was it. She came after us as though we infected her son with the plague."

"I'm sorry. I can't help you anymore because I quit. I wouldn't do what they wanted me to. So maybe let it die a slow death. Or have your parents that support you put recommendations on your website. I don't know, but I need to go. Best of luck to you."

My heart was heavy knowing what they were dealing with. I was only happy I didn't add to it with a story filled with lies. Since I resigned, I left work well before quitting time. I arrived home much earlier than usual. My boyfriend, Damien, was home. His car was parked out in front of the duplex we shared. I sure was happy because I needed a shoulder to lean on and a good stiff drink.

When I entered the apartment, I expected to see him in the living room with the TV on, but he wasn't there. I plunked the banker's box down on the dining room table then headed to the bathroom. As I turned the corner, I heard a moan. Then another, and then a series of *Oh yesss, Damie, just like that. Keep it up.*

What the fuck. Damie? He likes to be called Damie? I was with him for over two years and never knew that.

Using the bathroom fled right out of my mind. Seeing who my boyfriend was with and what they were doing, in *my* bed, took its place. I marched into the bedroom and got the shock of my life. Damien, or *Damie*, was going down on my best friend and apparently doing quite a fantastic job of it. His head was buried between her thighs and she was meowing like a starving cat. "Yessss, give it to me, right there. Oh, yesssss, Damie. Lick me good. Suck my bean. I love it when you do that little swirl. Yessss, that's my favorite. You know how to do it. You're the best pussy eater in the world."

He mumbled something about how great her pussy was, I think, but it was hard to tell for sure because he said it with his mouth against her. I was superglued to the carpet, rooted there by shock.

The worst thing about this was Damien had only gone down on me once or twice in the whole time we'd been together. He told me he didn't like to go down on a woman and here he was, the apparent master of it. That little fucker. I finally found my voice and decided to use it.

"Oh yes, Damie, give it to her good. You're the best

pussy eater in the world." I did my best job of mimicking my friend. I even added a meow at the end.

Damien flew to his feet, naked as the day he was born. It was quite comical at the time, seeing his dick bob up and down. I almost laughed, and would have, if I hadn't been so furious.

"Marin! What the hell are you doing here?"

"I live here. It's *our* home. *Our* bedroom. *Our* bed. Remember? Or has her pussy suddenly given you amnesia?"

I stood there with my arms crossed, acting brave, but inside I was a quivering mess and everything was beginning to crush into tiny pieces. This was the man who said only the day before —a measly twenty-four hours ago— that he'd love me forever. Who only last night told me I was the Yin to his Yang, the cream to his Oreo. What the hell happened between then and now?

"Uh, yeah, of course I remember."

"Then why the hell are you eating another woman's pussy in my bed?"

"It's not what you think?"

"It's not what I think? What … do you think I'm blind? You're naked and so is she. And from all accounts, both of you are having one helluva damn pussy party." I peeked around him to see if I could look her in the eye. "And Dawn! How could you? Of all people, I would've expected better from you. You're supposed to be my best friend." Then I aimed my gaze back at Damien. "You're fucking my best friend." I balled up my fist and nailed him with an uppercut to his right jaw. His head snapped to the left and he actually groaned. Loud. Dawn screamed. "Shut up you two-timing whore. You're next." I stomped over to the side of the bed, ready to lay into her with my fist, only Damien grabbed me from behind.

"Stop it. You can't punch Dawn."

"Let me go." I struggled like a demon-possessed madwoman until he released me. By this time, Dawn had rolled off the bed and I jumped on top of it, chasing her. "You fucking whore, get back here."

I did a flying leap, tackling her to the ground as she screamed. Then I grabbed her streaked blond hair and yanked it as hard as I could, practically pulling her to her feet. When I got a clear shot, I fired a jab at her cheek.

Damien seized me by the shoulders and dragged me off of her. Dawn screamed at the top of her lungs, "She's killing me."

"Shut the hell up, Dawn," Damien yelled.

I jumped on Damien's back and knocked him in the head. He shook me off and I fell to the floor, hitting my own head.

"Call the police," Dawn yelled.

"And say what?" Damien asked.

"She attacked us," Dawn said.

"You would've done the same. She caught us naked in her bed for Christ's sake."

I lay on the floor, catching my breath and stared at them. Then I sat up and in a defeated tone said, "You were the two people I trusted most in the world. Damien, just last night you told me how much you loved me. And you"—I pointed at Dawn—"you told me just the other day you thought Damien was going to propose soon." Tears rolled down my cheeks, uninhibited. "Were you two planning the wedding together and then figuring out a way you could still fuck around behind my back?" Suddenly, I was sick to my stomach at the idea of this. I stood up on wobbly legs. I stared them down with cold eyes and spewed, "You two deserve each other. I'll be back later for my things." Then I pointed to the bed and spat, "That you can keep."

I felt physically ill. Leaving the room, I only stopped to grab the banker's box on the dining table. Then I heard, "Marin, wait. Don't go."

Seriously? A million dollars wouldn't have made me stop. The idea of his hands on me after what I just witnessed was as disgusting as those of my former employer. But at least my former employer was sort of upfront about it. Damien had been lying and running around behind my back and how long had that been going on?

I drove until I pulled into my parents' driveway. Mom was shocked to see me. But one look told her more than she needed to know. When I broke down in her arms, she hugged me. I couldn't tell her for days what happened. It came out in pieces when I finally did.

Dad, being the lawyer he was, wanted to sue the magazine.

"How? There was no evidence or proof of harassment."

"I wish you had called."

"Dad, I couldn't work there anyway. They were unscrupulous. I don't want to work for a publication like that." He understood.

Then I told them about Damien and Dawn. Mom was hurt too because she really loved Dawn. We met right after college and were roommates until Damien and I moved in together. Dawn was the one who urged me to date him. I tried to piece in my mind when they could've gotten together, but it was a blank. I stopped thinking about it because every time I did, it upset me too much.

A MONTH LATER, MY PARENTS' frustration with me grew. I'd given up finding a job as a journalist. My attitude went to hell over the profession after my experience and though my gut told me I was wrong, my jaded belief had every news publication lumped in with *Newsworthy Magazine*. I no longer trusted any media source and gave up on the whole idea of working in journalism period.

I ended up bartending, coming home right before the sun rose, and sleeping until I had to be at work the next day. I dyed my hair the colors of the rainbow in an attempt the bring some cheer into my life. It didn't work. Mom and Dad flipped out.

"How will you ever find a respectable job now? I can see tinting your hair but that … that is downright shocking, Marin." Mom's eyes held a bucketful of disappointment. The daughter she'd been so proud of only a few years before was now letting her down. But I didn't have the energy to change. I lived in the lower level of their home, hiding from friends, and the only activity I had other than work, was riding my skateboard. It was something I'd enjoyed in my college years and hadn't done since I'd met Damien. I'd abandoned everything I did with him, ridding myself of the hurt he'd inflicted.

"You look like one of those skater kids I see at the park on weekends."

"Maybe I want to look like that," I said.

"But why?" Mom asked. Dad stared in mute shock.

I shrugged a shoulder and played with one of my new earrings. I'd had my ears pierced several more times, along with an eyebrow and my nose.

"Maybe I like that look," I said with defiance.

By now, Mom stood in front of me, inspecting me. "You never used to. Are you on drugs?"

"What?"

"Drugs? Are you taking them?"

Throwing my arms in the air, I yelled, "No. Just because my hair is colorful does not mean I'm on drugs. You guys are really something."

Dad stepped forward. "Young lady, do not use that tone with your mother. You have to agree with us on some things. There has been a drastic change in your looks and behavior. You don't socialize, you don't do anything but work in that bar, and skateboard. We're worried about you."

"Thanks, but I'm fine." I didn't need any reminders of what was wrong in my life. I was fully aware of everything. It was why I was a damn hermit. My intestines twisted in pain every time I thought of how I ended up in this place.

Mom tapped my arm. "Honey, you're not fine. Why don't you talk to someone?"

"Who?"

Mom and Dad glanced at each other before she answered. "How about a therapist to help get you through this?"

I held out my hand, palm facing them. "Oh, no you don't. You keep them the hell away from me. I'll figure this out. Just give me a little more time. Okay?"

FIVE MONTHS LATER, after I'd lost my job as a bartender for being consistently late and had nothing to do in over a month, Mom and Dad came into my room one morning and made an announcement.

Dad began, "This is it. We're done. You can't continue like this."

Mom stepped in. "Honey, we love you to the stars and

back, and then some, but you're wasting your life away. So, we've made some new arrangements for you."

"Arrangements?"

"Yes, arrangements," Mom said. "A friend of mine has a son. His wife tragically died in a plane crash and he is in need of a live-in nanny. You're hired. You leave today. You'll move in with him and take care of his two children."

"What? No. I can't. Nope. Kids and I are like oil and water."

"You don't have a choice, Marin. It's either that or the streets," Dad said. He was serious as hell.

"Dad, please." I used my best begging voice.

"Nope. I can't watch you live like this another day."

My stomach crashed to the floor. What the fuck was I going to do? I was an only child. I never even so much as babysat. I voiced those concerns.

"You'll figure it out," Mom said, sounding all chipper. "You're pretty resourceful and bright if I do say so myself."

Dad opened the blinds and added, "Take a shower and start packing. You need to be there by one."

"How old?"

"What?" Mom asked.

"How old? The kids." I figured I should know that going in.

"Oh, yes." She chuckled. "I guess that would be helpful. The daughter, Kinsley is six, or maybe she just turned seven, and the son, Aaron is ten months."

I was so fucking fucked. I'd never even changed a diaper and here I was getting ready to be a nanny for a ten-month-old. What the hell was I going to do?

Chapter Four

GREYDON—SIX MONTHS LATER

KINSLEY TURNED seven today and it was a disaster. When Mom brought out the cake, she threw a tantrum. She wanted to know when her mommy was coming to eat a piece.

"Kinsley, remember, she lives with the angels now," I explained.

"I want her to come and eat cake with me. Why can't she leave the angels just for one piece?" She stomped her foot as she spoke.

My heart had malfunctioned. Though I was a cardiologist, specifically an electrophysiologist, who repaired hearts with faulty rhythms, I was helpless. If someone needed a pacemaker, no problem. If they had an arrhythmia, I could do an ablation or get them back into rhythm by whatever means was necessary. I was the guy who handled the heart's electrical issues. But I couldn't fix my own broken down heart. All the circuitry had failed. The wiring was malfunctioning and nothing I did helped. It wasn't so much because of losing my wife. It was because of the kids, specifically my daughter. What was even worse, I watched my little girl, my adorable, sweet polka dot, and I was helpless to ease her pain and disappointment that her mother wouldn't be sharing her birthday cake this year.

"Hey, polka dot. Come here a sec." She walked over to where I stood. I crouched down to her and said, "Look, Mommy can't come. It's not because she doesn't want to, but because she just can't."

Kinsley pushed away from me and marched to the table where her cake sat. "I don't want this cake." Then she shoved it to the floor.

"Kinsley. Clean that up now."

She didn't pay any attention to me but instead ran up the steps to her room. Hudson's four-year-old son, Wiley, ran after her while Hudson chased him.

Mom grabbed my arm. "Grey, it's time to man up and stop being so self-centered."

"Huh?" My daughter had just exhibited a horrible act of rude behavior and Mom was telling me I was self-centered?

"You heard me. Your kids need you and you're not spending enough time with them. This is what happens. You can't blame her for acting like that. My guess is you haven't even explained that Susannah is never coming home again."

I was appalled. "I told Kinsley she was with the angels."

Mom put a hand on her hip. Oh boy, she meant business now. "For how long?"

"What do you mean?"

"How long did you say Susannah would be gone?"

An exasperated sigh exploded out of me. My head clanged. "I didn't."

"Kids need a time stamp on everything. You can't just say she went there. You have to say it's forever. And for God's sake, quit feeling sorry for yourself."

Now I was pissed off. "I'm not, dammit. If you want to know the truth, I'm mad as hell at Susannah. She was fucking her co-worker and then ran off on a business trip and got herself killed, leaving me holding the bag."

Mom's mouth flopped open for one second. But that was it. "Oh, and the plane crash was her fault I suppose."

"What?"

"The plane crash? It was her fault," Mom repeated.

"No, it wasn't."

"Like I said, man up. You need to put your feelings behind you and think of your kids."

"I am."

"Like hell you are. I'm sorry your wife wasn't faithful. I truly am, son. But had she come home, you would've fought and divorced. Would you be carrying on like this? You used to be the best father around. I was so proud of the way you were with Kinsley. I remember how she was when you'd come home from work. I saw that man, Grey. I witnessed it with my own eyes. I used to be here when Susannah traveled. That man is gone. You act like you don't give a shit about your children. The tenderness is absent. You're a completely different man, and you can't continue like this."

She was right. My mind flipped back to those days before Aaron was born, and I would be home taking care of Kinsley when Susannah was gone.

"Daddddddy!" She ran up to me with her arms held out.

"Hey there, polka dot. What have you been doing?" I asked as I

lifted her up in the air and spun her around. Her squeals of delight were like a balm to me after a long day at work.

"Playing with Gammie. We were making pictures. See?" She pointed to the table where her paper and crayons were spread out.

"Let's take a look." I carried her there, reluctant to set her down. She had a way of putting a warm glow in my heart. It was a kind of feeling that didn't come from anything else and couldn't be described unless you experienced it yourself through your own kids. We sat at the table, her in my lap, and she showed me all of her art drawings, which weren't much more than stick figures. Still, I ooohed and aaahed over them because my sweet, adorable child had created them for me.

"Let's put them up on the refrigerator because they're perfect. I love all of them." So, we went and stuck them there so I could see them every day.

"Grey, are you even listening to me," Mom said, bringing me back to the present.

"Yes, Mom. I am." Guilt stung me like a thousand hornets. My behavior since Susannah died had been horrible. But I couldn't seem to pull myself out of this … funk I was in. Was I making excuses? Maybe. But no matter what I did, including my visits to the shrink, nothing worked. I hated myself for it too. Mom was right. I needed to make some serious changes.

Dad and Pearson walked into the room. Dad said, "I got Aaron in the swing. How's the cake cutting going?" They took in the mess on the floor. Then Dad's head bobbed back and forth between the two of us and he asked, "Oh, boy, what did I miss? Did she tell you to stop feeling sorry for yourself?"

Pearson disappeared. I didn't blame him.

I huffed, "Yeah, she did."

"She's exactly right, son."

"You too, huh?"

"Yeah."

Even though I knew she was right, I still felt such a deep betrayal by what my wife had done, I wanted Dad's absolution. "Mom, tell him about Susannah."

"She was having an affair. He already knows."

"You can't do much about that now, can you, son?" Dad asked.

If I thought I'd get sympathy from my parents, I was dead wrong.

"If I could impart a little wisdom here, learned from my advanced age."

My brows shot up because my dad was in his early sixties but didn't look close to that.

"When you kids were born, and we were in the thick of things, we didn't think about the time factor. But then one day we woke up and in an instant, you were leaving for college. Time passes in a snap, Grey. I'm not kidding. I'm begging you, don't let what Susannah did ruin what you have with your kids. Love them. That's all you have to do. Other than listen to your mother."

"And on that note," Mom said. "I wanted you to know that I won't be coming in to help anymore because I've hired a nanny for you."

My mom just delivered the ultimate blow. The total knock out. "You did *what?*"

"She's my best friend's daughter. You remember Trish? Well, I figured I needed to step away from this damn catastrophe you have going on here. Marin McLain, your new nanny, will be showing up today at one. She'll be full time, live-in. Treat her kindly, son. I've taken the liberty of preparing one of your many guest rooms upstairs for her. It's the one on the end closest to the children's rooms. That way she can get to them faster than you since you're so preoccupied." She scowled.

"Mom. That's not fair."

"Fair has nothing to do with it. Selfishness, feeling sorry for yourself, that old woe is me attitude, has everything to do with it. Anyway, good luck." Then she turned to my dad and said, "Let's go say goodbye to the kids."

Pearson tiptoed back in. "Hey man, I think I'll be making tracks now too."

"Did you know about this?"

His sheepish expression was all the answer I needed.

"Do you really think I'm being selfish here?" I asked.

"The thing is, Grey, it's more of you not being present. I get what Mom is saying, and I also get how angry you are. But you can't do anything about it, so you have to move on."

Hudson had walked in while Pearson was talking. "Pearson's right. I was so pissed off at my ex that I let too much pass by. And in the end, it was really stupid. I missed too much of Wiley's life. Don't let that happen to you."

After they were gone, I mentally analyzed my behavior. While I may not be the same man I was six months ago, I loved my kids. I tried to be a good father to them. Gathering Aaron from the swing, I went upstairs to Kinsley's room where I found her drawing a picture.

"What're doing, polka dot?"

"Making a picture for Mommy."

"Can we talk a minute?"

She turned her hazel eyes to me, and I offered up a small smile. Because even after everything, all the horrible and hateful feelings, I still remembered that first night I met Susannah. Looking into my daughter's eyes brought it all back.

"Honey, you know when I said Mommy went to live with the angels?"

"Uh huh."

"Come here a sec." I was seated on her bed and patted

the place next to me. She came over and I picked her up, placing her on my lap.

"When I told you that, I meant she's there forever and not coming back. You remember when Gammie and Bebop had Tricks?"

"Uh huh."

"And Tricks died?"

"Uh huh."

"Tricks went to live with the angels too."

Her tiny rosebud mouth puckered as small lines formed when her brows drew together.

"Like she's with Tricks?"

"Yes."

"So like Tricks. I won't see her no more."

"I'm afraid not. I wish it could be different."

"Why won't the angels let me borrow her for a little bit every now and then cuz I wanna see her like now?"

Brushing her hair back, I said, "That's a very good question. But heaven needs your mommy a whole lot. I guess the angels need her too."

"But I need her more, Daddy. I miss her. See, it's my picture I drew to tell her how much." She pointed to what she had made. It was a drawing of a small girl with a bigger one and a large heart between the two. Or at least that's what I *thought* it was. While Kinsley wasn't bad at art, I had no misconception that she was Picasso or anything. My heart ached for this child of mine. Oh, how I wish I could tell her a different story. But I couldn't.

"I see. And that's wonderful. I'm sure Mommy loves it because I believe she can see it from heaven."

"You think?"

"I do."

"How come she didn't say goodbye."

"Because she didn't mean to leave. It was an accident,

polka dot." Fuck, this is so hard to explain. My chest aches just telling her this. "She would never have left you on purpose."

She balled her fists and rubbed her eyes. I pulled her close and hugged her. "I'm sorry, honey. But we're going to do the best we can together. Okay? I love you so much, and I know you miss her. But we're a team, you, Aaron and me." I wanted to squeeze her because I hated she was going through this. It was bad enough for an adult. But how would this affect her later on?

"I have another surprise for you."

"What?" She sniffed.

"We have a new babysitter coming today."

"Is she fun?"

She better be. "Why, yes she is. You're going to love her. Just wait till you see her."

"Can she sing and draw pictures?"

"Well if she can't, you can teach her. How does that sound?"

"Okay, I guess."

We went back downstairs and I dished out some ice cream instead of the cake that we wouldn't be eating. When we finished, I settled Aaron in the swing and we turned on the TV. About an hour later, the doorbell rang.

"She's here," Kinsley yelled, tearing out of the room and running to answer the door.

"Kinsley, wait." But before I could stop her, she'd managed to tug open one of the large double doors with both hands and then both of us stood there and gaped. Suddenly, Kinsley yelled, "Look, Daddy, it's a rainbow!" And that was an understatement.

Chapter Five

MARIN

DR. WEST and his two rugrats only lived about fifteen minutes from Mom and Dad. Given this, I waited until the last possible minute to leave—translation, until Mom and Dad shoved me out the door, tossing my two suitcases into the trunk of my Toyota Corolla.

Before I got in, Mom grabbed my arm and said, "Be nice to those kids. They're adorable and need a mother figure right now."

"You're joking, right?" I was the last thing that could qualify as a mother figure in anybody's book.

"No. You can do it, Marin, I know you can." She hugged me and gave me a peck on the cheek. Dad only glared at me—the biggest failure in his eyes. His high hopes for me had long ago been washed down the drain. The daughter who he'd wanted to go to law school was now on her way to being a nanny. Not that there was anything wrong with that, but it was something I was being forced to do. How fucked up was that?

When I got to the address Mom plugged into my phone, I did a double take. Then I checked to see if it was correct. It was. This place was freaking huge. I'd always thought my parents' place was big, but this was twice the size of their home. For whatever reason, I had it in my mind that I would be coming to a cozy home that would be cute and comfortable. This house looked imposing. The driveway circled around in front but also went around the back, only there was a gate that prevented me from going in that direction. So, I pulled up in front of the house and sat there for a few moments. I'd best get this over with.

A set of formidable wooden doors challenged me to ring the bell. I hadn't been this intimidated since my first job interview. Pressing the button, I could hear the buzzer ringing. I waited, patiently, because I figured with a house this large, it may take days for someone to find their way to the door.

When that blessed event occurred, I found myself facing two sets of eyes. One pair of hazel irises that grew incrementally the longer she stared at me, and another set of gray ones, framed by one of the most arresting faces I'd ever seen. A square jaw covered in sexy scruff peppered with a tinge of gray, complemented by a straight nose, and hair that appeared to be skillfully arranged, made for one perfect package.

The young girl was positively gorgeous. Her features resembled her father's, and then she blurted out how I reminded her of a rainbow only her dad's expression indicated I was more on the line of a freak of nature.

Deciding to jump right into this awkward situation, I said, "That's right. My name is Marin McLain and I happen to love rainbows and bright colors. What about you?"

"I'm Kinsley. I love bright colors too." She grabbed my hand and tugged me past her dad. "Do you like to color and draw pictures, because I got lots of crayons and stuff."

"Yeah, I do. We can color if you'd like. But how about I speak with your dad for a minute first?"

"Okay."

When I turned back to greet Dr. West, he was in the same spot, standing at the door. "You're Trish's daughter?" It was obvious I wasn't quite what he'd expected.

"I am." I held my hand out for him to shake. He finally did, although he seemed more than a bit reluctant to. I almost told him I wouldn't bite or give him the cooties.

"What's that thing in your nose?" Kinsley asked.

"It's a nose hoop," I said, explaining my piercing.

"Whatcha got that for?"

"Because I like it."

"Oh. Is that a nose hoop over there in your ear?" She aimed a small finger at me.

She was asking about my helix piercing. "No, that's an earring."

"Oh. Why do you got those flowers on your arm?"

Nothing got past this little girl as she asked about my tattoos. I had a series of intertwining red and pink roses that started on the underside of my arm and wrapped around my wrist. "Well, I happen to love flowers. Do you like flowers?"

"Yeah. I used to give my mommy flowers, but then she moved in with the angels and Daddy said she's never coming home."

Gulp. What do I say to that?

"I'm sorry, Kinsley. I bet she wishes she could come home, but I also know she's watching over you every day."

She scrunched up her nose and asked, "How'd you know that?"

"Because if she's with the angels, that's what she'd do. That's what angels do. Everyone has a guardian angel to watch over them. So, the way I see it is your mommy would be doing that too."

"Oh. Daddy, have you talked to her enough?"

Glancing at Dr. West, I noticed him staring at me. He was sort of a stiff looking dude, like his butt cheeks were probably clamped together tightly. "Kinsley, you should go and play. Or maybe go and check on Aaron for a minute so Marin and I can talk a second or two."

"Oookkaaayy." She skipped out of the foyer, leaving the two of us alone.

"I expect you'll want to show me around and all."

Taking his thumb and index finger, he massaged his chin. "Yes, of course. Follow me, please." He gave me a tour of the house, which was expansive. I mean h-u-g-e. There was a formal living room, which looked like it hadn't been used in a while, a family room, which was a total wreck, a smaller den, gigantic kitchen, formal never-used dining room, his off-limits office, a big laundry room, a media room—also a wreck, and then there was the upstairs. We hurried past his room which was at one end of the hall and had double doors. The hallway continued down to five other bedrooms. The kids occupied two and I was to have one next to theirs. Each of the bedrooms had its own bathroom. This house was palatial. Who needed all this room?

He cleared his throat. "I think you should know this house is on the market."

"Oh. I didn't see a sign out front."

"No, there isn't one. Showings are by appointment only."

His icy, clipped tone indicated I should've known that. The last place I'd lived, other than my parents', was a tiny one-bedroom apartment. How was I to know that?

"I see. Will you be moving close by?"

"Not too far. I want to stay close to The Oaks Day School, for Kinsley and then Aaron."

Ahh, she went to the elite private school nearby. "Of course. I suppose you want something smaller."

"Why would you suppose that?" he snapped.

His snippy attitude had me taking a step backward. "I, uh, well, that's to say, this is a really big place."

"The size of my home is not really your business, Ms. McLain."

Whoa. The dude was rude. "Okay then. I just thought—"

"About your thoughts. It may be best if you keep them to yourself," he barked. "I'm trying to make this as easy as possible for Kinsley and she won't need any added stress to the move."

"Yes, sir."

One slash of his perfect head was all I got as a response. Jeez, he sure was a fun prick. Most dads would like the input of their nannies. That was stupid. How the hell would I know? I'd never nannied before. Maybe I needed to be nannified before I started thinking like a nanny.

"On to the kitchen then."

He took me down the back staircase and I wondered how the kids were doing, so I braved the question.

"There are monitors and cameras all over. See?" He pointed to the wall where I could see a small video screen. On it were Kinsley and her baby brother. He was happily swinging in his swing. Dr. Grouch held his phone and said, "I have an app. You should download it too. I'll set it up for you. You can check the cameras from there as well."

"Uh, my phone's memory is shot."

A massive sigh of exasperation shot out of him. Then he snapped his fingers. "Give it to me."

"What?"

"Your phone."

I dug into my pocket and pulled my phone out. "Here."

"Jesus, how old is this?" Sharpness edged his tone.

"I don't know. A few years maybe."

He shook his head. "This won't do." Then he checked his watch. "After I show you where all the food and kitchen items are, I have to run to the hospital. Before I go, I'll stop at the phone store and buy you a new one."

"You can't buy me a new phone."

"Why not?"

"Because I won't let you."

"You will. This app is a necessity if you're going to work here and this dinosaur of yours would never allow it to be downloaded."

I shifted back and forth on my feet. This was super embarrassing.

"What?" he asked.

"I can't afford a new phone."

"Are you deaf or do you have an information processing issue?"

Was he always this offensive? I mean he was a doctor and they sometimes had that asshole reputation, but still. I was here to care for his kids you'd think he'd be nice to me. If I hired someone to feed my pet guppy, I'd be super nice to her because you never know. That person could let my guppy starve and how would I know?

"No! I have excellent hearing and I process information just fine, thank you very much." I left off *asshole* at the end because I was feeling a little nice.

"I said I would buy it. Follow me."

Damn was he ever demanding. He showed me where everything was and then left me to deal with the kids. Okie dokie. This should be interesting.

I entered the oversized family room and saw Kinsley tickling Aaron. He was giggling up a storm, which made me laugh. He was absolutely precious and I found myself melting in my Chucks.

"Hey there, guys."

Kinsley turned and said, "Watch this, Marnie."

"Er, Kinsley, my name is Marin."

"I know, but I'm gonna call you Marnie. It's more fun." Hmm. I guessed that was better than Barnie. I had a vision of that big purple dinosaur that I was in love with as a kid. *I love you, you love me ...*

She stuck her fingers into Aaron's ears and he giggled like crazy. It had me laughing right along with him.

"He really likes this." She did it again. I kept an eye on them and then asked what they wanted for lunch.

"Aaron usually eats a bunch of mushy stuff and I want French fries."

"Why don't we all go into the kitchen and have a look-see?"

Kinsley acted like I fed her a sour grape. "I don't think we like those."

"Like what?"

"Looksies."

I bit back my bark of laughter. "Oh, that's just a saying. Instead of looking and seeing what's to eat, I said look-see instead."

"Oh." She brightened up and grinned. "Come on. I'll show you our stuff."

She grabbed my free hand because the other was carrying Aaron and we went into the kitchen in search of food.

Then she put one hand on her hip and with the other, she pointed at two cabinets. "This one has the good stuff and that one has the yucky stuff."

"Yucky stuff?"

"Uh huh. Aaron's mush is in there. The yellow, orange, and green stuff and other yucky things." She made a face.

I opened the doors and saw oatmeal, jarred baby food, canned food, and things such as that. The other had snack food.

"Yeah, that's the good stuff," she yelled and clapped her hands.

Not really, but we'll let it pass. Maybe I could get them to eat some fruits and vegetables.

"What's in the fridge?" I asked.

"Over there." Her arm shot out like an arrow. Guess she wanted me to check it out myself. It held chicken, turkey, salad vegetables, carrots, celery, tomatoes, yogurt, cottage cheese, all sorts of fruit, cheese, milk, juices, and lots of other things.

"Looks like we have all sorts of goodies to choose from. Do you like sandwiches?" I asked.

"Yep. Peanut butter and jelly."

"What about turkey?"

"Nope."

"Hmm. Do you like carrots and celery?"

"Yep."

"How about yogurt?" She made a horrible face, so I assumed she didn't. "Where's the bread?"

She ran to a drawer and opened it. Inside revealed all kinds of bread, ranging from the sandwich variety to

English muffins and bagels. It was a bakery in there. Who ate this much bread?

"I'll get to work. Wanna help?"

She never answered but said, "You gonna make Aaron a sandwich too cuz you'll have to make his mushy?"

"No, I'll get his jarred food."

"Okay."

She sat at the table and eyed me as I made her peanut butter and jelly sandwich. I peeled and cut up a carrot for her, and then poured her a glass of ice cold milk. "Here you are, princess."

She giggled. "I'm not a princess. I'm a polka dot."

"A polka dot? How'd you get to be a polka dot?"

She pulled her shoulders up to her ears. "I dunno but that's what Daddy calls me. His big ole polka dot and Aaron is his curly Q." Aw, I didn't think that stodgy dude had it in him.

She ate while I fed Aaron his mushy stuff. I chuckled when he grinned with his mouth full, but I wasn't laughing so much when he spewed that mouthful out at me and covered me in orange carrots.

"Ewww, yucky. Aaron got his mushy stuff on you," Kinsley hollered as if I didn't notice.

My white shirt was now splattered in the stuff and I hoped it would come out.

"You shoulda ducked like Gammie does."

"I'll know better next time."

Later that night, when the kids were bathed, in their pajamas, and tucked into bed, Dr. Grouch came home. He took one look at me and said, "Your shirt is stained." I supposed he didn't think I had eyes or something. Then he handed me the new phone. "The app is already down-loaded and set up. Shouldn't be difficult to figure out. I also entered my phone number and the house line."

That's it. No *How'd the day go? Are the kids okay?*

He walked toward his office. Didn't go upstairs to check on the kids either. I scratched my head. What kind of a father was he? Didn't he care that he left his kids with a stranger all day? Was he even worried? I would've been frantic, and I don't even like kids. But I had to admit, these kids were super cute and fun. And they were growing on me … fast. It was bewildering how I didn't mind spending time with them one single bit. Even changing Aaron's diapers didn't bother me and I had never changed one before now. The way the dad acted made we want to spend even more time with them. No wonder Kinsley begged so hard for a bedtime story. I was going to do my dead level best to be a good nanny to them. I may not have great experience, but I could try. I used to be fun. Somewhere, deep inside, there was a purpose to my life. I hadn't figured it out yet but maybe this was taking me in that direction.

Chapter Six

GREYDON

AFTER I LEFT THE HOUSE, I hit the cell phone store and got Marin lined up since this was a priority. Then I headed to the Heart Center at the hospital. The electrophysiology lab was waiting for me.

"Sorry I'm late."

"No problem, Dr. West. We're ready when you are."

I had to induce an arrhythmia on a patient to figure out why he kept having them. The worst part of this procedure was keeping the patient calm.

"Mr. Fisher, how're doing?" I asked.

"I want to get this thing over with."

"Of course you do. And we're going to make that happen. We want you to relax so we're going to give you something for that. How does that sound?"

"Good."

"Dr. West, what insertion point?" the nurse asked.

"Wrist."

She prepped the patient as I asked, "Mr. Fisher, you recall how we discussed what I would do?"

"Yeah."

He was already loopy. Good.

"Let's go," I said to the nurse.

The nurse found the vein and I went to work inserting the sheath. Then I ran the wire or catheters through the vein up to the heart guided by X-ray.

"How you doing there, Mr. Fisher?" the nurse asked.

"Fine," he said, in a groggy tone.

Once the catheters were in the proper position, I sent electrical impulses through them to induce arrhythmias, mapping where they were stemming from. Mr. Fisher's didn't take too long.

One of the nurses called out, "Dr. West, patient is …"

"I've got it. V-fib. Mr. Fisher needs an ICD." An ICD was an implantable cardioverter defibrillator. It was a small device that we would plant under his collarbone which would automatically bring his heart back into normal rhythm. "Let's get this done." I had assumed this was the issue, but we had to be sure.

"Dr. West, we're ready."

All it took was a small incision using X-ray imagery and inserting the leads into the chambers of his heart where the problem was occurring.

"Let's give it a go."

While I was still inside with the caths, we tested it just to be positive it was operational and would bring him back into rhythm. Everything worked like a charm.

"Mr. Fisher, are you still awake?" I asked.

"Uh huh," he answered.

"I believe you're good to go."

"Okay."

All he wanted to do was sleep.

"Nice work everyone. Mr. Fisher, I'll see you in a little while."

I left the EP lab, talked to Mr. Fisher's family to let them know everything went well and went to the break room. I'd have to dictate his case and then chart it on the computer. I decided to check my phone to see what was going on at home.

Everyone was in the kitchen and Kinsley was telling Marin, who she was calling Marnie for some reason, that she only liked peanut butter and jelly sandwiches. Boy, did she pull a fast one on her. That stinker. I watched Marin to see how she handled the kids for a few minutes and was satisfied they were fine. Then I went back to work.

I was called down to the emergency department to check on a patient that came in with V-tach because I was the only cardiologist in the house. After reviewing all the tests that had been run along with the therapy that had been initiated, I consulted with the attending physician.

"He needs to be cathed. I'm sure he's blocked somewhere. I'll call in one of my partners."

"Thanks."

I headed to the doctor's lounge to call the service, checking to see who was on call. Then I placed a call to Josh and explained the situation. His expletive told me he agreed it wasn't good news.

"I'm on the way. ETA in twenty," Josh said.

"I'll relay that. Thanks."

When Josh arrived, I joined him in the cath lab, but when we got inside the patient's coronary arteries, what we found was worse than we had expected. We pulled every trick in the book, but he didn't respond. We shocked him three times but never could bring him back into normal rhythm and he flatlined.

Josh swore and I pulled off my gloves as I checked the

time. After pronouncing the time of death, I headed to the waiting room. This was the part of my job I hated the most. His wife looked up as I approached and she knew. They always knew.

"I'm so sorry. We did everything we possibly could."

She grabbed whoever it was that waited with her and broke down crying. I briefly thought that was what I should've done when I heard the news of Susannah. Instead, I was angrier that I never got the chance to tell her how I felt.

"Would you like to see him?" I asked.

"Could I?"

"Yes. Come with me." I took her hand and told the person accompanying her she could come along too. When I got to the door of the lab, I told them both, "He looks fine, like he's asleep, if you're wondering."

They followed me inside where she proceeded to sob even harder. I'd seen it many times. It was hard to let a loved one go, especially when only moments before you were talking to them, maybe even sharing a laugh or two.

"Take all the time you need," I told them.

Leaving, I informed the nurses to allow them to stay however long they wanted. "Text me if you need me."

"Sure, Dr. West."

I found Josh back in the lounge and he shook his head when he saw me enter.

"You know, it never gets any easier, does it?" he asked.

"Nope, never. In some ways, it gets worse. At first, I blamed it on lack of experience. I can't do that anymore. My skill level isn't going to get any better than it is now."

"You're right. I hadn't thought of that. I hate going home after losing a patient."

There was nothing to say to that. Going home these days was tough period. But adding a loss to it made it even shittier. It was getting late. I did a quick camera check and saw that Marin was putting the kids to bed. It was time to finish up my documentation and get out of here. When I was done, I noticed Josh was still there, staring at the computer screen.

"You okay?" I asked.

"I was about to ask you the same. Everything okay at home?"

I knew what he was referring to, but now wasn't the time to discuss it.

"It's fine."

"I thought after today, you might ..." he shrugged.

"My mom fired herself and found a new nanny for me."

"Yeah?"

"She was sick and tired of my rotten disposition."

Leaning back in the chair, he said, "You're not so bad."

"Come on, Josh. You can be honest with me."

"Okay, you're a fucking crab all the time, I admit. But damn, you have a good reason to be."

"Maybe, but I need to move on. It's just that ... I don't know. I'm still so fucking pissed."

"Have you thought about joining one of those support groups?"

"They don't have one for spouses who died suddenly right after you found out they'd been fucking around on you."

"Ouch. It must suck to hold that anger inside you, but Grey, you have to let it go."

"Now you sound exactly like my mom."

"Moms are smart like that."

I pinched the bridge of my nose to ease the ache forming there. He was right, Mom was right and so was the rest of the world. "I know, but the problem is I don't know how to do that."

"There has to be someone you can talk to about it."

"I have. Three therapists to be exact and they all said the same. Let it go. Only I can't seem to be able to do that." I squeezed my shoulder blades together because they were aching now too. I didn't mention the additional issue I had. There was the question of whether or not Aaron was even my son, which only added gasoline to the already flaming fire in my gut.

"And today didn't help either, did it?"

"Not exactly. I gotta go. The kids are already in bed and my status as father of the year just keeps getting worse and worse every day."

"Hey, Grey, if it's any consolation, you're one of the best physicians I've ever had the privilege of working with."

"Thanks, Josh. I'll keep that in mind when my kids don't know who I am in another year."

When I walked into the kitchen, Marin was there. She greeted me with a smile that quickly died when she saw the expression on my face. I noticed her stained shirt and saw in my head Aaron spitting out a mouthful of food at her. I almost laughed but didn't have it in me at the moment. He loved to do that. I mentioned the stain, then handed her the new phone right before I headed toward my office. I needed a few moments to decompress. Losing a patient really sucked it out of me. I thought about his poor family and how they were dealing with it. In my head, I ran through the steps we took just to satisfy myself we'd done everything in our power we could've. I sat in the dark, letting the calm wash over me. It helped some, but the continued presence of Susannah in this house always lingered. I would be happy as hell to get away from here.

My thoughts made a U-turn back to Aaron. A huge part of me wanted a sign or some way to tell he was mine. But the kid was looking more and more like his mom every day. Except for his eyes, which were gray like mine, he was Susannah in every way. And the eyes were problematic. I pulled the desk drawer open and looked at the picture of the guy my wife was fucking. Dark hair like hers and gray eyes like mine. What were the odds? Did I dare do a DNA test? Was it worth it? If I found out he wasn't mine, what then? Could I still love him?

That question plagued me constantly. The kid tugged at my heartstrings for so many damn reasons. I wasn't a heartless bastard. He'd never know his mother. And for all the shitty things she'd done, she'd always been good to her kids. I still wonder how she could've led such a duplicitous life. She sure pulled it off well.

Rolling my shoulders to ease the built-up tension, I decided to check on the kids. I headed upstairs and went into Aaron's room first. He was snuggled with his favorite stuffed toy—a gray elephant—and sleeping soundly. My little polka dot was fast asleep too. She was lying on her back, with an arm over her head and she'd kicked the covers off. I tucked her back in and stared at the little beauty. My heart squeezed as I gazed at her. She was growing up so fast and I was missing this time with her. Mom had preached to me about this and said I'd regret being away from her. I needed to do my best to be around the kids as much as possible. Before I left her room, I picked up a few of her scattered toys and placed them back in the bins where they belonged. Then I tiptoed out, closing the door softly behind me.

My stomach let out a loud growl, reminding me I hadn't eaten since breakfast, so I headed to the refrigerator in search of dinner. When I got there, Marin was in the kitchen, seated at the counter, sipping on some tea.

Not one for much chatter, I went about fixing myself a sandwich and salad and took a seat at the opposite end of the counter where my laptop sat. I intended to catch up on some journal reading I was behind on. But as soon as I opened the thing, Marin said, "That's a little rude, don't you think?"

I immediately stopped chewing and stared at her for a second. What the hell was she talking about. Was it rude to eat in front of her or to read?

After I swallowed my bite, I said, "Not following."

"You left and were gone for quite a while. Then when you came home, you never even asked about the kids. Don't you care just a little?"

"Excuse me?"

"Are you deaf?"

Who did she think she was? "No, I can hear just fine. I'm having trouble processing your interrogation of me."

"Why? Isn't it clear?"

"Why? I'll tell you why. It's none of your damn business. That's why," I snapped. I couldn't believe the nerve she had.

"I'm the nanny of your children, so it makes it my business. They wanted to see their daddy, but you came home too late and don't give enough of a shit about them to even ask how their day went."

This had become close to a shouting match. Before I said anything else I'd regret, I shut the laptop, picked up my dinner, and marched into my office. I was pretty sure smoke blew out of my nostrils by then and my appetite had disappeared. That girl was a piece of fucking work.

Once in my office, I threw my sandwich down and flopped

onto the chair. Now I needed to find a new nanny. I couldn't have her around fucking with my already screwed up existence. Before I could call my mom to complain, the office door flew open and she stood in front of my desk looking like the devil himself. Except this devil had hair the color of a kaleidoscope and it looked as though it was charged with electricity.

"Where the hell do you think you're running off to? I wasn't finished. Those are your children we're discussing."

"Exactly. *My* children. Not *yours*. You should keep that in mind."

"You're the one who should keep in mind you have kids to begin with."

I stood up so fast the chair flew back and crashed into the wall. "You presume way too much. You don't know a damn thing about me. How is it you've formed this opinion of me in the less than ten minutes we spent together? Is this how you treat everyone you meet?"

She snarled at me. "No. Only those who deserve it."

"I think it's best if you leave."

"I think so too. Oh, and those kids. They're the most adorable children I've ever met. They need a father. You should pay attention to them. Maybe hug and kiss them every now and again."

What the hell! "And what do you know about parenting?"

"Enough that I notice when kids need love."

"Oh, and mine never get any? Is that right?" Her mouth flopped open, then closed. She didn't answer. "Well?"

"I never said that."

"No, because you would've been a liar if you had. I love my kids but don't have to justify that with you or anybody else."

"Then why didn't you go upstairs when you got home?"

A huge rush of air left my lungs. I was tired. So damn tired. All I wanted to do when I got home was relax, see my kids, eat dinner, and go to bed. But here I stood arguing with the rainbow-haired nanny. What the hell happened to my life?

I rubbed my eyes and said, "Work was a ball buster. I lost a patient today. I came in here to clear my head. And, for your information, I did go upstairs and checked on Aaron, then my polka dot. Afterward, I went to the kitchen to make a sandwich. I hadn't eaten since breakfast. Then you lambasted the shit out of me. Satisfied?"

She stood across the desk from me in that ridiculously stained shirt and when I finished with my explanation, her head bobbed up and down once, and she said, "Yeah." Then she sprinted out the door.

I think my mother sent psycho nanny here to test me and I was going to kill her.

Chapter Seven

MARIN

JESUS SAVE ME. I just gave the man hell a thousand ways to Sunday and one of his patients died today. Oh my God. A sob exploded out of me as I ran into the laundry room to hide. When it came to shit like this, I was the weakest person in the world. *Marin did not deal with sad. Marin was awful at this.* How did he do it … tell the families that sort of news? Good Lord. It had to be the worst thing to explain that someone passed. Another sob burst out of me. I sat on the floor with a towel pressed against my face.

That was how he found me.

"What's wrong with you?" He stood in front of me like a soldier ready to do battle.

"Nothing."

"Don't lie to me. Ever. Lying is a deal-breaker. I hope that's clear. I can accept a lot of things, but lying is not one of them."

His stern voice made me flinch.

I nodded. "You had to tell that family someone they loved died." And I sobbed some more. *Just stop already, you big crybaby.*

He rubbed his jaw where the sexy scruff grew. Sexy scruff? What the hell. The man was old enough to be my dad. Okay, he wasn't *that* old. Our moms were besties so he couldn't be *ancient*. But I needed to find out. I couldn't be thinking someone was hot and them being my dad's age. That was just creepy and gross.

"How old are you?"

He blinked twice. "Forty-one. Why?"

"Jesus, you're old." I sniffed away the remnants of my crying jag.

He huffed and glared down at me. "I'm not old. You twenty-somethings think everyone over the age of thirty-five is old. Just wait. It'll be your turn one day."

"Yeah, but when I get to be that old, I'm going to be cool. Not stodgy and grumpy."

He grunted but didn't say anything.

"Is it hard?"

"Is what hard?"

He was so annoying. Didn't he pay attention? "Can you not follow a conversation? Is it hard telling a family that?"

"You know something? You're aggravating as hell. I can follow a conversation just fine, but you jump all over the place like a damn jackrabbit. And yes, it's extremely difficult. I despise it. It gets worse every time."

I crossed my arms and hugged myself, knees pulled to my chest. My heart banged at the thought of anyone having to do that. "I can't imagine."

His voice was low when he said, "Don't even try."

We were both silent, him standing and me sitting. I had

trouble wrapping my head around what he'd had to do today. Finally, I decided it was time we moved on.

"Are you gonna stand in here all night?" I stared at him like he was the lunatic.

"You came in here first." He stared right back at me,

That was a small detail I'd forgotten. I stood and led the way into the kitchen.

"You should know that I checked in on you and the kids throughout the day."

"Say what?" What was he talking about?

"The cameras. Remember? It's why I wanted you to have the cell phone? Which you should be paying more attention to while you work. I didn't put them in here for nothing. And another thing … you shouldn't judge people. And before you try to deny it, don't bother."

He was right. I did judge him.

"Right." Now I felt positively stupid. And awful. And a total moron.

His full sexy lips were pressed into a thin hard line. Then he added, "I knew you and the kids were fine. Polka dot likes you. You should also know she likes turkey sandwiches and played you on the peanut butter and jelly. She's tricky like that."

I snapped my fingers. "That little bugger. I'm gonna get her."

"Care for some advice?"

I tilted my head and thought for a second. "Sure."

"Don't give her a choice. Just fix something and she'll eat it. And stay clear of Aaron when you feed him." He circled his finger in front of my stained shirt.

"Yeah, I picked up on that right away. I was thinking I'm the one who needs the bib."

He laughed. A good hearty laugh. And it sounded better than us arguing.

"Hey, can we have a truce?" I held out my hand and he took it. His was warm and firm when he shook it. It felt … nice. I reluctantly pulled it away and felt my cheeks flush with heat.

"You were good with the kids. Much better than I expected."

That sort of pricked me in the wrong way. It's not like I'm incapable of doing anything. "Well, they're not the monsters I imagined them to be, either."

He scowled for a second then said, "I won't lie. I have stiff expectations."

My brow furrowed. "What do you mean?"

"Don't be ordering me around anymore," he snapped.

"Right, but I speak my mind and if I see something that isn't right, I won't sit by silently."

"Fine, but next time, I would prefer if you'd ask first before plowing into me like a howitzer and blowing me to smithereens."

I had no words because he was right, so I only nodded. I never asked or gave him a chance to explain, which wasn't fair at all. Assuming was so wrong. I needed to work on that. Actually, I needed to work on a lot of things, but we weren't going there.

"I also have some guidelines about their schedules, but you had them to bed early, so that's good. If they stay up too late, it ruins the following day for them. And Aaron needs his naps on schedule." He tapped the counter for emphasis. "I have everything written down for you on a couple of spreadsheets. Of course, when Kinsley is at school, you're one on one with Aaron. Don't leave him in the swing all day. I demand better care for him than that. He requires stimulation but also needs to learn to entertain himself. So, picking him up constantly, spoiling him, isn't good either."

My head spun with all of this. "I'll be honest. You're totally confusing me. Pick him up, don't pick him up."

"It's all on the schedule. A good balance is what it's about. Just check it if you have a question."

Jeez, the guy's a schedule Nazi. "Kinsley did say they weren't allowed too many snacks."

He nodded. "That's correct. I don't want them filling up with sugary crap. Fruits and vegetables are fine but not too close to meals."

"Got it. I saw all the fruits and vegetables in the fridge."

"Yes. Just be aware that Aaron can't chew everything yet. So be careful with what you feed him."

"Right. I checked with my mom about some of that today."

Then he showed me where the household credit card was for groceries and other things the kids might need. "If an emergency should arise, such as one of them gets injured and needs to go to the doctor, text me immediately along with 911 in the text. If I don't call you back right away, it means I'm doing a procedure and don't have my phone on me. Call my mother. Her number's in your phone too. She'll know what to do."

"What if it's just a fever or something that's not an emergency?"

"Text me and let me know. If I don't answer, call my mom."

"Okay."

"Any other questions?"

There weren't any at that time and I told him so. "I'll probably have some come up later, so I'll let you know then."

"The kids wake up early due to my schedule. I'm usually out of here by seven."

"Okay."

"Aaron will be the first with a dirty diaper, so be ready for that. I work out every morning so I won't be around."

"Work out?"

"Yes. There's a gym downstairs."

Gosh. It's a wonder his kids ever see him. "I see."

He eyed me for a second. "There's a treadmill down there if you're interested."

"Gee, thanks." Was he telling me I needed to work out? I did a quick glance down at my thighs and squished my butt cheeks together, so they got a little work out as I stood there.

"Kinsley needs to be at school by eight. You'll have a busy morning. I'm off to bed."

"Right then." I eyeballed him as he walked away. From behind he looked pretty damn good with that tight ass of his. Too bad he was an old geezer. And damn the dude had a temper. Granted, I did go off on him like a cannon. But shit, how was I to know one of his patients had died? Ugh, I can't even … How do doctors do that? I shuddered at the thought. Who in their right minds would want that job?

I climbed the steps and walked past the kids' rooms. The temptation to peek in was great, but I held back. And then I remembered I had the cameras. I went and got ready for bed. After brushing my teeth and washing my face, I did some more unpacking and then climbed into bed and turned on the phone. It only took a bit to figure out how to use that app. It was super easy. I picked each room where a camera was located and selected it to see. It was pretty fucking amazing this technology even existed. When I got to Kinsley's room, I saw her sleeping like a log, all spread out on her bed. Then I clicked on the camera in Aaron's room and was surprised to see Dr. West standing next to his crib. He just stared at the baby for minutes on end. Suddenly he dropped down into a crouch with his head in his hands. He appeared to be trembling. Was he crying? I had to be mistaken. Maybe he had a migraine or something, the way his hands furrowed in his hair. Should I go and check on him? I felt like I was spying though. After a moment, he got up and walked out. I noticed his face as he passed the camera and even though the picture was black and white, I recognized utter despair when I saw it. It had been there after catching my boyfriend fucking my best friend. But why would he look like that after watching Aaron? Was something wrong with the baby?

Switching off the app, I made a phone call.

"Hello?"

"Mom, what the hell is going on?"

"Marin? Whatever do you mean?"

"You know damn well what I mean. Dr. West. What's wrong with him? Or the baby? I just saw him on the camera."

"Camera? What are you talking about?"

"He has cameras everywhere in this house. To watch the kids. Anyway, he bought me a phone so I can too, but I just checked on the kids, and he was in the baby's room and I saw him crying."

"I don't know. Paige never mentioned anything about it."

"Well, something's up."

"Hmm. I can ask."

"No! Then he'll know I was spying."

"You weren't spying. Were you?"

"No! I was checking on the kids like I'm supposed to."

"Then ask him."

"No! I can't do that. He'll yell at me. He's such a grouch."

"Grey? He's not a grouch. He's only trying to get over everything."

"Mom, he's a grouch. Dr. Grouch. He's a grumpy old man."

Mom laughed at me.

"Marin, the man's hardly old."

"He is too. He's in his forties. That's old."

"Oh, honey, just wait. You'll be there before you know it."

What was she saying? "Seriously? I'm only twenty-six, Mom. Or have you forgotten?"

"No, I haven't forgotten. Your father reminds me every day."

"I'm sure he does. Well, I have to go. I'll be up at the butt crack of dawn."

She laughed again. "Welcome back to the real world. Your father will be thrilled."

"Night, Mom. I love you."

"Love you too, dear. I'll talk to Paige."

"Don't you dare mention a thing about this."

"I won't."

We ended the call, but Dr. Grouch stayed on my mind for far too long that night. The next day was going to be very long for me. I hadn't worked this hard since my days at the magazine. Dr. Grouch would probably find all sorts of issues with my nannying.

Chapter Eight

GREYDON

AS I WAS HEADED downstairs for my morning workout I heard Aaron crying. Marin was still asleep. I handled his diaper changing, which was what I'd hired her to do. I had to pound on her door several times to wake her up. It annoyed me that she hadn't heard him.

"Marin. Wake up." Jesus, she was supposed to take care of the kids and now I had to wake her lazy ass up.

"Uh, I'm up now," I heard her mumble.

"You should've set an alarm. Aaron needed your attention. Couldn't you hear him on the monitor? I'm too busy for this, which was why I hired you."

"Coming."

I set Aaron back in his crib since he'd stopped crying and carried on. I'd check on her in a couple of minutes to make sure she actually got out of bed. When I got to the treadmill, the app showed her changing Aaron's diaper. I shook my head because it had to have been obvious it didn't require changing. He was already cooing. I had to let this go. Satisfied all was in order, I cranked up the treadmill, setting the pace at a seven and a half minute mile. I needed to do about forty minutes and then hit the weights. Not working out yesterday had fucked with my emotions and I couldn't have another day like that. Not to mention, the patient I lost took its toll, so this work out was a necessity.

When my forty minutes were up, I was dripping. After guzzling down some water I did my usual bench and shoulder presses, dips, curls, flies, and abs workout. I added some leg presses today, although my legs were shot from the run. My muscles were like jelly when I trudged upstairs to the kitchen to make a recovery protein shake.

Marin was in there with the kids. Polka dot was dressed and ready for school.

"Daddy, you look like you played in the rain."

"I do?"

"Yeah."

"Good because I'm gonna give you a big ole hug."

"Ewww no. You're stinky." She pinched her nose.

I pretended to grab her and she let out a gigantic squeal. She hopped off her chair and ran around the table as I chased her. Once I caught her, I tossed her into the air, holding her away from me. "Should I or shouldn't I?" I asked.

"Nooooo!" she squealed again.

I laughed and set her down.

Aaron smacked his hands on his high chair and I patted his head before I went to make my shake.

"Morning," I said to Marin.

"Good morning. Looks like you went at it pretty hard."

"Yeah. I generally start Mondays out like this."

She carried a bowl of oatmeal to Kinsley and came

back for another for Aaron. Then she sat down to feed him. I observed her for a minute before I fixed my own breakfast.

Aaron was banging his fists and grinning and Kinsley tried to explain to Marin that she liked Fruity O's the best.

"You know, Marnie, Fruity O's are better for you."

Her use of the name, Marnie, had me hiding a chuckle.

"No, they aren't. They're filled with sugar. Oatmeal is best."

"But the TV says they're good."

"Of course it does. Do you know why?"

"Yep. Because they're good."

Marin shook her head. "No, because it's a commercial and they're trying to sell more."

Kinsley's brow creased. "Are they lying cuz lying's bad."

"They're not exactly lying. They're just not telling you everything about the product."

"What's the product?"

"The product is Fruity O's. It does have nutritional value, but it also has lots of sugar which isn't good for you."

"But Marnie, it tastes good."

"Doesn't oatmeal taste good?"

"Yeah, when you put lots of sugar on it."

I swallowed back a laugh. Polka dot was persistent. Marin had her hands full. Aaron banged his fists again and she shoved another spoonful of the gooey stuff into his mouth. He grinned.

"See, Aaron likes it."

"He doesn't count. He likes mush too and it's icky."

"Okay, short stuff, I give up."

"What's a short stop?"

"I called you short stuff, not short stop, but … a short stop is a position in baseball. Do you know what baseball is?"

"Yep. Daddy watches it on TV. It's a dumb game."

Marin sat straight up in her chair and tapped Kinsley on the arm. "Well, I figured you were a smart girl."

"I am a smart girl. Daddy says so." That earned me quite the reproachful look.

"A smart girl wouldn't have called baseball a dumb game."

"How come?"

"Because baseball involves lots of strategy."

"What's stragety?"

Marin laughed at the way Kinsley pronounced the word and corrected her. Then she checked the time and said, "We have to get a move on here, short stuff. Finish eating and stop asking me so many questions. I'll explain what strategy is on the way to school. Your oatmeal is getting cold."

"Okaaaay."

I had to admit, that funky looking woman had a way with my daughter. Kinsley seemed to have taken to her and Marin was comfortable with both kids. But right as I finished that thought, Aaron fired a shot at her, covering her shirt with a healthy dose of oatmeal. Kinsley exploded in laughter.

"You forgot about that," Kinsley said.

I walked over and handed Marin a towel to which she smiled her thanks. "Yeah, I sure did." Marin dabbed at her shirt, wiping the goop off.

"You need to angle yourself sort of behind him," I suggested. "I think he's in early training to become a marksman."

"Thanks for the advice," she said.

I drank my protein shake and headed upstairs to shower. By the time I came back down, the house was empty. I was more than a little disappointed I didn't get a chance to say goodbye to my daughter. I made a mental note to let Marin know that was one of my requirements.

My day consisted of nothing unusual other than my appointment with the psychiatrist, Mike Schellburg, who I was seeing at the end of the day.

When I got there, we started out with the usual how's it going.

And then I told him of my breakdown in Aaron's room last night.

"How bad was it?" he asked.

"Bad enough to bring me to my knees. I cried like a damn baby at the side of his crib. I couldn't stop staring at him. He's such a beautiful baby, Mike. And I love that boy. My heart … It's so difficult. He's the best baby. Better than Kinsley ever was at that age. Happy all the time. You should see him." I brushed away an errant tear. At least this was one place I didn't feel ashamed when a tear or two leaked out of my eyes.

"What are you going to do about it, Grey?"

"I have no idea."

"What do you want to do about it?"

Leaning forward, I rested my elbows on my knees. "I don't know. If I find out the truth, then what do I do if Aaron's not mine?"

"I think you know the answer to that."

"It's tearing me apart. Could I still love him?"

"Only you can answer that. What does your gut tell you?"

"The same thing it's been telling me from the beginning. To forget about it. But it keeps nagging at me and it's driving me nuts. I can't seem to drop it. I think it'll keep up until I learn the truth."

"Are you prepared to deal with those consequences? Because if you go that route, you may be raising a child that isn't biologically yours. Will you love him the exact same way you love your daughter?"

"That's the million dollar question, isn't it?" Rising to my feet, I paced the room, wanting to throw something. "Why the hell did she have to fuck around on me like that?"

Mike scribbles some notes on a legal pad, and then says, "No one can answer that except for the one person who's no longer here. Let's get back to your feelings toward Susannah. Do you still love her?"

"No!" And that was an emphatic answer.

"Are you sure about that?"

"Positive. My feelings for her died the day her lover's wife showed up in my office."

"Tell me something. What if Susannah hadn't died that day? What if you had gotten the chance to confront her? What would you have said?"

My response is immediate. "I would've asked her why, right before I asked for a divorce."

"What if she would've said she needed a distraction because she felt your marriage had gotten a bit stale. But that she still loved you and wanted it to work? What would you have done then?"

Once again, there was no hesitation in my response. "Here's the thing, Mike. Susannah and I talked a lot. There were always two things I would never abide and they were lying and cheating. I'd always been clear on that. So she knew my feelings on the subject. And they haven't changed. If she were alive, we would be divorced."

"And you're positive about this? There are children to consider."

"I'm as sure as there is breath in my body. She carried on an affair that lasted for over two years. How could I have trusted her again? This wasn't some random one or two night fling. This was a purposeful relationship. No, this marriage would not be in existence today and I can honestly say my feelings for her died right along with her."

"Do you feel enough time has passed since her death to allow for you to move on?"

"What do you mean?"

"Grey, you're still a young man. You need to look ahead. There's a possibility for future relationships in your life."

His statement stopped me in my tracks. "You've got to be kidding."

"Not at all."

"The last thing I want or need is another woman in my life." The idea left a bad taste in my mouth.

"You should think of your kids."

"I am thinking of my kids. Susannah fucked me over, Mike. Why on Earth would I want to risk that again?"

"Not all women are like her."

"Let's be clear. Once was enough to destroy any hope of finding another that isn't like her."

He shook his head. "You're jumping to conclusions. You can't lump every woman into that category. By doing so, you'd be missing out and so will your kids."

"First, there isn't any possibility of me ever putting my trust in another woman again. Second, I can raise my kids just fine. I would like to change the topic. What should I do about Aaron?"

"Only you can decide that. But not all women are like Susannah."

"Okay, we are having two dissecting conversations. One, I believe all women are like Susannah—liars and cheaters. And two, finding out about Aaron scares the shit out of me."

Mike chuckled. "I'll admit, this conversation chain is strange. One thing at a time. Women first. I disagree. Do you believe your mother is like Susannah?"

That was in insult. "Absolutely not."

"That's my point. You have to find the right one, Grey."

"My mom is from a different era. Things have changed since then."

"You have an answer for everything. If you seek, you will find, and you are unwilling to do that."

"Exactly. I have no desire to seek. Trust doesn't come easy, and the last time I tried, I ended up as nothing but a pile of ashes. It won't happen again. I won't allow it."

"Okay. We'll drop this for now. On to the DNA. I understand your fears. You don't have to do anything, you know?"

"Why the hell does he have to look exactly like his mother?"

Mike laughed. "Maybe it's God's way of giving you an answer."

"An answer to what?"

"To telling you what to do," he said.

"That's not an answer."

"Think about it."

"It's all I've been doing. And you know something? You're not helping much."

He chuckled. "I'm your psychiatrist. I'm not supposed to give you all the answers. I'm supposed to help you find a way to get back on track so you can figure these things out for yourself. My biggest concern is that you're not suffering from depression and you're able to function as a parent for your children."

"I'd be a liar if I said I was a happy man. But I'm not in the depths of depression either."

"I don't want you hiding in a dark cave somewhere, letting life pass you by. Understand?"

"Yeah. I do."

On the way home, my mind kept straying back to Susannah and what she'd done. All those damn pictures I'd seen of her with her lover. It still shook my foundation that she had done it for so long and I had never suspected a thing. My anger over it had lessened. She was gone and I had to get it through my head that there was no use in rehashing this. If she were still here, we wouldn't be together anyway. My parents were right. I needed to pull my head out of my ass and focus on my kids.

When I arrived home, the gate was open. I'd have to remind Marin to keep it closed. Even though the community here was safe, I didn't want to take any chances where the kids were concerned. I drove the car into the garage and grabbed my things. Walking into the kitchen was like entering a war zone. Aaron was screaming his head off, Kinsley was yelling, and Marin stood behind the counter holding a mop, her hair poking out of a messy bun in every possible angle, wearing the most exasperated expression possible.

"What in the world is going on?" I asked.

"The dishwasher is leaking everywhere and I'm trying to get it mopped up."

"Aaron won't stop screaming, Daddy."

"And why are you yelling?" I asked her.

"Because Marnie said the fucking dishwasher won't turn off."

Marin's expression was so comical. She looked like she wanted to crawl into said dishwasher.

"Okay, polka dot. But you don't have to scream."

I scooped up Aaron and noticed his diaper was full. "He needs changing," I said.

"Oh, no." Marin was clearly overwhelmed.

"I'll handle it." Then I walked to where she was standing and saw the water gushing out. "Did you turn it off?"

"I tried." Panic laced her voice.

"Daddy, Marnie said the fucking thing is broken."

"Kinsley, why don't you go in the other room and let us grown-ups handle it?" It was almost impossible not to die laughing at this scene. "What about the breaker box?"

Marin looked at me blankly.

"Shit."

"Daddy said a bad word." She scolds me for *shit,* but clearly has no idea about *fucking.*

"Not now, Kinsley."

I jabbed the off button on the dishwasher, but it was no use. "Here." I handed Aaron to Marin and said, "I'll turn off the breaker." I ran into the laundry room, located the proper one, and broke the current.

"That did it," she yelled.

When I came back into the kitchen, water still trickled out, but at a much slower pace.

"Oh my gosh, I was freaking out and didn't know what to do. Thank God you came home when you did. I'll grab some towels to soak this up." She handed a giggling Aaron back to me. He must've thought we were playing. Then she mouthed, "Sorry about the swearing."

I nodded. I would've kicked the damn thing in. "This is weird. This thing isn't even two years old." I stared at the boxy machine as though it were possessed. Then I grabbed my phone, searching for our repairman.

"Who are you calling?" Marin asked.

Holding up a finger, I began speaking. "Yes, Ralph? Greydon West here. Any chance you can make a house call tonight? Great. We have a possessed dishwasher. That's wonderful. We'll see you in about thirty."

"Wow. It sure pays to have connections I suppose." She reached for Aaron saying, "Here, I'll go change him now."

"That's okay. I'll do it. You look like you could use a break."

Her eyes widened a bit and she said, "Thanks. I'll get Kinsley's dinner started."

"What are you making her?"

"I was going to fix some chicken."

"Hmm. That sounds good." I was pretty hungry myself, but I didn't want her to think I was asking.

"You want me to make extra?"

"You don't mind?"

"No. I was going to do it anyway."

"Thanks. That would be great."

She snapped her fingers. "Oh, but maybe I should wait since that repair guy is coming."

"Tell you what. Why don't we all go out when he gets here?"

Kinsley jumped up and clapped her hands. "Yay. Can we get pizza?"

"I think we can."

Marin's hands flew to her hair. "Uh, why don't you three go and …"

"No. You hafta come too, Marnie," Kinsley shouted.

"I need to shower."

"Go. I'll watch them."

"Are you sure?" she asked.

Aaron started kicking his legs. "You seem to have forgotten something. They're my kids." *At least one of them is anyway. And it's time I start parenting again.*

"Right." She ran out of the room.

Kinsley tugged on my hand. "She's fun, Daddy. I want my hair to look like hers."

"Okay, polka dot. We'll have to see about that."

"And can I get a bunch of flowers on my arm too?"

Isn't this great? Rainbows and flowers. "Maybe one day when you're a grown- up."

Chapter Nine

MARIN

SCRAMBLING TO SHOWER AND DRESS, I did it in record time. My hair was still wet, but as I stared back at my scraggly locks in the mirror, I knew the only hope for them was a messy bun. So I wound them around the elastic and did the best I could. Then I ran back downstairs to the waiting hungry crew in the kitchen.

"Ready?" Dr. West asked.

"Yep."

We all loaded up in his car, the non-sporty one, which was still a big fancy SUV, and drove off to the pizza place. Kinsley chatted up a storm and it was super weird sitting next to him in the front seat. I couldn't help but compare my car to his. There wasn't a speck of dirt or a crumb in sight. Mine looked like it had been infested by a team of hungry toddlers on their break from daycare.

"Daddy, you shoulda seen Marnie today. She didn't know how to take me to school."

"What do you mean, polka dot?"

At this point, I wanted to slide under the seat because I knew what was coming.

Kinsley laughed as she told her dad what happened.

I PULLED into the horseshoe drive in front of the elite prep school.

"Whatcha doin', Marnie?"

"I'm dropping you off."

"It's not how you do it."

"Oh?" I was completely clueless. My mom always pulled in front of the school and just let me get out of the car.

"Only the big kids get to go in like this."

"Hmm. Okay. Tell me what to do."

"Ya gotta go over there." She pointed to the parking lot where I apparently had to park. I pulled the car over and did as she instructed.

"Now ya gotta take me into my classroom."

Shit. I looked like death on a stick. *"Okie dokie." That meant I had to get Aaron out of his seat too. It probably wouldn't be a good idea to leave him alone in the car. Better get a move on. As I got out of the car, I noticed I was still wearing my fuzzy bunny slippers. Wasn't this great. This was sure to make a great impression on these people. Gathering Aaron in my arms, Kinsley took my free hand and we headed for the door. In the meantime, I took a look around the parking lot. It was nothing but a sea of expensive cars. Next to my Toyota Corolla were Lexuxes, Mercedes, BMWs, Range Rovers, Audis, and even an Alfa Romeo. Now I knew I was in trouble—me in my oatmeal-smeared T-shirt with holes in it, baggy pants, and bunny slippers.*

"Lead the way, my dear," I said with much more bravado than I actually felt.

When we got inside, my worst fears came true. Every eye in the place was glued to me. I looked like a homeless woman compared to everyone else.

"You gotta stop there first," Kinsley said. She pointed to a glass window.

I stepped up to it and a middle-aged woman looked down her long thin nose at me and asked, "May I help you?"

"Yes. I'm Kinsley West's nanny and I'm here to drop her off."

"Hmm." Her eyes raked over my shirt as I cringed. I wished so badly that Aaron was as large as me so I could hide behind him. "Name?"

"Huh?"

"Your name?" She said each word with great precision like I was an idiot and didn't understand English.

"Oh. It's Marin."

"I see. Does Marin have a last name?"

Kinsley started laughing because she thought this whole thing was funny and I suppose through her child's eyes it was. But this woman was not nice.

"Yes, Marin does. It's McLain."

"Yes, I see you're on the list."

She was being a bitch. "You can go on." She leaned forward and said, "Kinsley, honey, you can show her the way."

Kinsley swung our joined hands back and forth and said, "Yes, ma'am."

Onward we marched. Women stood by and stared. As we passed I heard their whispers. They were all dressed to the nines and I mean the nines. Designer clothing that I probably never would own. Fine shoes and nice handbags. The women greeted Kinsley and gave me withering glares. I must surely smell or have some dreaded contagious disease by the way they acted. But if I cowered, I would let them know they affected me, so I stood ramrod tall and plodded on, smiling with the little girl who was oblivious to it all. When we arrived at her classroom, she took me inside and was so sweet. She happily introduced me to her teacher.

Mrs. Crawford didn't quite know what to say to me. She stammered for a long moment until Kinsley said, "I want rainbow hair *just like her and flowers on my arm too. I'm gonna ask my daddy if he'll let me."*

"I see. Well, Kinsley, why don't you take your seat so your er, uh, …"

"Marnie. Her name's Marnie."

"Actually, it's Marin," I said.

"Yes, well, I need to get my students gathered."

"Yes. See you after school, short stuff."

Kinsley hugged me and I left, taking the walk of shame for the second time. I would make sure I was dressed more appropriately for the pick-up. And with that, I stopped and returned to her classroom. Mrs. Crawford looked up as I opened the door. "Am I supposed to come in and pick her up here or will she come out to the car?"

"No, she'll come to the car."

"Thank you."

WHEN KINSLEY FINISHED HER STORY, Dr. West glanced at me and said, "I should've explained." And that was it.

If I expected the least amount of sympathy from the jerk, I was wrong. His hard-core gaze zeroed in on me until I practically shriveled in my seat. "I survived." I didn't mention how rude those women were. It didn't matter and besides, who wanted to act like that? My parents were well off but never raised me that way. They didn't spoil me with fancy clothes or fancy cars. I had to work while in school and earn my way. They believed if you wanted those kinds of things, you had to earn them yourself.

At the restaurant, we ordered pizza and I gave Aaron a bottle while we waited. Dr. West asked Kinsley what else happened that day and she recounted everything from the time I left her until I picked her up. She was extremely detailed for a seven-year-old. Maybe he'd browbeaten her from the time she could talk.

Then Kinsley threw me a curveball. "Marnie, tell Daddy about the songs we sang."

"No, I think you should."

"Marnie and me sang songs. Wanna hear us?"

One corner of Dr. West's mouth tugged upward. Good Lord, the man may actually have a bit of a sense of humor.

"Polka dot, you know how much I love to hear you sing."

Kinsley clapped her hands. "Marnie, let's do the spider one."

I was feeding Aaron while he sat in his seat, propped up on the table, so I said, "I only have one hand, Kinsley. Why don't you show him yourself?"

"No, I want you to do it too. Daddy, take Aaron's bottle." Dr. West and I were seated across from each other, so he grabbed the bottle out of my hand. I was so done.

"You ready, Marnie?"

Was Dr. West biting his lip? It didn't seem possible.

"I think so. Are you?"

"Yeah. Come on."

She put her hands up so her pinky finger touched the thumb of her other hand as I'd taught her and she began to sing, "The itsy bitsy spider ..." and I joined in, mimicking her hands. Aaron stopped sucking his bottle, his eyes widening, and he grinned.

With each word, Kinsley's tone grew louder until I'm pretty dang sure the entire restaurant was watching ... and listening. When the song ended, Dr. West, along with a few other kind people, applauded.

"That was fantastic," he said.

"Did ya like it?" Kinsley asked.

"I did. It was the best song I've ever heard. And Marin taught you that?"

Her head bobbed as she said, "Yep. I like doing that song."

We ate our pizza then, but he kept staring at me. It was strange really. And it made me feel weird.

Later that night, after we'd gotten home, I bathed the kids and got them ready for bed. Aaron was totally done after his bottle. Not knowing much about babies, all I could say was this kid was easy breezy. All he did was pee, poop, and eat. He cried, but only when he was hungry and his diaper was dirty. And cute! Oh my God, I could cuddle with the little guy all day. But for some weird reason, Dr. West didn't pay him a whole lot of attention. He was only about his polka dot, and not even that overboard on that, but not Aaron. Maybe he just wasn't a baby kind of guy.

When I finished putting Aaron down, I walked toward Kinsley's room, but as I closed in, I heard Dr. West's voice. He was reading her a bedtime story. So I went downstairs instead. The dishwasher repair guy had fixed the problem, so I reloaded the thing and set it to run. Then I threw all the towels we used to mop up the mess into the washer. I decided to hang out in the kitchen for a bit and was sitting at the counter, munching on an Oreo when Dr. West walked in.

"Oreos, huh?"

"Uh, yeah," I said with my mouth full. I didn't want to add anything else because nothing was worse than talking with your teeth covered in those chocolate crumb cookies, not that I really cared what I looked like.

"No milk?" he asked,

"Huh?" My mouth dropped open. He didn't look like the cookies and milk kind of guy. Then he broke into a deep chuckle. Hearing him laugh sounded completely odd.

His finger circled around as he said, "Your, uh teeth are a bit … chocolatey."

My hand flew over my mouth. Shit. I knew I'd make a total ass out of myself.

"You reminded me of polka dot when she eats those things."

Great. Just what I always wanted … to remind someone of their seven-year-old kid. Then again, she was adorable, so maybe it wasn't so bad after all.

After I swallowed, I said, "Yeah, they do create a dental catastrophe," I said.

"But so worth it."

Did he just say that? The guy actually ate them?

"For real."

"Kinsley loves you. She went on and on about you when I put her to bed."

Now my hand flew to cover my heart that just did a little flip inside my chest. I never thought I'd feel this way so quickly. "Really?"

"Yeah. She does. We do have a problem. She wants some flower tattoos and is under the impression that when she turns eight, she will be of age. I had to burst her bubble and explain that no, it's when she turns eighteen, and now she thinks that's a very old woman. But then I told her you were twenty-five."

"I'm twenty-six."

"Sorry. Twenty-six. And now she believes you are as ancient as the dinosaurs." He chuckled.

"Sometimes I feel that ancient too." I got up to put the Oreos away.

"Come on," he huffed. "*I* don't even feel that way."

I was about to come back with—*well, I've had a pretty shitty year*—but then I thought about what he'd been through and I stopped myself. I shrugged instead.

"You're lucky. You have two gorgeous kids. What can I say?"

He squinted. "Wow. Do I hear a little self-pity in your tone?"

My hands flew to my hips as I assumed the stance. "No." But there was.

"Do you work out? Exercise stimulates endorphin production, which can help with your mood."

My mood? "Not anymore."

"And …?"

Why was he so curious? I wasn't exactly comfortable telling this man why things went to shit and I quit working out. It wasn't like we were best friends.

"Things sort of happened."

He scooted his stool around to face me. "Honestly, I don't know very much about you. My mom only told me you were her best friend's daughter, you were trustworthy, and would do a great job with the kids. I think since I'm entrusting you with the livelihood of my children, your secrets are safe with me."

What the fuck!

"My secrets?" He wanted me to divulge my innermost private matters, things I would only tell my best friend.

"It seems you experienced something that caused you to quit working out."

My lips pressed together for a second. It angered me that he assumed so much. "I believe you have this impression of me that I'm not very smart and that I don't know much about the benefits of exercise. You have this assumption, like those women at Kinsley's school, that I'm just some uneducated bimbo because I have brightly colored hair and some ink, don't you?"

"Whoa, hang on a minute. Did I ever say anything about that?"

"You didn't have to and neither did those asshole women at The Oaks."

He stretched out his hand, palm facing me. "What happened this morning?"

I pinched the bridge of my nose to stem the headache that was sprouting. "Nothing."

"I thought I asked you never to lie to me."

"I'm not lying."

"Then you're withholding the truth." He was glaring at me again and it was extremely unnerving.

I blew out a lungful of air. "Apparently, there's a designer dress code requirement to walk into the place, and of course, I didn't quite meet the standards." I motioned with my hand up and down my body, indicating my lack of the appropriate attire.

"What does that mean?"

"It means that all the mothers in there were dressed in their fancy clothes, and my wardrobe was not in compliance."

"Hmm."

"Yes, hmm. You can probably see where this is going." Now that I'd picked up steam, I was on a roll. "What pisses me off is people automatically discount the fact that I'm a college educated individual who happened to resign from a job with a highly creditable magazine because I had conflicting views from that of my editor. He didn't like the fact I refused to concoct a story that didn't exist. And to top that one off, I cleared out my desk and went home early, only to find my live-in boyfriend screwing my best friend. So now you know my life story." *Why the hell did I tell him all that?* I puffed out my cheeks and stared at him like he was an apparition. Then I hopped off the stool and made tracks for the stairs. There was no way in hell I could look him in the eye after that word vomit fest.

Chapter Ten

GREYDON

"MARIN, WAIT."

She stopped, thank God. After that story, she couldn't just leave me hanging.

"What happened?"

Her head was bent at such an angle that I couldn't see her expression. "I just told you."

"No, I'm talking about your job."

A puff of air hissed out of her. "My boss wanted me to write an exposé about a daycare center, only he wanted me to embellish the truth. There was no story. I refused to lie and conjure up something that didn't exist. I wouldn't compromise my integrity or ethics, so I resigned."

"Jesus. Who did you work for?"

"*Newsworthy Magazine.*"

"Seriously?"

Her blue eyes grew stormy. "No, I just made all that up."

I flashed her an exasperated look. "Didn't you have any legal recourse?"

"Did you not listen? I resigned." She waited expectantly for me to say something but there was nothing for me to add. She shook her head a second and continued. "Yep. Marin McLain. Former writer extraordinaire. You can Google me if you'd like. I had larger than life dreams and here I am working as a nanny. Don't get me wrong. Your kids are awesome. But my goals were aligned much differently from this."

I had no idea what to say to her other than, "Have you tried to get another job?" When her expression crashed, I quickly added, "Okay, that was a stupid question. Sorry."

"Everywhere I applied wanted to know why I left *Newsworthy*. No one leaves a publication like that unless you get a better offer. I had zero references and if I'd said I didn't see eye to eye with my boss, that instantly labeled me. If I didn't tell the truth, they would want to call him for a reference. Then where would that have put me? It was a Kobayashi Maru scenario."

I raised a brow. "And yet you didn't think like Captain Kirk."

"What do you mean?"

Gesturing toward the stools, I said, "Take a seat."

After we were seated, I began. "Kirk beat Kobayashi Maru. Remember?"

"Well, yeah, by reprogramming the computer. How am I supposed to do that?"

"Think outside the box."

"I'm not following."

My laptop was on the counter, so I pointed to it. "You can write anywhere, correct?"

"Yep."

"Then do it. Freelance. Submit your articles to whichever publications will accept them. Prove your talent to the world that way. You have the skills. All you have to do is find the topics people are dying to read about."

"But most publications only accept articles from their employees."

"You're not thinking outside the box." I tapped my temple. "Start your own publication. Blog. Whatever. More people rely on electronic media anyway. Just do it. Change the rules. What's your passion? Write when Aaron is napping or on your days off. When the money starts rolling in, to the point you don't need to be a nanny anymore, give me some notice so I can find your replacement. But whatever you do, don't stop writing." I used my finger and pounded the counter for emphasis. She was entirely too young to give up on a career she loved.

Her eyes flicked between the computer and me. "You may have something there."

"No. I definitely have something here. You're only twenty-six. That's entirely too young to give up on something because some jackass wanted you to do something that was unethical. Write about that. Don't use names or places. Just tell about a hypothetical situation that exists. People love that shit."

"You think?"

"Yes. I'd read the hell out of something like that. It has mass appeal because it's happening today and it's ageless. Find topics like that. Or write about what happened to you today when you dropped Kinsley off. People automatically assumed you were uneducated because you didn't dress like they did."

A soft smile lifted the corners of her mouth. "Yeah. Yeah, that's something I could do."

"Marin, even if you don't post it anywhere, just write it. If you stop writing, you become stale. If you become stale, you lose your talent. It's as if I were to stop practicing medicine. I would lose my skills. You can't quit."

Maybe it was the urgency in my tone, but I had her agreeing with me.

"You're right. I'll start writing again. Even if it's just to scratch that itch."

"Exactly. And now, I need to scratch the itch to get some sleep."

"Me too. I promise to set my alarm tonight. Sorry you had to wake me this morning."

I clicked my fingers. "Oh, a couple of things. I like to say goodbye to Kinsley before she leaves, so if I'm not down from my shower, send her up to my room. And can you make sure the gate in the driveway is kept closed? Even though this is a gated community, I like that extra safety measure for the kids."

I turned to leave when I heard, "Dr. West?"

"Yeah?"

"Thank you."

She stood there smiling and it was the first time I paid close attention to her. She was pretty in a disarrayed fashion. Her crazy messed up hair and the rest of her was completely unconventional, but it somehow worked.

A COUPLE OF WEEKS LATER, I was in the process of shoving some lunch down my throat when Josh came into the break room.

"How's it going?" he asked.

"Not too bad today. You?"

"Same. Hey, my sister wants to know if you're dating anyone."

I almost choked on my salad. "Um, what?"

"Yeah, sorry. She needs a date for this wedding she was invited to. She doesn't know anyone to ask and thought about you."

"Oh." I relaxed. "For a minute there I thought she was hitting on me."

An awkward laugh chuffed out of him. "Uh, no. That would be rude."

"No, I'm not dating anyone. And I'd be happy to be her fake date as long as I'm not on call and my nanny can sit that night."

"I'll have her call you."

Later that day, my phone vibrated while I was with a patient. When I had a chance to check it, I saw a voicemail and call from a number I wasn't familiar with. The message was from Deanna, Josh's sister. I called back when I was done for the day.

The wedding was on Saturday and I explained that I needed to check with Marin first.

When I walked into the house, Marin and Kinsley were singing "Do your ears hang low, do they wobble to and fro?" I chuckled. Kinsley was practically screaming the words at the top of her lungs. I peeked into the living area and they were both doing a performance for Aaron. He sat in his swing with a goofy grin spread across his face as their animated gestures entertained him. The song was over in a flash, and he kicked his legs out whereby Kinsley proclaimed, "I think he wants to dance."

"He can't dance. He can't even walk properly. Look at him." Marin had taken Aaron out of his swing and he was running around, teetering this way and that, like a sailboat with a broken rudder.

"How do you know, Marnie? You haven't let him try to dance."

"I know. How can he dance when he can barely stand

up straight? How do you suppose he'll be able to tap out a tune?"

"Maybe he's got magic dancing legs. Look at how they kick out when he runs. Maybe they're special."

"They're special all right. He's going to be a punter for a football team."

"What's a punner?"

"A punter, not a punner."

"What's that?"

"It's someone who can kick a football really well."

"Nope. He's gonna be a dancer. See? Look at how his legs cross." Right about then, Aaron crash landed on his ass.

"Uh huh. I don't think that'll work too well in a dance," Marin said.

I swallowed a laugh so they didn't hear me. The two of them always had these comical interchanges between them.

"What kind of dancer anyway?" Marin asked.

"An Irish dancer. Like those kind that wear those clicky shoes." Then Kinsley took off and did her best imitation of an Irish step dancer. She looked like she was having some sort of seizure, the way her arms were so stiff and her legs kicked out at awkward angles until she caught sight of me. "Daddy!" She flew into my arms, Irish step dancing forgotten.

"How's my polka dot today?" I kissed her as I hugged her to me before setting her back down.

"Good. Aaron says he wants to be a dancer."

"He does?"

"Yeah. One that wears those clicky shoes."

"And he told you that?"

She nodded so fast, I got whiplash watching her. "But Marnie says he's gonna be a ball punner."

"Punter," Marin corrected.

"Polka dot, when did Aaron start talking?" I asked.

"He told me in my ear."

"Hmm. I see. And are you sure he can do it?"

"Uh huh. Watch his legs move."

"Oh, they can move all right. Hey Marin, I know you're not supposed to work Saturday night, but can I ask a favor? I need a sitter. Would you mind?"

Kinsley jumped up and down and Aaron let out a giggle.

"Uh, no, I guess that would be fine."

"Great. I really appreciate it."

"No problem."

Kinsley tore around the room like her hair was on fire. "Yay, Marnie's spending the night. Marnie's spending the night."

Marin chased her and grabbed her around the waist. "You little goofball. I spend every night here." Then she tickled her as Kinsley giggled something fierce. She eventually broke free yelling, "Daddy save me from the tickle toad."

"The tickle toad?"

"Yeah, that's what Marnie turns into when she tickles us."

"Is that right?"

Kinsley grabbed my leg and asked, "Daddy, are you going to a birthday party?"

"No, polka dot. I'm going to a wedding."

"A wedding?" Kinsley asked.

"Yes, it's a big party after someone gets married. You've been to one before, but you were a lot younger and don't remember."

"Oh. Who's getting a wedding?"

I smiled at her use of words. "Just a friend."

That must've satisfied her because she skipped away and went back to tickle Aaron. I turned to leave but caught Marin staring at me. I wasn't sure what to make of it, so I left. But the way her eyes drilled through me left me unsettled. I had work to do so I brushed it off. Once I finished my computer work, I went into the kitchen to find Marin feeding the kids. She rushed around telling Kinsley to hurry and finish.

"Why the rush?" I asked.

"It's my school program, Daddy. Aren't you coming to watch me sing?"

Marin's lips pinched together and her damning eyes told me more than I needed to know.

"I'm sorry, honey, I can't."

"But Daddy, I'm singing the spider song all by myself. And I practiced real hard to be good."

Fuck. I promised I'd meet Deanna for a quick drink tonight. The last thing I wanted to do was to take her to a wedding without the benefit of meeting her first.

I patted her head. "Polka dot, you're going to be fantastic. The best one there." I didn't risk a glance at Marin. She'd already scolded me with her scorching glare. And Kinsley's crushed expression was making me feel like a complete asshole.

"Come on, Kinsley, let's get your party dress on," Marin said.

"Party dress?" I asked.

She looked at Kinsley and said, "Um, yeah. You're gonna rock that spider something crazy, girly." She grabbed Kinsley's hand and said to me, "You wouldn't mind watching Aaron for a minute, would you?" Her tone was icy and carried more than a hint of reproach.

"No, that's fine." I checked my watch. I hope she didn't take long.

Over her shoulder, she asked, "Oh, and would it be too much trouble to change him for me?"

Christ, she made me feel like utter shit. It was deserved for missing my daughter's show. I took Aaron upstairs and changed him. When I had him freshly diapered, she walked into the room and picked him up. Without so much as a word, she gathered his things, put them in his bag while she held him as I stood by feeling like a jerk, probably because I was. Then she marched out and called for Kinsley. I didn't have the heart to walk out with them. Or maybe it was the lack of balls. Wasn't that something? The nanny made me feel two feet tall.

My meeting with Deanna was a waste. This wedding thing was nothing but a front. She was hitting on me from the moment I sat down and I almost told her to forget the whole thing, but then I'd have to face Josh. She wrangled a dinner out of me and by the time I got home I was beat—mentally and physically.

Walking into the kitchen, I almost jumped when I saw Marin seated at the table.

"Have a good time tonight?" she asked.

"Jesus. Don't do that."

"Let me tell you something *you* need not do. Don't disappoint your kids and leave them hanging. Your daughter waits for you to come home every single day. And then you pay her very little attention. This school program was very important to her. Was it asking that much to attend? And your son. You act like he's not even here most of the time. Start acting like a father before they forget who their father is." Placing both palms flat on the table, she pushed herself to her feet and then walked past me and went upstairs.

And didn't that just make me feel shittier than I already did?

Chapter Eleven

MARIN

SATURDAY ARRIVED and I decided to take the kids on an outing. We were going to eat a junkier than junk fast food lunch and then go to the local zoo. Every time they saw animals on TV, their eyes bugged out. I'd be damned if I was going to sit back and wait for Dr. Grouch to take them. So that morning, they ran around and as they watched their favorite cartoons, I planned the day.

Around eleven, the man himself came into the room and announced that we would have to leave for the afternoon.

"Why?"

"There's going to be an open house today. The realtor has requested the house be tidied up and that no one be around from one until four."

"Uh, okay." After I thought about it for a moment, a question popped into my mind. "How long have you known about this?"

"Since Wednesday. Why?"

"And you decided to wait until now to spring this on me?" I was grinding my molars to the point where I would probably need dentures by the age of thirty. Dr. Grouch would get the bill if I did.

"There's a problem with that? I thought since you planned to have the kids today that it would be fine."

"Of course. It's always fine, isn't it? But can I ask you something? Does it ever occur to you that your kids would like a moment of your time too?"

Who was this person? He stared at me as though I'd lost my last brain cell, but I couldn't care less. I didn't waste time waiting for him to answer but started picking up the room, making sure it was "tidied up" as requested. When I was finished, I scooped Aaron up and carried him upstairs with me. Kinsley's room was next, followed by Aaron's, then mine. After all the bathrooms were neat and organized, I ran back down to the kitchen, where I found Dr. Grouch sitting on his ass at the counter drinking a cup of coffee. That did it.

"Do you possibly think you can find time in your busy schedule to help me get the house *tidy*?" Sarcasm oozed from me.

The coffee mug stopped midway from the counter to his mouth. His eye twitched for a second, and he set the cup down. "I get the feeling you're upset about something."

"Wow, aren't you perceptive?"

"No need for sarcasm."

"Oh, there's a very big need." I walked past him, into the laundry room to deposit some dirty towels I carried down from the bathroom. Then I came back into the kitchen, walked up to him and grabbed him by the shirt. "I just want to say one thing. You are a terrible parent." He gaped at me, but I didn't give a damn. Let him fire me. Between carrying Aaron around and cleaning up the house, I was exhausted. I hurried out of the room to get the kids ready for our outing.

"Kinsley," I called out. "Come on, let's change clothes."

She followed me up into her room to dress. She was very obedient about doing what was asked of her. I changed as well because my shirt was damp with sweat. Then I dressed Aaron and gathered up Kinsley. When we all got back downstairs, Dr. Asshole wanted to know where we were going.

"On an outing. A *fun* outing." I stared pointedly at him. "We'll be back at four or later."

"You're not going to tell me where?" he asked.

"We're going to eat a junk food lunch and then I'm taking the kids to the zoo since they adore animals and have never been *in their life*." My statement had the effect I'd hoped. His jaw sagged open as we all traipsed out the door. That man was infuriating.

Both kids were happy as hell when we pulled into the junk food parking lot.

"We're gonna eat *here*?" Kinsley asked.

"You bet we are."

Aaron gnawed away on his chicken squares. It sort of creeped me out when I thought about what was actually in those little meat cubes, but I refused to allow myself to dwell on it. Kinsley munched on her burger and fries.

"This is the bestest food I ever ate, Marnie. We should eat here all the time."

"Tell your daddy that."

"Can we get some ice cream for dessert?"

"I think that's a great idea."

Kinsley clapped her hands. "Yay!" Then we bumped fists.

When she said that, Aaron pounded his hands on the table and yelled too.

"Marnie, why doesn't Daddy ever come out with us?"

That's the million dollar question, isn't it? "Oh, honey, I think it's because he has to work really hard."

"Yeah, but does he work all night too?"

"Hmm, not all night because he has to sleep."

"But what about after we eat dinner. Does he work then?"

"Sometimes he does."

"I don't want him to work all the time. It makes me sad." Her little voice had turned sad and it tugged at my heart.

"You should tell him that."

She played with her French fries and said, "I do sometimes, but I don't think he listens to me."

"Honey, sometimes, people's hearts stop working like they're supposed to, and he has to fix them so they don't have to be sick anymore." Her expression was so gloomy I needed to change the topic. "So, who's ready for ice cream?"

Aaron clasped his hands together. I messed up his already tousled hair. "You are?" He nodded, said some gibberish, and gave me a toothy grin. I laughed because his teeth were sparse and he was so damn cute.

"What about you, Kinsley?"

"Can I have a hot fudge sundae?"

"You sure can. Let's go."

We all ended up getting what Kinsley ordered. Aaron was a mess. I took several pictures of him with his face covered in fudge and ice cream. It was hilarious.

Then I asked Kinsley, "What kind of birthday cake do you think Aaron would like? It's almost his birthday."

"I think he'd like an ice cream cake."

"Great idea. I'll pass that on to your Gammie."

"Won't you get it?"

"Uh, I don't know. Maybe."

"Marnie, you gotta get it. It won't be no good if you don't. Your stuff is better than Gammie's."

My heart just banged a million times harder inside my ribcage. "Can I have a Kinsley hug?"

She stood up, crossed over to my seat, and wrapped her half-pint arms around me. "This is the best squeeze I've ever had."

Aaron pounded on the table and talked in Aaron-speak again. I asked him, "You want one too?" More gibberish came as a reply, so I picked him up out of his high chair and hugged the pieces out of him. He put his arms around my neck and did his best job at squeezing me back. These kids were situating themselves into a huge corner of my heart and it was starting to worry me. Walking away from them wouldn't be easy. It would be one thing if their asshole dad would give a shit, but from what I'd seen so far, he wasn't very invested in them. If he spent an hour a week with them, I'd be surprised.

"You okay, Marnie?" Kinsley wanted to know.

"I'm perfect because you two are my pals and we're going to have fun today. Are you guys ready to go see the critters?"

Kinsley laughed at my use of the word critters. "They're not critters, Marnie. They're animals."

"Right, then. Let's get a move on."

After making sure Aaron's fudgy face was wiped clean, we headed for the petting zoo. The kids were in critter heaven. And then we got to the llamas.

They gave us food to feed them and unfortunately, I was in the direct line of llama spit. No one warned us of that little issue with those particular creatures. Luckily, it got me in the shirt. Had it been Kinsley, it would've gotten her in the face. When it happened, she screamed, then yelled, "Ew!" Aaron laughed, and I rushed around looking for a paper towel, forgetting that I had Aaron's diaper bag on my shoulder. Once I regained my wits, I pulled out a wipe and cleaned myself off, then hurried us out of the llama pen.

"Why'd it do that, Marnie?"

"I have no idea, but no more llama petting for us."

"Yeah, that was icky."

You should've been me, I wanted to say.

"Okay, onto the next group of animals." We headed to the goats because Kinsley wanted to pet those. They tried to eat the diaper bag, so we didn't stay too long there either. Then we visited the geese, but they chased us all over the place. Those suckers were aggressive.

"Why are they so mean, Marnie?"

"I think they're hungry for Aaron's biscuits." I had teething biscuits in the diaper bag. "Maybe they smelled them."

That answer sufficed. So onward we went. Aaron was happy riding in his stroller and we walked along looking at the animals. I checked the time and noticed it was almost four.

"Are we gonna visit the monkeys, Marnie?"

"Yes, we are."

After the monkeys, we headed home. Kinsley's questions about their red butts were a little more than I wanted to answer. When we pulled into the drive, it was four fifteen. Dr. West's car was there, along with two others.

Aaron was fast asleep, so I gingerly picked him up and carried him inside.

When I got through the door, four sets of eyes turned my way. A couple, Dr. West, and another woman were seated at the kitchen table.

"Marin, Kinsley," Dr. West said.

I raised my finger to my lips, so they wouldn't wake Aaron, and carried him straight upstairs. Once I got him settled, I went to my room to change my offensive shirt. Seemed that's all I did these days. Then I ran back downstairs to make sure Kinsley wasn't in the way of the adults. She was in the living room with the TV on, sitting quietly.

"Marnie, who are those people Daddy's with?"

"I'm not sure."

"Can I have a juice box?"

"Uh, let's wait a bit."

We watched TV together until all the people left. Then Dr. West came in and announced, "We're moving. I signed a contract on the house."

Chapter Twelve

Greydon

MARIN AND KINSLEY stared at me like I'd lost my mind. "What's wrong?"

"What's that, Daddy? Moving?"

"We won't be living here much longer. We're getting a new house."

Kinsley's expression crashed. "But I like this house. Where will my bed be? How'm I gonna sleep?"

"In the new house. You'll love it even more. I promise."

"But I want to keep the room I got now. It has elephants and giraffes in there."

I sat down and pulled her onto my lap. "Polka dot, we'll put giraffes and elephants and anything you want in there. I promise."

"Angels? Can it have angels in there too? And do you think maybe one will be Mommy."

"Maybe so." I'd paint every fucking square inch of her walls with angels if that's what she wanted.

"What about Aaron? Where're we gonna have the ice cream cake Marnie's gonna get him?"

"Ice cream cake?" What was she talking about?

"You know. His birthday cake."

Oh, hell. He was going to be a year old and I had conveniently shoved that to the *do not disturb* compartment of my brain.

"We'll have it at the new house."

"Will Marnie's room be next to mine there too?"

"Yes, it will." I glanced at Marin and she was puncturing me with those damn eyes of hers. She had the ability to emasculate me in a millisecond with that look. Shit. I was handling this completely wrong. It didn't matter. I never expected the house to sell this fast, but that couple just moved here and wanted to close within the month. Thirty days. They gave me my asking price and this deal was too good to walk away from. My realtor already found another home for me. It was a brand new spec house that I had placed a contingency contract on and it was due to expire in forty-five days. This was a win-win for me.

I mentally ticked off a list of who needed to be contacted on Monday. Painters and movers to start with. The house was freshly painted, but I wanted Kinsley to have her giraffes, elephants, and angels if she wanted. And I wanted some changes made to the interior.

"Daddy, can we?"

"What?"

"Can we go to the movies tomorrow?"

"Oh. Is Marin taking you?"

When her happy face crashed, I knew she'd been expecting me to be the one to take her. "Listen, polka dot, Daddy will be really busy over the next few weeks with the move, but after that, we can go to the movies all you want. Okay?"

"Okaaaaay." She slid off my lap and with her head dipped, she slowly walked toward the kitchen. Marin followed her. Not able to face them any longer, I went upstairs to shower. The truth was, the remorse and shame that covered me was so thick, I didn't think I would ever rid myself of it. The wedding I had promised Deanna I would take her to felt like a noose around my neck. Why did I even agree to go?

It was after five when I went downstairs, dressed in my navy suit. The kids were in the living room with Marin, playing.

"Daddy. You're all dressed up," Kinsley said.

"Yep. I'm going to that wedding, remember?"

"Oh. I forgot."

"You guys have a good time tonight."

Marin's scowl made me feel extremely guilty about leaving the kids. It wasn't something I even wanted to do and it soured my mood even further.

When I got to Deanna's, she offered me a drink, but I declined. The remorse about spending so much time away from Kinsley was smothering me. But, I didn't want to ruin Deanna's night. One of her closest friends was getting married, so I pasted on a smile and pretended I was happy to be here.

The reception turned out to be a full-blown party with a twelve-piece band and a bar that served top shelf liquor. Deanna kept shoving drinks in my hand and before I knew it, I was not close to being sober. We took an Uber back to her place because driving was totally out of the question. When she was inside, I fully intended to take another Uber home, only she grabbed me and begged me not to leave her alone.

"Don't go, Grey. We've had such fun, I don't want you to leave. Please stay."

"But I have kids and need to get home."

She lunged at me with the intention of kissing me, but I moved at the last minute, causing her to crash to the floor. She tried to catch herself and ended up twisting her ankle since she was wearing spiky heels.

"Ahh," she cried out in pain.

I helped her to the couch, apologizing, even though it really wasn't my fault. She was the one who tried to kiss me, not the other way around.

"What am I going to do?" she whined.

"I'll get some ice. Hang on."

When I came back, I took her shoe off and asked her to put weight on it. She did. I was sure it wasn't broken, but the morning would tell the real truth.

I placed the ice on her ankle, which I propped up on the couch. After a few minutes, she asked, "Will you help me to my room? I'd like to undress."

Under ordinary circumstances, this question wouldn't have bothered me, but the way her voice had turned sultry sent alarms ringing.

"Um, Deanna, I'll give you a hand to your room, but then I have to leave."

"Leave? You can't leave me like this." She pointed to her foot. "What am I supposed to do? I can barely walk."

"I believe it's only a slight sprain."

"But it hurts," she whined again. Jesus, this had been a huge mistake to take her. And then drinking all that vodka. My head pounded already, and it wasn't even morning yet.

"Okay, let me help you."

I helped her up, and by all rights, she was a very attractive woman, but I just wasn't interested.

"Which way?"

"Over there." She pointed toward the hall. "My room's down there."

Her bed was covered with a red satin coverlet. It looked as though she staged the room. It had the appearance of a sexy boudoir. Deep red pillows were haphazardly flung about and a black silk robe lay on her bed.

"Can you unzip me?"

She turned her back to me and I undid her zipper.

"I'll give you some privacy."

"I'd rather you didn't."

"Uh, Deanna, I think we have different objectives. Mine was to see you safely home and then leave. Obviously, you had something else in mind. I'm sorry we weren't on the same page."

"That can always change you know if you give me a chance."

"I don't think so." I walked away, closing the door behind me. It left me in quite a quandary though. I was more than slightly inebriated and also concerned about her. What if she wasn't faking and something really was wrong with her ankle. I decided to sleep on her couch and take an Uber back to my car in the morning.

I should've taken one home that night.

The next morning, I was on the couch when something awakened me. It was Deanna's hand on my crotch.

"Good morning, big guy."

Fuck my life.

I slid her hand off me. "How's your ankle?" I didn't really want to know, but it was a diversion.

"Better." Then she opened up her black silk robe to reveal her naked body beneath. This woman was not taking no for an answer. Her hand moved back to my pants and tried to unzip them when I stopped her.

"I'm sorry, Deanna. Like I said last night, our paths aren't quite intersecting right now. I'm sorry." I gently pushed her hand away and stood up. It wasn't easy, because she was nearly naked and right in my face. But I managed it and groped for my phone in my pocket where I ordered an Uber.

"So you're really turning down a quickie?"

Giving her a regretful smile, I said, "Yeah, I am. I'm glad your ankle is better." Checking the app to see how far the Uber driver was, it showed he was a few minutes away. I decided to wait outside. It was too uncomfortable in here. What should my parting words be? Thanks for an awkward evening?

"I guess I'll be seeing you," I said.

"Yeah, I guess so."

I let myself out the door and waited. It wasn't long before the driver showed up. I felt like I was doing the walk of shame. It was awful. This was the last time I'd be going on any dates.

The kids were running around yelling and happy when I walked into the house. My head thrummed out some kind of hard rock tune I'd never heard before. All I wanted to do was go to bed.

"Daddy!" Kinsley collided with my legs. I picked her high up in the air, then hugged her.

"Hey there, polka dot."

"Daddy, you have pink stuff all over your shirt." I'd never bothered to check myself out, but I guess it was from when Deanna made her big kissing attempt on me. "What is that?"

Marin stood by and smirked. I'm sure she was enjoying this exchange.

"I think it might be lipstick."

"Lipstick? Why would you have lipstick on your shirt?"

"Because some women were at the wedding that I knew and they hugged me. It got on there by accident."

"Oh."

Marin glowered. She saw through my lie. But she didn't need to know the truth either.

"Daddy, you smell bad."

"I do?"

"Uh huh." Kinsley pinched her nose.

"Guess I need to go take a shower then." I put her down and climbed the stairs, passing by a grinning Aaron. That kid never had a bad day in his life. When I got to the bathroom, I looked in the mirror and grimaced. There was more than just a little smeared lipstick on my shirt. That stuff was all over my collar. Deanna did a great job of ruining my shirt. No wonder Marin had given me the stink eye.

Chapter Thirteen

MARIN

HE WALTZED in the door without a care in the world but looked like the biggest manwhore I'd ever seen. Did the man not realize he had a daughter? Granted, she was only seven, but still. And the stench ... how much alcohol had he consumed last night? Then he disappeared for hours. Again, an absentee dad. He was no longer Dr. Grouch or Dr. Asshole. He was Dr. Ghost.

I was supposed to have yesterday *and* today off, but I guess he forgot. Or just got drunk and laid and didn't give a shit. So I rolled in plan B.

"So guys, wanna go see a movie?"

Their eyes lit up, only Aaron's always did that when you asked him something.

"Can we get popcorn and Skittles?" Kinsley asked.

"You bet we can."

"Yay!"

Off we went and ended up seeing the cute movie about

the little minion characters. Oh, the kids laughed and laughed, even though I doubted Aaron knew what was going on. I laughed like they did, though I seethed inside. Over the past weeks, I'd had a few chats with my mom and explained some things about Dr. Ghost. I told her how I was going to all the parent-teacher conferences, with the kids in tow, how he practically ignored Aaron, and how he was never around. Mom was genuinely shocked.

"Well, darn it, Marin, I just don't know what to say."

"He's a dick, Mom."

"Marin, don't say that. He's been through so much."

"Yeah, well, don't make your kids go through it too. I'm just sayin'. Honestly, I'm their mom and dad rolled into one. And it's not fair to them. They are the most adorably perfect kids ever."

"Thank God for that. At least they're not hellions."

"He should be thankful, but he doesn't give a shit."

When we came home from the movies, Dr. Ghost was watching TV. "I wondered where you went."

My snarky mouth mumbled, "I'm surprised you even noticed we were gone."

Kinsley said, "We went to the movies, Daddy. Saw those minion things. They were funny."

"Minion things?"

"Jeez, you really are out of touch," I said.

He shrugged and said, "Can I have a word with you?"

We went to the kitchen and he said, "I'm calling the movers tomorrow. We only have four weeks and I'd like to move as soon as the house is painted. There are only a few rooms that need to be done since the place is new. We'll start packing up a room at a time. Then we'll get the kids' and your room done."

"That makes no sense. That'll put us between houses and living in two places."

"No, it won't. I have it all planned out with the painters on a spreadsheet. I talked to them this afternoon. It's all good."

He and his stupid spreadsheets. "Fine. Just tell me what and when I need to have it done."

"I'm hiring a muralist to paint the kids' rooms. I want them to have nice pictures of whatever they want. Kinsley mentioned giraffes and angels. She can decide what else she wants added and then the decorator will coordinate accordingly. But you'll have to pick out Aaron's."

"Me? Why me?"

"You're with him all the time." He said it like I was an idiot. Was he for real?

"Why not you? You're his father. Or haven't you noticed?" He glanced away and didn't look at me again.

"You'll do it. I'm never here."

"Oh, really. I wasn't aware." *Dr. Ghost.*

His mouth opened as though he wanted to say something but then clamped it shut. He rose to his feet and walked away. Everything about him was so weird. I needed to quit trying to analyze his craziness. This wasn't my business. Or was it? The truth was those children didn't occupy a corner of my heart. They now owned a large chunk of its real estate and my concern was genuine. I wanted things to be right with him because of those precious kids.

The night he talked to me about my writing, I had started a journal. Every day I wrote something, even if it was just a line or two. I looked back now and noticed if I would've charted his behavior, it would look like a zigzag. Why was he so mercurial? He seemed to have everything in life, right at his fingertips. I just couldn't seem to figure him out.

THE NEXT FEW weeks flew by. Between the end of the school year, Aaron's upcoming birthday with me trying to pull a family get together for him—and was that really my job?—and moving, I was at my wit's end. I had gone from being a bartender to being a full-time mother/housekeeper/and now moving coordinator. I didn't have a clue as to what I was doing. The jerkface even wanted me to direct the movers on moving day.

"I may be on call that day," he informed me.

"Oh, no, you don't. That's it. If you're on call, I quit."

"What! You can't quit."

"Says who? I can do what I want. Besides, you're the most ridiculous boss with the most absurd expectations I've ever encountered, and that includes my former unethical employer." There, I said it. He stood there staring at me as though I wore a black witch's hat. I wish I had those kinds of awesome powers at the moment. I would zap that ass of his, which was so damn tight it could probably snap a ten penny nail in half. I almost chuckled at my little joke.

"No, you can't possibly quit."

"The hell I can't. I will not be in charge of your move. That is your responsibility. This is your house. I've done just about everything else. Do you not see how wrong all of this is?" My arm swept out in front of me. I stood and waited for an answer. He only gaped at me like a stupid guppy. "For someone who went to medical school, you sure are as stupid as a box of rocks."

"I am not stupid."

"Then stop acting like it and take control of your own household. Be a man for God's sake." I stomped out of the room. My feet were beginning to ache from all this stomping. This man was grating on my last nerve. Then guilt rained down upon me as I thought about those sweet little angels who needed someone to love them. And I caved every time. Turning around I said, "Okay. I won't quit, but by doozy, you'd better take responsibility for this move." I aimed my pointer finger at him and added, "No on call tomorrow. Do I make myself clear? Or I'm out the door."

He raised his hands in the air and said, "Perfectly. No on call."

The man kept his word. He was there for the movers and all the unpacking of the boxes. It was a mess too with the kids to keep track of. I never could've done it without him. At the end of the day, he thanked me profusely. Over and over. He'd never done that before.

I gawked at him.

"What?" he asked.

"I, uh, I'm shocked." And I was … genuinely.

"Why?"

"You *never* thank me."

"Yes, I do."

Then I chuckled. It quickly turned into an all-out howl. Tears poured down my cheeks as I doubled over and slapped my knee. The man was delusional.

"What is wrong with you?"

I held a hand in the air, trying to catch my breath. When I could breathe again, I sucked in a lungful of air and said, "There's nothing wrong with me. It's you who has the problem." I walked away, hoping he'd ponder my statement.

Kinsley and Aaron were in the new living room where the electronic guru who Dr. Delusional had hired was hooking up the TV to the newly installed cable. Thankfully I had been forward thinking to have that done ahead of time because you-know-who sure hadn't. I had also made sure the water, gas, and electric would be turned on, reminding him he needed to transfer the service over. The guru was also outfitting the entire house with the camera system that the other house had. This one would be wireless and secure. As much as the doctor spent on this stuff, one would think he gave a shit about his family.

"Kinsley, Aaron, make sure you don't get in the nice man's way, okay?"

"Okay, Marnie." Aaron mumbled something unintelligible.

"Hey kiddos, I have an idea. I'm going upstairs to make up your beds. Why don't you guys come with me."

"Okay. Come on Aaron," Kinsley said.

He gave us both a slobbery grin. I picked him up and we climbed the massive staircase. This house was even larger than the last. Maybe Dr. Delusional wanted to be Dr. Disappearing Act so he could go missing in here and the kids wouldn't be able to find him at all.

"Marnie, do you like it here?"

"Um, yeah, I do. It's a real pretty place. Do you?"

"Nuh uh. Mommy won't know where we live now."

We were navigating the long hallway toward our rooms, so I stopped and dropped to my knees, as I still held Aaron. He thought I was playing, so he laughed.

"Honey, your mommy is an angel now, remember? She'll always know where you live. That's how angels work. They know everything. She's with you right now."

"She is?"

"Absolutely. And she already knows what your new room looks like and that it has giraffes, elephants, and angels on the walls. She also knows it has stars on the ceiling."

"She does?"

"Yep. And you want to know what else?"

"What?

"I bet she loves them and would tell you if she could."

Kinsley threw herself at Aaron and me, knocking us

backward. The three of us ended up on the floor in a big heap, laughing. That's how Dr. Delusional found us.

"What's going on here?"

Kinsley looked over her shoulder at him. "Marnie told me Mommy liked my new room and would always be able to find me."

"Polka dot, I'm pretty sure Marin is right." Without another word, he about-faced and headed toward his room, which was at the opposite end of the hall. So much for family time.

"Come on, short stuff, let's get those beds made up." It took twice as long with Aaron in the room because every time I put the sheet on one corner of the bed, he'd pull it off. He thought we were playing a game, and honestly, it was hard not to laugh at him. Cuteness all wrapped up in sweet was a hard combination not to love.

We finished in Kinsley's room, then went to mine. It was a wreck. I still had boxes to unpack. Kinsley opened one that wasn't taped and pulled out a couple of framed pictures.

"Who's this, Marnie?"

I looked up to see what she held, and what used to crush me to smithereens only pinched a little now. It was a picture of my ex and me.

"Oh, that's my old boyfriend."

"What happened to him? Is he an angel now like Mommy?" I wished I could tell her he was a cheating demon prick but that wasn't quite appropriate for a seven-year-old.

"No, sweetie. We just didn't quite see eye to eye and broke up."

"What does that mean? Broke up?"

"Well, it means he's not my boyfriend anymore."

"Oh, like Jordan and Brianna at school?"

"I suppose so, even though I don't know who they are."
I'm pretty fucking sure Brianna didn't find Jordan's face
buried in some other chick's pussy, but I didn't go there.

That seemed to satisfy her, so she put the pictures back
in the box. Then she opened a plastic bin. I was busy with
making up the bed, so I wasn't paying much attention.
Most of my focus was on the bed and Aaron. Suddenly, I
heard a buzzing noise. My head jerked up to find her
holding my vibrator. Fuck me.

"Kinsley, put that away!"

"What is it, Marnie? Is it a toy?"

"Yes. I mean, no! Put it back! Now!"

She laughed and ran out of the room, holding the
damn thing in the air. I scooped up Aaron and chased her.
I heard her laughing all the way down the hall. Dammit,
she better not ... and fuck me if she didn't.

"Daddy, look what I found."

Dr. Delusional walked out of his room, took one look
at Kinsley, and asked, "Where did you get that?" Then he
saw me chasing her. A smirk appeared on his scruff-
covered face, and then he broke into a howl. And Jesus,
help me, did he ever sound sexy when he laughed. After he
could finally speak, he said, "Polka dot, I believe the owner
of that would appreciate it if you would return it to her.
And you might want to turn it off first."

"What is it, Daddy?"

"I think you should let Marnie explain." It was the first
time he'd called me Marnie. He leaned his long frame
against the wall as he crossed his arms, waiting for my
explanation. Kinsley turned and extended her hand out to
me, with said vibrator in it.

I grabbed the damn thing from her and turned it off.

"Uh, Kinsley, like I said earlier, this is a kind of toy, but
it's for grown-ups." My face grew as hot as the Sahara.

"But how does it work?"

Dr. Smart Ass snickered, damn him.

"It's sort of hard to explain. It's a grown-up kind of thing. Why don't we go and finish in my room and then I'll read to you and Aaron."

"Do you play with it?"

"In a manner of speaking."

"But how?"

Jesus, please come into this house and rescue me from this travesty.

Right as I was opening my mouth to answer her, Dr. West said, "Polka dot, you're a persistent little thing, aren't you? Were you snooping in Marin's things? Is that how you found it?"

"Yes, Daddy."

"Come here, please."

She walked over to where he stood. "Remember what I taught you about that?"

"I'm not supposed to snoop."

"That's right. So what do you say to Marin?"

She turned to me and said, "I'm sorry."

Then he surprised me by hoisting her high into the air and saying, "Good girl." Then he planted a kiss on her forehead.

I scurried back to my room, tail tucked between my legs, vibrator in one hand, the other hand holding Aaron's as I practically dragged him behind me. I had to hide that damn toy somewhere. I stuffed it between the mattress and box springs before Little Miss Snoopy got back to the room so this didn't happen again. Then I quickly finished making up the bed and went into Aaron's room. His was easy since he was still in the crib. Kinsley hadn't reappeared, so I figured she was still with her dad. About damn time.

Aaron and I went back downstairs to the kitchen. This was going to be a bear of a task. Most of the unpacking had been done, but I had no idea where anything was. Dr. West and Kinsley walked in and she shouted that she was hungry. I didn't dare look him in the eye. That vibrator incident would never be forgotten. Rushing over to the refrigerator, I opened it up to inspect the contents, only to find there were none. Well shit. Then I blurted out, "I need to go shopping."

He bit his lips for a second and I just knew he was dying to say something. Thank God he didn't. Instead, he ran his hand through his hair, and said, "I really need to get my office arranged." Then his tongue poked the inside of his cheek. Why was I all of a sudden finding him so sexy? Ugh.

For once I didn't mind this task. It would get me away from this situation and by the time we got back, maybe he would've forgotten the sordid incident. "Come on kids, let's go to the store." I corralled them and off we went.

While we were there, I had Aaron in the baby carrier strapped to my chest, and Kinsley usually held my hand. But I was picking out meat for our dinners, and Kinsley hollered, "Look, Marnie, it's the man from the picture." At first, it didn't click, but when I turned to see who she was pointing at, it clobbered me like a giant log to the side of my head. Damien stood there, holding my former best friend's hand. They stared at me for a second and then laughed. They laughed!

My feet froze to the floor. I wanted to run, to hide, but I couldn't. Kinsley grabbed my hand and swung them like she always did. They walked toward us, their laughter replaced with giggles.

"Hmm, taking care of kids now, Marin? Looks like

you've done a great job of climbing up the career ladder," Damien said.

"Hi! My name's Kinsley. My brother is Aaron. What's yours?"

Bless her adorable heart.

"I'm Damien. This is Dawn."

"Hi there," Dawn said.

They looked from the kids to me. I smiled.

"So, Mare, what's up?"

"Not much. You?"

Dawn shoved her hand into my face and announced, "We're getting married."

"Congratulations. You two deserve each other," I said sourly.

"Hmm, looks like you got what you deserve too, Marin," Dawn said.

She was referring to my situation in life. Fucker.

"Yeah, well, just remember. Once a cheater, always a cheater." Then I grabbed the cart handle and pushed it away from them.

Kinsley asked as we walked, "Did they cheat in school on their tests?"

"Something like that. Okay, so what kind of fruit do you want, honey?" We finished shopping, loaded up the car, and drove home.

After what I just experienced, I wasn't in the mood to do all the unloading. So on my first trip in, I marched into the doctor's office and instructed him to get his butt outside and help me.

"Since when do you give me orders? I was under the impression you are my employee and not the other way around."

"Is that right? Tell you what. From now on we won't

have to worry about that employer/employee relationship."

I didn't give him the opportunity to object or to say a single word. Without a thought, I went out to the car, took all the grocery bags out, set them in the driveway and drove off. As I did, I saw him run out, waving his arms. My phone rang a few minutes later, but I didn't answer. It was over. He'd done his best to abuse my role as the nanny and I'd done my best to fulfill it. I couldn't do work for the ungrateful shit any longer. Working for him was like working for a ... well, there were no words for it.

When I pulled into Mom and Dad's driveway, their car was gone. That was probably a good thing. They would've told me to turn around and go back. But seeing Damien and Dawn, dealing with that, and then all the shit I'd been handling for the last few months, had done its best to piss me off something terrible. Maybe I needed to go back to school. Maybe law school. I don't know, but I had some figuring out to do.

Chapter Fourteen

GREYDON

I WAS UP SHIT CREEK. No, I was buried in deep shit. And it was my fault.

"Grey, whatever did you do to that girl?"

"Mom, I don't need a lecture now. Your help is what I'm calling for."

She showed up exactly like I knew she would. Dad did too. The expressions they both wore weren't anything I wanted to deal with at the moment. The kids were happy to see them, but I felt like a twelve-year-old again. Dad took care of the kids while Mom took care of giving me that talking down I had coming.

"What the hell happened, Grey? You will explain, or your father and I will leave."

"She quit."

Mom stared at me like I didn't have one ounce of sense. "I could slap you right now. I know that. But why?"

"She couldn't hack it, Mom."

"Grey?" The question begged for more of an explanation.

I scrubbed my face and skimmed over the sketchy details. She didn't buy it. Mom was more perceptive than that.

She took the *mom stance*, the one with a hand on one hip and a foot placed in front of the other. Oh, I knew that stance well. I'd faced it many times as a teenager. It was her combative posture and she was ready to duke it out with me. "Bullshit. You were an asshole to her, weren't you? What did you do to that girl? Your children adore her and she did everything in here but mop the floors. Oh wait, she did that too." Her pointer finger came up for that last remark.

"I have a housekeeper for that." My argument fell short.

"And you don't think the kids spill stuff every day? Do you see a dirty house? Is there laundry piled up? Are your children lacking for anything? Do your kids ever tell you they're hungry, tired? Do you see a complete mess when you get home at night or are your children bathed and ready for bed—not that you would know about that anymore? Oh, and how did the move go, by the way? Were your kids' rooms unpacked? Were their things put away? Their beds made up? Their toys put up? Their books put on shelves?" Sarcasm oozed from every one of her words.

When I stopped to think about it, that poor girl took on far more than a mere nanny should've had to.

She didn't give me the opportunity to answer before she charged on, her finger digging into my chest. "Oh, and when was the last time you helped Kinsley with her home-work? Attended a meeting with Kinsley's teacher? The school year is ending in a week. Were you even aware of that?"

"Shit."

"Shit is right. That about sums up your current parenting skills. You're pathetic. I thought I raised you better than this. What happened to you? You used to be *Father of the Year*. Where is that man now, Grey?" She held out her phone.

"What's this?"

"Call her. Right now. Because that woman, the one you let walk away, is the only hope your children have. She is raising them, Grey, and if for one solitary minute, you would pull your head out of your ass, you would notice that." Her tone gave me no opportunity for arguing.

My hands were fisted in anger, not at my mother, but at myself. "She won't answer. I've already tried."

"Don't be such a fool. She won't know it's you. You'd be calling from my phone."

I plowed a hand through my hair and blew out a puff of air. "I don't know, Mom. I really fucked it up."

"Don't use that word around me. You know how much I hate it. Call her this second. Yes, you've made a mess of things, but it's never too late to make amends. Grey, you have a huge heart inside that body of yours. Start using it, dammit." Her phone sat in her hand, like my lifeline. Marin was my only chance.

Grabbing it, I had to search for her number in my own phone in order to place the call. I was still surprised when she answered.

"Hello?" She clearly didn't know who it was.

"Please don't hang up. I was a first class jackass and I'm sorry. But the kids need you. And that may be another jackass thing to say, but it's true. I need you too. This house can't possibly function without you. I'm begging, Marin. Anything you want."

"Too late, buddy. I gave you multiple chances and you blew every one of them. I …"

At that exact moment, salvation in the form of my dark-haired polka dot, blew into the room yelling, "Daddy, Daddy, when is Marnie coming home?" It was impossible for Marin not to hear her.

"Baby, I'm not sure if she is."

"Why not?"

"Here, why don't you ask her." I handed her the phone. It may have been completely cruel of me to use my daughter as a weapon, but I needed that woman more than I needed anything at the moment.

Kinsley grabbed the phone out of my hand and asked, "Marnie, why aren't you coming home?"

I couldn't hear her response, but Kinsley said, "But I love you so much and so does Aaron only he can't talk right. Who's gonna take me to school and help me with everything? Mommy's with the angels and now you're leaving too. And who's gonna help Aaron with his dance lessons?" Then she broke into tears. I gathered her into my arms and handed the phone to Mom.

"Can you talk to Marin for a second, please? Tell her I'll call her back."

I carried Kinsley to the big leather chair in the office and sat down with her in my lap. "Polka dot, it's going to be okay. We're a big old team, remember?"

"I liked it better when Marnie was here. You work all the time."

My brittle heart exploded into a million shards. "I know you did. But we'll be just fine again, you'll see. Gammie will help and Bebop too. And maybe we'll find a different Marnie."

"I don't want another Marnie. Marnie was my friend."

We sat together for a long time, so long that I lost track

of time. How in the hell would I persuade her to come back? I smoothed Kinsley's hair and murmured soft words to her as I tried to figure out how to handle this. The main thing on my list was becoming a better dad ... like the kind I used to be. Then I heard a tap on the door and looked up to see Marin standing there. Kinsley's head was squished into the curve of my neck, so she didn't see her. I poked her on the side and said, "Hey, kiddo, you've got a surprise."

"What?"

"Look over there."

When she did, she rocketed off my lap, and bolted across the room like a slingshot, straight into Marin's arms. Marin's eyes were narrowed on mine. I got the feeling she was warning me and I heard her loud and clear. No more fuck ups. I dipped my head right before she and Kinsley left the room. I'd made up my mind to be the father I used to be, along with being a better employer. I didn't need a repeat performance of today.

A WEEK LATER, Kinsley had her end of the year school night and I was on call. I begged my partner to switch with me, but there was no way he could do it. His kid was also in some school program. I made the dreaded call.

"Marin, I—"

"I know. You can't make it."

"I tried to switch, but Josh's kid has his program too. I swear." I whined like a five-year-old.

"Listen to me. I don't care if you have to wear those green scrubs and one of those goofy hats. Your ass better be there or else." The call ended.

Fuck, she meant business. I checked the time and

prayed that at six forty-five, I wouldn't be in the EP lab doing a procedure on someone. The minutes ticked by and at six thirty, I warned the nurses I would be leaving but would have my phone. If anything happened, they were to text me. I would respond immediately. I begged God to give me a quiet night, at least until Kinsley was through with her part of the performance.

At seven, I ran into the school auditorium, dressed exactly like Marin described, and feeling like an idiot. But I didn't care. I hunted her down because if she didn't see me, my ass was finished. I finally located her, sitting off to the side, alone, with Aaron. There were empty seats around her, thankfully, so my long strides ate up the aisle and I sat down next to her.

She gave me a sidelong glance and then said, "You can take off that stupid hat. I don't think you need it in here."

I quickly yanked it off my head. She had a way of making me feel foolish. Then she plopped Aaron in my lap. He slapped me in the face the first chance he had and then laughed.

"Shh," I said. That made him laugh harder.

The music started up and the curtain opened. The first crew came out and they were the littlest things, cute as could be. They ran around in a state of confusion and the auditorium broke out in laughter. I relaxed more and more as the song went on. When it was over, the next group came out.

"This is Kinsley's group."

I perked up. She was dressed in a fish outfit. Well, sort of. I had no idea she even owned this. A smiling blue fish hat sat squarely on top of her head and she wore a blue sparkly shirt that mimicked fish scales and had a fin jetting out on the back. Her skirt had layers of sparkly tulle underneath it and the group sang "Under The Sea." They weren't bad, and I could pick out her voice because there were only ten of them. My heart soared for this precious little daughter of mine and then it sank for all the programs of hers that I'd missed. When she was done, I stood up like a fool and gave her a standing ovation. Marin grabbed my arm and jerked me back into my seat.

"What?"

"You're making a spectacle of yourself. Behave." This time her words weren't angry ones. They were filled with amusement and her eyes danced as they watched me.

"She was so good."

"Yes, she always is."

Now I felt even worse. Marin must've sensed that, because she said, "I have tons of pictures and videos saved for you."

"You … tons of videos?"

"Yeah. I was waiting for you to express an interest in your kids."

"I guess I deserved that." Poor Aaron had gotten rattled around with me standing and clapping, but he didn't mind a bit. He only grinned, like he usually did.

I looked down at him and thought about how his birthday had come and gone. I wasn't present for it— couldn't force myself to be there. The one year mark of his birth had left a sour taste in my mouth. Only now as I looked at him, I thought how all of this wasn't his fault. I kissed the top of his head, and damned Susannah again. Had I done something to send her into the arms of another man? Was I such a terrible husband? We never fought or argued. I thought we'd had a good marriage. How could I have been so wrong?

My phone beeped with a text. I checked it to find I needed to go.

Marin saw and nodded. I handed Aaron off and said,

"Tell my polka dot I'm so very proud of her and that I love her more than ice cream. I'll call as soon as I can."

She touched my arm as I was leaving. "Hey, I'm glad you made it."

"Not near as much as I am."

I turned to leave, but her voice stopped me.

"Don't forget your goofy hat." She pointed to the chair next to me where I'd left the damn thing. My goofy hat. That brought a smile to my face.

"Right. Thanks."

I thought about Kinsley's performance the whole night. But she wasn't the only one I thought about. Why hadn't I opened my eyes to what was right in front of them before?

Chapter Fifteen

Marin

DR. GROUCH WASN'T SO grouchy anymore. A change came over him the night after Kinsley's program and he was … nice to me. Really nice. He was actually considerate of my schedule and asked before he did anything. There were several times in the weeks that followed where he wanted my opinion on things. The man shocked me. It was so bad that at one point I only stared at him.

"What?"

I rubbed my eyes for a second. "What's happened to you?"

"What do you mean?"

It was out of my mouth before I thought about it. "You've changed. Dr. Grouch has disappeared."

"Dr. Grouch? I'm not a grouch."

I slapped a hand over my mouth and sputtered with laughter.

"You think I'm grouchy?"

Pulling my hand away, I announced, "Paging Dr. Grouch. Dr. Grouch to the heart center," in a formal tone. Then I bent over at the waist and laughed even harder at my little joke.

When my chortling subsided, I realized he wasn't laughing. In fact, he hadn't found any of this as funny as I had. I straightened back up to see he was more than a little irritated.

"I'm happy you find what I deal with on a daily basis as comical. And that when I have to tell a family their loved one has died, and I'm a little grouchy as you put it, you can find it easy to make fun of. Why don't you try putting yourself in someone else's shoes for a change, Marin? Maybe you wouldn't be so quick to ridicule."

"I wasn't ridiculing you."

"Sure sounded like it to me."

"And I wasn't making light of what you do. I was referring to the way you usually act around your kids."

"Yeah, well, sometimes it's a little difficult to shed what happens at work the very minute I walk through the door. Damn, you're a ball buster. Has anyone ever told you that?"

I backed up a step because someone had. My ex-boyfriend, Damien. He used to tell me that a lot but I always thought he was a pussy. He used to whine all the time. Like even when he got something as minor as a paper cut. One time he stubbed his big toe on the table leg and for a minute I thought he was going to cry. That's being a pussy, isn't it? Maybe I should've felt more sorry for him, but I told him to man up and quit acting like a baby. Now I felt kind of bad about it.

"I apologize for being disrespectful of your profession. I shouldn't have said that."

He sliced his head up and down once, and then turned

around and left the room. I watched his retreat with increasing regret and guilt over what transpired. If only he hadn't made that remark about his work. I knew it bothered him sometimes. But that didn't erase my belief he didn't spend enough time with his kids. They watched the door, especially Kinsley, every day for him to walk in. And when he did, some days he'd just briefly acknowledge them and take off for his stupid office. I should've kept my mouth shut. Things were going so well, with him being nice and I had to go and ruin it.

Since it was getting late, I decided to go to bed. I could watch TV on my iPad if I wanted or maybe I'd read instead. Or I could work on the article I'd started about what happened to me in my dream job, but words that used to flow seemed to have dried up on this topic. Maybe the timing wasn't right. There were a few books I had that, that I'd been waiting to dig into so that should keep me plenty occupied. And I could also write in my journal. When I got upstairs, I checked on Kinsley, and she was sound asleep, so I moved on to Aaron's room. But I stopped when I saw the doctor standing over his crib. I was getting ready to move on, but I heard him mumbling something. He was too far away for me to understand what he was staying, so I went to my room. He always acted so strange around that boy. I couldn't figure it out. No use in asking him why either. Like he'd tell me anyway. In most cases, he wasn't very forthcoming about things.

In the morning, the kids were cranky. Everyone was in a bad mood. I had a headache, Aaron was fussy, and Kinsley wasn't eating her breakfast. She was always agreeable about most things and it was unusual for her not to eat.

"I don't want this," she whined as I placed the fruit in

front of her. When I set her scrambled egg and toast down, which she always gobbled up, she said the same thing.

I felt her forehead and it was warm. "Hmm, do you feel okay?"

She shrugged. She wasn't a sickly girl, and in the months I'd been here, she hadn't been sick a day.

"Let's ask your daddy." I figured that would be the best thing.

I ran downstairs to where he was working out, something I never did, and *holy Jesus*. The man was running on the treadmill without a shirt, sweat streaming down him, and he was ripped and ... hot. How did I not know this? I'd been living under the same roof with him for how long now? Four months? And I had no idea this body existed under those scrubs he sometimes wore, or that stiff shirt and tie he wore to work. Christ almighty, why did I ever come down here? Now I'd have this image burned into my brain forever.

He pulled out his earbuds and huffed, "Yeah?"

"I, uh, erm," and I licked my bone-dry lips.

"What is it, Marin?" Impatience tinged his voice.

He waited for me to say something. Anything.

"Yeah. Uh, Kinsley. Yeah, Kinsley is, um, acting hot ... I mean weird."

"Which is it? Hot or weird?" He was obviously annoyed with me.

"Both. I was wondering if you could take a look at hot. I mean her." *Pull it together, you idiot.* My hungry eyes roamed over his delicious torso. Wait! He was an old man. How could he look this good? Men my age rarely looked like this. I was so consumed with lusty thoughts of him, I didn't realize he'd gotten off the treadmill and passed me.

"You going to just stand there or are you coming?"

Jeez, get your head out of your ass, Marin.

"Right, yeah, coming." He was halfway up the stairs, so I jogged up behind him, ogling his ass, and was huffing by the time I got to the kitchen.

He gave me one of those looks and said, "You should be in better shape than that, as young as you are. It's not good for your heart, you know."

"I do know. I'm not exactly an idiot. Time is a factor, or you probably hadn't figured that out."

"You can use the treadmill. Take the kids down there."

"Yeah, and that's so easy." Snarkiness ruled my comment.

"You don't want to wake up one day with occluded arteries. Oh, wait, you wouldn't wake up at all if they were occluded."

"Gee, what a lovely thought."

"Just telling you what happens when you don't take care of yourself."

"Let's focus on Kinsley, shall we?"

He turned to check out his daughter. "What's up polka dot? Not feeling so good?"

She scowled at him and I wanted to laugh. He looked at me and said, "Kids can be difficult."

"Aren't you a doctor?"

"I'm a cardiologist, not a pediatrician."

What the hell was that supposed to mean? Didn't he go to medical school? Didn't they teach him about the human body? Wasn't Kinsley a human? The way I figured she operated the same was as he did.

"That makes zero sense. She's a human."

He laughed. He fucking laughed at me. "Why is that funny?"

"She's a child. I was trained on hearts, not kids."

"That's the dumbest thing I've ever heard. So you went

to medical school and didn't learn a thing about the human body, only about a heart."

"No, that's not what I said."

"Is too."

"Is not."

He was so frustrating. "Stop it. What did you learn?"

"Hearts."

"Then you got screwed."

He stepped back like I slapped him. "I went to Harvard Medical School. I hardly think I got screwed."

"If you can't tell whether Kinsley is sick, I believe you did."

He clamped his teeth together so hard I heard them click. "Marin, all I'm saying is I didn't study childhood illnesses."

"Can you at least tell if she's got a sore throat? Like check in there or something? Don't you have a little black bag with one of those lights in it like real doctors have? Or one of those ear lights?"

He glared at me before leaving the room. I knew he went to his office and I had seen that little black bag of his in there. I'm not sure what was in it or if he actually used it. But it all seemed odd to me. I always figured you went to medical school and then got some kind of doctor training and then went to a specialty school. Guess I was wrong. He was special and just went to heart school.

Out he came toting that little black bag. He set it on the kitchen table and pulled out one of those things with a light on the end.

"Polka dot, open up so Daddy can see down your throat."

She did. All he said was, "Hmm. Her throat is fairly red. Does it hurt, polka dot?"

She gave him her usual shrug.

"Did you take her temperature?" he asked me.

"No, but I will." I ran upstairs and got the thermometer. Then I ran back down and stuck it in her ear. Seconds
later it beeped. "One hundred. Not too high, but no
wonder she's cranky."

"She's probably coming down with a cold," he said.

"She hasn't been coughing nor has she been
congested."

"It could be the early stages. My thoughts are to keep
an eye on her. Check her temperature every so often. If it
gets above a hundred and one, call the doctor."

"Okay." At least he went to a school that trained him in
more than just hearts.

So much for my plans for the day. The local library was
having a kids' day and I was going to take them there. But
now, that was out. We would hang around here until she
was better.

Dr. West was right. Kinsley ended up with a mild cold.
By the next day, she developed a slight cough and runny
nose. Nothing really bad, but enough to make her feel
puny. After that initial day, she actually perked up. Aaron
never got sick, thank God. And Dr. West even called
during the day and the next to check up on the kids.

Chapter Sixteen

GREYDON

I WAS SITTING at my desk, skimming through my emails when Josh stuck his head in my office.

"Hey, don't forget the office family picnic this weekend."

Shit.

"Damn, thanks for the reminder."

"Don't you put this stuff in your calendar?"

"Yeah, I do, as a matter of fact."

He let out a deep chuckle. "Guess you were trying to sneak out of it then, huh?"

"No, it just wasn't on my mind."

"So what was?"

Marin riddled with anxiety over a mere cold was. Last night, when I got home, she nearly assaulted me with questions. I assured her it was nothing and that kids got sick all the time.

"Not these kids. They haven't been sick a day since I've been here."

"You've only been here four months or so. Just give it some time."

I told Josh about it.

"Hey, consider yourself lucky. You actually found a nanny who cares. We've had terrible luck finding a good one."

"Is that right?"

"Yes, and the one I have now is obsessed with germs. She's constantly wiping everything off. It makes me crazy. I want to tell her to let the kids build up some immunities."

"At least you don't get reprimanded for not knowing pediatric diseases."

"Truth. Man, I bet you wanted to give her a real tongue lashing."

"More like a … never mind." For some reason, her bossiness had been kind of hot, not to mention our verbal sparring. And it rattled me to the core. She was the nanny, and off-limits. I kept reminding myself of that.

He turned to leave and said, "Saturday. Noon. Don't forget, asshole."

I gave him the thumbs up. Honestly, I wasn't looking forward to a Saturday afternoon picnic with the office staff. I wondered if Marin would be able to go. She could help watch the kids, which would be great.

That afternoon, after a relatively smooth day, I plopped my ass down into a chair in Mike, my psychiatrist's, office.

"So? What's new?"

"Things are better at home," I said.

"Oh?"

It always drove me crazy when he did this shit. Threw the ball right back to me with absolutely no advice.

"Why do you do that?"

"Do what?"

"Never give me advice."

"Grey, if you want advice, write to Dear Abby. So? Explain how things are better. Tell me about your engagement with your children."

He always found the snag, didn't he? I shifted in my seat. "Kinsley is in love with the nanny. She really adores her."

"Why the look?"

"The look?"

He laughed. "Your expression. If your brow was any more furrowed, you wouldn't be able to see."

I raised a hand to my forehead to ease the tension because indeed, he was correct. "She has a way with the kids that's … genuine. She … loves them I think."

He leaned closer. "That's wonderful. You must be happy about that, knowing your kids are with someone who genuinely cares about them. What about your engagement with them? Is it any better?"

I squirmed. "I'm working on it."

"Care to explain?"

"My nanny is on my ass constantly. She says I'm selfish."

"And what do you say?"

"It's difficult to argue with her, but she doesn't know the whole story either."

Mike leans back in his chair. I can tell by his expression he's not buying my explanation. "Grey, by your own admission, you were never this way with your children before. How can we get back to the real Grey? You're not a selfish man."

"I wish I knew. I'm trying. It easier with Kinsley, but Aaron, I can't decide what to do. She sees my reticence with him and takes it for selfishness."

"I see. Let's get back to the nanny. You're happy the kids get along with her."

"Uh huh." I nodded.

"But I sense there's more."

He was right, only I was unwilling to admit it. "More?"

"More than just the relationship between the kids and the nanny."

"What's that supposed to mean?"

He offered me one of his calm smiles. "Do you want me to spell it out for you, Grey?"

"You think I have a thing for her?"

"Do you?"

I swallowed. Why was it so hard to admit?

"Let's try another subject then since you're so … taciturn about this one. What about your decision on the DNA?"

The question hung between us, like a noose waiting to be tightened around my neck.

"Grey?" he prompted.

I gritted my teeth and admitted, "I don't know."

"You can't keep torturing yourself. You're eventually going to have to shit or get off that damn pot you've been on for how long now? Almost a year? Even I have to say it's a little ridiculous."

"Are you calling me out?"

"Damn right I am."

This was the first time he'd gotten tough with me. I didn't respond, only gaped at him because it had actually shocked me.

"Listen to me. If you know, you know. Aaron is yours for the long haul, whether you like it or not. If you get the test results and they tell you he doesn't carry your DNA, you will have the answer. If they do say he's yours, then you know. But this lack of knowing is disturbing you.

You're acting as though he's not yours anyway, so what does it matter?"

When I didn't respond, he continued, "Who would you give him to if the test shows you're not his father?"

"No one." I was indignant he'd even asked me that.

He leaned back, crossed his legs, and said, "Exactly."

Then another thought popped into my head. "Holy shit. Aaron may have half-siblings."

"Something else you may want to explore when he gets older, but that's up to you."

I knew Allie Gordon had two children, but I didn't know their ages. Did that give him a right to know them?

"Yeah, I need to get this done. If he's not mine, would I have a responsibility to tell Allie Gordon?"

He shrugged. "You may want to talk this over with your parents or brother, who's an attorney. They could give you better guidance on this issue. My role is to get your head straight. The bottom line here … or question … is what will you do when you find the answer? How will it change the way you treat Aaron?"

I knew I'd backed away from him and that needed to change. I had to get right in my head over it. Maybe this would be the first step.

"You've given me a lot to think about."

"I was hoping I'd given you a lot to act over. The thinking is what's killing you. It's time for you to make a decision."

"You're right."

He uncrossed his legs and said, "Good. I want to see you back in two weeks. And Grey? I want you to either have made a decision or have done the test by then? Are you good with that?"

"Yeah. I am."

After I got into my car, I googled DNA test kits on my

phone and ordered one. I still wasn't sure I'd actually go through it, but if I had it, maybe it would make the decision for me.

ON SATURDAY, we pulled up to the park for the office family picnic. Marin wasn't very excited about going. She tried to worm her way out of it, saying it wasn't appropriate for her to attend a family event like this since she technically wasn't family.

"It's very appropriate. You're there for the kids. And there'll be others there besides family." The truth was I couldn't imagine going without her.

But I was wrong. In the past when I'd come to these, I'd never paid attention to who attended them. No one had brought their nannies or anyone outside of their immediate families. Marin was right and it was obvious the situation was extremely awkward for her. However, even if I had known, I still would've wanted her here.

"Are you sure I shouldn't leave?" she asked.

"Of course not. You wouldn't be here if I didn't want you here."

"Everyone's staring."

Taking a quick look around, she was right. They were and it was rude. "Not everyone."

"Most of the women are."

"Ignore them." But it was easier said than done. I wasn't the one they were staring at. I did my best at making her a feel like she belonged, but it was a little weird. People would ask about her, but I actually knew very little to tell. I'd never taken the time to learn anything about her, which was inconsiderate and sheer laziness on my part. If I hadn't investigated where she went to school

—which was Emerson College, consistently rated the number one school in the nation for journalism—I wouldn't have known since I hadn't directly asked her. Ironically, Emerson was in Boston and I had to laugh since she gave me such shit about my Harvard education.

The thing that impressed me though was how well she handled herself. I thought we had a friendly staff until today. The nurses and office employees treated her like a pariah. Maybe it was because she looked different from the rest of them. Or perhaps they were protective of their little group. But I didn't like it and wasn't proud of them at all. I bit back several replies at times because children were present, but at our Monday lunch staff meeting, I would be sure to address this issue.

All the men tried to corral me over to where the corn hole contests were going on, but I declined because I didn't want to leave Marin alone with the kids. It wasn't that she couldn't handle them. It was because of the remarks I kept overhearing and it was pissing me off.

Josh's wife, who'd been very kind to me this past year, came over to speak.

"Grey, it's been awhile. I hope you're doing well."

"Ashley, it's good to see you. This is Marin. She takes care of the kids and she's been a lifesaver."

They greeted each other and Ashley was extremely warm to her.

She gestured to a group of people and said to me, "I was wondering if you would like to join us over there. I thought maybe the kids would like to play together with the others."

Marin glanced at me with eyes begging to say no. But Ashley wasn't like the women who had made snide comments and I wanted Marin to know that. "It's fine with me as long as Marin is okay with it."

Her brows shot up. She didn't expect that, nor did Ashley from the way she looked at the two of us. I was trying to make a point, which was Marin wasn't just some idiot to be treated poorly like the rest of the office staff was doing.

"Er, yeah. I think it would be great for the kids."

"Then let's do it."

As we walked, Ashley said, "Josh would kill me for mentioning this, but I heard your date with Deanna was a disaster."

I almost choked on my tongue. My eyes went straight to Marin. It wasn't like I needed her approval to date or anything.

"Uh, well, I didn't realize she thought of it as a date."

Ashley cracked right up. "You're joking, right?"

"No! Josh made it sound like she needed a stand-in for a wedding. When I met her, it was just as a friend."

"Come on, Grey. Take a look at yourself. You're the new Dr. McDreamy. Everyone is talking about getting their little paws on you. Or rather getting their paws in your …" She chuckled at her little joke, which I didn't find very amusing.

I glanced at Marin again. "Start spreading the news, Ashley. That's never gonna happen."

She grabbed my arm. "You can't be serious. You could have your pick of the crop. Heck, you could have the whole crop if you wanted it."

"I don't want any part of the crop. I only want to raise my kids."

I cut a peek at Marin, and she stood awkwardly with the children as we discussed the possibility of me dating someone. "Look, don't take this the wrong way. But I did that once and it ended up pretty badly. I'm not ever taking that chance again."

"Not all women are like Susannah."

Kinsley's head turned toward us at the mention of her mom, and she said, "Miss Ashley, you know my mommy lives with the angels now and I have angels in my room."

"Listen, let's not discuss this in front of the kids. It's not the most appropriate thing, wouldn't you agree?" I mumbled to Ashley,

"Yes, and I apologize," she whispered. And then she and Kinsley had a discussion about angels as we continued walking. Marin kept peering my way every now and again as she held Aaron's hand. No telling what the hell was running through her head now.

Chapter Seventeen

THE CONVERSATION between Dr. West and Ashley had been very enlightening. One, he hadn't liked his wedding-date-not-date. And two, he had no intentions of ever dating, even though he was the hot commodity at the hospital. I guess women went for old doctors these days, or maybe it was the money. But I had to admit the man was smokin' hot.

The kids had a great time playing, but most of the focus was on Aaron. He was clearly the center of attention with everyone oohing and ahhing over the little cutie. He'd run, full steam ahead, and then crash right into my lap, giggling like crazy. Then he'd take off again on repeat.

Dr. West had walked off a bit to where Kinsley was playing.

"You're a natural with him," Ashley said as she sat down on the ground next to me.

"He's so easy, anyone could be."

"He loves you. Look at him."

"This kid loves everyone. He's the happiest thing in the world. Hardly ever cries. I'm telling you, he's the perfect baby. Well, toddler now."

"Yeah, it looks like it." She huffed out a short laugh. "I wish mine had been that easy. Josh wants another one, but we just got over that difficult stage and I'm not quite ready yet for number four."

"Four?"

Her arm shot out in the direction of the men and she chuckled saying, "Right? Tell that dork over there."

"Wow, he really wants a fourth, huh?"

"Um, make that six. I would have to fall for an Irish Catholic. He has six siblings, so he figures it's normal. I'm going to look like that cow in the milk ads."

It was impossible not to laugh. "I didn't think people had that many kids these days."

"They don't. Joshua McBride is not normal by any means."

Aaron came back for round two hundred and fifty-nine interrupting us, and Ashley ruffled his wavy mop of hair. "Boy, does he ever take after his mother."

"Yeah? I never met her," I said.

"Such a tragedy."

"I know. I feel really awful for the kids, especially Kinsley. And Dr. West too." I didn't think of it much, but it must've been difficult to carry on after she died.

"Susannah was … different."

That took me aback. "Different? How so?"

"She was corporate all the way, if you know what I mean. Between you and me, I think she wore the pants in that house."

"Really?" This revelation shocked me. Dr. West seemed

so controlling. He didn't act like the kind of man that would let a woman push him around.

"I don't mean that in a bad sense, necessarily. I think he just deferred to her a lot. Let her handle things more at home, if you follow me. I suppose what I'm saying is whatever Susannah wanted, she got."

"I see." I really didn't, but I wasn't big on gossiping like this, so I didn't want to push her for more. I had to admit I was somewhat curious about her. Mom never said much and I'd never asked. It was sort of a topic no one ever spoke of.

"You're not even the least bit intrigued, are you?" Her eyes targeted mine and it was then I knew she had a motive for this *friendly* conversation. Ashley was peeling away the layers of my onion, or trying to anyway.

"Only in the sense where the kids are concerned. I really love those kids. They lack attention because he works so much. I worry about Kinsley missing her mom. Aaron won't remember a thing about her, unfortunately."

"No, he won't. Susannah was the type where if she were here, she would be on her phone, off to the side, dressed up in either very expensive jeans or something even better than that. She wouldn't sit on the ground like you and I are, nor would she let Aaron bulldoze her repeatedly. And Grey … he was really the mom and the dad in the house. He did everything for those kids when she was alive. Susannah was sort of hands-off with them."

This piece of information shocked me, but then again it didn't. I was under the impression that neither of them had paid a whole lot of attention to their kids and both were caught up in that uppity fruppity society stuff. Maybe I was off base here. So I did the only thing I could. I shrugged.

"Tell me, Marin. Grey is sexy as hell. It's hard for even

me to miss and I am head over heels crazy about Josh. I mean we can barely keep our hands off each other if you want to know the truth." She sighed. I really didn't want to know that little tidbit but whatever. "Aren't you the least bit interested in him?"

Now it was my turn to laugh. And I did. So much that I clapped my hand over my mouth. "Not at all. He's so old!" And I laughed again. The thought of being with him was ludicrous. Then I added, "Have you looked at us? I am not even from Venus in his world."

She squinted at me. "He looks at you differently than he does others."

"What's that supposed to mean?" This conversation had gotten super weird.

Aaron was charging me over and over and I held him a minute to calm him down. He was completely wired and when he got like this, he had a tendency to drop like a dead fly. We hadn't even eaten yet and it wouldn't be good if that happened way before his nap time.

"Josh's sister took him to that wedding. I'm sure you're already aware of that. She's gorgeous. And I'm not just saying that because she's my sister-in-law. She's also hot and sexy. We're really close. She wanted to go out with him, so I told her to go for it. It was bad advice. Deanna is great—a sweet person and I adore her. She drank too much and went a little overboard. I probably shouldn't be telling you this, but I get the sense that you're not the kind of person who runs around and gossips. I don't either even though it's looking like I do. Grey turned Deanna down. He had a huge opportunity and walked away. I was pretty shocked when she told me. And she didn't hold back. She was embarrassed about the way things turned out. Josh says the nurses at the hospital openly flirt with him all the time and he completely ignores it. Acts like they don't exist.

But today…" She aimed her finger at me. "He's into you, Marin. He pays serious attention to you."

I wanted to shove her shoulder like I would a good friend, only I didn't know her well enough for that. "Of course he does. I'm practically raising his kids. He's comfortable with me because I'm not a threat. He can act normal around me, but I have to say he isn't my cup of tea."

"Are you serious?"

"Totally. He's an ass."

She chortled. "So what you're saying is he's a doctor."

I jerked my gaze to hers and saw mirth in her eyes. I couldn't help joining in on the fun.

"What's got you two laughing so much over here?" It was Dr. West.

Ashley smoothly said, "Marin is such a joy. She's been filling me in on stories of the kids and how fun they are."

"Yeah, they love her too."

"Grey, this one's a keeper. If you ever want to get rid of her, send her to my place. I could use her with the team Josh is trying to build."

"I can see that," he said. "I came over to tell you two that lunch is ready."

"Great. I'm starved," I said.

We trucked over to where the food was being served. They'd hired a caterer to do this. Grey was helpful with the kids. He took care of Kinsley while I handled Aaron. Aaron loved the macaroni and cheese and the pieces of chicken fingers I fed him. I was a freak about him choking though so I only gave him the tiniest of pieces. Grey poked a little fun at me, while Ashley and Josh watched us with interest.

"He has teeth. He can gnaw on a little bit more than a tiny crumb, I promise."

"Nope. Not taking a chance."

"Marin, it'll take him all afternoon to eat."

"That's fine. I don't want it getting stuck in his trachea. Do you know how difficult it is to do the Heimlich on a thirteen-month-old? No thank you."

"I think you're going overboard with this. He's not going to choke."

I threw my hands up in the air. "Then you feed him and you watch him."

"Marin, this is—"

"No. Honestly, if you don't like the way I do this, then you can handle it."

By this time, I had gotten to my feet and he did too. He grabbed my arm, which wasn't something he normally did. "Please, sit. You're right. I shouldn't have butted in. You're wonderful with Aaron. Much better than …" And nothing. Better than what? I stared at him waiting and waiting. But he only cleared his throat and said, "Please eat. Your food is getting cold."

I dropped back down to the blanket and noticed Josh and Ashley were trying to hide their laughter.

"What?" I asked.

"You," Ashley said. "You sink your teeth into something and that's it."

"I can't help it. Babies choking freak me out."

Josh aimed his thumb at Ashley. "She's the exact same way. With number one, I figured we'd be doing baby food for life. By the way, you handle Grey well." And he chuckled. I had no idea what he meant.

I finished eating and feeding Aaron. Dr. West went off to play with Kinsley, but not much later he was back announcing it was time to leave. Kinsley whined, saying she wanted to stay. I didn't blame her. It was a fun outing for her. They never did family events and this had been a great one. Why run off like this?

"Is it ending soon?"

"No. I'm just ready to leave." He sounded a bit grumpy.

"But she's having a great time. Aaron's nap time isn't for another hour. Why not stay until then?"

He grunted out his response. "Okay. We leave in thirty minutes. Kinsley, go play, but when I call, you come. Okay?"

"Yes, Daddy." She scampered off toward the other kids.

"Was that really necessary?"

"What?"

"To tell her to come like that? She's very obedient. You never have to tell her twice."

"Are you dictating to me how to raise my children?"

Wow, where did that come from? "Don't I pretty much do that anyway? Raise your kids, I mean?"

His mouth opened and closed, and he pointed a finger at me for a second but then let his hand drop. After a moment, he left. Damn good thing he did. If he thought he could go pointing that doctor finger of his at me, he had another thing coming. I'd take that finger and stick it right up his butt. Hell, his butt was so tight, that finger didn't have a chance in hell of getting jammed up there even if I tried to hammer the damn thing in.

"Do I need to be afraid of you right now?" Ashley had walked up and I hadn't noticed.

"Why?"

"You look like Daenerys Targaryen from *Game of Thrones* when she's getting ready to unleash one of her dragons."

I pinched the bridge of my nose. "No, I'm fine. It's just … oh, nothing."

"Yeah, they're frustrating, aren't they?"

"I mean, she's having so much fun and she never gets to do stuff like this and he wants to leave for no good reason."

"And you told him this?"

"Well, yeah. Why?"

She only laughed. I didn't think it funny, but apparently, she did. "That is priceless. I love that you don't jump at his every whim." That was such an odd thing to say. She left me standing there trying to puzzle this out. All I knew was this group had my head spinning and I wasn't exactly sure I liked it.

Chapter Eighteen

GREYDON

I'M NOT sure if Marin worked for me or the opposite. She was calling the shots these days and it was difficult to argue with her logic. My reason for wanting to leave had everything to do with how the women from the office were treating her—snubbing her, whispering behind her back, and giving her those looks—but I didn't want to tell her that. This would be addressed on Monday. I'm not sure why they felt the need to do that, but I wasn't going to stand for it.

When we got home, Aaron was fast asleep, so I carried him up to his room. Kinsley was in need of a nap as well, so she tagged along behind me. I got her settled and then decided to do a quick workout. I grabbed some water from the kitchen and headed down. Why had Marin invaded my headspace so much? She'd taken over, like a fucking virus. I couldn't say no to anything she demanded. Why was that? Because she made perfect sense every fucking time and it pissed me off. They were my kids, so I should have the final say, right? But no. She was the one who got her way. And that's what sucked. She was making me lose my shit. I had to leave her during that damn picnic because it was either that or get into a bitch session. And wouldn't that have gone over well? I could just hear Josh on Monday giving me shit about it.

I was adjusting the weights on the leg press when I heard footsteps. Turning around, I saw Marin stepping onto the treadmill. She hadn't seen me yet because I was bent down, reaching for another plate. I took the pleasure of observing her for a minute. She looked good … really good.

"You finally decided to start exercising, I see."

"Eek!" Her phone flew out of her hand as she jumped in fright. "You scared me to death. Don't do that."

"I wouldn't have had I known you'd react like that."

"I always react like that when someone scares the crap out of me." She picked her phone up and stepped back onto the treadmill. "And just so you know, I've been exercising for a few weeks now. Only when Aaron is napping. Kinsley comes down here with me, so don't think I'm a neglectful nanny." Her sassy tone let me know she wasn't happy with my comment.

"I hadn't meant to infer that."

She stuffed her earbuds in and ignored me. I guess the conversation was over. After I worked my legs much harder than I'd intended, I moved to the bench press machine. It faced the treadmill, so I watched her run as I lifted. She had good form but was a bit slow. Maybe I could put her on a running program or at least offer her a few pointers. I finished my punishing set of chest presses, did some lat pulldowns, then walked over to the treadmill.

"Hey."

She yanked out her earbuds and raised her brows.

"You should pick up your pace some. I can put you on a program."

"Oh?"

"Yeah. Intervals. Go all out for about fifteen to twenty seconds, and then back off for a minute or two. Then pick it up again. Do this for twenty to thirty minutes three days a week. Then on the other three, try to pick up your pace where you can't carry on a comfortable conversation. Maybe you could run a 5k then."

Her head slanted and she paused the treadmill. "Has it ever occurred to you that there's a remote possibility I have one functioning brain cell in this skull of mine? And that perhaps I have some experience at this?"

"Er …"

"Yeah, didn't think so. I'm going to let you in on something. I used to run marathons. I've done ten and let me count." She paused and looked up at the ceiling. "Seventeen half marathons. I ran cross country in high school. I know all about interval training. In the old days, we called it speed work. Now non-runners fancied up the term with *interval training*." She finger-quoted the new term. "Give me another month, Dr. Know It All, and I'll dust your ass in a 5k." Then she flashed me a cocky—yes, a cocky—grin. "Care to accept this challenge?"

Well, fuck. I couldn't pussy out of this. I returned her little cheeky smile. "I'd love to accept your challenge." But then I thought how I needed to get my running ass in shape. If she was a marathoner, she knew what the hell she was doing. *Shit.*

Her cocky grin remained in place and I had an urge to kiss it away. "Since you're so damn smart, I'll even let you choose which one we do."

"It's a deal." I held out my hand and she shook it.

"Now leave me alone so I can get back to running. I don't have the luxury of a lot of time like you do. I actually work for a living."

"What?"

"You heard me." She waved her hand.

I turned around and could've sworn she flipped me off. The little shit. I was going to have to show her up on this 5k or else. I finished my workout and literally sprinted to my computer to Google upcoming 5k's in the area. There were a few about six or seven weeks from now. I'd have to see if my parents could keep the kids. Then I leaned back in my chair and chuckled. She totally dished it out to me. There I thought I was Mr. Knowledge and she showed me up. She even challenged me. A grin stretched across my face, which soon turned into a chuckle.

It lasted until I opened my desk drawer to get something and there sat the DNA kit I'd ordered. When it arrived, I'd stuffed it in there, still not knowing what to do. Maybe it was time. Maybe today was the day. Maybe knowing would put an end to all of this.

As I stared at it, time disappeared. My thoughts shifted back to Susannah and the day she told me she was pregnant with Aaron. I was overjoyed. After Kinsley, I was sure she hadn't wanted another. With her travel schedule and how invested she was in her career, she always said only one. She loved her daughter. I never doubted that. But when the second pregnancy happened, she wasn't happy about it.

"THIS IS GREAT. You know I've always wanted more than one."

"You have. Not me. I'm the one who has to carry it. This was unplanned, Grey."

"Yes, but you know how much I'll help raising it. I'm not an absentee father."

"Grey, I didn't mean to imply that. It's just ..."

"What?"

"I, uh, nothing."

THINKING BACK TO THAT CONVERSATION, was she trying to tell me something then? Or was I reading too much into it? I sat and stared at that stupid kit until Marin walked in and asked, "Have you figured it out yet?"

Did she suspect something?

"What?" I practically yelled.

Her eyes darted to me, and then the kit. It was plainly written on the box. *DNA Paternity Testing Kit.*

"Um, the race. Are you okay?" Her tone was soft.

When I didn't answer, she asked, "What's going on? I know it's not my business and you can tell me to butt out, but you have a really crazy look on your face."

"Yeah, well, it's not your business."

Both her hands shot up, palms facing me. "I get it." She started backing away.

"Wait." She loved Aaron and maybe she could help me think things through. "You ... I mean, are the kids up yet?"

"No. They're still sound asleep. Aaron will probably be down for another thirty and if Kinsley wakes up, she'll come down wanting a snack."

I shook my head. "So, uh, do you mind if I ask you something?"

She rested a hand on her hip. "Only if you want an honest answer because I'm not into blowing smoke up someone's ass just because I think it's what they want to hear."

"I already figured that out about you."

"So what's up? And I take it that it has something to do with what's in your hands."

I was holding the box and turning it around and around. "Yeah. Take a seat."

She ran her forearm across her damp forehead after she sat down. I took a deep breath and launched into the sordid tale.

"The day my wife died in that plane crash, I found out she'd been having an affair that had been going on for two years."

Chapter Nineteen

MARIN

IF A BOMB HAD GONE off in the room, I wouldn't have heard it. My jaw sagged. "Say what?"

"You heard me correctly. See, here's the thing." A pained look crossed his features as a cold stab wedged in my heart. "I don't know if Aaron is my son."

"Hang on. You mean she wasn't careful?"

"I don't know. She died, remember? I couldn't ask her."

"But he has your eyes."

"Yeah, about that. The man she was seeing had eyes the same color."

The coldness pressed down until I didn't know whether to cry or throw up. This was so sick. Who would do that? What kind of woman was she? I hated to speak ill of the dead but … then again, she didn't exactly know she was going to die either. "Surely she would've been smarter than that?"

He shrugged. "I never thought our marriage was terrible. Goes to show you how little I knew." He'd always seemed so strong, so powerful, but at this moment he was quite the opposite. Sitting across from me was a broken, vulnerable man.

I sat ramrod straight in the chair and mumbled, "Now it all makes sense. Why you're so detached from him."

He hung his head … was it in shame? I didn't know, nor did I care.

"I swear I don't mean to be that way. He's such a beautiful child."

Leaning over his desk, I said, "So what will you do if you find out he's not yours? Let the baby daddy have him?"

He lifted his head. "Not possible. He died too."

"So why even bother? Why torture yourself?"

His fingers dug deep grooves into his hair and it brought chills to my body. I didn't understand. Aaron was innocent. Didn't he see that? Anger spiked in me.

"You have the most adorable son up there. DNA be damned. He's your kid whether you choose to accept it or not. He's sweet and precious beyond words. God has blessed you with two healthy kids. Let this go and allow him into your heart. I can promise you one thing. If you don't, he'll eventually recognize it and will grow up to resent you. Then one day when you have the balls to actually treat him like he's yours, it'll be too late. He'll be lost to you. And the other thing—does it really matter either way? Answer that question. If you can honestly say yes, that you wouldn't love him just the same, then give him up for adoption. There are couples all over the place that would give their right arms to have a kid like him. Hell, give him to me. I'll gladly take him off your hands."

The misery staring back at me did nothing to soften me

towards him. He was only wallowing in self-pity. Yeah, it sucked that his wife cheated on him. Yeah, it was terrible that she may or may not have considered the consequences. But control what you can. That ship had sailed. It was time to move on. My heart ached something fierce for that sweet, adorable child that was missing out on the affection and love from his father and I wasn't going to back down on that.

"You don't understand."

"Oh, I do. I know what it feels like to be cheated on, but you have kids to think about. You need to bury those emotions and focus on them. They need you more than you need your self-pity."

"I'm not pitying myself."

"No?"

He could lie to himself, but I wasn't buying it. I grabbed that kit out of his hands.

"What are you doing?"

"I'm taking this."

"What will you do with it?"

"I'm not going to tell you. That way you don't have to worry about it anymore. Treat Aaron like your son, Grey. I'm not even kidding. You'll lose him before you even had him."

I left in a hurry before he had a chance to say anything. And there was something else. I had called him by his first name. It was something I had never done before.

Without looking back, I hurried up the steps and jumped in the shower. I didn't have much time before Aaron woke up. And about the time I was getting dressed, I heard him cry. As I sped toward his room, I was surprised to hear the doctor's voice from inside. He was in there talking to his son. Well, I'll be damned. I'm not sure how long this would last, or if it even would at all, but I'd take it just the same. They needed to bond again because they sure as hell hadn't spent time together since I'd started working here.

I was in the process of sneaking away when Kinsley careened out of her room, yelling at the top of her lungs. "Marnie, I'm hungry." She pushed past me into Aaron's room and in the process, it caused me to stumble into his room too.

Dr. West looked up at Kinsley's voice, but his eyes landed on me instead. Fire simmered beneath their surface and my hand flew to my pulse as it felt like the wings of a hummingbird fluttering in my neck.

"Daddy, you're changing Aaron's stinky. You never do that."

His gaze never left me as he answered, "Yes, I do, polka dot."

"Nah uh. Marnie does." Then she skipped around the room announcing she needed a snack. "Come on, Marnie, let's go find something." She took my hand and tugged me along behind her. I could feel Dr. West's gaze scorch my skin as he watched us leave. I braved a quick glance over my shoulder and his hands had stilled in their task as he stared. Why was he doing that? I shivered in response as Kinsley dragged me along. I couldn't get that intense look or the feeling of it out of my mind.

We were standing in front of the refrigerator and Kinsley asked, "Well can I?"

"Can you what?"

"Have a Popsicle? A red one?"

"That would be a no. You can have some fruit or carrots and celery, or half of a sandwich." I was having a difficult time concentrating because of my burning curiosity over the way he gazed at me. Kinsley pouted for a bit but then decided on some apple with peanut butter. She was a big fan of that. I gave her a glass of milk to go along with it and had the same for myself. That's how the doctor found us when he came down with Aaron.

"I think the boy is hungry." With those words, Aaron started kicking. But Kinsley said, "Nope. He wants to dance. See." I only laughed at her.

The rest of the day was sort of awkward until Dr. West said, "How about we go to dinner tonight?" Wait, what?

"Yeah!" Kinsley yelled. Aaron kicked his legs and talked in his own language.

"I think that's a yeah for him too," I said.

"I need to put him down so he can run that kicking energy off," Dr. West said.

"Maybe we need to start him on some foot drills and punting. I've never seen anything like it. But then again, I don't have many comparators," I said.

"He does seem to like to move them a lot."

"Constant motion," I said.

"He wants some clicky shoes," Kinsley said.

"I think *you* want some clicky shoes. And they're called tap shoes. Or, I'm not sure what the Irish step dancers call them." I quickly Googled them. "This is interesting. I found they're called hard shoes or jig shoes. The toe pieces and heels are made of fiberglass, so they produce better sound quality. That came from Wiki." They gave me blank looks. "I thought you might want to know."

"Can I get some?" Kinsley asked.

Dr. West answered, "Only if you're going to take Irish step dancing lessons. And you have to practice."

"Can I?"

"Ask Marin if she would mind taking you. And we'd

need to see where they are held too, because if it's too far, then no."

"Marnie, would you do it?"

"Only if it's not too far." So I found myself Googling Irish step dancing lessons and found a dance studio that was only about fifteen minutes away.

Dr. West asked, "Are you sure about this?"

"Yes, but Kinsley, you have to go through a complete session. No dropping out. Okay?" I said.

Her head whipped up and down so fast I couldn't track it.

"On Monday I'll call them to see when I can enroll you. How does that sound?"

"Oh, Marnie. Thank you." She wrapped her arms around my hips and hugged me. "Now can we practice?"

"Practice?"

"You know? Our step dancing."

We? There wasn't any *we* in this equation. "I'm not sure about that. You don't know the first thing about it."

"We can try. Come on."

At that moment, I had a good idea of what it was like to be in the military. Kinsley ordered me around like a drill sergeant. "Marnie, move that table. Don't forget the lamp. That chair's in the way. Now the rug."

"I can't move the rug. It's way too big."

"How will we make those clicky sounds?"

"We don't have any clicky shoes to begin with, so it won't matter."

"Oh, yeah. You gotta get that thing over there out of the way too."

"What thing?"

She pointed to the big toy box. "That thing with all the toys."

"That's clear on the other side of the room."

"But what if we crash into it?"

"Wait a minute. I'm not dancing, you are," I reminded her.

"Yes, you are too. You're gonna help. Now come on." She tugged on my hand. "Just move it."

She won. There was no arguing with that girl.

"Now get some dancing music for us."

Geesh. What else will she want? A five-piece band?

I asked the little device in the room to bring up some Irish dance music. Thank God for that. Soon it was playing and Kinsley was dancing.

"Come on Marnie, you gotta kick out your feet. Like this."

Swear to God, thought I was gonna die. I didn't know what the fuck I was doing. I never did ballet, tap, or any kind of dance, and here she expected me to pull an Irish step dance routine out of my ass.

So my feet and legs did their best imitation of what I *thought* an Irish step dancer would do, only I immediately got scolded.

"No, Marnie, you don't move your arms. Like this. See?"

I watched her and clamped my lips together. Her arms looked like they'd been stapled to her legs and her feet, well, I wasn't quite sure what to say about those. It seemed one went north and the other went south. And not in a rhythmic way.

"Now you do it."

"Oh, I'm not sure I can follow that."

"Pound your toe on the floor and then your heel and kick your legs out. Like this."

Good Lord, if I did that, I'd be in a wheelchair for life.

"Okie dokie." I went at it again and if someone

recorded this, it could possibly go viral on YouTube on how to make an ass of yourself.

When I finished, Kinsley said, "You don't learn fast, Marnie. Maybe you should just wait 'til we take lessons."

I wasn't sure how I was going to break it to her, but there would be no *we* in the lessons. Hopefully, she would figure that out when I went to buy her clicky shoes.

The couch was a welcoming reprieve, but as I went to take a seat, I noticed we'd had an audience. Dr. West stood there with a smirk on his face. How long had he been watching and why was he smiling like that? He looked like he carried some major secret. And I wanted to know what it was.

Without thinking, I said, "Why don't you give it a go? I think you could be the next superstar."

"Oh, I'll pass. Seeing this little dance performance was plenty for me." Then he waggled his brows. What the hell was that supposed to mean? Was the stodgy doctor making fun of me? My cheeks flamed as I turned to go and see where Aaron had gotten off to.

"Aaron is fine. He's right behind me if you didn't notice."

I hadn't. I was too busy trying to figure out what my employer was thinking. Then he had the nerve to shock me again.

"I was wondering if you'd be interested in taking the kids to that amusement park tomorrow. You know the one with all the kiddie rides?"

Who was this man? Had a good fairy invaded his body and taken over, because he sure was acting strange?

"Uh, sure."

"I'm listening to your advice if you're wondering."

"Oh." My tongue must've disappeared because I was incapable of forming a single syllable.

"Great. I was thinking we'd leave after we got home from church. Maybe around noon, if that's okay?"

He was asking me? And since when did he go to church?

"That'll be perfect. It'll give me a chance to do my run for the day." I winked at him and walked out, leaving him to ponder that.

Chapter Twenty

GREYDON

MARIN DIDN'T HAVE A CLUE. She had gotten to me — gotten behind the walls, the same ones I'd vowed never to bring down. Not only that, she made me hard, so fucking hard, harder than I'd ever been for any woman. My showers were getting longer and longer each day. And my analytical brain wasn't making any sense out of it. How could I be interested in someone who was sixteen years younger than me? Not to mention she was the complete opposite of Susannah, from her rainbow-colored hair, to her clothing, which wasn't anything close to designer labels. But there was something about her. Maybe it was her sass because damn if she didn't have plenty of it. Or maybe it was the fact she loved my kids. Or had the nerve to stand up to me and didn't care what I thought—or anybody else for that matter. It made me wonder how she'd acted when she'd taken Kinsley to school. Of course it was summer break now, but as I thought about it, when I went to that program, she'd been alone, no one within striking distance of her. It didn't seem to bother her, but who knows. If that had been Susannah, she would've been holding court.

The trip to the amusement park was a great idea. She handled the kids like an expert. When it came time for Kinsley to ride certain rides, she was adamant about her not going on one.

"Absolutely not."

"But why, Marnie?"

"You'll be sick afterward. And I'm not comfortable with you getting off and throwing up."

I chuckled at their banter constantly. Kinsley was persistent as hell and did her best at working Marin over, but Marin was tough. When it came to the important things, she stood strong.

"Marin is right, polka dot. That ride is way more than you can handle. Let's go."

Marin added, "No more arguments on it or we can call it a day."

"What does call it a day mean?" Kinsley asked.

"It means we'll just go home."

"But I don't want to call it a day and go home," Kinsley said.

"We won't if you don't argue with me," Marin said.

"Okayyy."

We walked around and took Aaron to the little helicopters. They strapped him in while Marin grilled the man about safety. It was clearly a ride for kids his age, as it claimed on the board up front, but she wasn't satisfied until she saw how slow it went.

"That thing doesn't even go off the ground," she commented.

"You expected it to?"

"Well, yeah. It's a helicopter."

"In name only. It's the impression they give."

Aaron was kicking his legs, as usual, and Marin snapped photos of him every time he passed us. She was going use up all the memory in that damn phone if she wasn't careful. Which reminded me.

"Hey, do you really have videos of Kinsley's programs I missed?"

"Sure do. I was waiting for you to ask for them." She combed through a gazillion pictures and handed me her phone. As I watched, tears sprung to my eyes and an immense pang of remorse plowed into me that I'd missed my daughter do these amazing things. I was mesmerized.

"Remind me when we get home, and I'll download these to your laptop."

After clearing the emotions from my throat a few times, I nodded. "Thanks. This means a lot."

We were headed to the car when I heard someone call my name. I turned to see Allie Gordon standing there with two children close to Kinsley's age or maybe a little older.

"Mrs. Gordon."

Her brows drew together as she took in the scene— Kinsley, Aaron, Marin, and me. A surge of pain nailed me for what this woman experienced. Her children—both girls —were holding each of her hands. "Yes, I see you're …"

"I should introduce you. This is Marin, my nanny, and these are my children." I hesitated to say their names. It was awkward as shit. All I wanted to do was get to the car and go home.

"Yes. I hope things are better…" She kept staring at Aaron. I looked at her daughters as well, though I couldn't see any resemblance between them and Aaron.

"We should be going," I said.

"Have a nice day."

We turned and left for our vehicle. Marin looked at me oddly while Kinsley asked, "Who was that lady, Daddy."

"Just someone I know, polka dot."

Seeing Allie had put a stain on our day. Too many old memories were conjured up. But I was glad the children had a blast even though I cringed at what they ate. As Marin reminded me, every now and again wasn't going to kill them.

When we got home, and the kids were out of earshot, she asked, "Who was that woman?"

"That was the wife of the man Susannah had the affair with."

"Oh, God. No wonder it was so awkward. She kept staring at Aaron."

"You noticed that too?"

"It was so weird."

"Honestly, I feel sorry for her, but I wish she hadn't approached us. There's really nothing to say."

"I agree. It made for an uncomfortable exchange."

Kinsley ran up to us then, cutting off the rest of that conversation. "Marin, I'll bathe the kids tonight." When I told her, I'd never seen such an expression of mortification. Even Kinsley looked taken aback.

"Daddy, you don't know how to do that."

"Yes, I do, polka dot. I used to give you baths every night."

"You did?"

"Come on, let me show you."

The entire time, Kinsley would say, "Marnie does it this way and Marnie does it better like that." By the time I finished, I was pretty fucking sure Marnie was the expert on everything. Aaron was fussy during his bath, but I attributed it to him being tired. It was a long day in the sun and he looked somewhat flushed. Perhaps he'd gotten a little burnt.

We all traipsed back downstairs, but Aaron remained cranky. Marin felt his head and claimed he was warm. "Maybe he has a fever. Let me get the thermometer."

Sure enough, he was running a temp of one hundred. I wasn't concerned since it was so low. But not Marin. Panic was her middle name all over again.

"The thing about kids, Marin, is they catch things. They have little illnesses. He'll be fine." She ignored me. By the time we put him down, she was convinced he was dying.

I grabbed her shoulders and said, "You have to stop this. You're scaring Kinsley and quite honestly, it's way overboard. Kids pick up viruses all the time. Kinsley did when she was his age. This is borderline neuroses. I love the fact you're so concerned, but please calm down."

"Right. You're right. I don't know why it worries me so much."

"We gave him acetaminophen and he'll be fine in the morning. He probably caught a little bug. By the way, I'll be leaving early. We have a staff meeting and I need to do some things in the office beforehand."

She nodded, saying, "Okay."

"You know how to reach me if you need me."

I left her standing there. I would check on Aaron again before I went to sleep, but I was sure he was fine. Being at that picnic yesterday exposed him to a lot of people and he just probably picked something up there.

The next morning, I left early because my plans were to address the way the staff had treated Marin. On my way out, I checked the camera in Aaron's room, but he was sleeping soundly so I decided not to disturb him. That comforted me because sick babies usually didn't sleep like that.

My office was more quiet than usual since I was the first to arrive. Emails had accumulated over the weekend which I took care of. Then I got to work on deciding what to say to the staff. The physicians and nurse practitioners didn't know I had this planned, which was done on purpose.

Everyone was surprised to see me in my office when they arrived. When we were all in the kitchen, which was where we held our meeting because it was the only room in the building large enough to seat us all, John began with the usual housekeeping items. After that, some other things were addressed. When he was finished, and everyone was getting ready to dart out of the room, I stood and asked for their attention.

"I'd like to address something. On Saturday, I witnessed some of you exhibit rude behavior toward the woman who takes care of my children. I'm not going to name anyone, but you know who you are. First, it more than disappointed me. You were hired as employees in this office because we thought you were professionals. What I saw was not professional at all. It was small-minded and petty. Second, I'm not sure why you thought it was necessary to treat her that way, but I would appreciate if we have any other office functions where she is present that you treat her with the courtesy and respect she deserves. If you find that you can't, see me afterward and we can arrange for a separation package for you. Thank you for your time." As I walked past everyone, you could've heard a pin drop in the room. I believe I got my point across, loud and fucking clear.

Ten minutes later, Nicole poked her head into my office and told me my first patient had arrived.

"Thank you, Nicole." The warmth that we used to share was gone. The woman I thought was kind and caring wasn't. What she had done to Marin was unacceptable. Nicole had acted like she was better than Marin and it really bothered me.

My first patient was in a gown, waiting for me. He should've had an EKG, but hadn't. In the past, I would've let it slip. Not today.

"Excuse me, Mr. Jeffries, I'll get the nurse in here right away."

Storming out the door, I called, "Nicole!" She was sitting at the nurse's station, which was in the center zone in the office.

"Yeah?"

"Where's Mr. Jeffries' EKG?"

"I haven't gotten to it yet."

"Why is that?"

She looked at the nurse sitting next to her.

"Don't look at Sharon. I'm talking to you."

"I … I don't know."

"Go and do it. There's no point in examining him without one. You should know that. Let me know when it's done."

"Okay."

"And Nicole? That's unacceptable. You know every patient should have one *before* I get in the exam room."

"Yes, Dr. West."

I stayed on her ass all day long and by the middle of the afternoon, Josh hit me up. "Hey man, what's up with you today?"

"Me? What do you mean?"

"Your attitude toward Nicole."

"Long overdue. She's way too slack and I've had it up to here." I slashed my hand across my neck.

"Hmm. I didn't know it was that bad."

"Josh, how many times do you go in to see a patient and an EKG hasn't been done?"

"Never."

"My point exactly."

"Get rid of her."

"I'm going to if she doesn't straighten out. Just making her day miserable first."

All the things I'd let slide over the years, came to an end today. She was going to have to work from now on if she wanted to keep her job. Dr. Nice Guy was gone.

At the end of the day, she knocked on the door and came into my office. "Have I done something wrong?"

"Just the things I've called you on today. Do your job, Nicole. You know what the requirements are."

"But, I've been doing it this way all along and you've never said anything."

"Yeah, and that was my mistake. I've been doing your job and mine so what am I paying you for?"

"I get the feeling you're angry."

"I am. For the reasons above." My eyes bored into hers until she looked away.

She eventually said, "I'm sorry. I know I was one of the girls who was rude to your nanny."

"It was worse than rude. You whispered to the others about her behind her back. You made offensive comments about her hair and the way she was dressed. You acted as though she was beneath you somehow. I expected better out of you."

"But we're protective of you."

"I'm a grown man who doesn't need protection, but you don't protect someone by hurting another. Especially if it's someone they care about. Did you stop to think about that?"

"You care about her?" The way she said it indicated her shock and disbelief that it was even remotely possible.

Leaning back in my chair, I crossed my arms. "That's none of your business. However, your holier than thou attitude where Marin's concerned is a bit disturbing."

Her hand flew up. "No, it's not that."

"It doesn't matter. You're my employee and you're not doing your job. Is there anything else?"

"No, I guess not."

Her question rang in my head. *You care about her?* Did I? I *desired* her, yes. One thing was true—I was not happy to hear those women speaking poorly of her. I wanted to see Marin happy. Seeing her happy made me happy. *Shit.* That gave me more insight. And then there was something else. Lately, every time I looked at her, I saw something other than the nanny. My brain said—*oh man, don't think that.* But her eyes called my name, even if she didn't think they did. I lusted after her to the point it was painful. And dammit, she was pretty. No, it was more than that. She was beautiful from the inside out.

Josh stuck his head in and asked, "Hey, you up for the poker night tonight?"

"No, I—"

He sat down in the chair Nicole vacated. "Come on. You haven't been in months and the guys are about to write you off. You know we don't do late. We start at six thirty and you'll be home by ten, tops. Besides, it'll do you good. And Ashley raved about your nanny. Now she wants Marin's clone. So, your kids are in good hands. And you're not on call tonight. I just checked."

Shit. He's covered all the bases.

"I have to run over to the hospital to check on a couple of things."

"So, do it and come on. Don't be such a loser, man.

You need a guy's night out and you know it. When's the last time you had one?"

"I can't remember." It was the truth. It was before Susannah died. "Okay, I'm in. See you at six thirty. Your place?"

"Yeah."

It was already past five-thirty, so I needed to get a move on. I called the house from the office phone and no one answered so I left a voicemail, letting Marin know of my plans. It had been such a busy day and I'd meant to check on Aaron during the day but with everything happening here, I didn't have a chance. When there weren't any texts on my phone by noon, I figured he was fine. Then I grabbed my stuff off the desk and made tracks for the hospital. I needed to sign some things on a few patients, which always took longer than expected, and then I was back in the car, headed to Josh's.

Poker night was always a great time. There were eight of us and the guys yanked my chain about not being around for so long. I kept my drinking to a bare minimum —only two beers for the night—and at ten-thirty, I was opening the door to my car. It was then I noticed my cell phone on the seat. It must've fallen out of my pocket when I got out of the car. Picking it up, I saw the battery was completely drained. I set it on the charging base of the console and headed home.

By the time I got there, the phone had enough juice to power on. When it sparked to life, about twenty texts from Marin and some from my mom lit up the screen. They sent my heart rate to about two hundred beats per minute and all the air went surging from my lungs.

Chapter Twenty-One

MARIN

AARON WOKE up and his fever had worsened. He was fussy, but not all out crying. I gave him more medicine and prayed he'd get better. But by noon, it developed quickly into a cough. Again, I thought maybe he had a cold, so it wasn't too much of a concern. Only he progressively got worse throughout the day. After sending multiple texts to Dr. West in the early afternoon, which went unanswered, I was at my wit's end.

Late in the afternoon, I broke down and called my mom, crying.

"Honey? What's wrong?" She knew it was bad since I wasn't the type to cry very often.

"It's Aaron. He's sick and I don't know what to do. I've called Dr. West. He's not answering and neither is his mom."

"Don't you remember? We're all out in Vegas for the next four days."

"What should I do?" I asked in a panic.

"Tell me everything that's going on."

I explained it all and between Mom and Paige, they decided I needed to call Aaron's doctor. When I did, he suggested I take him to the hospital urgent care.

I texted Dr. West again, letting him know what was going on and still no response.

Packing up a sick child, along with Kinsley was no picnic. I didn't know how much time it would take, so I wisely brought Kinsley some snacks because my appetite was nonexistent. We got to the urgent care and it was packed. They must've felt sorry for me since I was in tears because I didn't have to wait too long.

They ushered us back and a nurse came in to take Aaron's blood pressure and temperature. Then someone came in the get some blood samples. It scared Kinsley and she started crying, along with Aaron. I wasn't much better but trying my best to hold it together. Why the hell wouldn't Dr. West call me back? Had something happened to him?

The lady was really fast and she gave both kids stickers, which appeased Kinsley more than it did Aaron. He was coughing up a storm by now and breathing weird. How could he go from feeling fine yesterday to this sick so quickly? It was scaring me something fierce.

Another nurse came next and took us down to radiology. They wanted an X-ray of his chest, which made sense since his cough sounded so awful. We waited … and waited … and waited. I was super anxious because Aaron's coloring had gone from pink and flushed to ashen. He was whiny and his breathing sounded even worse than before. I wondered if he had asthma or something.

After a whole fucking hour, they took us back. Kinsley

and I had to wait in one area while they took Aaron into the X-ray room. Kinsley cried when they took him away.

"Where's he going, Marnie? What are they doing to him?"

"They're taking a picture of his lungs."

"But why can't you do that with your phone?"

"Because with this special machine they can see inside his body. Like through here." I pointed to her chest.

"You mean like Daddy sees inside of a heart?"

"Kind of like that, yes."

"I don't want Aaron to be sick. How's he gonna dance with me if he's sick?"

"He's going to get better. That's why we're here."

"I'm scared, Marnie. Where's Daddy?"

Good question. I'd like to know that answer too. "He must be working."

"Can't you call him on the hospital phone?" Why the hell hadn't I thought of that?

"Maybe. We'll try when we get done with Aaron's X-ray."

Pretty soon, they brought the little guy out, and he was so listless, I almost wished he was screaming and crying again. I hugged him tight to my body and felt how much he was burning up.

"Where do I go now?"

"Someone will come to escort you back to urgent care."

"Just tell me how to get there and I'll go myself." I was tired of this waiting game.

"You have to have an escort, ma'am."

My patience had run out. "Look, he's really sick and waiting here isn't doing him any favors. I'm pretty damn sure I can follow directions on how to get back there. Just tell me where to go, or I'll figure it out on my own."

He gave me the directions and off we went.

"You were kinda mean, Marnie."

"Yeah, I was, wasn't I? I just want Aaron to get better."

"Me too."

We walked back to where we started and I went to the nurse's station. I immediately got someone's attention. "He's really sick. He's gotten even worse since we've been here. Can you just have a doctor come in? And in the meantime, can one of you page Dr. Greydon West. I'm not sure if he's in the hospital, but if he is, tell him his son is in the urgent care."

Damn. If I had known that would've had the effect it did, I'd have done it sooner. Those people snapped to attention like I was a five-star general.

"This is Dr. West's son?"

"Yes. I put it down on the information I had to fill out if you'd bothered to read it."

"We'll get a doctor in here right away."

I barely had time for my ass to hit the chair before a doctor rushed in. He introduced himself and went to work on Aaron right away. The labs had come back showing an elevated white count meaning he had an infection.

"My suspicion is pneumonia. I want to see his chest X-ray first. But I'll be honest. I'd like to admit him. This is a pretty sick little guy you have here. We're going to start fluids on him right away and antibiotics since he does have some sort of infection. Let's get things moving so we can get him up to PICU."

"PICU?"

"Pediatric ICU."

"ICU! Oh God! Is he …?" I didn't dare utter the words, but I immediately thought he was dying.

"We need to keep an eye on his oxygen levels and make sure, for at least the next twenty-four to forty-eight hours, things don't go south. I want a pediatric pulmonary expert to handle this."

"Things go south?" I screeched. Kinsley started crying.

"Marnie, I'm scared."

"I know." I patted her shoulder and hugged her to my side.

The doctor quickly interjected, "It's going to be fine. Don't worry. The good news is he's been sick for less than a day."

"How could this happen?"

"Pneumonia in children under two can do this."

I was close to breaking down but knew I couldn't. Kinsley was here and she was hugging my leg, crying. The doctor crouched down and pulled a lollipop out of his pocket, handing it to her. She shook her head, not even wanting it. "Don't worry, your brother will be fine."

About an hour later, we sat in the PICU unit. I was in a quandary. The nurses kept coming up to me, telling me young children weren't allowed in the unit.

I wrung my hands. "I don't know what to do. Dr. West isn't returning any of my calls or texts. His parents are out of town. I don't have anyone to call to keep her. What am I supposed to do? She can't stay home alone." I tried to text my mom again and Paige, but now they weren't responding. They had tickets for a show, so they probably had their phones turned off. If I could get in touch with one of Grey's brothers, maybe they could help. Only I didn't have either of their numbers.

That's when I broke down. Tears didn't roll. They practically spurted out of my eyes like a busted hose. Kinsley cried too, asking me if Aaron was with the angels now.

"No, baby, he's not. He's right here." I lifted her up on

my lap and held her. We both bawled like a couple of babies.

The nurses left us alone for a while. I checked the time and it was nine o'clock and no calls or texts. I shot Dr. West another one, although I don't know why. I told him Aaron was in the PICU with pneumonia and if he cared at all about his child, to please respond. They didn't allow kids up here and I was in a bind with Kinsley.

Ten minutes later, another physician came in and introduced herself. She was the pulmonary specialist who would be taking care of Aaron. His X-rays showed pneumonia in both lungs.

"He's a lucky guy you brought him in when you did."

"How in the world did this happen so fast?"

"It was brewing for a day or two, but that's how it can be with kids under two and people over sixty-five. But when it takes hold, it can spread like wildfire. I'm pretty sure he'll be fine. However, I want him here for at least twenty-four hours, just to be sure. We should see a good response to the antibiotics we have running by then."

"That sounds good."

"I'd tell you to get some sleep, but I doubt you'd follow those instructions."

"No, you're right. Thank you, doctor."

She checked him over and then left. There was a recliner and a hard chair in the small glass cubicle, so I let Kinsley sit in the recliner, where she fell asleep, holding her stuffed giraffe I'd brought for her. I covered her up with a blanket I found in the tiny closet.

All I did was stare at the machines, looking at numbers I had no idea what they meant. Suddenly, the door slid open and he was there. Two long strides swallowed up the floor as he went to the computer near Aaron's bed, furiously typing on it. The monitor jumped to life at his commands, instantly filling with information. I watched as he scanned it before he went over to his son and placed a hand on his head for a second. Then he turned toward me.

That's when I came to life. I stood up and walked over to him. Then I balled up my hand and punched him. My weak fists pounded his chest, shoulders, anything they could touch until I collapsed against him in a wall of tears. He held me as I sobbed, rubbing my back and hair, but didn't utter a word. Then he pulled me away from him and just stared at me … until his mouth crashed onto mine in a bruising kiss.

Every word of reproach, every incensed thought vanished. Even Aaron's illness evaporated for a moment. All I knew at that moment was what his lips and tongue were doing to me … and how they singed mine, how my skin was scorched, my belly tightened, and that I wanted to clench my thighs, drop to my knees and do dirty filthy things to him. My fingers dug into his arms, holding on for dear life, knowing that if I let go, the terrible world as I knew it would crush me again, and I couldn't bear for that to happen. I wanted this … this lust. This *desire*. I wanted to explore it, wanted it to devour me. But I also wanted the safety, the warmth, the comfort, the strength his body provided. The last six hours had been sheer hell and I wanted it to disappear and for Aaron to be healthy, and for all my worries about him to fade away. This kiss, this passion that was escalating between us was only a fantasy, a dream to carry me away for one tiny moment.

But it did end, and when he looked down at me, I only saw wonder in his beautiful gray eyes. It hadn't been a fantasy at all and I didn't imagine it.

His hand slid to my cheek as he said, "Jesus, Marin, my phone fell out of my pocket and I didn't know anything until a few minutes ago. I'm so very sorry." Then his warm, protective arms wrapped around me and held me tightly again before moving away to check on Aaron. "According to his chart, he has pneumonia and they have him on antibiotics."

After I filled him in, he said, "I owe you everything." He reached for my hand. But this was so confusing to me, I drifted out of his reach.

My hand touched my lips—which still burned from his kiss—for a second, and then I said, "Kinsley isn't supposed to be in here. They've been giving me hell about it. I didn't know what to do ... there wasn't anywhere for her to go."

His hand tore through his hair. "Shit. I'm sorry. You must've had the worst day."

I shuddered. "Not the best."

"Why don't you go home and I'll stay here with Aaron? Get some rest. If anything happens, I'll call."

I swayed on my feet. "That's probably a good idea. We still have a problem though. We'll have to find another sitter for Kinsley."

"Don't worry about that. I have backup. People I used before you."

"Good." I started gathering my things and woke Kinsley. When she saw her daddy, she jumped out of the chair.

He grabbed her and they clung to each other. "Hey, polka dot. You're going home now with Marin so you two can go to bed."

"Are you gonna sleep with Aaron?"

"I sure am."

"Did you bring your jammies?"

"No, I'll just sleep in my clothes."

"Oh. Then good night." She gave him a loud smacking kiss on the mouth. Hmm. He had one sexy mouth, for sure.

We left with him promising to call if there was anything to update me on.

When I crawled into bed, exhaustion claimed me, but I could still feel the burn of Grey's lips on mine. Something primal had been sparked deep within me. Why did he have to go and do that?

Chapter Twenty-Two

GREYDON

WHEN I WALKED into Aaron's room and saw her sitting there, the ache in my chest grew exponentially until my heart nearly vaulted through my ribcage. Between Aaron and Marin, I was sure I would need the services of one of my partners. You never want to see one of your kids so sick that they've been admitted to the PICU. I couldn't take a solid breath until I was able to read his chart. It still wasn't easy and wouldn't be until he was out of the danger zone … until I was comfortable knowing he was having a positive response to the antibiotics.

Then there was Marin. Dealing with her was like dealing with a wounded tigress. She came at me, claws exposed, but was harmless because she was so exhausted. And didn't that make me feel even more like shit. It had all been a terrible series of mistakes, but still, I should've been more careful with my phone … paid closer attention to my shit. So yeah, I accepted full responsibility for that.

Then something hit me when I saw her. Passion never swept me away. I wasn't that guy. But when I stepped through that door, molten heat poured through my veins, unhinging me, and I couldn't have stopped myself, no matter what. This had been brewing for some time now. If I were honest, it was why I was so defensive about how the office staff had treated her. She didn't deserve it, true, but it hit me harder because I had *feelings*, intense feelings for her. But this couldn't happen. I would never allow my heart to get wrapped up in a woman again. The pain was too great and not worth the risk.

But seeing Marin sitting there, looking like she'd been through hell, had opened up something inside of me ... something I thought had died. When she started punching me with her weak blows, I was done. I had to find out, to taste her, and so I did. I kissed her. It was undoubtedly the most inappropriate time and place, but I couldn't take it back now. And wouldn't if I could. That kiss only made me want more. ... made me want it all. And if she was willing, I aimed to go after it, God help me.

After keeping watch on Aaron for a few hours, I settled down on the recliner for an unrestful night. The beeping of the machines made it difficult to get much sleep at all. At first light, I texted the staff on the group messaging we'd set up for emergencies such as this, letting them know I needed to cancel out my day and why.

Josh was the first to hit me back.

Josh: You okay? Is Aaron?

Instead of going through all the texting, I decided to call him.

"Hey man, what the hell happened?" he asked.

I explained everything, down to my phone situation.

"Shit, I bet you freaked."

"Yeah, when I got home and saw that Aaron was in the PICU, I about lost it."

"Hey, I'm glad he's doing okay. Is there anything I can do for you? Other than practice stuff?"

"Now that you mention it, do you guys have a good sitter that can watch Kinsley. I know Marin will want to come and see Aaron and I can't be here all day tomorrow."

"Hang on."

I heard him checking with Ashley in the background. "Ash says to have Marin drop her off here and she'll handle it."

"No, I can't do that. She has her hands full."

"She insists. Besides, the nanny comes during the day and Kinsley will have a good time. She can even spend the night if she wants."

"Are you sure?"

"Grey, you know us. We wouldn't offer if we didn't mean it."

"Thanks, I'll let Marin know. Both our parents are in Vegas together, or I wouldn't be asking."

"Not a problem. Give Marin Ashley's number. You have it, right?"

"Let me check." I quickly scanned my contacts and saw that I did. "Yeah, I've got it. Thanks, man. I owe you."

"Yeah, when our brood is the size of a baseball team, we'll hit you up." I chuckled. Just then, Aaron started crying.

"Hey, Aaron just woke up. I've gotta run."

I checked on him and was pretty sure his diaper needed changing.

"Hey, buddy. How's my boy?" I rubbed his tummy, but it didn't help. He was safe in his bed, so I searched the room for a clean diaper and finally found one. Then I went about changing him. He still cried afterward, but a nurse arrived and checked his IVs.

"His sedation has obviously worn off," I said.

She stared at me for a second.

"I'm his father."

"Hi, I'm Cathy, his nurse for today."

I got up and went to the computer and started typing.

"Sir, you can't do that."

I ignored her.

"Sir! Mr. West."

Annoyed, I said, "He hasn't had any sedatives since I got here and the last time they were administered was at nine thirty."

"Sir, I'm calling …"

"It's *Dr.* West, not Mr. West, and I have access to all his medical records as I'm on staff here at the hospital. Now, why has my son not been attended to? This is the PICU and no one has checked on him for at least three hours."

Eyes resembling ping-pong balls nearly popped out of her head. "Um, sir, I mean, Dr. West, we monitor the patients from the station out there." She pointed to where a group was seated and looking at all the monitors.

Scowling, I asked, "Doesn't the I in PICU, mean intensive? He hasn't had any hands-on care in quite a while. How can you do that from out there?"

"But …"

"Who is Aaron's attending physician?"

"It's Dr. Sutton."

"When will she be making rounds?"

"She's here now."

"Good. I'd like to speak to her. Oh, and so you are aware, sedation was ordered for Aaron every eight hours. It's eight o'clock. He's well past his last dosage."

She went to leave, but I stopped her. "Aren't you even going to check your patient?"

Cathy scurried back to Aaron to check his diaper.

"Too late. I already changed him because you didn't bother to do so."

She was clearly flustered by now but did what she was supposed to and left.

Dr. Sutton—Jane—came in about ten minutes later.

"Grey, you're stirring things up in here."

"I hope more than a little. They needed a little stirring. Quite frankly, I'm disappointed in the care Aaron's received."

"I totally understand. That won't happen again. I got on them about Aaron's meds. His IVs are good. We're going to do another CBC and a white count with a differential to check on whether or not there's an improvement over yesterday's."

"Yeah, I saw that left shift with the neutrophilia." That was a clear indication of infection.

"I think we'll see improvement. I want another chest X-ray later today as well. If by tonight, I'm seeing a steady improvement, we can move him out of here and into a regular room. And if this improvement continues at a rapid rate, which I have no reason to think it won't, then he can go home the day after that. We'll switch him off the IV antibiotics to oral. Sound like a good plan to you?"

Nodding, I said, "I'm just overwhelmed at how quickly this developed."

"Like I told your nanny, he's under two and kids can be very vulnerable to pneumonia. You're lucky she had the foresight to bring him in. I won't explain the outcome to you if she hadn't."

"You don't have to. I know."

Jane left and Cathy practically ran in here and hovered

over Aaron. She gave him more sedation so he would sleep, and was in and out like an overprotective mother. Jane must've really given them a dressing down.

I called Marin and woke her up, but also scared the hell out of her.

"Dr. West! Is everything okay? How's Aaron?" she yelled into the phone.

Laughing, I answered, "He's good. It's after eight, so I assumed you'd be awake or I would've waited to call."

"It's after eight?" she screamed.

"Yeah, sleepy head."

"Ugh." I had a vision of her flopping back on her pillow for some reason. "I'm sorry I overslept."

"Don't be sorry. You deserve to sleep. And don't you think you need to stop calling me Dr. West?"

"Um, okay."

"I think you should start calling me Grey."

"Grey?"

"It's my name, you know."

"Y-your name," she stuttered.

Chuckling, I said, "Yes, Grey, short for Greydon."

"I knew that." She paused briefly, then said, "I mean, okay."

"The reason I'm calling is I need a favor. Can you bring me some fresh clothes? I've been in these for a while and they're awful. I want to run down to the doctor's lounge and shower. Oh, and Ashley said for you to drop Kinsley off at their place. They want her to spend the night so that'll free you to come here."

"Are they sure?"

"Absolutely. I asked and Josh said we could return the favor when their brood was the size of a baseball team."

She laughed. I actually loved the sound of it. "I love it when you laugh."

"Er, uh, thanks. So, what should I bring you to wear?"

"Jeans and a decent shirt will be fine."

"Um, do you need, erm, like, ah, underwear or anything?" she squeaked out.

I bit my lip to keep from laughing. It was interesting that this conversation was causing her to sound so awkward. I wondered if she was blushing. "No. Unless you want me to wear some and, in that case, they're in one of the drawers in the closet."

"What about socks? Or shoes?"

"Yeah, I'll be needing those too. Socks are in the drawers. Shoes, use your own judgment." I wanted to see what she'd bring. "There are some duffle bags in there too. Oh, and can you bring a toothbrush and toothpaste? You'll find some in my bathroom. One of the drawers. Just dig around in there." Man, I imagined her squirming.

"Sure. I have to shower and bathe Kinsley. We were so tired last night we fell straight into bed. And then breakfast. Is that okay?"

"It's perfectly fine. I'll see you whenever you get here."

"O-okay."

"And Marin?"

"Uh huh?"

"I liked kissing you last night. More than a lot."

I hung up before she had a chance to respond. Let her think about that when she was digging around in my closet, looking in my underwear drawer.

Chapter Twenty-Three

Marin

DID HE NEED UNDERWEAR?

Unless you want me to wear some.

What the hell was I supposed to do with that? Take him underwear or not? The thought of him *not* wearing any was hotter than flames charring my skin. But did I want him to know that? Sweat seeped out of my pores as I thought about it, and the more I did, my heart tapped out a rhythm that had me wondering if I should call him back. Only because I was worried about my damn health.

Kinsley pushed my door open and ran into my room. "Marnie, I had a bad dream."

"You did?"

"It was about Aaron and that he went to live with Mommy."

"Oh, sweetie, come here."

She climbed up on my bed and I hugged her. "Aaron's

getting better already. I just talked with your daddy and he told me so."

"He is?"

"Yep. And I bet his legs will be kicking again in no time. And guess what else."

"What?"

"You get to go to Ashley and Dr. Josh's today and play. You even get to have a sleepover."

"I do?"

"You sure do. Doesn't that sound fun?"

"Yeah! Do they eat good stuff over there? Like snacks and cookies?"

I hid a laugh. "I bet they do."

"Can I call Daddy?"

"I don't see why you can't. Here." I hit his number and handed her the phone.

"Daddy!"

I heard him call her his polka dot and then tell her about Aaron getting better.

"I get to have a sleepover party tonight."

They talked a bit longer and then ended the call.

I brushed her thick hair off her forehead and asked, "Feel better now?"

She nodded.

"Good. And now we both need to bathe since neither of us did last night. So why don't I get your bath ready or do you want to take a shower so you can wash your hair too?"

"Shower, please. I can do it myself cuz I'm a big girl." She spread her arms out for emphasis.

"Okay. Make sure you rinse your hair really good and put the conditioner in because if you don't, it'll hurt when we comb it."

"I know. Ouchy." She grimaced.

"Right."

We both went into her bathroom where I got the water going and set everything out for her. She was pretty good about this. "Do you want me to stay in here while you shower?"

"You don't have to."

"All righty. I'll be in and out if you need me." I wouldn't take mine until she was done, just in case. While she showered, I decided to pack Grey's things. It felt completely weird thinking of him like that. But then again, it had always felt so stiff and formal calling him Dr. West. But he *was* stiff and formal most times. And grouchy. Hopefully, he was changing.

I slowly opened his bedroom door and walked in. I'd only been in here once, and that was before all his furnishings and belongings were moved in. The room was massive. It was actually two rooms—a bedroom with a small sitting area off of it. It had a fireplace in it, which I thought was so romantic the first time I saw it. The bathroom was palatial—like something out of a magazine, but then so was the rest of the house. When I entered the closet, I didn't know where to begin. It was kind of sad in here since this was built as a his and hers. The hers side was completely empty obviously. It held massive built-in dressers and shoe racks and shelves and anything your heart could possibly imagine. A giggle burst out of me because all my things would fit in less than a quarter of this space. Moving over to his side, I found a suitable duffle bag to hold everything. Then I located his jeans. It was easy because everything was very organized. Next, I grabbed a dark grey shirt and then hunted for a pair of socks. I opened drawer after drawer of ties. Good lord, how many did the man own? And folded shirts. He had an endless supply. Before I got to his sock drawer, I found the stupid underwear drawer and much to my shame, my fingers buried themselves in pair after pair of them. There were cotton boxer briefs, regular boxers, silk boxers, bikini briefs, and tightie whities. The man must have an underwear fetish because there was every style of men's underwear imaginable. And I pulled every type out and inspected them. Before I knew it, I'd made a mess of the damn drawer and realized when he went to fetch a pair, he would certainly know an underwear spy had been in here lurking.

"Marnie! Marnie where are you?"

Fuck! The drawer was nothing but a heap of unfolded skivvies. What the hell was I supposed to do?

"I'll be there in a minute."

I started to fold a few but knew it was hopeless, so I just threw a pair in the bag, not really paying attention. I figured while Kinsley was watching something on TV, I'd sneak back up here and rearrange it. On the way out, I grabbed a pair of shoes and tossed them into the bag too.

"I'm here."

"Whatcha got there, Marnie?"

"I'm taking this to your daddy when I go to the hospital later."

"I'm hungry."

"Let me get you some breakfast and then I have to shower. But first, did you comb your hair and get all the tangles out?"

"Yep."

"Okay. How about waffles today?"

"Really?"

"Really. Let's go."

After she was settled, I told her to watch a video when she was done. I showered and then quickly dressed in jeans, a white T-shirt, and sandals. Then I remembered about Grey's toothbrush. I stopped in his closet to quickly fix up his underwear drawer and did the best I could, but it wasn't anywhere near what it looked like when I opened it. The thing was, I couldn't remember exactly how it was organized and I was sure he would never find anything when he went in there the next time. I was so screwed.

The bathroom was another story. I eventually found a toothbrush, but it was after opening drawer after drawer. Standing in here made my heart twinge all of a sudden. Here was this man living in the beautiful place, but he had no one to share it with. If I were him, I would want somewhere small to live so I wouldn't have to stare at so much vacant space. It would only remind me of all that I had and lost.

Kinsley was eager to get to the McBride's house. Once there, Ashley assured me everything was fine and she could stay as long as need be. When I left her, she was already playing.

Grey was happy to see me when I walked into Aaron's room. I had worried about his reaction toward me, and to be honest, I wasn't sure how things should be between us. My concern was unnecessary. He immediately came to my side, pulling me into his arms. His embrace took me by surprise. But his kiss really threw me off kilter.

I dropped the stupid duffle and clutched his shirt at the waist. Jesus, what was going on with this man? Had the stodgy old doctor disappeared? Was I falling for this older dude? I mean the guy was in his forties, way older than anyone I'd ever dated. But he was also way hotter than anyone I'd ever dated either.

"Are you okay?"

My head bobbed. "Yeah, you?" I hardly recognized my breathless voice.

"Fine. I had to ream an ass or two, but things are better."

"What happened?"

"The care in here wasn't up to par. That's all. It's great now."

I looked at him. Really looked and noticed the dark circles under his eyes and the lines of stress he was attempting to pretend weren't there. The urge to press my fingers to them was overwhelming.

"You need to go home and sleep."

"No, I'm not leaving. Let me shower and I'll feel better."

I gave in and gently smoothed my fingertips over the space below his eyes. "You're tired. You can't hide it."

He took those fingertips and pressed kisses to them. "I've gone far longer than this without sleep. Thanks for bringing my stuff. I'll be back."

He left and I checked on Aaron. He was still asleep, which I supposed had to do with the drugs. I ran my fingers through his soft curls and held his chubby hand. He was so stinkin' precious. I loved this kid and started to ponder what I would do when I didn't have this job. The scary thing was how attached I'd become. And then … what about Grey? What were *we*? That was even weird to think about. How had we gone from being almost completely uncommunicative to this? And I had barely given him a glance before. Oh, I noticed him all right, but a much older him than me. That was then. Now, all I thought about was that strong jaw covered in scruff, chiseled cheeks, those large eyes that were thickly fringed in dark lashes, and his sexy mouth. I pressed my fingers to my lips thinking of how his had crushed mine last night and that it triggered an urge for more. I remembered how my hands seized his arms, feeling the strength of his rigid biceps, and recognized the safety they brought. How had I missed so many things about him?

Grey was a man who commanded the room. When he was in it, people took notice. I saw that at the picnic. And it wasn't that he tried. It just happened.

Aaron kicked one of his legs, and I smiled, thinking of Kinsley. I still held his hand and he tried to pull it away, so I let him. He rolled to his side and whimpered. The IV must've tugged a bit, so I rearranged it to give it more line. Ugh, I hated seeing him like this. My eyes welled up with tears and I scrubbed them away.

Two hands clamped down on my shoulders and I jumped.

"Sorry, I didn't mean to frighten you." Then he asked, "Why are you crying?"

"Seeing him with that IV is killing me. I know he's uncomfortable."

The pads of his thumbs stroked my cheek to wipe the tears away. "Please don't. I'm hopeless seeing you cry." Then he held me to his chest. "IVs aren't that bad and the sedation will help with it. But I don't want him to continue with that. Since he's had some really good sleep, I want to talk to Jane about getting that reduced."

"Jane?"

"His doctor. Jane Sutton."

"I see." I should've known they'd know each other.

"I have a question. Did you have fun poking around in my underwear drawer?"

Holy shit. I stepped out of his embrace. "Uh, why?" I asked, cringing.

He smirked. "Because you stuck Christmas underwear I got as a joke in the duffle bag. They have a reindeer nose with bells on them. Did you really want me to wear them?"

My hands flew to my face in horror. Oh. Jesus. "I grabbed the first thing my hands landed on," I mumbled.

"Is that so? I'm pretty sure those things were buried in the back of the drawer."

I spread my fingers apart to see he was grinning at me. "Stop it."

"Did you inspect all my underwear?"

"No," I lied.

"Yeah, you did. Admit it." He pulled my hands down and held them. I tried to tug them away, but he wouldn't let me. "Well?"

"I was going to grab a pair, but your drawer was so damn organized that I started admiring all the different styles and then Kinsley called me and I was sort of busted."

He chuckled. "If you want, I can model them for you."

"Oh, my God." I would never live this down.

My face burned with embarrassment. His hand brushed across one cheek and he said, "I didn't take you for the shy type."

"I'm not shy. This goes way past shy. This is like a home invasion."

He bent down and pulled those damn underwear out for me to see. "I can't believe you brought these for me." He laughed as he held them up against his hips. Not only did they have a reindeer nose, it was exactly where his penis would be with jingle bells dangling by his balls. I'd really done it this time.

"I swear I didn't even look at them."

"Uh huh. So, the way I'm thinking is what's fair for the goose and all."

"What do you mean?"

"I think I need to get a good look at your underwear drawer."

"You'll be greatly disappointed, I can promise you."

He waggled his brows. "You have no idea I may be a granny panty kind of guy."

A huge snort of laughter busted out of me. It was so loud Aaron cried out. "If you're into granny panties, you're dead to me."

Now it was his turn to laugh. "Yeah, that was kind of bad, right?"

"That would only confirm that you are definitely an old geezer."

He grabbed me around the waist and pulled me against him. "I can show you things that will prove to you I am *nowhere near* an old geezer. Which brings me to my next point. I would very much like to pursue this thing between us, Marin. That is if you're willing."

"What if we don't work? Then what happens to me as *the nanny*? I love your kids and it scares me that I'll never see them again."

"I've thought of that too, but if we don't try, we won't know, will we?"

"No, but I'm not sure I could live in your house if things between us don't work."

He brushed my hair back. "I have a very good feeling about us. You're the only person I've been interested in since Susannah. I never thought I'd date again. Here's the thing. You're not someone I ever would've given a chance either. We're so different. But I can't stop thinking about you. Please say yes."

"We'll be practically cohabiting."

"We will be cohabiting. There is no practically about it. But you'll keep your room and I'll have mine. We won't compromise that for the children's sake."

"Okay. We can try, but I have to tell you, this scares me. A lot."

"Don't be afraid, Marin."

"I don't want to get hurt."

"I know. And I won't be the one to do that."

Weren't those the promises they always made? Damien said that to me and look what happened. But I did know one thing about Grey. His wife had cheated on him and he wasn't very happy about that. He wasn't the cheating kind so if my heart were to get broken it probably wouldn't be because of that.

Chapter Twenty-Four

GREYDON

MARIN SURPRISED ME, she really did. I suspected all along she would push me away. But she didn't. Now all I wanted to do was learn everything possible about her. We were stuck in Aaron's glass cubicle all day, so we might as well start now.

I began with questions about her college days and why she chose journalism.

"My dad had visions of me practicing law with him but I'm afraid I was a huge disappointment. I had this urge to write. In high school, I would sit for hours, creating these stories and handing them in to my teachers. They encouraged me to study creative writing and literature, but it wasn't for me. My interests were more in current events, so I turned toward journalism. When I was a junior, I had this amazing teacher who helped me after school each day, He taught me how to craft journalistic articles. My school didn't have a journalism class until you were a senior. He was the one who encouraged me to go to Emerson. So, there's that."

"And you graduated magna cum laude?"

She squints at me. "How did you know that? I never told you."

"My mom did. I did ask a few questions about you after you came to work for me. I didn't know what your degree was in though until you told me. And after I found out you went to Emerson, imagine the good laugh I had over the shit you gave me about Harvard."

Two bright spots of pink dotted her cheeks. I reached out to brush the back of my hand over them and felt the heat radiating off her. "Don't be embarrassed. I have a tendency to act like an ass. It's a defense mechanism when I'm challenged. Or when I'm pissed."

Her hands covered her cheeks after I took mine away. "I hate that I get so red like that."

"I think it's sexy."

"Can I ask you something?"

"Sure." I wanted her to feel she was able to question me about anything.

She tilted her head and appeared hesitant for a second before she blurted, "Why are you so distant with the kids?"

No toe dipping with this one. She took the plunge, head first. "I wasn't always. I've not been in the best place and I … it's been hard. It's not right, I know. I try. You don't see it, I'm sure. This sounds like I'm making excuses. Before Susannah died, I was in the thick of things with them. When it was just Kinsley, I did it all. You probably can't picture it, but it's true. I was Mr. Mom. What she did really destroyed me and it wasn't just the cheating. It was the effect on the family. It was the destruction of trust. And the lying. Those were always my two deal-breakers and she knew it. We'd talked often about it. She traveled a lot for her job and I put my trust and faith in her and there she was, cheating for over two years. It shook the foundation of everything for me."

Marin was silent for a moment. "They need you, Grey. Go back to them."

Those words were an arrow to my heart. I vowed to make a change starting today.

"It may seem like a mountain, but it's not. Take it a day at a time," she said.

"You're right and I'm such a shit."

She rested her hand on my arm. "Not a shit, just an absentee dad. And it's an easy thing to change. So why cardiology?"

My mind reeled with how I had to change things at home, but I answered her anyway. "Nice diversion. When I was in medical school, I did my cardiac rotation and that was it. I knew if I couldn't do cardiology, it would crush me. That's how important it was to me."

"Why so?"

We're seated, she on the recliner and me on the hard chair. I scooted closer to her and picked up her hand. "Some people think it's the God syndrome—you know where people feel like they're God saving other's lives. But that's not it for me. I found that saving someone, preventing them from dying, and keeping them with their loved ones longer, made being in school and all the years of residency and fellowship worth everything. There are a lot of jobs out there that people love. But I am crazy about what I do. I know without a doubt I made the right choice."

"What would you have done if you wouldn't have gotten into the cardiology fellowship? Isn't that how it works?"

"Correct. You do a medicine residency, usually, and

then apply for a cardiology fellowship. As for an answer, I don't know. I didn't have a Plan B."

She taps my arm. "No Plan B?"

"None. Other than I figured I would keep trying until I got accepted."

"But you did."

"I did."

She squeezes my hand when she says, "And you came to your hometown. Why?"

"I was done with Boston. I stayed there for my residency and ended up becoming chief."

"Chief? Is that like some special pow wow society?" She smirked.

Was she serious? It was hard not to laugh. "You really don't know?"

"I assume it's some kind of fancy title."

"It's the Chief Resident in the Department of Medicine. It's a position you strive to attain as a medicine resident."

"I see. Were you ever worried about being accepted?"

"Not really but I wanted to leave Boston and come to Manhattan. My first choice was Weill Cornell in New York. I did my three-year cardiology fellowship and two-year electrophysiology fellowship there. After five years at New York-Presbyterian, I was ready for a change. That's when we moved up here and the rest you can probably deduce on your own."

"Hang on a sec. You went to medical school for four years. Then you did a residency for what? Three years?"

"Yeah."

"Then you did another five years in fellowships?"

"That's right."

"That's a total of ..." She looks up at the ceiling while

she adds in her head. "That's twelve years. That's a really long time!"

"I was glad when it was over. But the truth is, during my fellowships, it was hands-on learning that was invaluable. The final two years was incredible."

"Really? I would think it was torture."

"Not at all. It was where I learned to induce arrhythmias in people and bring their hearts back into normal rhythm."

She made a face like she just swallowed sour milk. "Ugh. I'm not sure that's good or bad."

"Let me explain. Sometimes the heart gets off its normal rhythmic pathways. The electric circuitry gets screwed up. Often, it's benign and the person can just live out a normal life with no harm. Other times the arrhythmia is deadly and doesn't allow the heart to pump blood properly, so without shocking it back into normal rhythm, the person will die. Drugs can control this, sometimes not. My job is to find out why it's happening or where the arrhythmia stems from. So, I go into the heart and locate it. Sometimes, I have to induce the heart to have one when I'm inside so I can see what's going on to make the proper diagnosis. If I think it's treatable with drugs, then we go that route. If not, we implant an ICD or an implantable cardioverter defibrillator. It will shock the heart back into normal rhythm if it has an arrhythmia. Sometime a person won't even know it's happening."

"That sounds horrible."

"It's not as bad as that. The patient is sedated and we talk them through it."

"Don't you have to cut them open?"

"No, we go through the wrist or the groin, like when you have a heart catheterization."

"Oh. That sounds much better. Are they scared?"

"Yeah, but I do my best to calm them down. And the drugs help relax them too."

Suddenly, Aaron let out a yell. She jumped up and ran to his crib. "He's awake," she said to me. Then to Aaron, she said, "Hey buddy. How's my guy?" He let out a gusty cry. She picked him up to comfort him, swaying back and forth with him in her arms. "It's okay, buddy, you're going to be fine now." His cries changed to whimpers and he quieted down as his little hands clung to her arms.

"Do you think he's hungry? He hasn't eaten since yesterday."

"Probably. We should get him some food. Let me ask the nurse." But I didn't have to because she came striding into the room.

"How is he?"

"Maybe he should eat?" Marin asked.

"Let me check." She went to the computer and it said he could have juices and light foods.

When they brought it in, he sucked it down like no tomorrow. The kid was probably starving. I would talk with Jane when she came in later.

Marin and I held Aaron a lot that day, only because we didn't want to keep sedating him and he was so crabby. It was probably the IV along with the fever he was still running. It wasn't nearly as high and Marin agreed he looked much improved over when she brought him in.

It was lunchtime and I ran down to the cafeteria to get us some food. The nurse suggested we both go, but Marin refused to leave Aaron alone, so we ate in Aaron's room.

"This isn't bad," Marin said. "I was expecting something terrible."

"No, it's pretty good, actually. Hospital food has improved a lot over the years."

A young woman came in and said she was going to

take Aaron down to radiology to get another chest X ray. Marin jumped up to go with her and she stopped her.

"He'll be in good hands, I promise. We won't be gone long." She pushed his bed, along with his IVs out of the room.

"He'll be fine," I comforted her. "They do this all the time."

"Not to Aaron they don't."

I stared at her. "You're very protective of him."

"Is that bad?"

"No. It just surprises me."

"Why?"

"You've only been around him since the beginning of March and it's July. The bond you've developed with him is strong."

"I can't help it. At first, it was because you didn't pay him any attention, so I felt really sorry for him. And then it was because he is so damn precious."

My silence had her grabbing for my hand.

"What is it?" she asked.

"The DNA test. Do you still have it?"

"Yes."

"I think I want to know."

"Grey, what will you do? Because if Aaron's not yours, I can tell you this. It will make no difference to me at all."

The truth was, I had no answer. "I don't know. My gut aches with the thought of it. It's been killing me forever and my shrink keeps badgering me about it."

"Your shrink?"

I help up my hands. "Guilty as charged. I've been seeing one since Susannah died. I had so much anger, there wasn't any way for me to handle it. Hence, my shrink."

"Thank God. But you don't look like the shrink type."

"Why not?"

"Oh, God." She dropped her head onto her lap. "Don't get mad at me when I tell you this."

Her words were muffled, so I asked, "What?"

Sitting up straight as a board, she said, "Promise you won't get mad when I tell you this."

"Okay."

"When I first met you, you seemed to be so starchy. I can't imagine you sitting in a psychiatrist's office, pouring out your heart to her."

"Hmm. Starchy, huh?"

"Yeah, with all your ties and white shirts."

"I do have to dress appropriately for work, you know."

"The doctors I've gone to don't dress up like that."

"And my shrink is a man."

She waved her hand. "Whatever. Why do you all dress like that? It would make me uncomfortable."

"Really?"

"Yes."

"I've never thought of it that way."

She circled with her index finger in front of me. "Now this, I like. But that tie stuff. It's great if you're going somewhere and everyone is dressed up. But it puts me off as a patient."

"I can't wear jeans in the office."

"Why not? My doctor does."

"Duly noted. Can I ask you a question now?"

She dipped her head. "Sure."

"What made you dye your hair those colors."

Her hands instantly flew to her hair, smoothing it down. "It was a moment of rebellion. I wasn't in a good place and I thought it would give me a sense of … freedom."

"And did it?"

"Yeah, it did. It was so different from my real color that it set me apart from the old Marin. And my dad about flipped."

I had to laugh because I'm sure he did. Her dad was a lot like my own father— fairly conservative in dress. The change most likely threw him for a loop.

The door to the room slid open then and Aaron was delivered back to us, whining away. Marin picked him up and he calmed down some. Maybe we'd have the results of his X-ray soon.

I checked the computer, but nothing was entered yet. His blood count results were in and they were definitely better than the previous ones.

"There's a big improvement in his blood counts," I told Marin.

"Thank God."

"I'll bet his X-ray looks better too."

About an hour later, Jane came in to give us the news that he was improving.

"I think we can get him moved to a regular room. How does that sound?"

"Great. Can he eat?" Marin asked.

"I think so. He hasn't had any vomiting or diarrhea, so we should be safe in that regard. I'll order a normal diet for him."

"Thanks, Jane. What's next?"

"Let's give it one more day. I'd like to try switching him to oral antibiotics tomorrow morning. That way, if we see a spike in his temperature, it'll happen before we discharge him."

"Good plan."

"Ugh, he has to keep the IV one more night?" Marin asked.

"I'm afraid so, but I'll order a light dose of a sedative so he'll sleep."

The fact they kept sedating him wasn't something I was thrilled about. "Is the sedation necessary?"

"Grey, I know you don't like it, but Aaron needs his rest. Kids don't like IVs and with his age, and the fact that he's not comfortable with the fever, I think it's best. I'd rather do that than hit him with a heavy dose of a narcotic-laced cough medication."

"Ok," I said.

"I promise, it'll only be enough to relax him to get him to sleep. And I won't have them administer it until after he eats his dinner. So let's see about getting a room then."

Marin tapped my arm. "I'll give Ashley a call to let her know what's going on."

"Good idea."

As Marin walked out of the room to do that, I picked up Aaron. He was adorable, as Marin had said. Why couldn't I just drop the paternity stuff? Why couldn't I let it go? Did I hold a grudge against Susannah for cheating on me? Or was it more than that? Aaron didn't deserve this at all. Neither did Kinsley. But I needed to know for some torturous reason.

When Marin returned, I said, "I'd like for you to go home and get that kit. I want to know."

"Grey." Her voice held a warning. "That's not a good idea."

"It won't change anything. Aaron is mine either way." Who was I convincing more, Marin or myself?

She blew out a long breath. "You should let it go."

"You're probably right. But then again, you haven't been in my shoes for these past several months. You haven't experienced betrayal like this. And I'm not talking about Susannah and our relationship. I'm speaking of the kids and what she did to our family."

Her hands assumed the prayer pose. "But Grey, that is your relationship, isn't it? Your family? And won't it put a bigger wedge between you and Aaron?"

"How can it? I've already said I'd accept him as my own, no matter what. It wasn't his fault what she did."

"No, so why pursue it?"

Aaron was still in my arms and I felt his soft curls beneath my chin. He shifted in my arms and his eyes caught mine. Lashes damp with tears from crying, he latched onto my shirt with his tiny fists and a hint of a lopsided grin appeared. The ache in my chest deepened, making it hard to breathe because he was the one who had suffered. This beautiful, innocent child. I kissed his cheek and hugged him closer.

"Well big guy, looks like you're feeling better, aren't you?"

One of his legs moved a bit. It wasn't quite a kick, but it was better than nothing. I peered over the top of his head to see Marin watching us.

"Get the kit. I promise as long as there is life in me, I will not hurt this child." I would not let the ghost of this sin —if it was a sin to find out the truth—haunt this son of mine.

Chapter Twenty-Five

MARIN

THE KIT BURNED a hole in my bag as I walked back into Aaron's room. Grey was seated in the recliner, but immediately stood when I entered. My expression must've told him everything, but he didn't back down. I pulled the kit out, only the nurse walked in, so I crammed it back in my bag.

"We have a room ready for little Aaron on the pediatrics floor. They're on the way to move him now." She smiled. "I'm sure you're happy to see him get out of here."

Grey was the one who did the talking while I listened. My mind was wrapped around that stupid DNA kit in my bag. I was still going to do my best to talk him out of it, even though his mind was made up.

He and the nurse were talking when another person showed up and introduced herself as Tracy from the pediatrics unit. "I'll be taking Aaron down to his new room now." She got all his equipment ready and then we took him right in the portable crib down the two floors to the other room.

She chatted all the way and exclaimed how cute he was. "I'm sure you're ready to get out of that unit. All the parents are so happy to move to the floor."

"Yes," Grey agreed. I think he was ready for her to stop talking. She chatted on and on about how the hospital ran things, not aware he was a physician. She was only trying to help and didn't know any better. I would've engaged with her, but my brain was still wrapped around that stupid box in my bag.

After she got Aaron settled, she wrote his nurses' names on the whiteboard in his room and while she did that, Grey went to log into the computer in the room. She must've heard him, and she started to say something, but he held out his hand. In it was his hospital badge.

"Oh, Dr. West. I wasn't aware."

"It's fine. I never checked his last X-ray report and I wanted to take a look at it."

"Oh." She let out a nervous laugh. "I guess it's okay."

He pulled up both X-rays and sighed. "What an improvement."

"That's good news. I think he has a meal on the way too. If you want to grab something to eat, feel free. I can feed him," Tracey said.

"No, that's fine," I said. "I'll do that." Tracy nodded and left the room.

Grey asked, "Are you hungry?"

"A little."

"It is dinner time already. I'll run and get us something. What would you like?"

"A sandwich. I'm not picky."

He left and I picked Aaron up to snuggle. I couldn't wait to get him home. "One more day here, little guy.

Then we're home free where you can sleep in your own bed and see your big sister. How does that sound?"

He grabbed my shoulder and patted it. I wanted to kiss him to pieces and never let him go.

"And one more thing and listen up good. Don't you ever do this to me again, you hear? You scared me to death. I didn't know ..." I got too teary-eyed to continue, so I just hugged him.

Grey came back with our dinner and we were alone again. After we ate, he brought up that damn kit. I yanked it out of my purse and handed it to him.

"Let it be known I am not in favor of this."

"I am aware. And to you, I promise this won't change anything between Aaron and me. I am his father. Do you understand?"

"Yes."

He opened the package and took out the cotton swabs. He used one on his cheek, then he swabbed the inside of Aaron's while his son watched him curiously. When he was finished, he put them in the appropriate containers and packaged them up as the directions stated. Then he handed it to me. "Will you mail this for me?"

I didn't bother with an answer, but I grabbed the package and stuffed it back in my purse.

"Thank you."

That evening, I sat in the recliner, after thinking over everything, and still had a difficult time understanding Grey's need to know. His voice startled me out of my thoughts.

"Why don't you go home, Marin. Get some sleep."

"I was going to suggest you go home and that I stay here tonight."

He wrapped his warm hand around mine. "Aaron is my son, my responsibility. I want to stay with him. You've done so much, a lot more than I could've asked. Get some rest. Kinsley will be home tomorrow and Aaron is still not well. I have to go back to work and catch up on the patients I've missed. They've had to double book me, unfortunately."

"You're sure?"

"Yes. I can sleep here. These chairs fold out into beds and they have linens for them. I'll be just fine. Oh, and do me a favor."

"What's that?"

A wicked glint sparked in his eyes. "I want you to sleep in my room tonight."

This request came out of nowhere and I was totally unprepared for it. "Your room? Why?"

His sexy mouth curved into a smile, one that would be stamped in my memory for hours, if not days. "I want to think of you sleeping there, naked, so the next time I'm in bed, I can dream about doing dirty things to you."

I swallowed the mass of lust that had embedded itself in my throat. It was like dislodging a giant rock, stubborn as hell, and refused to budge.

"Grey," I whispered.

"Hmm?" He had the look of innocence on his face.

"I, uh …" my voice trailed off.

"Go. Call me when you get home. When you're naked."

I nodded because it wasn't possible to form words. Who was this man? How had I thought him stuffy? This was a sexy as hell Grey and it made me wonder what he was going to say when I called. It also made me wonder what our first time would be like.

"Oh, one more thing, Marin." He wrapped his hand around my neck and gave me a searing kiss.

At first, I gawked at the man and then gulped. As I

hurried from the room, I noticed how wet things were between my thighs. I hoped the drive home was fast because I didn't want to get myself off on the way there. That would not be cool. What if I got in a wreck? That would be awful. I could imagine the headlines. *Woman Found With Pants Unzipped and Private Bits Exposed After Five Car Pileup.* Not cool at all.

I made the drive in record time, watching the garage door open and wishing it would speed up. It had been so long since I'd felt any sexual desire that mine was on hyper-drive right now.

Turning the alarm off, I dashed up the steps, made a quick stop in my room, and fished around under the mattress for my vibrator. Then I gazed at it like a drunken fool. Oh my gosh, I forgot to call Grey. I grabbed my phone and hit his name.

"That was fast. You must've laid the lead on the gas pedal," he said, chuckling.

I fake yawned and said, "Yeah, I'm so tired."

"Uh huh. Before you take that tired self of yours to my bed, I want you to do something. Are you naked yet?"

"Uh, no."

"Take off your clothes and get in the bed."

"Uh, I'm in the bed."

"Sweet dreams, Marin. Think of me." And he hung up.

I hung up and my hands shook. I powered up my vibe and thoughts of sexy Grey popped into my head. It wasn't difficult to get close to orgasm. I'd been close when I left the hospital. I slid my rabbit in and out of me, pumping slow at first, but then picking up the pace. Each time I thrust deep, that perky rabbit nose tickled my clit, and in no time, I orgasmed, calling out Grey's name. Then I wondered if he had a camera in there. Oh, God! How embarrassing. I jumped, almost right out of the bed, as my phone rang. *Fuck. Who was it?*

Checking the caller ID, I saw Grey's name. "Hello." My voice shook.

"I miss you. What are you doing?"

"Um, reading."

"Reading? Is that all?"

"Yes. No." I giggled, which sounded stupid.

"Marin, what exactly are you doing in my bed? Describe to me in detail."

Oh, God. What the hell was I going to say? "Um, nothing. I'm laying here."

"Marin." He said my name with a warning.

Shit, shit, shit. "Ijusthadanorgasmwithmyvibrator," I blurted.

"Are you dripping wet?"

"Uh huh."

"Text me a picture of yourself."

"No! I can't do that."

"Sure you can. Just keep your head out of it, then no one will know it's you except for the two of us."

I thought about it for a second and decided I could never do that, but instead, I sent him a picture of me, covered up to my neck. He laughed when he got it.

"You are such a chicken."

"Yes, I am. And you will have to wait to see the real naked me in person, Dr. West."

A deep chuckle came back to me. "I can't wait for that and to get inside of you. I'm going to have fun teaching you some things."

"Do they teach you those *things* in heart school?"

I had an image of him shaking his head. "Hardly." Then I heard a deep chuckle.

"Good. I was a bit worried."

"Don't be, Marin. But I want you ready tomorrow night."

I tugged the sheet close to my chin. "We can't do this with the kids in the house."

"They sleep, remember?"

"But it's inappropriate."

"Let me make that determination. Go to sleep. You're going to need it for what I have in mind." The line went dead. Oh my. And here I thought Dr. West was a straight-laced tight-assed dude. Who would've thought he was so dirty minded?

Chapter Twenty-Six

GREYDON

THE NEXT MORNING, Marin tiptoed into Aaron's hospital room. But after she heard him jabbering, all the quietness about her disappeared.

"He sounds so much better." A gigantic sigh rushed out of her.

"He is. Woke up like usual, demanding his diaper be changed." I watched her as she lifted him out of the crib. He pawed her face and she kissed his hand.

"Hey, buddy. Are you happy today?"

He smacked her in the face. "Ow. You better watch it." Her fingers dug into his ribs until he laughed, but it turned into a coughing fit.

"Oh, no, I'm sorry, baby boy. That sounds so nasty."

"Yes, that's what pneumonia does. They put him on a nebulizer to help break all that up."

She pointed to a bag and said, "I brought you a change of clothes so you could shower."

"Ah. Did you get stuck in my underwear drawer again?"

Her cheeks flamed scarlet and her attempts at hiding it failed.

"It won't work. But don't worry. You'll get used to it."

"Used to what?"

"My sexual innuendos."

Watching her responses made me think of an innocent naive woman, but I knew she was anything but that.

"I'm going to buy ear muffs for your son."

"Why?"

"So, he doesn't get tainted by your dirty mind."

I wrapped my hands around her waist from behind and drew her against me. Being much shorter than me, I was able to rest my chin on the top of her head. "You're the one I'm interested in tainting, not him." Then I kissed her neck, right behind her velvety soft earlobe. "I can't wait to crawl into bed with you tonight."

"Grey, someone might walk in here."

"What if they do? Is there a law against me embracing you?"

"I'm your nanny!"

I laughed so hard and it felt better than ever. I'd laughed more with her than anyone in my life, including Susannah. Now that I thought of it, Susannah and I hardly ever laughed together.

"Marin, I believe you're my kids' nanny, not mine. But, if you want to play nanny to me, I'm all in."

She looked over her shoulder at me and again, flushed with embarrassment. Aaron kicked his legs, so I took him from her.

"He wants to get down and run around," I said. With the door shut, there was no harm in that, so I set him on the floor and watched him waddle around. He crashed into

Marin's legs and garbled out something. It was good to see things returning to normal.

"Why don't you shower? I'll be his watchdog."

"Thanks. I won't be gone long," I said.

AARON WAS RELEASED LATER that morning and I returned to work. The pile-up of patients from the last couple of days was hell. I worked like a maniac to see everyone. Luckily, an electrophysiologist from the other hospital had filled in for me on a few cases. By six o'clock, I finished up, but I still had some charting to complete. As I sat at my desk, my phone dinged with a text.

What time will you be home?

It was Marin. Those words brought a smile to my face.

Seven—I hope.

She hit me back with: **Tough day?**

I've had much worse. But it's about to get better.

Her response had me chuckling. **Oh? Care to explain?**

I'd rather show you. But I'd make a fool of myself when I moaned.

She sent me an emoji with a shocked face.

See you soon.

I hustled my ass off to finish up and was out the door an hour later. When I walked in the house, Kinsley practically attacked me.

"Daddy!"

I picked her up and swung her high in the air. "Polka dot! I feel like I haven't seen you in a very long time."

"Because you haven't." She flung her arms around my neck and kissed me on the nose. "Did you miss me?"

"More than chocolate."

"I missed you more than ice cream."

"I missed you more than ice cream with chocolate on top."

"I missed you more than ice cream with chocolate and whipped cream on top."

We could go on and on like this, but I needed to check on Aaron. "How's your brother doing?"

"Good. But his legs aren't kicking as good. I don't know if he's gonna be a dancer anymore."

"Hmm. Let's see. Where is he?"

"In the swing."

We went into the living area and Marin was sitting with him.

"Hey," I said.

"Hey to you. How are you?"

"Hungry and tired."

"Good because I have lasagna in the oven," she said.

The little guy was heavy-lidded and sleepy. "Looks like someone is ready for bed."

"Yeah. I was giving you a few more minutes before I put him down."

"I'll do it. While I'm up there, I'll change and be back down for dinner."

"Thanks."

"Marin, don't thank me for putting my own son to bed." I picked Aaron out of the swing.

"Daddy, I wanna come with you."

I held out my hand and said, "Let's go."

We got to Aaron's room where I changed his diaper and then set him in his crib. His eyes were half closed already. Bending over, I pressed my lips to his forehead and covered him with his favorite blanket.

"Can I kiss him goodnight too, Daddy?"

"Sure, polka dot." I picked Kinsley up so she could kiss him. Then we left the room after I shut the light off.

"Why don't you read Aaron a bedtime story like you do me?"

"He's not old enough yet, but when he gets to be two, I'll start doing it, like we did for you."

"Did you used to read to me when I was two?"

"I sure did. That's how I started calling you my polka dot. You had this little book where the girl wore a polka dotted dress that you always wanted me to read for you."

"Oh. Maybe you can read that for Aaron too."

"Maybe I can."

She followed me into my closet where I took off my shirt and tie and changed into something more comfortable. Then we went down to the kitchen where Marin was serving up the lasagna.

"Polka dot, do you want some?" I asked.

"Nope. I ate already with Aaron."

"When someone offers you something, you should say, 'No, thank you.'"

"Even if I want some?"

Marin's shoulders shook as she turned away to hide her laughter.

"In that case, you would say, 'Yes, please.'"

She pursed her tiny mouth, then said, "No, thank you, Daddy."

"Good girl."

The three of us sat at the table and ate while Kinsley talked about how Aaron needed to work on his kicks. "Maybe I can help him and show him when I start my Irish dancing."

"Oh, shoot," Marin cried out.

"What is it?" I asked.

"I forgot to call the dancing studio to check."

"Don't worry. Call in the morning."

"Yeah, Marnie. You were scared about Aaron. Hey Daddy, how'd he get ammonia?"

Marin kicked me under the table and I bit down on my lip. "No one really knows. It just happens sometimes."

"Will I get ammonia?"

"I don't think so, honey. You don't need to worry about that."

"Oops, I forgot." She jumped out of her chair and scooted out of the room.

"Where did she go?" I asked.

"I don't know, but that ammonia thing was too cute."

Kinsley charged back into the kitchen carrying a large sheet of paper. She slapped it on the table, saying, "I made this for Aaron today."

It was a picture of Aaron, Kinsley, Marin, and me all holding hands. Aaron was naked except for a diaper and he had a gigantic pacifier in his mouth. I'm not sure why she'd drawn that because he'd give up his pacifier months ago. The picture was adorable and funny at the same time. I held out my arms to hug her.

"Kinsley, this is fantastic," I said. "You're becoming quite the artist."

"I know."

"Honey, when someone compliments you, you should thank them."

She quirked a brow, exactly like her mother used to do. "Even when it's from you?"

"Sure. It doesn't matter who it comes from, and that includes Marin."

"Thank you, Daddy."

Marin picked it up and said, "I told her too bad she wasn't in school right now. She could've entered into the art contest."

"She sure could have."

We cleaned up the dinner dishes and I put Kinsley to bed. She wanted me to find the polka dot story to read to her.

"Honey, I'm pretty sure that it's boxed up in the attic with the rest of your baby things. You're going to have to pick out something else." She settled on a different book and after a few chapters, she was nodding off. I kissed her, covered her up, and turned off the light.

It was only eight o'clock, but I was exhausted. Marin was in the den when I got back downstairs. "I'm not sure how much longer I can stay awake."

"You look super tired."

"I am. Why don't we go to bed?"

"Good idea."

After turning everything off, we walked up the stairs, and when she started heading toward her room, I asked, "Marin, where do you think you're going?"

"To bed?"

"Exactly. But why are you going that way?"

"Because that's where my bedroom is."

Cupping her neck, I brought her close to my body. "But you're not sleeping in your room." Then I ran my tongue down the side of her neck, stopping at her pulse point. I felt the thrumming of her heart beneath my mouth as I gently nipped and sucked. My thumbs circled the peaks of her nipples, which were pebbled under her bra. She hummed her pleasure. "We can continue this my room, or I can undress you here in the hallway."

"The kids?" she whispered, her voice husky with desire.

"Are asleep, and there's no need to whisper."

"But ..."

"This way." I steered her into my room.

"I need to wash my face and brush my teeth."

"You can do that in here," I said.

"Not my face regimen."

"Oh, you have a regimen?" I smirked.

"As a matter of fact, yes."

"Then go, but your sexy ass is sleeping with me."

"Yes, sir. Did I tell you that you're a bossy boss?"

I slapped her ass and said, "You're wasting time."

By the time she returned, I was in bed with my teeth brushed and face washed. I lifted the covers and said, "Get in here." And then it hit me ... her scent. Images of what I imagined she did last night spiked my desire, fueling my passion. Inhaling, I said, "I wish I could've been here last night with you."

A flush rose from her neck to the crests of her cheeks. "I do too. You could have shown me those *things* you mentioned." She smirked. Before she could offer up any other sassy comments, I took her chin between my thumb and finger and gently teased her mouth with mine. I began at one corner and lazily worked my way to the other. My teeth grazed her upper and lower lips and sucked on the bottom one before I pushed my tongue into her mouth. Our tongues met, hesitant at first, but the kiss quickly grew more demanding and frenzied. My mind became buzzed with the headiness of how the atmosphere sparked between us. The heat between us amped up and I couldn't get enough of her, of her lips, or her mouth. I had never wanted a kiss to go on like this. It was intoxicating and I was drunk with lust.

"I have wanted you so long ... Jesus, Marin. The number of showers I've taken and masturbated to thoughts of you naked, your legs spread, with that fucking vibrator in your hand, and me watching you use it on yourself. I have been so fucking hard for weeks now with these dirty thoughts of you."

My hand slipped under her camisole and tugged on her nipple, which was as hard as my cock. These damn clothes were useless and in the way, so I sat up and pulled her along with me.

"I can't wait to see you … to touch this, your body. To taste every inch of your skin. You have driven me half out of my mind with lust."

"We have to get rid of this." I waited for her permission before yanking her cami over her head, "And these." My fingers hooked around the elastic of her panties and with one quick motion, I pulled them off.

Her hand reached out for my shirt. "What about you?"

I stood up and took off the T-shirt and boxers I was wearing, my motions frantic. "For your information, this was for your benefit. I usually sleep naked."

"What about the kids?"

"What about them?"

"What if you're naked and they come in here?"

"Aaron can't get out of his crib yet, and Kinsley never gets up. If she were to come in, I'd tell her to go back to her room and I'd meet her in there."

"What if she were sick or had a nightmare?"

"I'd hear her and check the camera. And she's only had one nightmare that I can recall."

"You have an answer for everything, don't you?" she asked.

I climbed into bed and situated myself next to her. I brushed her hair off her face. "I didn't have anything close to an answer for you when you walked into my life." My fingers weaved into her thick multi-colored locks. "You, with your colored hair, piercings, and tattoos. I didn't quite know what to make of you."

"And what do you make of me now?"

"I'm not sure. I laugh a lot more. I won't say you didn't piss me off, but I love your passion. It inspires me."

"Can I tell you something? And promise you won't get mad?"

I brushed her hair back. "This seems to be a recurring theme with you."

She laughed. "I thought you were the stuffiest asshole I'd ever met."

For some reason, I couldn't stop kissing the corner of her mouth. "Stuffy, huh. I thought you said I was starchy."

"Yeah. I had all sorts of nicknames for you."

"Like what?"

She ran her finger across my lips. "Dr. Grouch, Dr. Ghost, Dr. Delirious."

"Why Dr. Ghost?"

"You were never home and would disappear for hours into your office."

"And Dr. Delirious?"

"Because you thought you were nice to me when in actuality, you weren't."

"I see. How about I show you how nice I can really be?"

"Oh? And how are you going to do that?"

"Like this." Her tits were perfect and I couldn't wait to suck on her nipples. I kissed my way down to her breasts, taking my time drawing each of her nipples into my mouth until they were stiff little peaks. She murmured her pleasure, but this was only the beginning. Working my way down her body, I got to the juncture of her smooth, creamy thighs, and spread them wide enough for my head and shoulders to fit.

"Bend your knees." She complied and I pushed her legs up a bit. My tongue swiped the seam of her pussy repeatedly until she huffed. When she became slick, I spread her lips using my thumbs and tunneled my tongue inside of her.

She raised herself to her elbows and watched. "Ahh," she moaned.

My tongue trailed to her clit, circling it, and using a finger, I slid it inside her. She was drenched and I spread her wetness around, adding another finger inside. Locating her G-spot, I massaged it, while my tongue worked a rhythm on her nub.

"Don't stop. Yes, right there." Her nails scored my shoulders, then my head, as I kept up my ministrations. She tasted divine, and I didn't want this to end. When had I ever thought that before?

"Oh, Grey, that's perfect. Yeah, that." I flicked my tongue harder and faster. "Yes, I'm coming." Her muscles clenched down on my fingers as the contractions of her orgasm took hold. I didn't stop my motions until her spasms ceased. She was breathless and covered in a fine sheen of perspiration.

"You taste even better than the scent you left behind." Wondering how she tasted had been driving me crazy. "Not to mention, you have the prettiest pink pussy."

A flush swept from her neck to the top of her forehead.

"Did that embarrass you?" It surprised me my dirty talked shocked her so much.

"A little."

"I'm only being honest. So, for the other part. I haven't been with anyone but my former wife for the past twelve years. After she died, and I found out about the affair, I got tested, so I'm safe."

"I'm safe too. After I caught my boyfriend screwing my best friend, I also got tested. I haven't been with anyone since then."

"Are you on any kind of contraception? I'm sorry this

is such a sterile topic, but I thought it best we have this discussion before we go any further."

"I'm glad you brought it up because if you hadn't, I would have. I'm on the pill and have been for years, so we're good."

"Thank God because I can't remember the last time I used a condom."

She laughed. "Oooh, you poor thing. That would've been terrible, huh?"

"Not at all. I would do anything to have you."

I crawled up her body to kiss her smiling mouth. Next I raised her leg near the crook of her knee and my stiff cock found her entrance. I worked my way in slowly, to make sure she was comfortable. But also so I wouldn't come all over the place. It had been so long, I was afraid I wouldn't last.

"Is this okay?"

"It's perfect."

My hips rocked against her as I watched her face. The expressions that flitted across it told me I was doing this right. Her panting increased and her fingers dug into the muscles of my ass.

"I have to get you to come fast because I'm not going to last. It's been way too long for me. Sit on my cock, facing away from me."

She straddled my hips. Her ass was gorgeous. My head swirled with so many thoughts of what I could do to that, but instead, I sat up, pulling her against my chest as I leaned on the headboard. Massaging her clit, I rocked my pelvis into her. She tried to spread her legs wider, but I said, "No. Keep them the way they are. It causes more friction."

Between my finger and the added pressure, within minutes, she said, "I'm coming."

My pace increased, and moments later, I joined her, groaning out my own climax. When my cock finally stopped pulsating, I panted, "You were worth waiting for."

She leaned her head back to look at me and said, "It was more than worth it." When she tried to move, I clasped my arms around her.

"Where do you think you're going?"

"To the bathroom. To clean up."

"Not yet."

"What do you mean?"

"I'm not done with you. Just because I'm an old man doesn't make me a deadbeat between the sheets."

Chapter Twenty-Seven

MARIN

GREY WASN'T JOKING. Not in the least. How did I ever think of him as a starchy old geezer? He made Damien look like a clumsy teenager when it came to sex. I probably came more in one night with Grey than I did in the two plus years I'd been with that loser.

"Tell me if I'm hurting you."

"I will," I panted out the words. This was what? Round three. Or was it four? How did he rebound so quickly? I was standing, bent over the bed, and he was banging me. I wasn't even joking. Each time he plunged into me, the contact made a bam-bam-bam sound. Maybe I should call him Dr. Bang from now on.

"Can you rub yourself?" His husky voice came from over my shoulder and it sent my blood racing through my veins. Jesus, how could that be? I wanted him to devour me, to inhale me. His hand gripped my hip, fingers almost bruising, yet I wanted more.

My nails clawed the sheets. "I can't. I ,,, I'm ..."

I should've known he'd handle it. His finger ended up between my legs, where it pressed and rubbed in a gentle motion. Not beat it to a pulp like dumbass Damien used to do. Shit. I needed to quit comparing the two because quite frankly, there simply was no comparison. My hips were repeatedly shoved into the mattress as he grunted and normally that wouldn't have been my thing. But this man's sexy sounds were beyond description. They had me grinding my ass back into him.

"Shit, Marin. Keep that up and it'll be over before it ever started."

He hiked one of my legs up and oh, my effing God, his cock slammed in deep and I gasped as it nearly collapsed me.

"How's that?" he asked.

"G-good."

"Only good?"

"P-perfect. D-don't s-stop."

He swiveled his hips and then thrust, swiveled, then thrust. Swivel thrust, swivel thrust. I was done.

"Ahhhh," I cried as I came. This night would be the ruination of me. If he and I didn't work out as a couple, I would have to join a nunnery.

Suddenly, he groaned and I felt him pulsing inside of me.

"God, I love that," I said.

His cock throbbed and I clenched my inner muscles against it.

"Fuck, Marin. You'll get me going again. And what is it you love?"

"The feel of you coming inside of me."

"That's good because we can make that happen a lot." He pulled out and I whimpered.

"No," I whined. "I like you in there."

"You don't exactly look comfortable." I wasn't, but it was a small price to pay for what he'd just given me. "Come on. Let's clean up," he said.

"Now you're ready?" I joked.

"It is after midnight, you know."

Crap. That meant only six hours of sleep unless Aaron slept later than usual.

"Maybe Aaron will sleep in," he said, reading my mind.

"I was just thinking that. But you have to go to work."

"I'm going to skip my workout. I think tonight sufficed."

We walked into the shower and rinsed off. "This is a magnificent shower." It was huge with dual shower heads and sprays running up and down the sides.

"Feel free to use it any time you want. It also converts to steam."

"That might look a bit weird to Kinsley."

He shrugged and said, "Soon we'll spend a lot more time in here getting dirty instead of clean." His mouth found mine and we ended up making out.

"We could get real dirty in here," I said.

I was careful not to get my hair wet and we finished up quickly and went back to bed. My body ached deliciously in all the right spots.

"Are you sore?"

"A little, but how can I not be?" I laughed.

"I'm sorry I got carried away. I overused you."

"I don't think so. I liked it … a lot. Walking may be a little difficult tomorrow, but it was worth it."

He pulled me against the expanse of his chest and said, "I can't wait to see if you limp in the morning." Then he pressed a kiss to my temple. "Goodnight sweet Marin."

"G'night." I was already drifting.

It wasn't Aaron who woke us in the morning, it was Kinsley. We were both in a deep sleep when I heard, "Daddy, did Marnie have a nightmare?"

Oh shit. Oh fuck. Oh noooooooo.

"Uh, what did you say, polka dot?" Grey's voice was heavy with sleep and oh, God, was it hot as sin.

I was alert and wide awake, only I pretended not to be. Grey's usually clear mind was foggy, or at least that's how he sounded. Maybe even slightly disoriented, as though he was struggling to piece together where he was.

"Did Marnie have a bad dream?"

"Um, I don't know. Why do you ask?"

"Cuz she's sleeping with you like I used to do if I had a bad dream."

Then he abruptly sat up like someone stuck him with a cattle prod.

Double fuck.

When he did that, he took half the covers with him, exposing my nakedness.

"Daddy, why isn't Marnie wearing her jammies?"

He slammed back down onto the bed.

"Um, why don't you go back to bed, polka dot, and I'll be in your room in a minute?"

"Okay."

As soon as the coast was clear, I scrambled out of bed and got dressed, saying the whole time, "Holy shit. Holy shit. What are we going to do?"

"Nothing. We're going to do nothing."

I stopped and stared at him. Then I launched into a verbal stream of exasperation. "You don't have any idea what you're saying. I'll be here with her all day long and she's going to ask me a million questions. She's not just going to drop this and move on. I know how that smart little brain of hers operates. Trust me on this, Grey. We have to come up with something plausible."

"You're serious?"

"Damn right I'm serious."

He thrust his hands into his already messy hair. And didn't that just make me want to kiss him again?

"Don't do that," I said, flustered.

"Do what?"

"That hair thing."

His mouth gaped and he only stared.

"You look way too sexy like that and I don't need sexy Grey right now. I need analytical Grey."

The idiot burst out laughing.

I clutched my hands together. "What is so damn funny?"

"You are," he said, pulling me into his arms. "Why can't we tell her the truth?"

"Are you serious? And say what? That I slept with you naked and we screwed our brains out last night?"

He cupped my face and said, "Not that, but a less pornographic version of it."

"Such as?"

"We came in here and started talking. Before we knew it, we fell asleep."

His hands ran through my hair and were very distracting. "How do we explain my nakedness?"

"Your shirt was dirty and you didn't want to sleep in a dirty shirt."

I patted his cheek. "I'm going to let you give her that explanation. Let's go to her room now." I grabbed his hand and tugged him down the hall. She was sitting on her bed playing with a herd of stuffed animals when we entered.

"Good morning little lady," I said.

"Marnie!" She jumped up and held out her arms.

I kissed her cheek and hugged her.

"I saw you sleeping in Daddy's bed."

"He told me. I was tired last night."

"Me too." By this time, I'd already dropped her back down next to her pile of critters.

"Polka dot, you asked why Marin slept in my bed."

"Uh huh. She didn't have a bad dream about a monster?"

"No, baby, she didn't. But we were talking and both got really sleepy. She just fell asleep."

"How come she was naked? Marnie, do you like to sleep naked? Maybe I should sleep naked too."

Oh brother.

"Sweetie, she spilled something on her shirt, so after she fell asleep, I didn't want to go get her pajamas, so I just took her shirt off. You know how I do that for you sometimes?"

"Uh huh."

"Well, I didn't have any pajamas to put on Marin, so I just let her sleep like that."

"Oh."

"Marnie, did you like Daddy's bed better than yours?"

I was not expecting that question at all. I stuttered out my answer. "I, uh, that's to say, his bed was, er, very big."

"Did you sleep a lot?"

"Umm hmm."

"Good. Maybe you can sleep there more cuz it's a big bed, isn't it, Daddy?"

"It sure is, polka dot. Now, are you ready for some breakfast? I have to shower and Marin has to check on Aaron first, though."

"Okay, I'll play in here for a while."

"Good girl."

We left her to her animals and parted ways in the hall where I mouthed to him, *that was close.* He only smiled back.

Aaron was awake in his crib, smiling and making funny noises. When he saw me, his legs kicked around the way they used to. Not quite as exuberantly, but he was on the way to being himself again.

"Hey there, little guy. You're feeling better, aren't you?" I picked him up and rained dozens of kisses on his cheeks until he giggled. But his giggles turned into a cough, so I waited until he stopped. Then I nuzzled his neck and really got him chattering. "There's my little fella. I missed you." He grabbed my hair and yanked. "Ouch." His fist was strong again. Thank God.

"Come on, let's get that diaper changed." I placed him on his changing table and cleaned him up. Then I changed his clothes and we grabbed Kinsley from her room to go get breakfast.

"Aaron! You're ready to kick again." She patted his legs as he kicked in my arms.

"Marnie, I think he wants to run around."

"I think you're right, but let's wait until we get downstairs." Once we got in the kitchen, I put Aaron down and he teetered around with Kinsley giving him a hand. Then I fixed our meal. Aaron gobbled his up which was a relief. When Grey came down, our plates were all cleaned up.

"Can I fix you something?" I asked him.

"Thanks, but I need to get a move on. I'll grab a protein bar." Then he shocked the hell out of me when he leaned over and kissed me.

"Daddy kissed Marnie. Daddy kissed Marnie."

"That's right, polka dot, he sure did," Grey said, right

before he kissed her, then Aaron, and walked out of the house.

"Is Daddy your boyfriend?" Kinsley asked.

How the hell was I supposed to answer that?

Chapter Twenty-Eight

GREYDON

WHAT THE HELL had I been thinking to have kissed her on the cheek like that? It was an impulsive decision. She'd been sitting there and it just happened. I could imagine the questions Kinsley hit her with. Now that I was away from her and didn't have sex on the brain, the ramifications of our actions sunk in. It had never been my intention to get involved with another woman, or at least until the kids were grown. But Marin broke every rule in my book. She wasn't someone I would ever have given a second look to under any other circumstance. How should I handle this?

I wondered how she would answer Kinsley's questions because there would be many I was sure. My phone pinged several times, but I ignored it. I would check it when I got to my office. I was pretty sure I knew who they were from. A hearty laugh ripped out of me. When was the last time that had occurred? I couldn't even remember. And I owed it all to Marin.

I walked into the office and things were sparking to life. Nicole was already there, a pile of charts on my desk waiting.

"Dr. West, here's your schedule for today. You have three procedures at the hospital beginning at eleven."

"Thanks." I reviewed everything and started work.

My patient load was heavy since I was still catching up. My first patient was already in the exam room, and thankfully his EKG and all other studies were in there. Nicole had started doing her job as she should've been all along.

By ten thirty, I was on the way to the hospital. My procedures went well, but the day was flying by. By afternoon, I hadn't had a chance to do any charting. It looked like I would have to wait until the end of the day. I grabbed a bite to eat on my way back to the office and gobbled it down before I saw the afternoon patient load. By five thirty, I was stuck with charting a day's worth of work.

Texting Marin, I let her know I'd be late. **Don't hold up dinner for me. It's been a rough day.**

She answered back. **It's fine. I'll have something waiting for you.**

I was finally able to leave at seven even though there were a few things I'd left undone. Rubbing my eyes, I was glad to be heading home.

On the way home, I mentally ticked off the emails I'd gone through right before I left. There was one that I needed to discuss with Marin, I was fairly excited about it as long as she was in.

The kitchen was bright and full of sunshine when I walked into the house.

"Daddy!" Kinsley yelled as she flew into my arms.

Lifting her high in the air, I said, "Hey there sweet

thing. What have you been up to today?" I planted kisses all over her cheeks as she giggled.

"Teaching Aaron how to kick and dance. Look."

Aaron was wheeling around the kitchen, holding his stuffed monkey, and laughing as his legs did their funny kicking motions.

"I think that's his specialty run, polka."

"I think he's gonna be an Irish dancer like me. He wants clicky shoes. Marnie got me some today."

"She did?"

"Yeah, but they have to get here."

Marin clarified things a bit. "I signed her up for classes. They don't start for another six weeks and the kind instructor gave me the link to the website where I could order the shoes."

Kinsley jumped up and down. "Yay. I can't wait. I'm gonna practice every day. And so will Aaron."

"Honey, I don't think Aaron will be able to dance. Remember what I told you earlier? He's too young," Marin said.

Kinsley ran up to Aaron and grabbed his hand. "It's okay. I can teach him myself. He doesn't have to come with me."

Marin and I shared a look and I shrugged. "Whatever you say, Kinsley. Will you watch your brother a minute? I have something to discuss with Marin."

"Are you gonna kiss her again?" Kinsley asked.

"Maybe. Do you want me to?"

"Yeah. I think she likes it." Then she puckered up her lips and kissed the air.

"I'll do my best. We'll be right in the next room, okay?"

"Okay."

I took Marin's hand and we went into the den.

"She was filled with all sorts of questions about kissing after you left."

I pulled Marin against my chest and pressed my lips to hers. "I probably shouldn't have done that. I put you in a bad position. I'm sorry."

"It's fine. Is this what you wanted to discuss with me?"

"Actually, no. I have something to ask you. I've been asked to speak at a conference in Vienna at the end of next month. It's a pretty big deal and I'd love for all of us to go. That is if you'd be willing to come along. I wouldn't be able to take the kids, obviously, if you don't come too."

"You want me to come to Vienna? As in Vienna, Austria?"

"Yeah. Is that something you'd be interested in? We could make it into a vacation. The conference is only a day and a half. My talk is only an hour long, so I wouldn't be tied up for very long."

"And you could get away?" she asked.

"Sure. The practice has things in place for conferences. I would get someone to come in and take my calls. Not to mention, it's over a month away, so I have time to plan. Please say you will."

She clapped her hands. "Yes! I think it would be great for the kids too. Aaron won't remember much, but Kinsley would love it."

"Great!" I hugged her. "I'll let them know and then make all of our reservations. Do you have a passport because I have to get the kids theirs?"

She touched my arm. "Yes, I do and Grey, I'm honored you asked me."

"I'm honored you accepted. I wouldn't have gone without you." I kissed her again on the cheek and we went back into the kitchen to find Kinsley trying to teach Aaron special kicks.

"Do you think she's ever going to give up on this?" Marin asked.

"Only when he can talk and tell her to stop."

The knocking on the back door surprised the two of us, but I went to answer it. When I looked out to see my parents, I was even more surprised.

"Mom, Dad, what are you two doing here?"

"That's quite a greeting," Mom said sourly.

"No, it's just that I didn't know you were coming."

"We've been out of town and knew Aaron had been sick. We wanted to check on him since we just got back."

"Oh, right."

Mom rushed over to pick him up and Aaron smacked her on the cheek. "He must've made a nice recovery," she said, smiling.

"Yeah, but he was pretty bad. Thank God, Marin was wise enough to get him to the hospital when she did."

"Oh, Marin, how can we ever thank you?"

"Mrs. West, there's no need for thanks. I only did what I thought was best."

"Your mother said she'd never heard you sound so worried."

"I was. It was awful. But all is well now, as you can see for yourself."

Mom's eyes bounced between Marin and me. One thing my mother wasn't was stupid. She was very perceptive and I was fairly certain she was picking up on certain cues. By this time, I didn't give a shit, so I walked up to Marin and put my arm around her.

"Marin did a stellar job and if my cell phone hadn't fallen out of my pocket, I would've been there to help her. But I wasn't, so it was all on her shoulders."

Mom continued to absorb the scene for a moment. Then she smiled. "Well, I'm happy to see you two getting along. For a while there, I was sure you were going to kill each other."

"Yeah, that's over, isn't it, Marin?"

"I hope so."

I pulled her against me. "It is."

"Gammie, I'm gonna take those Irish dance lessons and wear those clicky shoes."

Mom bent down and said, "You are? That's fabulous. Maybe you can teach me how to do it?"

"Nah, you're too old. But I'm gonna teach Aaron."

Mom laughed. "You can't fault her for her honesty."

My parents stayed a little while and then wanted to know if they could bring us some dinner.

"I've made dinner already, Mrs. West. Would you like to stay?"

"Oh, that's so sweet of you. But I wouldn't want to intrude."

"It's no intrusion," Marin insisted. "I've made plenty of chicken casserole. The kids have already eaten. Please stay."

"Are you sure?"

Marin insisted and they ate dinner with us. I told them about the Vienna trip. They were excited we were going to take a vacation. Dad suggested a couple of places to stay if we couldn't get accommodations at the hotel where the conference was. He and Mom had traveled there a few times over the years and always said it was one of their favorite places.

"Marin, you must visit the catacombs under St. Stephen's Cathedral. It's quite interesting if you love a bit of dark history."

Marin's eyes brightened. "Oh, that's a definite yes," she said. "Would it be okay for the kids?"

"I don't see why not. You can't really see much down

there. The story about them is fascinating. You should also see the Schonbrunn and Hofburg Palaces. There is so much to see there, Marin. And the shopping—oh, you'll love it, but the children may get bored. However, they will love the Prater, which is a large park and the Tiergarten Schonbrunn, which is the Vienna zoo."

"Oh, they love the animals."

Kinsley shouted, "Yay. Do they have llamas because Marnie doesn't like llamas."

Everyone turned to Marin whose cheeks had already turned crimson. "The llamas sort of spit on me when I took the kids to the zoo. I'll stay clear of them the next time."

"Ewwww, it was icky," Kinsley said, shaking her head.

"I can imagine. We'll make sure there'll be no llama visits on this next trip to the zoo," I said. I wonder why she never mentioned that to me.

Marin shuddered. "Either that or I'll wear a plastic raincoat."

Mom said, "Rick and I just love Vienna. Maybe we can dig up some of the places we toured so you can see."

Dad said, "Great idea, Paige. I'll see if I can find those files I kept."

"Thanks, Dad. That could be helpful."

After we bathed the kids, Marin refused to sleep with me that night. I tried my best to persuade her, but she wouldn't cave. There was nothing I could do so we went to our separate bedrooms, me with an erection that would have to be tended to … alone.

When I was in my room, I sent her a text.

You're cruel. I haven't been this uncomfortable since I was a teenager. I'll text you after my hot, soapy, and very lonely shower.

The only thing I received back was a laughing emoji. Guess she didn't feel too sorry for me.

It didn't take long for me to rub one off, seeing as I was stone hard. Jesus, it seemed like ever since Marin moved in I was spending more time jacking off than I had since before Susannah. Since Susannah had died, and even before then I hadn't had much of an urge. Marin was triggering all sorts of desires in me that I'd thought had ceased to exist long ago. This was certainly an unexpected but pleasant surprise.

I dried off and before climbing into bed, I grabbed my iPad so I could catch up on my medical journals. I was a bit behind on my reading. Midway through the first journal article, my phone pinged with a text. When I opened it, it was a picture of Marin, offering up a sexy smile.

Miss you already.

Glad she was thinking of me, I hit her back with—
You could always fix that, you know.

When she didn't answer, I assumed she fell asleep. We'd been up late last night after all. I finished reading and turned the light off, even though it was still early. But then I heard my door softly open and close. The sheets lifted up and she slid in next to me.

"I guess you broke your own rules, didn't you?"

"Before we do anything, set your alarm for five thirty. I'm not getting caught again."

"Yes, ma'am."

I did as she asked and before I could finish, she was straddling my hips.

"Someone is very eager."

"Yes, someone is. This girl didn't get a hot, soapy shower to relieve herself."

"What happened to your rabbit?" I was very curious about that.

"My rabbit doesn't compare to you," she whispered. Even though it was dark, the moonlight revealed her clear blue eyes as they penetrated my own and suddenly I was at a loss. I wanted to grab her and do all sorts of things to her … fuck her, lick her pussy, kiss her until we were both senseless. But then her fingers whisked over the skin on my abs, and I sucked in my breath. Blinking, the spell was broken.

I brushed the back of my hand over her nipple. "And here I thought I was nothing but an old geezer."

"You are. But that doesn't mean you don't know what to do with your, um …"

"My what?"

"You know."

I pulled her down to press my mouth up to hers. "I want you to tell me, Marin. I want you to say filthy things to me, just as I want to say them back to you."

"Uh, what kinds of filthy things?"

"You first. What doesn't your rabbit compare to?"

"Your cock."

"What do you like about my cock?" I whispered against her lips.

"Everything."

"Be specific, Marin."

My thumb massaged a circle on her neck and I felt the motion of her swallowing.

"I like how it—"

"No it. Refer to *it* as my cock."

She swallowed again. "I like how your cock makes me come."

"Is that all?"

"No."

"What else?"

"I like how it, um—"

"Don't close your eyes. Look at me when you tell me how much you love my cock."

Her startled eyes stared into mine. She was turned on by this. Her dilated pupils and damp skin told me what her words didn't. I ran my tongue over my lower lip because more than anything I wanted to taste her. I wanted my tongue between her thighs.

"Go on," I prodded.

"I like it when your cock is deep inside of me."

"Why?"

"It turns me on. The friction of it. It hits so many places that … I don't know. I, uh, it's just that, it's fucking amazing."

Her plump lips were less than an inch away that I had to taste them, feel them against my own. So I crushed mine to them, greedily exploring the rest of her mouth. She ground her pelvis against mine, rocking into me, she was soaking wet. I flipped her onto her back and wasted not one more minute.

When I was between her legs, I said, "I've thought of this all day. I love your pretty pussy, the taste of it, your scent. I can't get it off my mind. And it's a damn good thing you like my cock." My mouth latched onto her and she cried out. Only once. When she came, and I lifted my head, I realized why she'd been so quiet. She'd put a pillow over her face.

This was something we'd talk about later. Right now, I wanted to fuck her.

"On your knees."

She scrambled to obey. She just came and her swollen cunt begged for more. I placed her hands on the head-board and widened her legs. The curve of her hip, the arch of her back, beckoned to me. I slowly entered her from behind and I heard her suck in air. Even though I'd rubbed one off earlier, I was more than ready to have her tight pussy wrapped around me.

"Tell me if this is good."

"Yeah," she answered, her breath ragged.

At first, I moved slowly, then a bit faster. Pulling her hips closer to mine, I picked up the pace. In and out, in and out. She was tight, so damn tight. I slipped my fingers around in front of her and pinched her clit, working it between my thumb and forefinger. Her low moan told me how much she wanted that. I pushed into her harder and lost myself.

"How close are you?" I asked. I needed to orgasm so badly. I wanted to feel her tensing up on my cock.

"Now. I'm going to come."

Her ass bucked against me when it hit, and her muscles clenched down on me in a rhythmic fashion. That's when I let go. It was unreal pumping into her, feeling her gripping my cock that way. When it was over, we toppled over on the bed, both of us covered with perspiration.

My arm was still around her, my fingers on her clit, pinching it.

"Have you ever had a multiple orgasm?" I asked.

"Ha. I barely had one before you. If you don't count my rabbit-gasms that is."

"What do you mean?"

She shrugged it off by saying, "My sex life wasn't that epic, to be honest."

I shifted to my elbow so I could look at her. "All I can say is it wasn't because of you." And I kissed her gorgeous mouth, tugging on her lower lip with my teeth.

"You really mean that, don't you?"

"Of course I do. I wouldn't say it otherwise."

Then she graced me with the most amazing smile. "Thank you."

"You're welcome. Now I think it's time we get some sleep."

"Yeah, I agree. And don't forget about the alarm."

"It's already done, remember?"

My phone rang then. I picked it up and saw it was the hospital. "I wonder why they're calling. I'm not on call tonight."

"Maybe they got confused."

"I better take this." I answered the phone. "Dr. West."

"Dr. West, it's the Heart Center. We thought you might want to know that your father has just been brought in."

"Shit. I'm on my way."

Marin was already sitting up.

"It's my dad. He's in the hospital."

"Go. Let me know what's going on."

"I will."

I dressed in record time and prayed that Dad would be okay when I got there.

Chapter Twenty-Nine

MARIN

GREY LEFT and I threw on my robe and went to my own room. Before I got into bed, I put on my pajamas and said dozens of prayers that everything would be okay. There wouldn't be any sleep for me because I was worried sick about Rick. He looked fine when they were here tonight. I wanted to call Paige but didn't want to disturb her. I called my mom instead.

"Marin, what's wrong?" It wasn't even that late, but I could tell I'd woken her up.

"Mom, I wanted you to know that Grey got a call. Rick was taken to the hospital. You may want to give Paige a call."

"Oh, no. Is everything okay?"

"I don't know. Grey is supposed to call me."

"Okay, I'll call her. She may need someone there if Hudson or Pearson can't get there."

"Great idea because Grey will be with Rick."

"Thanks for calling, honey."

This waiting game was terrible. If I didn't have the kids to care for, I'd be at the hospital too.

I pulled out my iPad and tried to read but ended up reading the same paragraph a dozen times and couldn't remember anything about it. An hour later, I was downstairs watching TV when a text from Grey came in.

Dad has heart block which means he needs a pacemaker. He'll be fine. Waiting for the EP to get here since I can't do the procedure.

Why can't he do it? Doesn't he do those types of things as an electrophysiologist?

Why can't you do it? I wasn't sure I'd get a response. Then I added **Thank God he's going to be okay.**

I could see the little blinking dots, so I waited for his answer to come in.

I can't do procedures on family members.

Dang. I was aware of that. I didn't want to sound stupid, so I just texted **Right. Please keep me posted.** And I added a heart emoji not thinking about the heart thing.

Cute was his response. Then he sent one back.

Not much later, Mom called.

"Rick is going to be fine. He has some sort of heart rhythm thing and has to have a pacemaker. And I'm angry with you."

"With me? Why?"

"Paige was glowing over how you and Grey are all lovey-dovey. You haven't mentioned a word about this to me. And I'm your mother."

"Er, well, we're not all lovey-dovey and it's sort of new."

"All I can say is she's over the moon about it."

"Over the moon?" I repeated.

"Hello. She never thought Grey would take an interest

in another woman for as long as that man breathed air after what he went through. And now here you are, and according to her, all he did was stare at you."

"Oh, Mom, I think she's exaggerating a bit."

"I don't know, Marin. Paige isn't one to do that, especially when Rick is sick like this. She was very matter of fact about it."

"Interesting."

"My thoughts exactly. So, tell me your version."

"We sort of mended our fences after Aaron's illness and … I don't know, Mom. He's been really nice."

"Nice? That's all you have to say about him? You used to think he was a pompous ass."

"I never called him that."

"No, but you inferred it. You said he was an old man or something of that nature." She would have to remind me of that.

"Okay, Mom, he's not old. He's … mature."

"It's nice to know my daughter is coming to her senses. Anyway, please let me in on these things. I am your mother after all. And honestly, Marin, Grey is a much better catch than Damien ever was."

"Mom! Please don't compare the two. Besides, he's my employer. I need to be careful here."

"Honey, you know I'm right about him." If she only knew how right she was. My face was already on fire just thinking about it. I could almost feel his cock sliding into me. And those eyes of his … the way he looked at me. I had to swallow away the tangle of emotions … and desire.

"Marin, are you still there?"

"Oh, yeah, Mom. I'm here."

"I'll call you if anything else comes up."

"Thanks. I'm up, so don't worry about waking me." I didn't bother to tell her that Grey was texting me too. Now we had the moms gossiping about us. Great, just great. I could already see them conniving on how to get us together. Then a thought slammed into me. I wondered if they had this planned all along. No freakin' way. My mom would never go that far. Or would she?

At about five a.m., I finally gave up the ship and went to take a shower. As I washed between my legs, all sorts of wicked thoughts played through my mind. I had never been this sexually attracted to a man before. Grey ignited all my hormones to life, apparently. My hand worked its magic on me and I came to visions of Grey's head between my thighs. He was unabashedly forward and knew exactly what turned me on. Was that the doctor in him or was he just that much more experienced than me? I'd never been a prude about sex, but I'd never had a guy to make me feel the way Grey did. I wasn't afraid to use my own hand during sex, but it still wasn't great like it was with him. I'd always thought I just wasn't that sexual. I sure was wrong. I could have sex ten times a day with Grey.

I had just gotten back downstairs and put the coffee on when Grey walked into the house.

"Hey," I said. "How is he?"

"Good. Pacemaker is in and he'll be fine. He's going to have a complete work up though. I want to know what caused the heart block in the first place."

He came and hugged me tight.

"Is it unusual to have that?"

"Yes, for someone like Dad, without any underlying causes. That's what we'll be looking for."

"It's good you're checking then. How's Paige?"

"She's fine. My brothers showed up right before I left. It was good of you to call your mother. Mom had someone to wait it out with her."

"I didn't know if either of your brothers would make it in."

"Hudson couldn't leave Wiley and Pearson ... I think he was with a woman because he didn't return my calls."

"Glad it all worked out though. Are you hungry?" I handed him a cup of coffee.

The pressure of his gaze made me blush. "Yeah, for you. Are the kids up yet?"

I checked the clock to see it was almost six. "No, but they will be soon."

"We have time." He grabbed my hand and dragged me into the laundry room.

"Really? The laundry room?"

His tongue sketched a pattern across my neck down to my shoulder. "It's better than the bathroom."

"Not yours. You have that awesome shower."

He shut the door and shoved my chest against it. Then he pushed my yoga pants down to my ankles and I heard his hands fumbling against the scrubs he still wore from the hospital. Then his expert fingers brushed up and down my seam.

"How can you be this wet already?" he asked.

"I, uh, think about having sex with you a lot."

His breath fanned across my neck as he answered, "You do?"

"Yes, I do."

"I'm glad I'm not the only one." And he pushed the blunt head of his cock inside of me.

"Ahh," I moaned.

"You like that?"

"Yesss."

"And this?" He pulled out long and slow and then shoved back in, only this time he ground himself against me. Both my arms were raised above my head as he thrust in and out, over and over.

"Oh, I like that too."

"Good, cuz you're really gonna like this."

And he proceeded to fuck me exactly the way I needed, long and slow at first, and then frantically hard as though we were seventeen and our parents would be walking through the door at any second.

"Fuck, Marin. Tell me you're going to come because I can't hold back much longer."

One of his hands moved to my hip and the other wrapped around my waist, pulling me against him.

"Yes, I'm close."

"Use your hand. Like now."

I dipped my fingers where I could rub my clit and I was there in seconds.

"I love your ass. It's so fucking sexy the way you hike it up when I fuck you from behind."

What? I hike my ass up?

"And your pussy is so tight that when you come, it clenches the hell out of my cock."

"Ahh."

"Do you like it when I talk to you like that?"

"Yeah." I was panting from my orgasm, but no man had ever spoken to me like that.

Then his hand slipped between my legs to where we were joined and he slid a finger backward. "One day, I'd like to try this."

"You mean … that?"

"Yes, that."

He wanted my ass.

"Oh."

His deep chuckle shook us both. "Is that all you have to say?"

"Uh, okay?"

"You're not opposed to it?"

"I'm not really sure." While he was talking, his finger was touching me back there. It tickled. Of course he didn't do anything but touch. I'm sure it wouldn't tickle if he did *that*.

"If you are, you can say so." He pulled out then and I turned to look at him.

"You know I speak my mind."

"I do." One corner of his mouth lifted. Why did he have to be so sexy when we were trying to have an important conversation?

"I'm actually not familiar with that, so I don't quite know what to expect."

"We could explore."

"Is it safe?"

He still wore his stupid green hospital shirt, so I lifted it and ran my hands underneath. His skin was warm to the touch and slightly damp.

"Marin, I would never cheat on you. You should know that after what happened to me. And I would never do anything to you that wasn't safe."

I lifted my chin and found myself staring into his flinty grey eyes. The dark striations had me sinking into their depths and I knew without a doubt that was one thing I'd never have to worry about.

My palm caressed his cheek. "Yes, I do know that."

"But we don't have to think about it yet. Now let's go eat. I'm so glad today is Saturday and I don't have to work."

"I wish I could say the same." I pinched his ass.

"Oh, by the way, Hudson is going to spend the night tonight here with Wiley. It'll be easier with him visiting Dad in the hospital. And Kinsley will love it. But don't worry. I have no plans to abandon you with the kids. I'll be here."

We walked to the kitchen, hand-in-hand, and he suggested we make pancakes for breakfast.

"What's this *we* thing?" I asked.

"I know how to make pancakes."

"You do?"

He grabbed me by the waist and hoisted me up onto the counter. "Sit there and watch." He pulled out the giant griddle, which I had never used, a mixing bowl, whisk, measuring cups, and a few other items.

"I'm impressed," I said.

"Why?"

"You actually know your way around here."

He poked the whisk he was holding at me and said, "Just wait. You haven't tasted my pancakes yet. They're the best."

While he was busy making the batter, I leaned over to the coffee pot and poured a cup for each of us.

"What time is Hudson coming over?"

"Yeah, about that. He has to go back to the city and get Wiley who's with the au pair, and then return here."

"Oh, too bad he just didn't bring him when he came this morning. I could've watched him."

"That's what I told him, but he wasn't sure and I wasn't available to talk. It's not that bad of a drive though … less than an hour."

"True. I could always go if he doesn't want to."

"That's a kind offer, but that would be a lot of trouble since you'd have the kids."

"It's a suggestion if he changes his mind."

I watched Grey as he poured the pancake batter onto the hot skillet.

"Thank you, but he's probably already headed back

into Manhattan. He was there when I came out and said he would only stay a short while. I'm expecting him later this morning."

"Sounds good. You look like a pro with that, by the way."

"Told you I was an expert at pancakes," he said, wielding the flipper.

"Hey, are you going to make extra for the kids?"

He placed a finished stack on a plate that was sitting on the counter. "Sure. I'll keep them in the warming drawer for them."

Hopping off the counter, I went to the refrigerator and pulled out the butter and syrup. Then I put the syrup in a cup and stuck it in the microwave to heat it up. I tore off some foil to cover the plate of pancakes. Grey finished cooking, loaded up our plates, and I put the extras in the warming drawer.

My teeth sank into the first bite and they melted on my tongue. I hummed with delight. "These are fantastic."

He grinned. "Told ya I was the pancake master."

"You've been holding out on me."

"Only on the pancakes. I did give you a little breakfast sausage earlier."

After nearly choking on the bite I was swallowing, I recovered and said, "I believe it was a large breakfast sausage. You should never sell yourself short."

He snorted. "I'm glad you appreciated the sizable portion."

"I certainly did. Not only that, I enjoyed how the portion seemed to be so lively."

"It did have a mind of its own, didn't it?" He waggled his brows.

"Now that you mention it, it did."

"That devil can be like that sometimes."

"Well, don't let me stop it. I kind of like the little devil."

"I thought you said it wasn't little."

"I did, didn't I?"

He put his fork down, pushed our empty plates aside, and pulled me over to his lap. "If you don't stop all this sexual innuendo, I'm going to end up fucking you on the counter and how will that look if Kinsley walks in?"

"Not very good, I'm afraid."

And speak of the devil, a small voice interrupted us saying, "Marnie, is Daddy kissing you again?"

Chapter Thirty

GREYDON

SHIT. Maybe I should be a little less obvious.

"Good morning, polka dot. Maybe I was kissing her again." I shifted Marin and she moved off my lap to sit back in her chair. "Does Marnie like sitting in your lap?"

"Well ..." I stuttered.

"I was there because I thought I had something in my eye," Marin said, coming to my rescue. *Nice save,* I mouthed, while Kinsley was looking at Marin.

"Did Daddy get it out?"

"He sure did."

Then Kinsley turned toward me and asked, "Did you kiss it and make it better for Marnie?"

"I hope so."

"Good cuz I don't want Marnie's eye to hurt."

Marin tapped Kinsley's arm and said, "Oh, sweetie, you don't have to worry. My eye is perfectly fine." Then she asked, "Hey short stuff, are you hungry?"

"Uh huh."

"Your daddy made some of his famous pancakes for breakfast. Do you want some?"

Kinsley's eyes sparkled. She loved my homemade pancakes. "Yes, please. With lots of syrup."

"How about having a seat right there and I'll fix you up a plate?" Marin said.

Marin started to get up, but I said, "I have a better idea. You stay put and I'll fix polka dot's plate. But first, I want a morning hug and kiss from my favorite girl." Kinsley flew into my arms and I felt hers circle my neck. I loved the way she felt and it made me think how much I missed holding her and of the days when she was Aaron's age.

Then she asked, "Do you know how, Daddy? To fix up my plate?"

"Of course I do. I used to fix your plate all the time. Don't you remember?"

"Maybe. Can I have the Dory plate?"

Marin stood and said, "I see Aaron's awake. Let me go change him and bring him down while you handle the pancakes."

She went up the steps while I took care of Kinsley.

"Daddy, is Marnie gonna be my new mommy?"

"Why do you ask that, sweetie."

"Cuz you kiss her. You didn't use to kiss Mommy like that. Do daddy's kiss mommies?"

Jesus, this kid was observant. And come to think of it, Susannah and I were never affectionate with each other. I hadn't thought much of it, but I never had much of an urge to touch her like I did with Marin. Even when we initially started dating.

"Sometimes daddies kiss mommies and sometimes they don't. I guess it depends on the mommies and daddies."

"Okay. If Marnie is my mommy, will you kiss her all the time?"

"Would you want her to be your mommy?"

"What would happen to Mommy if Marnie is my mommy?"

"What do you mean?"

"Will Mommy still be with the angels?"

I dropped down next to Kinsley and looked her straight in the eyes as I took her petite hands in mine. "Honey, your mommy will always be with the angels. Forever and ever. And she'll always watch over you. Forever and ever. You don't ever have to worry about that."

"So, if Marnie is my mommy my real mommy will be there too?"

"Always. But polka dot, are you worried about this?"

Her expression was solemn as she gazed at me with eyes exactly like Susannah's. "No, I just don't want Mommy not to be an angel no more."

Hugging her to my chest, I swallowed the tight lump that had lodged there. "Oh my sweet girl. Your mommy will be an angel for the rest of time, so you don't ever have to worry about that. Okay?"

"Okay."

"And you know something else? Your mommy only wants you to be happy just like I want you to be happy because we both love you more than the moon and the stars, okay?"

"Okay. I love you too, Daddy." My heart filled with so much joy to hear those words from my precious little girl.

I smoothed back her silken hair. "Sweetheart, are you happy with Marin here?"

"Yep. I love her a lot. She's fun and likes to sing and stuff. Sometimes she draws pictures with me too. And she hugs me and Aaron all the time."

"Good. Then that's all you need to worry about. That and eating those pancakes I'm about to fix for you. And guess what?"

"What?"

"Guess who's coming to play with you today?"

"Who?"

"Wiley."

She clapped her hands. "Yay. I like Wiley. Do you think I can teach him how to kick and Irish dance?"

Oh, boy. "You can try. But maybe he'd rather play with toys."

"Maybe Marnie can teach us some new songs. Or we can draw princess pictures. I like princesses."

Maybe this was going to be torture Wiley Saturday. Between Kinsley and Aaron, the kid was never going to want to come back. When Marin brought Aaron down, the first thing out of Kinsley's mouth was how she was going to teach Wiley how to dance and draw princesses.

Marin buried her face in Aaron's neck, laughing, and he giggled because most likely it tickled.

"See, Aaron wants to do it too," Kinsley yelled in excitement. Aaron's legs kicked like crazy and Kinsley pointed at him. "Look. He wants to dance with me."

That poor kid. He didn't stand a chance in life.

"Polka dot, I just don't want you to get your hopes up in case Aaron wants to play sports."

"Why would he want to do that? Sports are boring. He could dance and have way more fun. And wear sparkly costumes and look cool, right Marnie?"

"Uh huh." Marin abandoned me for the laundry room. I knew she was cracking up in there, leaving me alone to handle my daughter.

"Hey, kiddo, are you gonna talk us to death or are you gonna eat?"

"I'm eating, see?" She took a bite of pancakes.

I let Aaron burn off some energy while I got his breakfast of mushy stuff ready. Marin still hadn't reappeared. When she did, she made an excuse of washing towels. I was already feeding Aaron.

"I thought you were napping in there."

"Marnie doesn't never nap, Daddy. Only us kids."

"I see," I said to my omniscient daughter.

Then I told her how Bebop was in the hospital because his heart had gotten sick.

Her brows furrowed. "Did you fix it up, Daddy? Should I make him a picture to make him happy?"

"I did, but he'll be there for another day or two, so we can make sure it's okay. I want you to come with me later this morning to visit him. And I'm sure he'd love a picture."

"Okay. I can kiss his heart and make it better."

"I think you can."

"Will Aaron come too?"

"No, honey, he's too little. He'll stay here with Marin."

Kinsley looked at Marin and said, "Marnie, while we're gone, you can give Aaron some dance lessons. That way he'll be better for when I get home. Make sure he doesn't move his arms when he kicks."

Marin saluted her and said, "Yes, ma'am."

Kinsley giggled. I handed Aaron off to Marin for the remainder of his breakfast and took my daughter upstairs to dress. While I was up there, my brother called.

"Hey, man, I'm headed back your way. It's okay to stay tonight, yeah?"

"Yeah, I already talked to Marin."

"I'm looking forward to meeting her. Mom is … well. she couldn't be happier you're with someone, Grey. But I have to say … the nanny?" He was obviously shocked by the sound of his comment.

"We're not together *together* like Mom wants to think. I'll tell you more when I see you."

"So, in other words, you're just fucking her."

"Ouch. That sounded harsh."

"Hey, man, I'm all for it. You deserve to have some fun."

"Yeah, but I have kids to be concerned about. And to that point, do you always use that language in front of Wiley?"

"Just because you have kids doesn't mean you can't have a good time. Take it from me. As for Wiley, he has headphones on. We'll talk about this later. I'll be there in forty-five to an hour."

He'd only been trying to make me feel better but all of a sudden guilt sunk its vicious claws into me. Was I doing Marin wrong by this? Did she expect some sort of long-term commitment? I know I expected her not to fuck around on me and I wouldn't do that to her, but I also had no illusions of any kind of serious relationship either. We should probably discuss this. Soon.

When Kinsley was dressed, I sent her downstairs, took a quick shower, and then dressed. As I was coming down the stairs, I heard Kinsley and Marin arguing.

"He may be a great dancer, but he may also want to play soccer or football. We just won't know until he gets a little older, honey."

"He's gonna be a dancing star and won't wanna to do anything else. Just like me. I'm gonna to be on TV someday with my clicky shoes."

"That's great. Kinsley, you should always dream big and never give up on your dreams."

"And Aaron will be dancing right along with me."

"He just might do that."

I wondered if I needed to be worried about her conviction. If Aaron refused to dance, she might be terribly upset. I'd ask Mom about it. She may have some sage advice.

Hudson arrived and it was easy to see by his reaction to Marin that he was more than a bit astounded by her appearance. Maybe he expected a Susannah look alike. She definitely was not that. I'm pretty damn sure her rainbow hair threw him because his jaw sagged open, but her sass set him back.

She stuck her hand out and said, "Hey, I'm Marin, the nanny, although Kinsley calls me Marnie. I'm sure your mother has told you all sorts of things that may or may not be true. And you can close your mouth now because I'm fairly certain you didn't expect anyone with rainbow colored hair or tattoos either. But don't worry, I'm not the least bit offended. And yeah, I do realize that Grey is old enough to be my father."

Then Hudson broke out in a hearty laugh. "Now I see why you like her." He shook her hand and said, "It's a pleasure to meet the woman who has set my boring brother on his a ... er, bottom."

"Thanks, I think."

"Oh, it's definitely a compliment," Hudson replied.

Marin grinned and Hudson cocked his head and stared. "You're quite stunning."

"Hey, don't even go there. And what's this about me being old enough to be your father?" My hackles rose.

"Calm down. I was just thinking how refreshing she was."

Marin added, "You mean you didn't notice our age differences?"

Hudson was comparing Marin to Susannah, whom he never liked and made no secret of. "I got you," I said.

"This conversation is getting confusing. I'm in the dark and maybe it's best I stay that way," Marin said.

"I'll tell you later when there are no little ears around."

Hudson pointed to his son and said to Marin, "That one is trouble. I'm just warning you in advance. He may look like an angel, but he's not. Trust me. His name is Wiley and that's exactly what he is."

Marin laughed. "I'll admit, I don't have a ton of kid experience, so I'll take your word for it."

"Hey guys, I hate to break this up, but we should be going. I want to check on Dad."

"Go. I'll hold the fort down."

"No, we're taking Kinsley and Wiley too."

"You just made my day very easy," Marin said.

Hudson and I grabbed the kids and set off for the hospital. On the way, the conversation turned to Marin. I had to remind him about the ears in the back seat. Kinsley was asking Wiley all kinds of questions about what games he liked to play, so I was confident we were safe.

"I like her," Hudson said.

I navigated the car out of the neighborhood. "I do too."

"She's not mousy. And she's nothing like——"

"Yeah, yeah, I know." I jerked my head toward the back seat so he'd get my meaning.

"I wasn't going to say the name. Don't worry."

"I'm the one who's worried. We started this thing and I never set her straight on where I stand."

"What do you mean?" he asked.

"You know? About the relationship thing."

"Jesus, Grey. Just because you're, you know, doesn't mean you have to have a relationship."

I rubbed the back of my neck. "Yeah but you know who"—and I aimed my thumb toward the back seat—"has seen us in a compromising position."

"Are you serious?"

"Yes. It was a mistake. We fell asleep."

Hudson had a good belly laugh over that one.

"Cut it out. Now I'm in much deeper than I intended."

"That pun was definitely intended," Hudson said, still laughing.

"You're an as ... er, jerk."

"True. But still. How do you know she wants more?"

"I get that feeling." And I did.

"You two need to talk. Clear that air. And Mom says you're going to Vienna."

"Yeah. I've been asked to give a talk, so we're going to make a vacation out of it."

"Bro, that's awesome. I think you need this. How long since you've taken a trip like this?"

"Can't even remember."

"See, I like her even better. She's getting my brother to take a well-deserved trip. This may even let you know things about your so-called un-relationship."

He laughed again. He was really loving this.

"Are you having a great time because you disliked the last person I was involved with?"

"Let's be clear. You know I never hid that. However, I never in a million years wanted you to go through what you did. I would've carried that pain for you. I hope you know that." His tone told me how serious he was.

I glanced at him because we were stopped at a traffic light. The love that shone from his eyes hit me all the way deep into my soul.

"I love you, Hudson."

"I know. Now get your head out of that dark tunnel it's been up and start living again."

A horn honked behind us and I noticed the light had turned green. I took a deep breath as I headed for the hospital. It was time to start living again and the trip to Vienna was a great way to do just that.

Chapter Thirty-One

MARIN

WHEN THE CREW LEFT, I called my mom. My hair looked like a herd of critters had taken up residence in it and I decided it needed help. I wanted to see if she could watch Aaron while I went out to get it worked on.

"Mom. Are you busy?"

"Not at all. Why?"

"Can you watch Aaron? I need to get my hair done."

She laughed at me. My mother.

"What's so funny?"

"I see you've finally gotten tired of that mess you created."

"Mom, that's not true. I just need a haircut." I'd never admit she was right.

"Really?"

"Yes."

"That haircut wouldn't have anything to do with that man you're living with, would it?"

"Mom!" She could be so exasperating.

"Who's doing it?"

I told her where the salon was.

"Why don't I just meet you there?"

"You don't mind?"

"Of course not. I've been dying to see you get rid of that debacle you made. I'll never understand why you ruined your beautiful hair."

"Who said anything about getting rid of it?"

"Marin, I hope you're joking."

"Meet me in fifteen." I ended the call before she could say anything else. The truth was, I wasn't getting rid of it altogether. But, I was changing it up some. I wanted to get a purple balayage with hints of pale blue and pink in it. I was super excited about it. I was pretty sure it would look good in my dirty blond hair.

When I got to the salon, Mom was there waiting. I handed off Aaron to her with instructions and his diaper bag. The girl escorted me back and I knew I would be there a while. When I told her what I wanted, she got very enthusiastic.

"That will look awesome on you."

The whole process took about two hours. When I walked out, Mom clapped her hands. "I love it!"

"You do? I wasn't sure you would since it has all the tints in it."

"No, it's beautiful on you, Marin. It really suits you."

"Thank you."

"And it does something magical to your eyes. Wait until Grey sees you."

I waved my hand. "Mom, stop."

"I'm not joking." She handed Aaron's diaper bag to me.

"Thanks so much for taking care of him."

"It was nothing. This child is so sweet. But he has an abundance of energy."

Picking him up, I said, "He sure does. Those legs are constantly moving."

"You know, you're a natural at this."

"Who would've thought I'd like it so much?"

Mom kissed my cheek and said, "Me. I always thought it."

We walked out together and said our goodbyes.

When I went to get Aaron out of the car, he was fast asleep in his car seat. I gently extracted him and carried him upstairs to his crib. After tucking him in, I went back down to the kitchen to see what I had for lunch. That's when everyone else came home.

Kinsley ran in and yelled, "Marnie, where's your rainbow?"

"It's still here. See? Only it's lighter." I picked up a chunk of my hair to show her.

"Oh, I like the other rainbow better." Then she ran off with Wiley in tow. I straightened up to find Grey gawking at me. Hudson was also staring.

"You two okay?"

"Uh, yeah. I uh, I'm okay," Grey said, still checking me out. Two steps later he was in front of me, holding a piece of my hair between his fingers, and rubbing them back and forth. "Fuck me," he said. Before I knew what he was up to, he grabbed me by the neck and kissed me. Not some gentle, quick peck on the lips kind of kiss. This was a full-on, push the tongue into my mouth, take possession of it, devour me right here, kind of kiss. He may have even growled. I'm not quite sure because the blood roared in my ears as my heart kicked up a beat that rivaled any music I'd ever heard. Warmth curled in my belly, spiraling out into my limbs. His other hand cupped my ass and squeezed as he pulled me into his chest when suddenly we both heard his brother clear his throat.

"Excuse me, but you two do have company, you realize?"

Grey released me and I pressed my lips together as the heat from what transpired between us blazed to a thousand degrees.

"Sorry," I mumbled.

"No, she isn't," Grey said with a smirk. "And neither am I. I'm only sorry we can't go upstairs and—"

"Okay, I get it. Spare me the details," Hudson said.

Grey leaned into me and said, "You look stunning."

"Thank you."

Hudson said over Grey's shoulder, "I agree."

Grey turned around and said, "Would you stop eavesdropping?"

"I'm not. Besides, it's rude to talk behind your company's back."

"You're not company. You're my brother."

In order to break this up, I asked, "How's Rick?"

"Good. Really good. He has a little bit of plaque on one of his coronary arteries, but other than that, he's good."

Hudson walked over to the refrigerator and grabbed a cold beer. After he popped off the top, he said, "I'm glad dogs don't get that stuff. Or rather when they do, it's usually too late to do anything about. If people didn't feed their pets table food, animals would be so much better off."

Hudson was a veterinarian. "How many dogs do you have?" I asked.

"We have three. Which reminds me. When are you going to get one?"

Grey looked at me in question and I said, "Oh, no. I have the kids to take care of."

"I want a dog, Marnie." Kinsley came tearing into the room right then and overheard Hudson. "Uncle Hudson has dogs."

"Yes, I do. And they're fun. Ask Wiley."

"I have doggies," Wiley yelled. "Scooter, Roscoe, and Flimsy."

"Flimsy?" I asked.

Hudson shrugged. "She has one ear that won't stand up, so we called her Flimsy. But kids need a dog."

"I don't have time," I protested.

"They're so easy. Crate train them. It doesn't take long to house break them."

"Easy for you to say. You have so much experience. Tell you what. How about we get a dog, but you train it and when it's ready it can move in with us?"

"Fine," Hudson answered without hesitation.

"Are you serious?" I asked.

"Yes. That's how easy it is."

"You're delusional."

"What kind of dog do you want."

I said, "I'd love a mini Golden Doodle," while Grey said he wanted an Irish Wolfhound.

"What? An Irish Wolfhound? Those things are gigantic. Besides, they shed all over the place. A mini Golden Doodle won't shed and they're small."

Grey shook his head. "Those things are goofy looking."

"They're cute."

Hudson held up his hands. "You two duke it out. I'm going to watch the baseball game."

Kinsley ran in and said, "Daddy, I want a golden noodle. Like Marnie wants."

"It's a Golden Doodle, polka dot."

"We can name her Marshmallow," Kinsley said.

"You're outvoted, I'm afraid. We'll get a mini Golden

Doodle named Marshmallow. And she'll be sweet and huggable."

He threw his hands up in the air and left the room.

"Marnie, are we getting a Marshmallow?"

"I don't know, honey. You'll have to ask your daddy."

That's what he got for letting Hudson get away with the dog thing. I had two kids here and the last thing I needed was a puppy to raise. Good Lord. I didn't know the first thing about dogs.

I joined the guys in the den where they were watching TV. Kinsley was trying to get Wiley to dance and after a while, she gave up and danced by herself. The men decided we would all go out to dinner after they went back to the hospital to check on Rick.

"Are you sure you don't need to spend more time there?"

"No, Mom shooed us out earlier. I think it wears Dad out having so many people in there. Mom said he didn't sleep much last night. Hospital rooms are noisy," Grey said.

"When will he be released?"

"Tomorrow. We'll go over in the morning and I'll stay until he's out."

"That's great." I saw how relieved Grey was as he spoke. The tension that was present earlier in our conversation about his dad was no longer there.

We ended up at the pizza place for dinner that night. It was something that appeased everyone's varied tastes—especially the kids. Kinsley was excited and she made me sing the Itsy Bitsy Spider song with her as she tried to teach it to Wiley. This time she wasn't nearly as loud as the last time we were in here. Grey ended up telling that story.

"Everyone was staring at our table and I thought

Marin was going to die. Her face was as red as the sauce on the pizza."

"Marnie is a good singer though, isn't she Daddy?"

"She sure is."

"But she can't dance as good as me. She doesn't know how to kick right."

"Kinsley, tell me about your dancing," Hudson said.

"Oh, God." I buried my face in my hands.

"Man, don't even go there," Grey said.

"Uncle Hudson, I'm getting some clicky shoes and you'll have to come watch me. Aaron's gonna learn how too. Maybe Wiley can too."

"Wiley? Dance?" Hudson asked.

"Don't say we didn't warn you," Grey murmured.

"I'm learning Irish kick dancing. I was teaching Wiley today. Didn't you see?"

"Honey, it's step dancing," I corrected.

"Yep." She nodded. "I can teach you if you want."

Hudson's brows shot up. "Uh, no thanks, but I'll come watch your recitals."

"Okay."

And that was it. Grey and I were shocked she didn't go on and on about it. Maybe it was dying a slow death and we were getting to the end of it.

Rick was released the next day and went home with strict instructions from his son. Grey came home with Hudson and it was funny to listen to him talk about bossing his dad around.

"You boss everyone around. I don't know why you think it's so funny," I said.

He gave me an odd look. "I am not bossy in the least."

"Sure you're not." I grinned and walked to the laundry room to toss some things into the dryer. When I came out, the kitchen was empty. Everyone had scattered to places unknown. I searched for Grey and found him in his office.

"Hey," I said. "What's going on?"

"Hudson is packing up. He needs to get home. I wanted to ask you. Do you have any idea when those DNA results will be in?"

My heart skidded to a stop. I never told him I'd forgotten to send them in. I had meant to tell him, but then things between us heated up and it completely slipped my mind.

"Um, about that. I forgot …"

"You did what?" Anger punctuated his words.

The gray in his eyes grew dark and stormy, instantly chilling me. I rubbed my arms in response, then quickly said, "No, wait. I planned to, but then things happened between us and I got sidetracked and then—"

Ice coated his words. "Marin, how could you? What gave you the right to make that decision? You had no business doing that."

I shook my head saying, "But, but—"

Hudson poked his head into the room. "Am I interrupting something?"

Grey responded, "Yes!" At the same time, I responded, "No."

Hudson was caught between two walls.

Immediately, I responded, "I forgot to do something and now Grey is furious with me."

Hudson chuckled. "No surprise there."

"Hudson, this is a bit more serious than that."

"Yeah, it sort of is."

Grey shot back, "Sort of?"

"Sorry. Can I help?" Hudson asked.

"Maybe." I looked at Grey then Hudson. It might not

have been my place, but maybe his brother could talk some sense into him.

Grey huffed out a breath. "It has to do with Aaron and the DNA testing."

"We're not back to that, are we?" Hudson asked, shaking his head. It was obvious he didn't agree with Grey on this.

I opened my mouth to speak, but before I could even get one word out, Grey started in.

"We never left it. All I want to know is the damn truth. I asked Marin to send in the kit, but without consulting me, she unilaterally decided not to. And I'm pretty fucking pissed off about it."

"You don't understand—" again I tried to interject something only Hudson jumped in first.

"I see your point, but I see hers too. She was only protecting you." Hudson's gaze bounced between the two of us.

Jesus, that's not what happened, but no one would give me a chance to utter a damn word.

"Oh? How?"

"Because what if you find out Aaron isn't yours? Then what are you going to do? Send him away? Or put him up for adoption?" Hudson asked.

Just when I thought it couldn't possibly get any worse, Kinsley darted into the room and asked, "Daddy, why are you gonna send Aaron away? Don't you love him no more?"

Chapter Thirty-Two

GREY

GREAT! Just fucking great! How could I have been so care-less to get carried away by my anger? I should've shut this conversation down or at least had the forethought to close the office door. Now my little polka dot thought the worst. This was not exactly what a seven-year-old needed.

"Kinsley, honey, I would never in a million years send Aaron away. I love him more than a thousand chocolate sundaes with marshmallows on top and whipped cream too."

"Why did Uncle Hudson say that?"

"He was talking nonsense, honey. You don't ever have to worry about Aaron going anywhere."

Tears created rivers down her sweet pink cheeks making me feel like a first class asshole for even thinking about that DNA shit. Picking her up, I held her close until her sobs eased. But the deep ache in my chest wouldn't go away any time soon. Oddly enough, seeing her like that made me not care about knowing anymore. Her anguished words made me realize this DNA crap didn't matter. I loved Aaron regardless of what the test would say, so what difference did it make?

"Come on. I think this calls for a red Popsicle. What do you think?"

She sniffed, then bobbed her head. I carried her into the kitchen where we each grabbed a Popsicle. Then I took a seat at the kitchen table and she sat on my lap as we ate our frozen sticks together.

"Better?"

She nodded. "I don't want Aaron to go away. He's my baby brother and I love him lots."

"I know you do and I'm glad. You're the best big sister in the world."

"Do you love Aaron, Daddy?"

"I love him more than I can say." And it nailed me in the heart and soul. Those words were the honest truth. He was the most adorable, loving child. I couldn't ask for anything more.

"Do you love Marnie?"

"Wh-what?" Her question came out of nowhere and really threw me.

"Marnie. Do you love her? I do. I love her like I love Mommy."

What do I say? I wasn't sure if I loved her. I loved to be around her. She certainly made me happy. But *love* ... that was a fucking huge word in my personal dictionary.

"I know you love her, polka dot. Marin is extra special."

Her beautiful innocent eyes dug into mine for the longest time. I'm not sure how long she burrowed holes in me with those orbs of hers before she hopped off my lap and trotted away. An uneasy sensation settled over me—as though she hadn't been exactly pleased with what she read in mine.

As I sat there, Hudson and Marin came in.

"I'm sorry, man. I didn't know she would come in," Hudson said.

"It's not your fault. We all should've been more careful." I ran a palm over my face.

"I've gotta be going. I know you're going on vacation soon, but if you get a chance, come and hang out in the city with me. Marin, it was great meeting you." My brother hugged her and then left.

"Grey, I'm sorry. It was a mis—"

I held up my hand. "Hear me out. You were right. I didn't realize it until Kinsley told me how much Aaron meant to her. She's right. I adore that kid … truly love him. It doesn't matter what the DNA says. Throw the damn thing away. I don't need to know. But …" I nailed her with my gaze, "I wish you had told me. I felt betrayed, and that didn't sit well. I trusted you, Marin and that really hurt."

I got up and went upstairs. It was mind-blowing how much I was reeling over what she had done. Trust was huge for me after what I went through with Susannah. The ache in my heart was hard to take and the bitterness of betrayal kept nagging at me. Is that what she'd done? Maybe not, but it was how I felt. How could my emotions be so strong? I knew it was irrational, but all I saw were those damning pictures of my dead wife and how I'd been lied to for at least two years.

My other concern was that Kinsley didn't experience any effects from this. She'd been through enough with losing her mom. The last thing she needed was to stress over how she might lose her brother too.

A soft knock came at my door. When I opened it, Marin stood there, her hands knotted.

"Can I come in?"

I waved her through.

"I'm so sorry. I should've explained things to you. But things got crazy between us after Aaron came home and I swear I just forgot. It totally slipped my mind that day, but it wasn't intentional."

"Wrong thing to say. You did do it intentionally. If you hadn't, you would've mailed that kit immediately."

"True, but I was referring to telling you about it. But, Grey, I—"

"Marin, you have to understand something. I have a huge issue where trust and lying are concerned after what I went through. You knew that. Not telling me just blows my mind."

"I understand. But I don't know what else to do or say other than I'm sorry. Please tell me what I can do?"

Her pleading voice let me know she was sincere.

"I just need some time."

She bowed her head and left the room. That was all I could give her right now.

The following week passed with me in a state of numbness. It wasn't like when Susannah died. This was different. I was trying to figure out my feelings where Marin was concerned. I hadn't wanted a relationship of any kind, but my emotions were tangled up in her, like it or not. She had become my navigator. Not so much in the sense of guiding me through life, but she was the one who set me on the track of getting my head straight and seeing the light again.

My phone rang, disturbing my confused thoughts.

"West here."

"West here too."

"Hudson, what are you doing?"

"Bugging the fuck out of you."

"Yeah, you are. What's up?"

"Have you figured your shit out yet?"

"What do you mean?"

"About Marin?" he said.

"No."

"Get your head out of your ass, man."

"I'm … I don't know. She wasn't honest with me, and I'm not sure I'm ready for a relationship."

"Listen, she made a mistake. You can't project what happened between you and Susannah on her. Besides, who's ever ready, you idiot? It just happens. If you wait much longer, you're going to be a grandpa."

"Haha, funny."

"Seriously, man. Let all that baggage you're hanging onto go, and have fun."

"I don't have any baggage."

"Really?" His laughter rang through the phone. "You're so overloaded with it, your spine is practically bent in half."

"Hudson, have I ever told you that you're an asshole?"

"You just did."

"I'm hanging up now."

"Have fun with her in Vienna. And hey, if you don't, I'm coming over there and stealing her from you."

"The fuck you are." I hung up that time. He really was an asshole. The idea of him stealing Marin from me had my jealousy meter swinging over to the red zone. What the hell was that telling me? If I didn't care for her, I wouldn't be jealous if another man were interested in her.

Then things started happening. We all went to the grocery store that weekend. I offered to go with her out of the blue and she took me up on it. While we were there, I paid attention to all the guys eyeing her. They didn't just glance at her. Their lecherous gazes roamed all over her sexy body. She'd been running a lot. We were gearing up for our 5k we were doing next Saturday. She was wearing running shorts and a tank top. Marin was built like an athlete and had strong legs and muscular arms. And her ass ... I licked my lips as I watched her bend over the fruit to inspect the melons. Christ, why hadn't I ever come to the store with her before? The other men noticed her too, but I scowled at them as they watched her. One of them got a little too close and I bumped into him.

"What are you looking at?" I asked.

"Uh, fruit." The guy looked at me in confusion.

"Right. Move it, bud."

"Grey, you need something?" Marin asked.

You bet I do, only if you gave it to me here, I'd get arrested. "No, I'm fine, thanks." I smiled at her. Damn, she was hot.

"Daddy, can we get some ice cream?"

"Sure, polka dot." She put her hand in mine and I said, "Let's go pick out some flavors." But then I thought of Marin and all those men in the produce section checking out her luscious ass, and I hesitated. "Hey, Marin, how long will you be?"

She eyed me curiously. "Not long. Why?"

"Nothing. Let's wait on Marin, polka dot."

"Okay, Daddy."

Aaron was in the grocery cart chatting happily, so I went up to him and picked him up. "Where to next?" I asked Marin.

"You don't shop much, do you?"

"Yes. No. You do it for me."

"Come on, let's get it done. We are TeamShoppers today."

"Yay! TeamShoppers, Daddy!"

We flew through the store and I was more interested in the men than in what we bought. I found myself agreeing to all sorts of crap and when we were unloading the bags, I kept commenting.

"You told her it was fine. I even asked you about that twice," Marin said.

"I don't know where my head was."

"You kept staring at those men in there like you wanted to punch them. What's going on with you?"

She had seen me doing that. Hmm.

"Who wants to go to the pool today?" I asked, changing the subject.

"I do, I do," Kinsley shouted.

"Let's eat lunch and then go."

I got the kids ready and was waiting on Marin, but she never came down. I went to up to check on her and she came to the door, still in her running clothes.

"Aren't you coming?"

"I didn't think you meant me."

I narrowed my eyes. "What do you mean. I always include you."

"Yeah, but ever since …" she trailed off as her gaze dropped to the floor.

"This is for the kids, Marin."

She raised her head and the sparkle that used to always shine in her sky-blue eyes was gone. The corners seemed to tug downward and the violet shading beneath them told me she hadn't been sleeping well. How long had this been going on and how had I missed it? Was I so self-centered that I didn't see the suffering she was enduring?

"Okay," she answered.

"Get ready, the kids are restless," I snapped, pissed off at myself for being so inconsiderate, but as I was walking down the stairs, I realized how my comment sounded and wasn't I the biggest dick around?

She came down in a cover-up and it wasn't easy hiding my eagerness to see her in a bathing suit. Things were so hectic at the house with Kinsley jumping around and Aaron excited, I wanted to get out of there as quickly as we could. We went to the country club and when we arrived, she was instantly jittery.

"What's wrong?"

"I feel out of place here."

"It'll be fine. I promise." It wasn't like she hadn't been here before with her parents.

We walked to the pool and I picked up some towels and selected our chairs by the shallow end. We laid out our stuff and the kids were anxious to get in the water. I was helping Aaron when I lifted my head to see Marin slipping off her cover-up. I gulped. I would've choked, but I didn't have any saliva. Shit, she looked like a goddess in her bikini. Her tits were perfect and her legs were long and lean with a hint of muscle showing. She was extraordinary.

Her hair was wound up in an elastic band and she smiled at me right before she jumped into the water. It was only three feet deep, but her skin looked like silk and I wanted to run my tongue all over her.

I happened to glance across the pool and saw that not only the men were ogling her but so were the women. *Eat your hearts out, suckers. She's mine.* But was she? I was going to have to work to make that happen. And starting now, I would do my best.

As we were swimming—me teaching Kinsley how to kick and hold her breath underwater, and Marin holding Aaron in her arms—one of Susannah's old friends came up to us.

"Hello, Grey. It's nice to see you out and about."

"Hi, Carrie. Yeah, it's a great day for the pool."

"And who is that with you?"

"Carrie, this is Marin McLain. Marin, this is Carrie Lord."

"Marin. A pleasure to meet you." She was acting like it was anything but. And then she launched into why she really came over here. "Grey, I heard you hired a new nanny. Is this the one?" She'd taken her sunglasses off and her eyes raked Marin over from head to toe.

Marin didn't wait for my response. She jumped right into the conversation. "Actually, yes, I am."

"Marnie can sing. Why don't you sing for her Marnie?" Kinsley wasn't doing her any favors right now.

"Polka dot, Marin doesn't need to sing right now."

"Oh, but that would be wonderful, wouldn't it, Kinsley?" Carrie said.

"Actually, my throat's a little sore today," Marin said. "We'll have to do it another day."

"Oh, I'm sorry to hear that. Well, I do hope you have yourselves a wonderful day." She snickered.

"You too." She sauntered off and I wanted to slap her smug face. Carrie always did think she was better than everyone else. Come to think of it, she was one of Susannah's best friends. Had Susannah acted that way too, and had I been oblivious to that fact?

The rest of the time at the pool, Marin was subdued. I decided to call it a day and go home. On the way, I asked, "How about we all go and get an Icee?"

"Yeah," Kinsley shouted.

We stopped for one and then went home. Once the kids were out of earshot, I said, "I'm really sorry about the way Carrie treated you. She never was very nice."

Marin shrugged. "It's not your fault."

No matter what I did that night, Marin never brightened up. When I had a chance, I slipped into the office and called my brother.

"Grey, what's up?" Hudson asked.

"I need to ask you something and be honest with me. Was Susannah a pompous bitch?"

"You really want the truth?"

"Yes."

"Well yes, she was."

"How bad was she?"

"She wasn't nice, Grey. She thought she was better than the rest of the world. Even when the two of you were dating. But Mom and Dad told me to stay out of it and that it wasn't my place. Mom said I would understand one day when I fell in love. She was right. So, I kept my mouth shut. I always figured you two were happy together."

"You know, so did I, only now I don't think I was. I think we were two entirely different people. And how can it be possible to live with someone for all those years and not know that?"

"Married couples stop communicating. They take things for granted. Maybe that's what happened with the two of you."

I rub my aching forehead. "I don't know. I only know I don't want that the second time around."

"Then don't let it happen."

"Thanks, Hudson."

"For what?"

"For being honest with me."

I guess it was true what people always said. You turned a blind eye to the truth because you didn't really want to face it.

Chapter Thirty-Three

MARIN

JOURNAL ENTRY: *I'm not sure what to do to change his mind about me, but my heart is not in a good place. Every time he looks at me I want it to be the way it was. His trust in me is gone and I don't know how to earn it back. Understanding how he feels, how his mind works, because he was so completely destroyed by the betrayal of his wife, I honestly can't blame him. And even though I didn't do it intentionally, I can see why he would hold back from me. When there is so much at stake and you've lost so much in the past, the last thing you'll ever do is repeat those mistakes. I thought I'd never trust another man again and here I am, miserable as hell, for the very same reason.*

WE WERE STANDING IN LINE, waiting for the starter's pistol to fire. Instead of being focused on my strategy of how I was going to dust Grey's ass in this 5k, my head was off somewhere else. He hadn't been himself lately. He wasn't exactly ignoring me, but the warmth wasn't there like it used to be. And now my heart ached with the emptiness from it. In that short time, we had been intimate, I had gotten used to feeling his hands on me, pressing into my flesh, touching me the way no man ever had before. He'd left my body craving for him to the point where I was physically miserable. I'd never imagined it could be like this … this desperate carnal desire.

Wanting to change this disastrous train of thought, I shook my arms and ran in place a few seconds when the blast of the pistol rang out. I took off, and heard Grey yell behind me, "Remember to pace yourself."

Yeah, right. I had more electric energy shooting through my nerves right now than a high voltage power line. My feet had wings attached to them—or that's how they felt. Maybe the goddess Nike was with me today and victory would be mine. All I thought about was marathon sex with Grey, him thrusting into me, and how I missed our nights together. His voice, his breath, his scent, his mouth, his tongue, his gaze …

Before I knew it, I was crossing the finish line and setting an unbelievable personal record for myself. My time was 17:49. And then my legs promptly buckled and I fainted.

I woke up to a group of three unfamiliar faces hovering above me.

"Miss, are you okay?"

"What happened?" I mumbled.

"You won! First female. And then you hit the pavement. It's not that unusual."

"Ugh." I struggled to sit up when I saw Grey run up to me.

"Does anyone have a stethoscope?" he yelled.

"I don't think that's necessary," I said.

A medical team showed up and he grabbed the stethoscope someone was pulling out, and called out, "I'm a cardiologist." Then he listened to my heart. "Your heart sounds fine, but I want an EKG on you."

"I just passed out. I pushed myself too hard."

"She set a record for the fastest female on this course," someone said.

"I set a new PR," I said, finally sitting up.

"How do you feel?" Grey asked, grabbing my arm.

"Tired."

"We're going to the office. I want to check you out."

It was useless arguing with him, so we didn't even stay for the awards ceremony. I had always wondered about where he spent his days and now I was going to find out. Only I never envisioned it would be this way. We entered through the back door and I followed behind him as he led me through a maze of halls.

"This is the wing I practice in." There was a nurse's station and a bunch of exam rooms nearby.

"I didn't think your place was this large."

"Yeah, it's pretty busy here." His answer was curt and non-committal.

We went into a room and he hooked me up to an EKG machine. I had all these sticky tabs on me with wires attached. When he was done, he showed me the results. It meant nothing to me as I didn't know how to interpret it.

"Your EKG is beautiful. It appears you are perfectly normal."

"I told you I just pushed myself too hard. I didn't leave anything on that course. I was out to win." I punched his shoulder as I got to my feet. Then my hand fell because we had stopped being playful with each other and the gesture felt awkward. The whole situation felt awkward.

"Congratulations. You beat me fair and square." His

steely eyes bored into mine and my feet froze to the floor. We were so close that for a brief moment, I imagined he was going to kiss me. Only my disappointment skyrocketed when he took a step backward and pushed the machine against the wall. "I guess we should get home."

I dropped my head to stare at my shoes. "Yeah. I could use something to eat and drink." A sad smile lifted the corners of my mouth as my soul ached for some small gesture of affection from him. How I longed for the days when we had that easy banter going. I wished we could get that back somehow.

"Grey—"

He offered a brief smile that matched mine. "I could use a bite myself. Let's go," he quickly said, cutting me off.

We left the office and went home where the kids were waiting. Kinsley was excited to hear about our race. Paige and Rick had watched them and knew something was up with us, but neither of them asked.

Kinsley ran up to me and asked, "Did you beat Daddy?"

"As a matter of fact, I did."

She clapped her hands and yelled, "Marnie won. Marnie won."

I took Kinsley's hand and said, "You shouldn't gloat, honey."

"What's that?"

"It means you should also be happy for your daddy."

"Daddy, did you run fast?"

"Not very fast. Marin was much faster."

"Girls are fast, aren't they?" she asked Grey.

"Yes, they are," he answered.

Paige and Rick left soon afterward. Things were a bit stilted in the house and they probably just wanted to get away from it all. We thanked them for helping out and reminded them we'd be leaving for Vienna in a few days.

"We hope you have a lovely vacation. Rest and enjoy yourselves," Rick said.

"Dad, if you need anything at all, you know who to call."

"Son, I'm fine and will be fine, but yes, I do."

They hugged the kids, Grey, and then Paige squeezed me hard when she hugged me. "Thank you for loving my grandchildren so much." I had to suck back the tears.

Later that night, after the kids were in bed, I knocked on Grey's closed bedroom door.

"Yes?"

"Can I speak with you, please?"

The door opened and he stood there, shirtless with a pair of jeans on. Why the hell did he have to do that and why the hell did he look so sexy?

"What is it?"

I sucked my lips into my mouth for a second. "I've been doing a ton of thinking these past few days, way more than I should, and after we get back from Vienna, I'm going to help you find another nanny. It's time for me to move on."

He opened his mouth to speak, but nothing came out.

I wanted to say, *fight for me, dammit.* But I didn't. I wasn't going to beg him when he'd obviously given up on us already.

"I see. Kinsley will be devastated."

I fisted my hand and pounded my chest. "This isn't about Kinsley. I love her and Aaron, more than I probably should, but at some point, I have to think about myself. Right now …" I waved my hand as my voice cracked and I swallowed and bit back the tears. I didn't want him to see how wrecked I was. Because the truth was, I loved him … was in love with him. I'm not sure how or why I'd let it happen, but I did, and it was too late to do anything about it. I was in damage control at this point. I had to reconstruct the pieces of not only my heart and soul but the rest of me before it fucking destroyed me. And the worst thing about it— somehow this was my fault. I would bear this burden for the rest of my life because there would be no replacement for Grey.

I was unsuccessful at willing myself not to cry. But I was determined he would not witness the flood I created, so I spun around and fled to my room. He called my name, but I ignored him. I flung myself on the bed and bawled my eyes out. It was three forty-five when I woke up, still in my clothes from the night before. How the hell would I get through a vacation pretending everything was fine?

ON THE WAY to the airport, I continued to question the logic as to why I was even going on this trip. Grey's distance toward me hadn't improved. I told myself I was going for the kids and that was it. It was extremely difficult being close to him and yet feeling so far away at the same time. He acted like a stranger whenever I was around. Every time I caught him looking at me, which was a lot, he'd jerk away as though he'd been caught doing something wrong.

I pretended everything was fine in front of Kinsley. The last thing she needed was another disappointment in her life. She'd already lost her mother, so I didn't just want to walk away leaving her with abandonment issues. This worried me to the point sleep was barely possible anymore.

These were things we should've considered before we ever got involved in the first place.

The flight was long, but we checked into our suite at the hotel and it was going to be tight. It was spacious and beautiful, but much more suited to us when we were a couple.

"Marnie, are you and Daddy gonna sleep in the big bed together?"

My head jerked in the direction of Grey. This was an unexpected question. I didn't want to give her the impression that everything was fine when it wasn't, but I also didn't want her to think we were having issues. Then she would worry. What should I say?

Luckily, Grey came to the rescue. "Polka dot, I thought it best if Marin slept in the room with you and Aaron."

His words whipped through me, flaying me to the marrow of my bones. Every shred of hope I held inside of my heart was now crushed until nothing remained.

"Come on, Marnie. Let's go look."

But I was rooted to the plush carpet, unable to breathe. If I dared, I would give my broken self away.

Kinsley scampered off to the other room as I stood there, arms wrapped around my midsection in a poor attempt to stop the burgeoning ache from spreading.

"You okay?" I heard him ask.

Fuck no, I'm not okay. I'm in pieces scattered on the floor. Can't you see?

Why didn't love come with an instruction manual and a warning label. *Handle With Caution,* or better yet *Danger Ahead—Stay Away.*

"Marin?"

"What?" I snapped.

"Are you okay?"

I stared at him, quivering lip and all, and said, "Oh,

Grey, do you honestly have to ask me that? Can you not for once open your damn eyes and see?" Then I shoved a fist in my mouth to stop the sob from bursting out and went to the other room to collect myself. I had kids to take care of and they didn't have to witness the horrible shape I was in.

Chapter Thirty-Four

GREYDON

BLUE EYES that used to sparkle like the sky on a bright summer's day were lifeless and without joy. Surely, I was the source of the pain lurking within their depths. I had forgiven her for the DNA kit. But the trust issue was something different. Why couldn't I move past that? My head was trapped in what Susannah did. Everyone I discussed it with said I couldn't compare the two. But I did, wrong or right.

The way I figured, I'd get over it when the time was right. But the way she figured, that decision wasn't mine to make. She'd already made it. She was leaving us, so I was already separating from her—physically and mentally.

Kinsley ran up to me and grabbed my leg. "Daddy, I think Marnie has a tummy ache."

"Why do you think that, honey?"

"Cuz she's in the bathroom and it sounds like her tummy hurts."

"Okay. Why don't you stay here while I check on her? I don't want you going outside of this room. Promise, polka dot?"

"Promise. Can I watch TV?"

"Sure." I turned it on and found something in English for her to watch. I hadn't located the DVDs we'd brought yet, but I needed to see if Marin was okay first.

I stood outside the bathroom door and heard muffled noises. I didn't think she was ill. It sounded more like she was upset and crying. This wasn't an ideal situation. Maybe I should sleep in here with the kids and let her have the big room.

After a few knocks on the door, I tried the handle and found it unlocked.

"Hey," I said. She was sitting on the side of the tub with her head in her hands.

"I guess a closed door doesn't mean privacy to you," she murmured.

"Kinsley thought you were sick."

She wouldn't lift her head.

"Marin, maybe it would be better if you took the larger room and I stayed with the kids. That would give you more space to yourself."

She pushed to her feet and walked over to the sink. After she blew her nose and wiped her eyes, she said, "This trip was a mistake. Maybe I should go home."

Oh shit. I couldn't stay here without her help. "Please don't leave. I need your help."

"You really don't understand, do you?"

Her eyes glistened with tears and her lashes were wet with the remnants of them.

"Yes, I do. I know you need your space from me and you're moving away from me ... from us, but—"

Her brow creased and she said, "That's not it at all."

She clasped her hands. "I love you, Grey. There, it's out even though I swore I wouldn't say it. Do you know how difficult it is being close to you when you can barely stand to be near me?"

When she said those words, I nearly stumbled. It was sheer force of will that kept me standing on my two feet. "I … I didn't know."

"Of course you didn't. You're so damn wrapped up in your own head over what happened to you and your dead wife."

"That's not fair."

"No? What's happening between us isn't fair either. I didn't ask for this."

"Neither did I," I growled.

The handle on the door jiggled and I knew who it was. Aaron was on the other side. "We'll discuss this later when we have some privacy." I opened the door to see the grinning face of my son. I picked him up high in the air, kissing his neck, and he kicked his legs. Then I carried him into what was to have been my room and dragged my huge bag over to the room the kids were in. Kinsley followed.

"Whatcha doin', Daddy?"

"I decided I'm going to have a spend the night party with you two while we're on vacation and we're going to let Marin have the big room."

Kinsley's hazel eyes popped with gold sparks. "Really Daddy? You never have a spend the night party with me or Aaron."

"It's time we started. Won't it be fun?"

"Yeah. You can read us stories all night long."

"Don't forget, you still have to sleep."

"We can after you read us the stories."

I laughed at my daughter with all the answers. After

my luggage was settled, we took Marin's and placed it in the big room. Kinsley looked sad.

"What's wrong, honey?" I asked.

"Won't Marnie be afraid in here all by herself?"

"She'll be fine."

Marin was seated on the bed and Kinsley jumped up next to her. "You won't be scared, Marnie?"

"If I am, I'll come and get you and you can sleep with me. How does that sound?"

Kinsley clapped her hands. "Yay. I can sleep with Marnie in the big bed."

I may have created a monster with this scenario. "Polka dot, you can only sleep with Marin if she gets scared, okay?"

"Okay, Daddy. But can you help me find the DVDs cuz there's nothing to watch on TV. I don't understand what they say sometimes."

That made Marin laugh and she offered to help Kinsley find them while I took care of Aaron.

Later that evening we walked around outside and found a quaint little restaurant for dinner. During dinner, I'd catch Marin wiping her eyes. I knew she didn't want any of us to see, but she couldn't hide all the tears. Afterward, we came home and went to bed.

My conference wasn't until the following day, so I thought we could make a trip to the zoo. Upon checking with the concierge, I arranged for transportation and we left later that morning.

Kinsley went crazy and Aaron loved it too. The zoo offered feeding of many animals, including arctic Siberian tigers, and giant tortoises. Even I was amazed by it. Then we visited the koalas where Kinsley asked if we could have a pet one. She begged and begged, but I told her she'd have to settle for a stuffed one instead.

Marin was quiet as she took it all in. I knew she enjoyed the animals, but she wasn't as expressive as she usually was.

"Come on, Marnie. Let's go see the pandas," Kinsley said. She grabbed Marin's hand and they walked toward where the pandas were kept. I pushed Aaron in his stroller and he constantly reached for things. Even though he was getting tired, he was still curious and good-natured. We took a break after we watched the giant pandas play around and Kinsley decided she wanted one of them too.

"Honey, it seems like you want one of everything here," I said. "We'd have to get a bigger house to fit them all inside."

"Nope. Not all. Not one of those giant turtles. They didn't smell so good."

Marin laughed. It was so good to hear that sound.

"Short stuff, I didn't smell anything."

"Neither did I."

Kinsley pinched her nose and said, "I did. It was yucky."

"You must've been close to their stinky," Marin said.

"Turtles make stinkies?" Kinsley asked.

"Yeah. All animals do. Just like people."

"How come?"

Oh, God, I'd missed these conversations between the two of them.

"Because they just do." Marin looked to me for help, only I smiled and shrugged. She discretely flipped me off so the kids couldn't see. I hid the huge grin that covered my face.

"Because why?"

"Well, if you eat, you make a stinky," she answered.

Kinsley wrinkled up her little brow something furious. "Nuh huh. That's not right. Is it, Daddy?"

"Afraid so. Marin is right."

"Ick. I'm not gonna eat no more."

"Any more," Marin corrected.

Kinsley's face looked like she just ate a lemon. It was so funny that I snapped a quick picture of her. Then I said, "Speaking of, I'm starving."

"Me too," Marin said.

"Let's find lunch." I checked the time and was shocked to see it was almost three. "Geez, it's almost supper time. How about we get a huge snack, like some ice cream, and then after we see a couple more animals, head back to the hotel for dinner instead?"

"Yay! Ice cream," Kinsley yelled.

"I didn't think you were going to eat anymore," Marin said.

"But I'm hungry so I gotta."

She tickled Kinsley in the ribs. "That's what I thought."

We found an ice cream parlor and all got sundaes made with gelato. And they were delicious. Then we were off to see the penguins, elephants, and our last stop was at the coati display. One of the zookeepers had one on a leash and Aaron went crazy over it. I'm not sure if it was its long striped tail or its long nose, but the kid loved that thing. It was gentle enough to pet, so Aaron ran his chubby hand along its back and kicked his legs in excitement. I think he would've stuffed the thing in his diaper bag if he were capable of it.

As we walked away, he kept looking back with his little arms stretched out. Marin took a ton of pictures of him with it and I couldn't wait to see them all. Both kids fell asleep on the way back to the hotel.

"Maybe we should order room service tonight," I

suggested. "With both of them asleep, I hate to wake them up."

"I'll do whatever. It doesn't matter. But I think they both had a great time."

"I do too. That was a great experience for them." And a better one for me watching them.

When we got to the suite, I suggested putting them both to bed.

"If we do that, they'll be up all night," Marin said as she was sitting down with Aaron on her lap. I had the stroller in one hand and Kinsley in the other. She looked up at me and jumped back to her feet.

"Sorry. I wasn't thinking." She grabbed the stroller and I laid Kinsley on the couch.

"What should we do?" I checked the time. "It's already nearly six."

"I say we order dinner and then wake them up to eat. Afterward, we bathe them and put them to bed."

I stretched out the kinks in my back. It wasn't hard to notice her staring at me and my dick jumped to life. Maybe I needed to jump in the shower while we waited for the food and I could take care of business.

"Fine. I'm gonna shower. Will you order dinner? I'll eat whatever."

I hurried out of the room with her staring at my back. I didn't want her to notice the damn bulge in my pants. That was something I didn't want to contend with right now. I had enough going on in my head.

Chapter Thirty-Five

Marin

GREY HUSTLED out of the room like I was contaminated. I thought we'd had a great day too. Goes to show what I knew.

I checked out the menu and ordered a ton of stuff. Pizza for the kids with some spaghetti on top of that. The pizza here looked different from what we ate at home, so I needed back up just in case. Then I ordered salads and some Weiner schnitzel. It was supposedly the hotel specialty, but then again, it was the specialty of Austria so how could I go wrong with that? I added several desserts, drinks, and some sides. They said it would be at least forty minutes. That would give me time for a shower too as long as Grey didn't take too long.

I was scrolling through the pictures I'd taken today when he came out. His hair was messy and damp from his shower. I'd expanded a photo I'd taken of him watching the kids and had been staring at him. It had captured every perfect feature of his face—from his intense gray eyes to his full sensuous lips. My fingertip had been tracing those lips when he walked into the room.

"I'm out if you'd like to shower."

"Ayy," I yipped and jerked at the same time. My phone went flying out of my hand and landed at his feet. I reached for it, but my hand collided with his. When I looked up, our mouths were only inches apart. The oxygen trapped in my airways, and everything in my body tensed. All I wanted was to act like he didn't affect me, but that wasn't possible. That was like eating a habanero pepper and pretending your mouth wasn't burning like the fires of hell.

He picked up the phone and went to hand it to me, only at the last minute, he glanced down. Then he saw what I'd been staring at. *Him.* He scrolled to find more pictures of him. Oh, the kids were in them, but they weren't the focal point. He was.

"May I please have my phone?" The humiliation was beyond anything I'd ever experienced. It was worse than leaving *Newsworthy Magazine* with my banker's box. It was worse than seeing Damien and my former best friend in the grocery store together after they'd gotten engaged. How had my life gotten so off track?

He kept scrolling.

"Grey. Please."

Perhaps he saw something in my eyes, or maybe it was the way my voice quivered when I asked, but he handed the phone over and I darted to my room. I went into the bathroom, stripped, and took a shower so I could wash away the layer of shame that clung to me and seemingly didn't want to let go.

Grey's conference was the next day and a half. Maybe I would check into getting my ticket changed after that.

Staying here with him was worse than I ever imagined. My heart was already in need of his medical services. If I stayed the rest of the week, there wouldn't be anything worth fixing afterward.

I didn't have a computer with me, and changing tickets on my phone was a pain. The hotel had a business center so I could do it there. The next day I would make arrangements after Grey left for his conference. He would be tied up for only a day and a half. I could leave after that.

In the morning, I took the kids downstairs to eat breakfast and then went to the business center to check on flights. I could get on a different one in two days. I changed my ticket, which was easy since we had first class seating, and then we made plans. The park was nearby, so we started there and the kids loved it. By the time we played on all the swings and other amusements it offered, it was already time for lunch, so we left and found a place to eat. Then I remembered Paige talking about the catacombs beneath St. Stephen's Cathedral, which was close to our hotel.

We rode back to the hotel to drop off the stroller. I opted to use the backpack carrier instead since according to the information, I would have to navigate stairs. The church was built in the 1500's. The work on it began in the twelfth century but wasn't completed for three hundred years. Beneath it laid the catacombs and Ducal crypt dating back to Archduke Rudolph IV whose remains had been there since 1365.

We entered the gothic cathedral and Kinsley asked, "Marnie, I didn't bring my church clothes. Are we going to church?"

Laughing, I answered, "Not exactly sweetie. We're taking a tour of what's under the church."

"What's under the church?"

"Just some things from ancient Vienna."

"Okay. But will there be things for me and Aaron to play with?"

"Not really, but this won't take long. I promise."

We went to where the tour started and lucky for us, we didn't have to wait long. The guide opened the gate and we walked down a flight of steps. We entered a crypt directly beneath the church where he explained how it had been refurbished and looked newer now. It was where the Vienna bishops were laid to rest. It was a good thing the tour guide had a heavy accent and Kinsley couldn't understand him because I think this was a little too morbid for a small child, even though Paige had said it was okay.

Then we moved onward into the depths of the catacombs. I stayed toward the back of the group in case Aaron cried. I didn't want him to disturb the tour. Even though he never did, I just took the extra precaution.

As we walked deeper and deeper into the cavernous area, it got cooler and cooler, and darker and darker.

"Marnie, are there monsters down her?"

"No, short stuff. No monsters." My voice was firm, although this place gave me the creeps like nothing I'd ever seen.

"I'm cold," Kinsley said.

"That's because we're way underground." I did worry about Aaron being cold, but hopefully, we would be out quickly.

The group stopped and the guide directed us to look in the barred windows on the right. Kinsley was too short, thank God, but you could still see the skeletal remains of bodies inside. It was the most disturbing thing ever. My skin crawled so much I rubbed my arms.

We walked farther on. To our left was another larger room. One by one each person would look inside.

"Marnie, what are they looking at?" Kinsley asked.

"It's only an empty room."

"I wanna see."

The rest of the group moved on as she asked me to hold her up to see inside the barred window. I didn't want to and was telling her so. All of a sudden a thunderous boom shook the walls around us, and I stumbled to my knees. What the hell.

"Marnie?"

Then another one hit. But this time I was slammed into something and hit the side of my head so hard that everything spun. Then rocks and debris rained down on me. Initially, I was confused and dizzy.

Shit. Kinsley. Aaron. I rolled on my back and covered Aaron with my hands as much as I could. All the lights went out, so it was black as coal inside. It was impossible to even see my hand in front of my face.

"Kinsley? Where are you?" I called out.

"Marnie? I'm scared. I can't see," she cried.

The explosion, or whatever it was, must've knocked out the electricity.

"Hang on a second. There must be emergency lighting down here. It will probably come on any minute. But it didn't. I fumbled in the side of Aaron's pack to find my phone. Then I had to figure out where the damn flashlight button was. When I turned it on, I found Kinsley. She was farther down from me.

"Kinsley, I'm here. Are you hurt?"

Then she started crying. Fuck, oh, fuck.

"Hang on, short stuff. I'm coming." I checked Aaron and he was fine. My legs were scraped, but I was ok. My head throbbed something fierce, and my shoulder too, but otherwise I was fine. I crawled over all the rock and debris and made it to where Kinsley was laying. Her forehead and leg were cut and bleeding.

"Can you move?"

She was sobbing so hard, I'm not sure she heard me. I kissed her cheek. "Kinsley? Honey, can you hear me?"

"Marnie? I'm scared."

So am I. "It's okay. We're okay. They're gonna come and get us. They know we're here."

"Who knows? Did you call Daddy?"

Fuck me. He had no idea where we were.

"Yeah. He knows. And the tour people know too."

I aimed my flashlight around to find that the walls on either side of us had crumbled down trapping our exits out, and cutting us off from everyone else. Then I aimed it to my left and, oh fuck, fuck, fuck. We were surrounded by piles of bones. They were every-fucking-where. Why the hell had I chosen this place to tour … and with the kids? I had to make sure Kinsley didn't see that. Oh, God. Please get us out of here.

"Marnie, call Daddy."

"Yeah. I'll call Daddy."

But when I tried, there was no signal.

"Did you try?"

"I can't, honey. There isn't a signal down here. We'll just wait."

"I'm cold." She was still sobbing. I was close to that point, but I forced myself to remain calm.

"Come here." I got Aaron out of his pack and sat him on my lap and then pulled Kinsley next to me. While we sat there, huddled together, my brain scrambled for ideas of how there might be something I could do.

"Kinsley, I need your help. You have to be a big sister now, okay?"

"Okay."

"I want you to hug Aaron and watch him. Don't let him run around. Can you do that for me?"

"Don't leave me, Marnie."

I put my hands on her cheeks. "Listen up, my brave, sweet girl. I am not leaving. I'm going right over there"—I pointed to where the rocks were blocking our exit—"to try to clear a way for us to get out of here. You can do that, can't you?"

Her head bobbed.

I used my phone to guide me to the pile of rubble that blocked our exit. "Is anybody there?" I yelled. "Help! Can anyone hear me?" I tugged on one of the rocks to see if I could move it, but they were wedged in so tightly they wouldn't budge. "Help me! We're trapped in here."

When that didn't work, I tried the other end that was blocked, doing the same thing. I didn't give up. Hours passed and I would periodically go to each end and yell.

"Marnie, I'm thirsty."

"Here." I handed both of them some water. I was always prepared with the kids. We'd been down here for four hours. Surely someone would help. They had to know we were trapped by now. Every twenty to thirty minutes I'd keep yelling and shouting just to make sure. In between those times, I told the kids stories, made things up, did everything I knew. Aaron slept part of the time. He was oblivious to our distress, thank God. And thank God I had brought a mobile battery with me because when my phone started dying, I panicked until I realized I stuck it in the pack. It would've been torturous to be stuck down here in absolute darkness.

After ten … ten excruciating hours, someone finally answered my shouts.

"We're coming. Please be patient. We know you are there. We are clearing the debris."

"I have two small children with me. Can you call their father?"

"Yes, I believe he is already here."

"Did you hear that, Kinsley? They're getting us out."

She was still whimpering off and on and I was so worried about her. It wasn't like her to act like this. Aaron, on the other hand, had only fussed when I wouldn't let him run around. It was too dangerous in here to allow that. So, he'd sit in my lap and kick out his legs.

The stabbing pain in my head persisted from where I'd hit it and my shoulder also ached. But my main priority was getting these kids to safety. They hadn't eaten anything since lunch and only had water to drink. I was out of everything and if we didn't get them out of here soon, I was afraid they'd get dehydrated.

We were all huddled together in the chilled air, trying to stay warm, when a ray of light broke through. Then it grew until finally a man in a hard hat climbed in.

"Hello, are you okay?" he asked in a heavy accent. "I'm here to get you out."

"Thank you. Yes, we're fine. Here," I handed Aaron to him.

He took him and asked, "Can you walk?"

"Yes." Kinsley and I followed, navigating our way through the rubble. When we climbed over the debris to the other side, a team of search and rescue workers waited to escort us to the outside. When we got there, it was dark, and Grey was waiting.

"Thank God you're safe." And then his arms were around us all, even me.

My head swam and overwhelming dizziness made it impossible to stand. I clutched his arm as I began to crumple.

People were clustered around me when I came to and

was lying on a stretcher. They wheeled me into an ambulance and drove to a nearby hospital. It happened so quickly, I didn't have time to ask about the kids. The hospital staff was very accommodating, but I didn't speak the language and was frightened. Were the kids okay? I was more worried about Kinsley than Aaron, but no one seem to know anything.

A doctor came in and rattled off something, but I didn't understand him. He only smiled, patted my hand, and left. Soon they took me to another room to do a scan on my head. As I laid on that hard surface, I sobbed. The person running the machine came out and instructed me to be still. Her English wasn't great, but at least I understood her. I sucked it up and after the scan, I was returned to my curtained off cubby. Being alone was awful and I wished there was someone to sit with me. But I knew Grey had his hands full with the kids.

A different doctor came in this time—an English speaking one— and said I'd suffered a severe concussion but would be fine. They wanted to keep me overnight. I had also injured my shoulder, but he said it wasn't serious and could be tended to after I got home.

"Do you know what happened?" I asked.

"It was a gas explosion of some kind," he said. "It happened near the church, so the section of the catacombs you were in was affected because that's where the gas lines ran. They are still investigating it."

"Are the kids okay?" I asked, grabbing his arm as he tried to move away.

He was puzzled by my question. "The kids?"

"Yes, I was with two children."

"I'm sorry. You came in alone. They may have taken them somewhere else. Were they injured?"

"Yes. One had some cuts and bruises and was very shaken. The other one was fine."

"Perhaps they determined the hospital was not necessary."

"Maybe." Then I asked, "When can I fly?"

"Tomorrow would be fine."

I wouldn't miss my flight, so that was good. The sooner I could get out of here the better. This trip had turned into a catastrophe.

They moved me to a room and there was still no word from Grey. I didn't expect one because he had enough on his hands without me.

Every time I thought about Kinsley, I had to force back the sobs. My heart hurt for her. The poor thing had been so frightened.

Eventually, I fell asleep, but every few hours, they'd wake me up to check my blood pressure. In the morning, the doctor came to visit and asked how I was feeling.

"Sore, and my head still hurts. Is that normal?"

As he looked through my chart, he said, "It will probably hurt for another day or so. Abstain from any activity where you risk falling. You don't want to hit your head again. Other than that, you're cleared to go, but get your shoulder checked out when you return home. I suspect it's only bruised, but it's best to be safe."

"Thank you."

The hospital ordered a cab to carry me back to the hotel only I didn't have a purse or anything to pay. I went to the room but had to knock since I didn't have a key. Grey opened the door and looked awful.

"I need my purse to pay for the taxi that brought me home."

"Marin, I … it's been a mess here with Kinsley."

"It's fine. I'll be right back."

He reached into his pocket, pulled out his wallet, and handed me a bunch of euros. "Here. That ought to be enough."

I went back down and gave the guy a huge tip for having to wait.

Back upstairs, Grey explained that Kinsley had to go to the hospital too, but they took her to a different one. "And then I had Aaron to contend with."

"How is she?"

He ran his hand through his hair. "I'm not sure. Why did you take them there? She said you left her." His tone was sharp, piercing.

He stunned me with his accusation. "Left her? I didn't leave her … would never leave her. I was with them the entire time. And I went because I didn't think … it was my fault, yes, for not investigating the place. But I never expected anything like that to happen." Tears formed in my eyes, and soon they turned into trickles sliding down my cheeks.

Stormy gray eyes stabbed mine, chilling me to the bone. Why would he possibly think I would do anything to harm the kids? That thought hurt more than anything and only solidified my decision to leave.

"I, uh, I would like to check on her if I could."

A brief slash of his head was all I got.

"Grey. I should never have gone there in the first place. It was horrible." I shuddered and turned so he couldn't see the pain in my eyes. Then I went to Kinsley.

"Short stuff, are you awake?" I whispered in case she was asleep.

"Yeah."

"What's going on? Are you hurt?"

"My leg hurts."

I bent down to check it out. "Can I kiss it to make it better?"

"Yeah." So, I did.

"How's that?"

"Okay."

"Only okay?"

"I didn't like that place, Marnie."

I brushed her hair off her face. "Guess what? Neither did I. We won't ever go back there, okay?"

Her head dipped up and down.

"Wanna come and watch some movies?"

"Okay. Marnie? You said you'd never leave and you left." She started crying and wrapped her tiny arms around my neck. I cried right along with her.

"I didn't leave you, sweetie. I had to go to the hospital for the night."

Through her sobs that hacked my heart into more pieces than it already was, she begged, "Promise you won't leave no more."

I said the only thing I could think of. "Give me a hug you big goofball." I couldn't give her that promise because in another day I would be breaking her heart again and I couldn't bear to think about it.

Chapter Thirty-Six

GREYDON

MY COMMITMENT TO do the talk was fulfilled in the morning while Marin and the kids were off somewhere. After lunch, I was sitting in on one of the other talks, and we all heard the explosion. It was close to the hotel so one of the physicians went out to inquire what happened. He came back with not much of an answer. I called Marin and never got a response. She wasn't answering any of my texts either, so I immediately knew something was wrong. A little later, I left the conference and checked with the hotel. They had just received word about the gas explosion. The authorities were shutting down all gas lines until they could determine where it stemmed from. I tried Marin repeatedly with no luck. It was really worrying me because it wasn't like her to not let me know her whereabouts. Then information started coming in about the explosion and how it affected the catacombs beneath the church. Things began clicking together as I remembered what Mom had told her about that tour of the catacombs. My chest instantly felt like it was being crushed and I couldn't push away the ache in the back of my throat. I rushed over there, but they wouldn't let me near at first … until I explained how I thought my kids were down there.

They allowed me through the cordoned-off section where the rescue teams had been established. There were about thirty people trapped. At first, they didn't know how serious it was. As time passed, they eventually began to feel confident they could get everyone out, but they weren't sharing much with me. The language was a barrier with some of the workers, although they tried their best to communicate what they could. A translator arrived and kept us up to speed, but the weight on my chest kept getting heavier, making breathing a struggle.

If anything happened to them … what would I do? And Marin, the way I'd been treating her. Acid seared my gut with the thought of it. How could I have done this to her? How could I have pushed her away like this? I was such a monumental idiot. She'd done nothing but bring brightness into my soul. She was completely selfless, only thinking about doing what was best for the kids. I swallowed and the bite of pain over every moronic thing I had done, sent nails shooting straight into my heart.

Approximately seven hours after the explosion hit, they broke through to the first group. There were about fifteen people, but Marin and the kids weren't among them. I tried to ask about them but wasn't able to. The lead on the search and rescue said he would find out who the tour guide was and they would establish when they had everyone out.

One of my colleagues came later and waited with me. I'm not even sure how he found out I was there, but it was a relief because he spoke both languages and was a huge help. He discovered that the tunnels had been blocked in several areas and they were breaking through one by one. They were confident everyone would be out soon.

When they got to the last blocked section, they found Marin and the kids. At my first glimpse of them, the band around my chest eased and my lungs instantly expanded. I could breathe again and for a moment I was actually light-headed. Tears welled up in my eyes and I was giddy. Yes, giddy. I trembled and when they ushered them close to me, I pulled them all against me. The man in the hard hat handed Aaron over and all three of us stood there in an embrace. That is until Marin collapsed.

"Hey, somebody help," I yelled.

"Daddy! What's wrong with Marnie?" Kinsley was sobbing hysterically and I could barely understand her. Everything broke down at once. My joy at having them all here was short-lived.

A medic ran over and soon a gurney appeared. Marin woke up, but Kinsley was inconsolable, screaming about the monsters in the dark place. She totally freaked out. I had Aaron to deal with, who also was crying. Then I noticed blood on Kinsley and a medic was speaking to me, only I couldn't hear him because Kinsley was crying so loud.

My colleague touched my arm and said, "Grey, she should be checked out." Then he spoke to the medic. But Kinsley wouldn't let me go. So, I had to ride in the ambulance with her and Aaron. It was a total shit show.

I wanted to check on Marin, but there was no time. My daughter needed me. When we got to the hospital, I figured I'd check on Marin then, but they took her to a different one.

As it turned out, Kinsley only had some minor bruising and a few lacerations. But they were concerned about

PTSD, as was I. They ended up giving her a mild sedative because she wouldn't stop screaming. I had never seen her like this and it was frightening.

My colleague was waiting for us in the waiting room and drove us back to the hotel.

"I don't quite know how to thank you," I said.

"No thanks necessary. I'm just sorry your trip to my home has been so troubled. Can I help you up to your room?"

"No, that's fine. But can you find out where they took Marin?" I gave him her full name.

"Yes, and I'll text you the information."

"Thank you."

When I got to the suite, I put Aaron to bed. Kinsley wouldn't stop crying again. Her sedative had worn off, so I had to give her another one. She was inconsolable and it freaked me out. I was exhausted and at my wits end. She finally calmed down about the time the sun was rising, so I climbed into bed, not thinking I'd sleep. I was wrong.

The knock on the door woke me up. Marin stood on the other side. She looked terrible—like she had been through the worst experience of her life. And she had. But I'd never seen her look more beautiful in my life. I wanted to pull her into my arms and hold her forever. Only she had to run down and pay the taxi driver.

When she got back to the room, I went off on her. All I could think of was how Kinsley said the place scared her and that Marin left her. Without thinking, I accused her, even though those were the words of an overreacting child and a father who'd had more than he could handle. It wasn't the least bit fair to her and I was a total ass.

She tried to explain, but it was no use. She went to see Kinsley and the timing wasn't right at all for us. We needed to talk. There were so many things I wanted to tell her …

things I had fucked up that needed to be fixed. But Kinsley needed us both, so I figured it would wait until the time was right.

Once again, I screwed that up. This seemed to be the story of my life. I needed someone in my head constantly saying—*Don't do it, man.*

The following morning, I quietly got out of bed so as not to wake Kinsley, and took Aaron into the other room to change him. When I got there, Marin's door was open. I entered it only to find it empty. All her things were gone. On the bed was a letter.

GREY,

Under the circumstances, I thought it best if I leave. Simply put, it's just not possible for me to share this suite with you. When we decided to take this trip, I thought I could handle it. I see now it was a mistake for me to come. I'm so sorry. And I'm sorry about what happened in the catacombs. It truly wasn't a place for kids. I should've investigated it more. I pray that Kinsley is all right. I love her and Aaron very, very much. Please tell her I'll see her when you return home.

Marin

WHAT THE HELL was I going to tell my polka dot? She was in the worst shape ever—even worse than after Susannah died. It was ridiculous for us to stay too. I quickly called the airlines to see what times the flights were. It was only six thirty. There was a nine thirty flight. We could make that.

I rushed around like a maniac. I took a shower with Aaron. Kinsley didn't need one. She could go home without one. I woke her up, then stuffed all our things into the suitcases.

"Get dressed, honey. We can't spare even a minute. We're leaving and a taxi is picking us up in twenty minutes. You need to brush your teeth and wash your face. Hurry, hurry."

She was groggy but did as I asked. The bellman arrived just as I was zipping up the last bag. We had so much shit, but that was fine. The thought of going home made me smile.

"Where's Marnie?"

"Um … she caught the earlier flight because there wasn't room for us all." I hated lying, but I didn't have it in me to tell her the truth.

She didn't respond and the last thing I needed was for her to know Marin left us. I was going to pull every trick out of my bag to get her back.

The bellman loaded our stuff into the waiting taxi while I settled our bill and off we went. We went through the airport and Aaron was in the carrier on my chest, Kinsley was hanging on one hand while I pushed a carry-on with the other. It wasn't exactly a picnic traveling with two kids alone.

I didn't get a seat for Aaron since he was under two. For takeoff, he was in my lap and then during the flight I put him in the seat with Kinsley. They watched movies together until he got too fidgety, and then I took him. He slept some and I'd put the seat into the flat bed position. He was always so good. Thank God he wasn't a whiny flier.

We landed and went through customs, with Kinsley asking a bunch of questions.

"What is that machine for? Why do they ask you that?

What are they doing there?" Trying to explain immigration to a seven-year-old was nearly impossible.

"Why can't we all just have one big place where we all live, Daddy?"

"Good question, polka dot."

The car service I'd ordered while waiting for our baggage had arrived and drove us home. I was never so happy to get there in my life. All I had to do now was reconstruct the shambles of Marin's heart. But hey, wasn't that my job? Wasn't that my area of expertise? I hoped it was because I wanted nothing more than to have her back here.

"Daddy, I'm hungry."

Kinsley pulled me away from my planning. "So am I. How about we order pizza?"

"Good."

I called Mom and Dad to let them know we were back.

"Hi Mom."

"Grey, where are you?"

"Home."

"As in here?"

"Yeah, Mom. Are you busy?"

"No. What do you need?"

"Can you come over? We just walked in and my hands are full. There isn't any food in the house and I need to pick up a pizza."

"I'm on the way. Where's Marin?"

"That's a long story and please don't bring it up when you get here," I mumbled so the little ears in the room didn't hear.

"Fine. Your father and I will be there shortly."

And they were. They walked in and Kinsley ran up to them jabbering on about the scary place with the monsters.

"What on Earth are you talking about, honey?"

"Gammie, Marnie and us got stuck in the scary cold place."

"Grey?"

"There was an explosion while they were touring the catacombs and they were trapped down there for over ten hours."

Mom stumbled to the closest chair. She sat at the table for a few minutes to collect herself.

"Mom, are you okay?"

"Yes, son, I am. It's my fault. I'm the one who suggested she go there. I can't imagine what it was like for Marin down there. She must've been terrified. That place is …" She shuddered.

"Mom," I said, my tone carrying a warning as I flicked my head in Kinsley's direction.

"Gammie, we were cold and hungry and Marnie had to go to the hospital."

"Is she okay?"

I answered. "She had a concussion. But she's fine."

Mom grabbed my arm. "Trish hasn't called. When did she come home?"

"She caught an earlier flight so just today. I'm sure she hasn't had a chance."

Mom wasn't buying it at all. Her eyes fastened onto mine and she read things that only a mother was able to.

"I see. You'd better get this figured out." That was all she said about it. "What do you need for me to do?"

"Can you stay with the kids while I grocery shop and pick up the pizza?"

"Of course. Your father and I would love to."

I was only gone for an hour and came home with enough pizza for everyone and also food for Aaron, who

Mom had already fed. There was baby food in the cabinet, which he happily gobbled down.

While I was gone, Mom helped Kinsley bathe while Dad bathed Aaron. Their bags were unpacked and the clothes sorted for washing. They really worked fast.

After we ate, Mom pulled me into my office while Dad occupied the kids.

"What the hell is going on, Grey?"

"What do you mean?"

"Don't you dare play stupid with me. When we were here before you left, things between you and Marin were strained. What caused it?"

"Me, okay? I'm the dumbass who ruined it all. But now I'm going to fix it."

"Did she really have to come home because there wasn't room on your flight? Kinsley said she hurt her head in the explosion."

The tension in my neck was about to cause a migraine. I took a deep, pained breath. I didn't need Mom to add to the guilt that was already weighing me down. "Mom, the situation wasn't ideal." I reached into my back pocket and pulled out her letter, handing it to my mom.

Mom took it, unfolded it and then started reading. Her brows lowered and her lips pursed as she read on. "Oh, Grey, what have you done to the poor girl?"

"I screwed everything up, Mom. It's my fault. I'm the one to blame."

"How so?"

"It had to do with the DNA kit."

Mom's eyes narrowed. "Are you back to that again?"

I fisted my hands. "No! I'm done with that and I told her. Aaron is and will always be my son. But she lied and I was hurt and furious over it."

"Lied?"

"I asked her to send the kit off and she never did. O1 she said she would."

"She said she did, but didn't. Is that it?" Mom asked.

"Not exactly but it's all semantics. I trusted her to do it and she didn't. She took it upon herself to act on my behalf without consulting me and I was angry over her decision. I'm over that now, but during the time I was deliberating, I pushed her away. Now I have to bridge the gap I created. She's in love with me. Or more to the point, she was in love with me. After that explosion and when I didn't know whether or not she or the kids were okay, I realized just how much she meant to me. I love her too. And now I have to fix things."

"My God, you're dense. How did you ever make it through Harvard?"

I blew out a long breath full of frustrations. "I have no idea."

"Good luck with getting her back. You'd better figure out a way to tell her you won't make the same mistake again."

I let out a self-deprecating laugh. "I hope she believes me."

"Grey, you may be many things, but you're not a liar."

"True, but she has no basis to believe my actions will hold merit."

Mom's penetrating gaze had me glued to the floor. Then she asked, "How much do you want this woman in your life?"

"More than anything."

"How much are you willing to risk in order to get her back?"

"Everything but my kids."

"Then find a way to prove it."

"How?"

"Figure it out, son."

Mom walked out, leaving me standing there. I was bereft and didn't know what to do. But I had to come up with something, and it had better be epic because I needed Marin in my life as much as I needed food, water, and air. Each day without her was leaving me weaker and weaker. It was draining the happiness out of my soul. Marin had recharged my batteries, only they had never been fully charged to begin with and now I was experiencing life the way it had been before her and it sucked.

That night when I was in bed, I texted her to see if she'd made it home okay and to let her know I was thinking of her.

You don't have to text me back, but I did want you to know that you're always on my mind.

I didn't hear from her and hadn't expected to. I checked in to see if she needed me to bring her things to her. I received no response. I gave her daily updates on Kinsley's progress, because as much as she hated me, I knew she still loved my daughter. But it also occurred to me how very little I knew about her. That set the stage for my plan on how to get her back. Over the next few weeks I decided to send her daily texts, asking her specific things about herself.

What's your favorite color?

If you could go anywhere in the world, where would it be?

What's your favorite song?

The beach or the mountains?

Sunrise or sunset?

Favorite movie?

Favorite Disney character?

Chocolate or vanilla?

Hershey Kisses or Peanut Butter Cups?

Pizza or burgers?

The questions went on and on. I was relentless.

After a week, she finally broke down and her first response was **Will you stop texting me?**

Not a chance. I need to know these things. As the song says—*I won't give up on us even if the skies get rough, I'm giving you all my love, I'm still looking up.*

I didn't hear from her for another day. Then I got **You are the most annoying person I've ever known. Leave me alone.**

Ignoring her, I kept up the questions. Then she came back with **Why are you doing this?**

Because I believe in us!

Go away!

I didn't. I persisted.

She texted me back with **Why do you need to know this stuff?**

Meet me for dinner and I'll tell you.

A few more days passed and no response.

Then she texted **No. Seeing you will hurt too much. It would remind me of how you pulled my heart out of my chest and ripped it into tiny pieces. You're supposed to fix hearts, not destroy them.**

Oh Jesus. Oh God. If words had the power to destroy, hers had just mutilated me, completely butchering my heart and soul. And I deserved every single one of them. **I swear by everything I own, everything that's in me, I won't ever hurt you again. Like I said ... *I won't give up. I had to learn what I got, who I'm not, and who I am.***

She didn't respond so I sent **Please.**

No. Leave. Me. Alone.

So, I did. For a while. But it didn't settle with me. The bit she said about me fixing hearts was true and I had done the opposite to her. I wouldn't give up until she found someone else, or I was dead.

Thought you might like this. It was evil, but at this point I was desperate. I sent a photo of the kids.

Nice try.

Then one night, without my knowledge, Kinsley got a hold of my phone. She texted Marin. The next morning, I saw it.

Miss U. U coming bak?

Marin must've figured it was Kinsley because she hit her back with **Miss U 2** and two heart emojis.

That's when I made the move.

Please meet me for dinner. Just once and after that, I won't ever ask you again.

I heard nothing for hours. But then …

Where?

I gave her the name of the nicest restaurant in town and the time.

You can even drive yourself if case you want to leave early.

Fine. Only if it will stop these annoying texts.

Not a chance. *We've got a lot to learn. God knows we're worth it. I won't give up. I'm here to stay and make the difference I can make.* I stuck in a heart emoji.

She agreed to meet me the following night. This was it. My one and only chance and I'd better make it right. I made sure I was out of the office by six. The reservation was for seven fifteen. I arrived at seven, just in case. I asked for the most private table they had so we could talk. I gave the hostess Marin's name and description so she could escort her back. The setting was perfect. I'd ordered a bottle of wine and waited. Seven fifteen came and went. Seven thirty did too. The waitress stopped by several times. When seven forty-five arrived, I knew she wasn't going to show. I checked my phone and figured she could've at least texted me. I had hurt her, yes, but I thought she'd at least have the decency to tell me she wasn't coming.

"Sir, are you sure you don't want to order something?"

"You know what? I'll just have the check, please."

"Yes, sir."

She came back and set the bill down. I gave her my credit card and realized that Marin never knew I loved her, that I still love her. I never had the chance to tell her and now it was looking like I never would. Even though Marin had given up on us I would never do the same. She had probably moved on but that would never happen for me. She was mine, now and forever, and I would have to figure out a way to make her see that.

Chapter Thirty-Seven

MARIN

MY DAMN CAR wouldn't start. Of all times for this to happen. Why now? Appeared to be a dead battery, or so Dad thought. Then when I went to text Grey, my stupid phone also had a dead battery.

"Ugh!"

"What's wrong?" Mom asked.

"My phone's dead and I was supposed to meet Grey at seven fifteen. He's going to think I stood him up."

"Use mine."

I grabbed Mom's phone but then realized I didn't know his number and the damn thing was stored on my phone.

"Shit, shit. I don't know his number. Who even knows anyone's numbers these days."

"Come on. Get in the car. I'll drive you," Dad said.

"I'm still going to be late."

"Don't worry. He'll wait. If he's not there, I'll take you to his place. And you can explain."

"Thanks, Dad."

I leaped out of the car but asked my dad to wait, just in case Grey had already left. The hostess walked me back and I saw Grey was paying the bill.

"I'm sorry. Don't leave. My car wouldn't start and I couldn't call because my phone was dead. Clearly, not my day. Let me run outside and tell my dad he can leave." Grey's expression was priceless. His mouth hung open and I casually said, "What? Did you actually think I would stand you up? Please." I rolled my eyes, all the time I snickered to myself.

I hurried outside to tell Dad he could leave, then rushed back in. "Woo, I'm exhausted from all that. Can I have some of that wine?" I asked. "Or did you drink it all because I'm so late?"

He finally broke a smile. "I actually did think you stood me up."

"I'm sorry. Dad thinks my battery is dead. The damn thing wouldn't even make a sound. And well, it was a mess. And that car never lets me down. I went to call you on Mom's phone but ... I didn't know your number."

I barely got that last word out before he grabbed my hand and pulled me over. His lips were on mine and he was hungrily kissing me, as in devouring me. All my talk about staying strong and not succumbing to his sexual advances if he made any, went flying out the window. I was gone. Dead. Completely fucked.

He released me and I said, "Well, I'm glad we got that settled. So, what did you want to discuss?"

The man rumbled with laughter and did I ever miss that sound.

"Pink, huh?"

"Guilty as charged. My room at home is still that color. Love it. Look at this hair. Don't you see it?"

"I should've known. And sunrises. That surprised me since I had to wake you up on your first day of work."

I twirled a piece of my hair. "Uh, that was when I was coming down off of my old lifestyle. I love the mornings."

"Pride and Prejudice."

"I've watched that movie maybe fifty times."

"Why?" he asked.

"I adore Mr. Darcy. He was such an ass at first, but then he was such a softie. And he truly wasn't an ass. He was just … shy. And Elizabeth was plain. But so perfectly beautiful on the inside and out."

"Exactly like you."

"What did you say?"

"You're beautiful on the inside and out. You're not flashy. You're not heavily made up. You're absolutely perfect. Just like Elizabeth Bennett."

"You've seen the movie?" I asked.

"Never, but I've read the book."

"And?"

"It's a classic. I didn't care much for it at the time, but I was an ignorant kid. I reread it when I was in medical school and loved it."

I leaned back and appreciated the glow in his eyes. "Why?"

"Because it was about a man who people perceived completely wrong. That happens a lot with the way doctors are regarded."

"So, in other words, you're not proud."

He leaned closer and steepled his fingers. "Not at all. I'm humbled by my patients when they are so appreciative of what I can do for them. I won't pretend to think I'm not good at what I do because I'm damned good. I'm thorough and don't take anything for granted when it comes to my patients. But I'm not proud. And I don't wear the white coat like a badge of honor either."

"Why not? Is it not an honor?"

"In some ways, yes. But the way I see it, it's my duty. I took the Hippocratic oath and as long as I practice, I will live up to that oath to the best of my ability."

I was seeing him in a new light, a revealing light, and it was frightening.

"Why am I here, Grey?" I thought I'd get that out of the way.

"I would've thought that was rather obvious."

"I need to hear your version. Before you tell me, you have to know that I can't go through anything like we did again. It was excruciating. I crawled home twice with my tail between my legs. A third time is not an option."

"There won't be a third time, Marin." His silver-gray eyes locked onto mine and he began. "After Susannah, I swore there wouldn't be any other women in my life. My heart was so brittle, it didn't have the capability to feel, let alone beat. And to be honest, it wasn't because we had some sort of undying love, because we didn't. I just refused to put myself or my family through anything like that again. But you walked through the door with that hair, those piercings, and tattoos, I didn't know what to think. I couldn't get over the way you spoke to me for one. You really just didn't give a shit. And then Kinsley calling you Marnie. I would watch the two of you interact while I was at work. Susannah was never so hands-on with the kids. You both laughed all the time. You even made me laugh. When I was home, I would eavesdrop on your conversations and they were downright hilarious. And the way you handled Aaron, and how fast you bonded with him, had me stepping back and examining my own feelings concerning him. I would go into his room at night and question why I had to know about his parentage so much … why it even mattered. But then one day, I saw you in a different light altogether. It was right when I showed up at Kinsley's school program. You made fun of my goofy hat. But it was more. Much more. After the office picnic, I knew it. I tried to push my feelings away, tried to resist, but the night I came to the hospital, it was hopeless. I told myself it was just sex, only I knew that wasn't true. Even Hudson gave me shit about it. But when everything happened with the kit, it crashed down around me and all I focused on was Susannah's betrayal. I couldn't get it through my thick skull that you were different. We were different. Blame it on my stubbornness, my stupidity. I accept total responsibility for it." He slashes his hand through the air as though he was angry. "When you walked out of those catacombs, all I wanted to do was hold you forever. But it was so chaotic with Kinsley screaming and you fainting. Then you were rushed away and we went to a different hospital. I was a fucking mess, Marin, crazy with worry. Kinsley had to be sedated in order for her to settle down, and I had Aaron to deal with. But I was so out of my head over the two of you. Shit. I didn't know if I was up or down. I couldn't even call to check on you. But my colleague did and found out you were okay. I'm sorry I'm rambling, but there is so much I needed to tell you because I never got that chance in Vienna. Then I struck out at you and I have absolutely no excuse whatsoever for that. I should've been pulling you into my arms and kissing you instead. I was just crazy that day." He let out a long huff. "Anyway, the whole point of this is I love you, have loved you, probably since the day you knocked on my door. Only this obtuse idiot didn't recognize it. When you left

Vienna, there was no use staying. I packed up the kids and left too."

"I don't know what to say."

"You don't have to say anything." He laughed awkwardly, then said, "I just word vomited all over you."

"That was an awful lot, I won't lie."

He glanced away then back at me. "May I ask you one thing?"

"What?"

"Don't give up on us yet? Because if there's one thing I've learned in life, it's that when you see something you want, don't ever give up. I'm not ever going to give up on us, Marin."

Chapter Thirty-Eight

G REYDON

MARIN HAD LISTENED, so there was hope. I was determined not to give up even if she told me no.

"I swear, if you give us a chance, I'll do everything in
my power to make you happy," I said.

"Grey, it doesn't work like that. I can't just pop up and
say—okay, it's all fine now."

"I understand. You need time. And I plan to earn back
your trust in me."

"It's not just that. You crushed me, Grey."

"I realize that." I blew out a breath. "It's a definite
no then."

"I didn't say that either."

I nearly tore out my hair in frustration. I was a lost
man, a ship without a mast, drifting hopelessly along.
Where do I go from here? How do I win her back ... find a
way into her heart again?

"What can I do? Everything I have is yours, except the kids."

"What if I want those the most?"

A grin played at the corners of my mouth. She would go for them before anything else. "Figured you'd say that."

She hugged herself. "Here's the thing. I don't care about materialistic things. I'd rather live in a small three-bedroom house than a palatial mansion. I don't care about fancy clothes or cars. My parents didn't raise me that way. You know my dad, right? He's very successful, but we always lived modestly. I wasn't raised with all that stuff so the designer handbags or shoes mean nothing to me. All I want is happiness."

"Done."

"Grey." She said my name in a warning tone. "I don't want mercurial moods either."

"I swear, Marin, I'll make you happy. I will. Think back to the way it was before. Put yourself back to then. It can be that way and I'll be the Grey you fell in love with. We'll hire a nanny and you can go back to work if you want."

"I don't want someone else raising our kids."

"*Our* kids?" I couldn't help the smile that formed on my mouth.

A bright pink flush spread from her neck up to her cheeks. I always loved that she blushed so easily.

"I'm not questioning it. It's the opposite. I'm ecstatic you think of them that way. And I know without a doubt that they love you."

She was silent.

"You need time. Not to mention we need to eat dinner." I flagged the waitress over and ordered for both of us.

When the waitress was gone, I asked, "Is everything okay?"

"I'm just thinking." She was fiddling with her napkin.

"About?"

"Us."

"Care to enlighten me?" I asked.

"Not really."

I reached over and took one of her hands in mine. "Mom is going to watch the kids for me so you can take all the time you need." She stared at her lap and didn't respond.

"WHAT'S WRONG?"

"I was thinking about us."

"Marin, I want to ask you to please not base your decision on the kids. I know you love them and I know how worried you get over them. If you and I don't work, she'll be fine. She asks about you and I know you two are texting. Mom told me."

Her watery smile let me know that's what she'd been thinking. I wanted her decision to be based on what was right and not the children.

"Grey, I love your kids, but contrary to what you're thinking, when it comes to our relationship, I'm being completely selfish in making this decision. You're probably aware Kinsley and I have been seeing each other. Paige has been great in helping with that. She's also been instrumental in me getting my things out of your house. But Kinsley keeps asking when I'm coming home."

"Yeah, she asks me that every day. I've been brutally honest with her, Marin. I've told her we are working on grown up things and that I'm hoping you'll come back, but I'm not really sure if you will."

Sadness clung to Marin's features. "She's told me as much. I've explained it the same way. She tells me everything you say. Sometimes I feel like I'm gossiping with a friend."

"She does have that older air about her on occasion, and then other times she's my little polka dot again."

"And that sweet Aaron is still kicking those legs. I think he's going to play soccer."

"Maybe so. At least he'll put the kicks to good use that way."

We ate our dinner, continuing our small talk and then I drove her home. She had to direct me because I'd never been to her parents' house before but when I pulled into the driveway I casually said, "There's not a chance I can talk you into coming home with me, is there?"

"Um, no. But dinner was good, and thanks for explaining everything to me."

"Marin, I meant every word."

"I know you did. I don't doubt your sincerity. It's just that"—she pressed her hand to her heart and continued —"I still remember how utterly shattered I was and I won't allow myself to even feel a shred of hope until I know without a doubt that this is for real."

I looked at my lap because I'd never felt shame like I did right now. But I had to man up. Marin deserved that at the very least.

"I understand, but …" I turned toward her. "I'll never treat you like that ever again. And … you'll never find anyone who loves you as much as I do. That was my second biggest mistake. Not telling you. Not telling you how I felt. But that was because I was blinded. Blinded to my feelings. I was stuck in the past. I'm not stuck anymore and I'm not that guy either. I know what I want and she's sitting right next to me. She has the biggest heart and the most beautiful soul I've ever encountered in my life. All she has to do is say the word. But one thing you should know

… I'm never going to give up on us, Marin." I picked up her hand and kissed her knuckles. "Ever."

"What was your first biggest mistake?" she asked.

"You don't know?"

"I want to hear your answer."

"Not trusting you. Not believing you. I should've known in my heart you'd never do anything that would shake my confidence in you. If I hadn't been such an idiot, we wouldn't be in this situation right now."

Then I got out of the car and walked around to the other side and helped her out.

"You're really serious, aren't you?"

"You haven't even begun to see how serious I am." I walked her to the door, kissed her cheek, and said goodnight.

The next day I called a florist and arranged for two dozen white roses to be delivered to her home. I noted the address last night when I dropped her off. On the card I wrote:

MARIN,
You're my one true love who owns my
heart and these roses are a symbol of that.
Love, Grey

THIS WAS ONLY THE BEGINNING. I was going to spoil her if it killed both of us. She didn't like materialistic items, but there were other ways. And it was starting now.

A FEW NIGHTS later when I came home from work,

Kinsley was running around the house with a small leather book in her hand.

"Whatcha got there, polka dot?"

She did her one shoulder shrug, saying, "I dunno. It was in Marnie's room."

"You know what I've told you about going through other people's things." I held out my hand and she handed it over. Curiosity got the best of me and I found myself opening it. It was her journal. Flipping through the pages, I was stunned to see the number of entries. They began shortly after she started working here. The last entry was written right before we left for Vienna. She must've forgotten to take it with her.

I'm not sure I'll ever find a way to get Grey to forgive me. He doesn't know the truth about what happened, but does it really matter anymore? He thinks so little of me now, why would he stop to listen? His trust in me was destroyed by one stupid mistake. Why didn't I tell him that I did send it in, but I sent it in late? Would it have changed things between us? Does it even matter anymore? He believes the worst of me even though I would never have betrayed him in a million years. I could never do that to someone I loved, even if I didn't agree with what he wanted. I'm sure this trip will be a disaster, but a promise is a promise and I am good for my word.

Shit. Shit. Shit. Marin sent in the DNA kit but didn't tell me. She never lied. She forgot but sent it in late. I am the biggest fucker that exists. Why didn't she say something? My mind sped back to that day in my office and I remembered her trying to say something but Hudson and I kept interrupting. She probably tried and just gave up. Christ, didn't this just make me feel even worse than I already did. Fuck my life. No wonder she thought I was the biggest asshole that existed. I had lived up to that description time and again.

Now it was time to really go to work. Over the next

couple of weeks, I put into motion several things. In our texts, she had mentioned she'd always loved animals, but never had the opportunity to have one. We'd talked about getting the dog, but she didn't want to because of how busy she was with the kids. In one of our conversations she'd said she wished animal shelters had more funding. So, I sent a huge donation to the local animal shelter in her name.

She'd also talked about getting involved with sick children at the hospital. I sent a donation there in her name. Then I hired someone with a therapy dog to spend time on the pediatric floor. That was all done under the Marin McLain donation. My brother helped find the perfect therapy dog for this.

When Marin received the letters on these, she went nuts … in a positive way.

My phone rang at work, but I couldn't answer it. When I finally got back to her, she was more excited than I'd heard her in weeks.

"That was so awesome. Thank you for doing that."

"Since you don't like designer handbags, I figured I'd spend the money elsewhere."

"Great idea. I think I want to own a therapy dog and do that now."

"Really?" This surprised me.

"Yes. It would be a way to give back."

"Hudson could help."

"You think?"

"He's the one who hooked me up with this owner so I'm sure he could."

"Thank you, Grey."

I went out on a limb and asked, "Hey, do you want to go to dinner?"

"Only if the kids can come."

"Only if we can talk first."

"Yeah, that's probably a good idea, isn't it?"

"Uh huh."

"Okay. When and where?"

We decided on a coffee shop near the house at six the next night. I didn't tell the kids because I didn't want to get their hopes up. Well, it was just Kinsley really. Aaron didn't know anything yet.

I asked Mom and Dad to stay late and I met her after work. She was waiting for me when I got there. It was comical really.

"You're early," I said.

"So are you. But I didn't want to take a chance on my car not starting this time. I don't have the best of luck." I leaned down to hug her and damn, she smelled like heaven.

"God, I could eat you."

"Excuse me?"

"You smell great." Then I laughed. "That wasn't the most appropriate thing to say, was it?"

"No. It shocked me. But I do miss our sexual banter."

"I can rectify that." I winked at her.

"I'm hoping you can."

"Does this mean what I think it means?"

"Do you think we can try?"

I took her hand between both of mine. "Marin, I don't want to try. I want to marry you."

Her chin dropped, her eyes popped open wide, and she said, "You what?"

"I want to marry you. I want to spend my life with you. I want you to be by my side, to walk with me through thick and thin, to keep me warm at night, to share my bed, and I want you to be the mother of my kids."

Chapter Thirty-Nine

MARIN

MY HAND COVERED MY MOUTH, mostly so I wouldn't cry and make a fool out of myself, but also because he'd totally shocked me. When he said he wanted me, I assumed it was back in his life, but not as his wife.

"Marin, I've never wanted anyone the way I want you. Ever."

He emphasized ever, so I knew what he was saying. I couldn't breathe.

"I love you. If you want, I can play the *I love you more than* game." It was the game he played with Kinsley. I wanted to laugh. I really did, but I was still trying to breathe.

"Jesus, are you okay over there? You're scaring me."

Then he went into action, got up, came over and kissed me. That's when I grabbed his shirt, pulled him closer, and then broke free. I sucked in a lungful of air and said, "I love you too." Then I kissed him again "Do you really want to marry me?"

"Of course I do. That's not something I'd ever joke about." He kissed me this time.

"Okay, but can we take it slow. Like maybe get to know one another better?"

"Absolutely not."

My jaw sagged. "What?"

"I am not ever going to risk losing you again. We're eloping."

"Are you serious?"

"Is this the face of a joking man?" he asked as he took his seat again.

He wasn't kidding. "No."

"Marin, we are in love, and as long as I live I will never love another woman the way I love you. I can also promise you that you will never find anyone who will love you more than I do. We've already muddled through the crap, why do we need to wait?"

"I guess I'm worried you'll decide you don't want me or something."

He leaned across the small table and took my chin between his thumb and finger. "That will never happen."

"How do you know?"

"Because I've missed you these past several weeks more than I ever thought possible. Life is completely and utterly miserable without you. And jacking off in the shower is a pitiful replacement for you."

"Grey!" I jerked my head around to make sure no one heard him.

"It's true. Sex with you is amazing. Can you deny that?"

"I can't say. I've never had sex with me before." I couldn't stop a smirk from forming.

"Just for that, I'm going to make you pay."

"How's that?" I asked.

"You'll see."

"Oooh. I'm intrigued."

He smirked. "Just wait. But hang on. You're already talking about sex therefore you agree it's amazing, right?"

"Oh, it is amazing. I can't deny that."

"Then what else?"

"If you ever have any trust issues before you fly crazy on me, talk to me."

"Done."

"And we're a team."

"Absolutely," he agreed.

"What about more children?" I asked.

"I'll do whatever you want. I'd have a dozen if you were agreeable to it, but somehow I don't think that's something you're interested in."

"No, not twelve, but I'd like two more." After being with Kinsley and Aaron, I'd decided having kids was a lot more fun than I'd ever imagined.

"Done. Anything else?"

"And I'd like to work?"

"You can do whatever you want. If you want to stay at home, fine. If you want to work, fine. If you want to get a therapy dog, fine. All I want is your happiness."

A warm glow took root in the pit of my stomach and began to grow, expanding to my chest. My lips stretched out in a humongous smile. "You really are serious?" I had to ask.

"Never been more serious. I'll give you whatever you want, Marin. You already have my heart. The materialistic stuff is nothing when you don't have love."

I jumped out of the chair and almost knocked his over. He was getting to his feet, but I wasn't making it very easy for him. Then my feet were off the ground, wrapping around his waist, as he swung me around in a circle, his hands on my hips.

"Yes," I said.

"Yes to what?"

"To eloping."

He set me down. "When?"

"When can your parents keep the kids and when can you take the time off?"

"Good questions. Let's get those ironed out and then we'll plan. But there is something I need to do first."

"What's that?"

"You'll see. Let's go home."

I grabbed his arm. "What are we going to tell Kinsley?"

"Nothing yet. But are you coming back to the house to live?"

"Yes. I still have a few things there anyway. I just need to pack what's at my parents."

"Let's get that now. I'm not in the mood to wait."

"You really are impatient, you know."

"So I've been told."

We went to my parents and while we were there, Dad and Grey disappeared while I went to my room to pack real fast. Mom came in to help and I relayed what was going on.

"Marin, you're sure about everything?"

"Yeah, Mom, I am."

"I knew you two would work things out. I'm so happy for you."

I didn't tell her everything. I decided to wait until the kids were told. That would only be fair.

Grey carried my bag out and we left. When we arrived at his house, his mom was one gigantic grin.

"Trish called, so I already knew. Thank God, you two finally came to your senses." Kinsley was in the other room, so she spoke freely. I only shrugged.

I'm glad to be back. I missed the kids so much. All of a sudden, a whirl of motion slammed into my legs.

"Marnie! I missed you!"

"I missed you too, short stuff."

We hugged for a good long time and then all decided to go out for spaghetti and meatballs.

"Aaron can get lasagna. It's mushy enough for him," Kinsley said.

"Yes, it is," I agreed.

Aaron was a solid red mess before dinner was over, but he didn't mind. He never minded when he was a mess. I was glad they invented baby wipes. I went through half a container.

"Paige, what did you do when your kids were little?"

"I didn't feed them lasagna," she laughed. "But I went through a lot of dirty bibs and towels. And diapers. We had disposables, but they weren't as good as what you have now. Well, when Hudson and Pearson were born they were, but not Grey. We used cloth ones for him."

"Ugh. How did you do that? That must've been a lot of work."

"Oh, it was. But I didn't know any different," she said. "He used to have to wear rubber pants over the diaper."

Kinsley thought that was so funny she wouldn't stop laughing. Then we all laughed too because the idea was so ludicrous.

"Daddy wore rubber panties." Her giggles were contagious.

"I bet that was a sight," Grey said.

After dinner, Grey suggested we all go get ice cream, but Aaron was asleep in his carrier, so Paige and Rick went and picked some up for us and brought it to the house while I put Aaron to bed. I was nuzzling his neck, inhaling his sweet baby scent when Grey walked in.

"You want two, huh?"

"Yeah. This kid is so precious. I never thought about having any until him. He melts my heart every time I look at him. And then I look at Kinsley and see how much fun they are at that age and I know I want them."

"I'll be happy to provide you with the means."

"I'll be happy to let you."

He kissed me and desire raged between us.

"Grey, we can't. Kinsley is downstairs and your parents."

"Right. Let's go."

When we got back downstairs, Grey looked at me and said, "I think we should tell Kinsley."

"Tonight?"

"No use waiting."

"What about our parents?"

"Kinsley should know first. She's the most important one, other than the two of us."

For some reason, I was suddenly nervous. What if she didn't want me as her step-mom. What if she threw a tantrum?

"What is it?"

"What if she resents me?"

"You don't honestly think that, do you?"

"I don't know what to think."

He took my hand and said, "Come with me."

She was watching TV and Grey said, "Hey, polka dot, Marin and I have something we need to talk to you about." He turned off the TV and she looked at us expectantly. "You know how I kiss Marin sometimes?"

Kinsley started kissing the air and laughing. "Like this?"

"Yes, like that. Well, we love each other very much and we want to get married."

"What does that mean?"

"It means that Marin will be my wife and I'll be her husband."

She scrunched up her mouth. "Is that like a mommy?"

"Not exactly. Your mommy is with the angels and will always be with the angels. But Marin will be my wife now. She'll be what's called a step-mommy, but you can still call her Marnie if you want."

"Can I call her Marniemom?"

"You can. Is that what you want to call her?"

Kinsley looked at me and laughed. "Yeah. I like that. Marniemom." Then she frowned again.

"What is it, honey?" Grey asked.

"Will Mommy get mad at me cuz I'm calling Marnie, Marniemom?"

Grey picked her up and sat down on the couch with her on his lap. "Mommy would never get mad at you for that. Remember, Mommy's an angel now and angels only want what's best for you."

"Really?" She was looking at me when she asked that.

I answered, "Your daddy is right. Angels look out for you and your mommy would never get mad at you for that."

"Then I'll call you Marniemom for now."

"That's a deal." And I high-fived her.

When Paige and Rick walked in the back door, Kinsley ran up to them and hollered, "I'm gonna have a Marniemom. I'm gonna have a Marniemom." Then she ran around in a circle.

"What on earth?" Paige asked.

"What she's saying is, we're going to get married," Grey said.

"Oh my gosh!" Paige set the bag of ice cream on the counter and rushed up to me to hug me. "Thank God! I prayed over this one."

"You sound like you never pray, Mom."

"You know what I mean, son. When's the wedding?"

"We haven't decided yet, but my parents don't know yet."

"Um, I sort of asked your father when we were there earlier tonight."

"You did?" I said, shocked. I didn't think he would ever do that.

"Of course I did. I didn't want our mothers chasing me down and killing me later."

That got a good laugh out of Paige.

"What did my dad say?" I asked.

"I won't be repeating that," Grey said. "But, Mom, we're eloping."

"Grey, you can't do that to Marin. She's never had a wedding nor has her mother. Every girl deserves a wedding. Trish will be devastated if you elope."

I hadn't given that a thought. One look at Grey and I could tell the decision was mine.

"Let's talk about this later," I said.

And we did. After the hottest sex I had in weeks and after coming several times.

"My mom was right. You deserve your special day. I won't take that away from you. In my heart, you're already mine, so I'll leave it up to you."

"Can I talk to my mom? I just don't want there to be any regrets."

Paige had been right after all. An elopement would kill Mom.

"Oh, honey. My only child eloping? At least consider a destination wedding."

"Okay, Mom. Let me talk with Grey. Or better yet, why don't you all come over and we'll talk about it? Then I don't feel like I'm going back and forth."

So, the following weekend, my parents, his, and the two of us had a chat. Everyone agreed to a small wedding. But then that turned into a guest list of over four hundred. In the end, we decided on a destination wedding.

Our destination was Paris, the city of love. We were to be married at the hotel Le Bristol with a reception to follow. The hotel was in the heart of Paris, just steps from the Champs-Elysées and the Louvre. It would take place in early October, only six weeks from now, which meant I was on overdrive in getting a dress. Kinsley was my only bridesmaid, and she would throw white rose petals as I walked down the short aisle.

The moms were planning everything for the wedding and reception, leaving Grey and I to handle the marriage licenses. We had our passports and everything necessary for travel from our trip to Vienna, so we were set. After the wedding weekend, our parents were taking the children off to Disneyland Paris and Grey and I would be honeymooning all over France for two luxurious weeks.

Mom and I were leaving the store after my final dress fitting, which I was happy to say was a smashing success. I walked out the door and crashed right into Damien and Dawn. Needless to say, all of us were equally stunned.

"Well, hello Marin. Are you still a nanny?" Dawn asked, snidely.

Mom, not waiting for my reply, jumped in to answer. "No, she isn't. She was just getting fitted for her wedding gown. We are all jetting off to Paris next week for the big event. Marin won't be working much anymore, Dawn.

What about you? Where are you working these days?" Mom, who was by no means a snob, looked down her nose at Dawn and I had to hold back a laugh.

"Paris? As in France?" Dawn asked.

"Yes, unless it's relocated to Italy," Mom answered. I snickered. "Marin is marrying a cardiologist."

Dawn's eyeballs almost rolled out. "Nice." She didn't mean it.

"Congratulations. I'm happy for you," Damien said.

"Thanks. Come on, Mom. We have lots of things we need to do before we leave."

"That's right, dear. You have to pick up your trousseau."

My trousseau. Oh my God, she really overdid with that. "Nice seeing you two." I wiggled my fingers as we left.

As we got further away, I said, "Mom. My trousseau? What the hell. Who even says that anymore?"

"I know. I couldn't help it. Those jerks deserved it. I had to rub it in." I could only shake my head.

The week arrived, our bags were packed, and all eight of us boarded the flight to Europe. This time, Grey and I held hands as we did, Aaron on Grey's back, Kinsley holding Paige's hand. We took up a chunk of the business class cabin, and the flight attendants were excited to hear we were traveling to Paris to get married.

"She's gonna be my Marniemom," Kinsley announced.

"She is?" one of them asked.

I had to explain the name thing. They brought out special gifts for the kids—coloring books, and since Aaron was too young, they gave him a stuffed animal. Kinsley wanted one too and they were happy to hand one over.

"Do you realize we haven't even known each other a year?" I asked Grey.

"I do. But when you know, you know. I'm not eighteen, or twenty. I know what I want in life, and it's you."

"I'm not even thirty. Tell me I shouldn't be scared."

He cupped my face and kissed me. "Don't ever be afraid. I have your heart in my hands and I'm the best when it comes to hearts."

"Daddy's kissing Marniemom," Kinsley announced.

"She's spying on us," I said.

Grey was frowning.

"What is it?" I asked.

"Do you have doubts about us?"

"I love you. So, the answer is no. I'm just insecure about the minimal amount of time we've spent together," I said.

"I'm not. At all."

"I keep thinking about my last relationship."

Grey took my hand. "And you told me that it was never good like what we have. Stop doubting yourself."

"I'm really insecure, aren't I?"

"Yes, and I can't figure it out. You have everything at your fingertips. And I'm going to give you the world. It's only begun, Marin. Just promise me we don't need to have this conversation again and that I'll see you walk down the aisle in five days."

"I promise."

And I kept that promise. When our wedding day dawned, all my hesitation vanished, and it was as though I had breathed fresh air into my lungs. My head had cleared and oddly, I felt like my life began that day. Marin McLain had been reborn.

Chapter Forty

GREYDON

THE WEDDING WAS TAKING place in one of the opulent ballrooms whose windows overlooked the Eiffel Tower. It was grand. The hotel had arranged an arbor we would stand beneath and it was adorned with a multitude of flowers that matched the ones in Marin's bouquet. We'd opted not to see each other before the wedding. I wanted my first look to be when she walked down the aisle on her father's arm.

When she did, I got the *wow* factor. Her gown was simple, off the shoulders, exposing their creamy flesh, going down to a deep V neck showing a good deal of her sexy cleavage. When she got close enough, her sparkling blue eyes lit up the room and my own nearly watered with unshed tears. She was radiant and stunning. Around her neck was a simple strand of pearls I had gifted her earlier that week, and she wore diamond studs in her ears. Her engagement ring sparkled; it was the one thing I had insisted upon. She balked, of course, but after hours at the jewelers, we finally settled on a two-carat solitaire. Today she would be getting two eternity bands to wear on either side. One was for our eternal love and the other was for the eternal love of our kids and our future children. She didn't know about that one and I would give it to her later tonight.

Our vows were traditional because we decided to follow along with *the sexy French version*, as Marin claimed. I laughed at her. "But they'll be in English," I had said.

"It doesn't matter. Whatever they say is sexy with that French accent. I'd rather hear them speak than me."

I'd give her anything she wanted, so I agreed.

The funny thing was, her eyes were glazed as she stared at me and I'm not quite sure she even heard the minister in his sexy French accent after all.

When he said I could kiss the bride, I took great pleasure in that. People cleared their throats, including him. Then he said, "And I thought we French were amorous." Turning to our guests, he announced, "I'd like to present to you Dr. and Mrs. Greydon West."

The room exploded in applause. Having a destination wedding, we didn't expect to have many guests. We were wrong. Over seventy-five people accepted. We were thrilled they wanted to join us in Paris to celebrate.

Josh and Ashley were some of the first to congratulate us afterward.

"Marin, your dress is out of this world," Ashley said, hugging my wife.

"Thank you."

"And what a place. This hotel." The women chatted while Josh congratulated me. My brothers were also there man-hugging me.

"Dude, you finally did it," Pearson said.

"What are you talking about? You're the perennial bachelor," I said. "He who will never be married."

"There's a reason for that. I'm an attorney. I see what happens in divorce court."

"You just have to pick the right one," I said.

"I'm proud of you, bro," Hudson said.

"Hey, there's hope for you. Look how I came to my senses." Hudson backed away, his hands raised. "I enjoy being the bachelor for now."

"You deserve the best, man, after everything you went through." Pearson and I hugged again.

"Thanks, Pearson. And when are you at least going to settle on dating the same girl more than once?"

Pearson wore a sheepish expression. "Who knows?" He was the womanizer in the family.

"Hey, I may have found Marin a therapy puppy," Hudson said.

"Yeah? Where?" I answered.

"There are some puppies at the local breeder near my office, but there's one that's showing a lot of promise."

"Thanks, man. Keep me updated on that."

The band struck up the wedding song and Marin and I came together for our dance. We'd chosen "I Won't Give Up" by Jason Mraz. After all, I had texted her the thing and annoyed her with it, but she confessed it was what swung her to my side after all. At the end, I kissed her honeyed lips. Then her dad took his turn. They'd chosen "Forever Young" by Rod Stewart. As they danced, my eyes sought out Kinsley and I knew it wouldn't be long before I'd be doing the same with her. A grin grew across my face as my heart warmed with those thoughts.

Marin was back by my side and then Kinsley ran up to us because we'd planned on a group dance. It was Justin Timberlake's "Can't Stop the Feeling. She loved the movie

Trolls, so that was a no-brainer. When it started playing, we pulled out the sunglasses I had stashed in my pockets and went to town.

"Marniemom, you have to hold your arms stiff, like this."

Oh, boy, the step dancing dictator was back. Marin played along but then I grabbed everyone's hands to save us all because no way in hell was I going to Irish step dance. We circled around and did all sorts of crazy moves. It distracted her enough so she didn't care anymore.

The hotel had arranged for a babysitter. We required a substantial number of references and did a complete check on her before we agreed. The hotel assured us they also did security checks on the sitters they hired, so we felt safe. I bought a portable camera to leave in the room, just in case. Every so often I'd check it to see how Aaron was doing. He seemed to be having fun with her, so I was good with that.

As the night progressed, I led my wife to the cake, where we did the required cutting. And then I whispered to her how I wanted to blow this joint.

"Can we?" she asked.

"Mrs. West, it's our wedding. We can do anything."

"Mrs. West, huh. I like the sound of that."

"Good, because it is your name now." And I quickly kissed her.

She laughed, saying, "We have to make an announcement."

"Then let's."

We pulled the wedding director aside. Since we weren't leaving the hotel, Marin had opted not to change into another outfit.

The announcement about us leaving was made and everyone gathered around, sending us off. Kinsley wanted to go to bed with us, which made us laugh.

"Marniemom, can I sleep with you and Daddy tonight."

Marin looked at me for an answer.

"Not tonight, polka dot. You're staying with Gammie and Bebop, remember?"

"Oh, yeah. Goodnight." She kissed us both, then scampered off. She was going to be exhausted and cranky tomorrow since she stayed up so late tonight.

When we got to the room, I couldn't wait to get Marin out of her dress. The dozen buttons in the back took longer than I wanted and her body shook as I tried to undo them.

"Hold still. You're making this harder."

"That's my goal."

"Huh?"

"To make it harder."

I spun her around and kissed her. "Do you want me to shred this gown to pieces?"

She bit down on her lips to keep from laughing. "No. But you're so funny, Grey, when you try to do things you find difficult."

"I'm trying to get you naked."

Her hand reached behind her and tried to grab my crotch.

"What are you doing?"

"I'm playing with you," she said.

"You're incorrigible."

"I know."

I finally got the last dreaded button undone and slid the blasted dress off her shoulders … and oh my … fuck me. She was wearing a cream-colored bustier with a matching thong that had dainty ribbons on the side.

"Are you trying to kill me, Marin?"

"No, but tell me. Was it worth the wait?"

"Every fucking button." I stared at her for what seemed like days. "You are every man's dream." My finger traced the top globes of her creamy breasts and then dipped down into the valley between them. "God, I don't think I've ever seen anything so beautiful." I kissed her neck then, breathing in her scent. "I want to gaze at you all night."

Her hands reached for me, unknotting my tie, then undoing my shirt buttons, one by one. Soft hands slid under the fabric and her heat warmed me to the bone. When her hand landed on my chest over my heart, I was sure she felt it pounding and the surging of my blood through my veins. Even though we'd had sex many times before, I felt like it was our first time.

My arms circled her and I undid the bustier and watched its slow fall to the floor. She was left standing in the sexy thong, which I intended to remove with my teeth.

Dropping my head, I took one nipple into my mouth and sucked until I heard her gasp with pleasure. I flicked my tongue across its rock-hard peak until her fingers sunk into my arms. Repeating this action on the other nipple, my fingers sought the place between her thighs that I knew she wanted me to touch. Sliding her thong to the side, I dipped my fingers inside her, only to find her dripping wet. Moving to her clit, I massaged her until she arched her back and moaned. She was so ready and so was I.

"I want to lick your pussy. I've been waiting for this all day."

Picking her up, I carried her to the bed and set her on the edge. Then I finished undressing. She watched me with eager eyes as I knelt before her. Taking one of the ribbons of her thong, I used my teeth to untie it. Then I did the same with the other.

Holding it up, I said, "I want you to buy a dozen of these. They were made for you." Then I tossed it aside.

I spread her lips apart with my thumbs and licked her from her opening to her clit. She was sitting up, leaning back on her elbows, watching me. My mouth moved to her inner thighs, sucking and nipping at them. I worked my way to the backs of her knees and up to her pussy again.

"What do you want me to do?"

"Exactly what you're doing," she said.

"This?" I slid a finger inside.

"Yes."

"And this?" My mouth landed on her mound and I sucked.

"Oh, yeah."

"And what about this?" My tongue circled her clit and flicked it.

"Yeah."

Then I pressed on her G-spot, and using my tongue, I massaged her clit.

"Oh, yeah." She buried her hands in my hair and her moans drove me on. I lifted my eyes and noticed she'd thrown back her head and was no longer watching me. It wouldn't be long. And it wasn't. Her inner muscles clamped down on my finger and a series of contractions hit. I loved it when she climaxed. She arched into my mouth and ground herself against me.

When her orgasm died down, I pushed her back farther onto the bed, put her legs over my shoulders, and found her entrance with my cock. Then I slowly pushed inside, rocking in and out at an achingly slow pace because I didn't want to come just yet. But it got to the point I couldn't hold back any longer.

"I'm going to come," I whispered. "Are you close?"

She barely spoke, only nodded that she was. And

then it happened, this crazy climax. She stopped breathing as I watched. Her hand squeezed mine and maybe I stopped breathing too. I don't know. It wasn't like anything I'd ever experienced. Her orgasm lasted a very long time.

"Wow," she said afterward.

"I think you just had a multiple orgasm."

"It was really weird."

I grinned. "Weird good or weird bad?"

"Weird good as in more like making love and not just sex." Her palm cupped my cheek. "Besides, anything sexual with you is good."

"I hope so."

"Grey. You should know that by now."

I kissed her. "Did I tell you how beautiful you are?"

"Yes. Did I thank you?"

"I don't know. Your sexiness put me in a daze." And it had.

She play punched me. "You're crazy."

I laughed along with her.

It registered then that I'd made love to my wife. *My wife. The love of my life.* It was hard to believe, yet it was real.

"What are you thinking? Your brow is furrowed." She took a finger and rubbed my forehead.

"I just made love to *my wife*. And I love how that sounds."

"Yeah, me too."

"Close your eyes." When they were closed, I reached into the nightstand and grabbed the box I'd put there earlier. Then I slipped on the other band I bought for her. "This is for the eternal love of the children we have and the ones we will have in the future."

Her eyes popped opened and she blinked several times. "Oh, Grey. It's beautiful. Thank you." The kiss was even more perfect than the ring. "It looks gorgeous with the diamond and the other band."

"I knew it would."

"I have something for you too." She got up and went to the bureau where she pulled out an envelope. Then she handed it to me as she got back in bed. "This is for you."

I opened it up and grinned. "The test results."

"Yes. But let me explain."

It was my turn to interrupt her. "Before you say anything, I need to give you something." I got out of bed and reached into the side pocket of my carry-on bag, where I'd stashed her journal. "This belongs to you. I didn't read it all, if you're wondering, but I did happen to see your last entry."

Her furrowed brow told me she didn't know what I was referring to. She flipped open her journal and I saw when it became clear. "You know?"

"Yeah, and I couldn't be sorrier than I already am."

"Every time I tried to tell you, you wouldn't let me get the words out, or something would interrupt us. I just forgot when Aaron was in the hospital and I sent it in much later than I originally said I would. But you were so angry with me, I couldn't explain it to you. You'd lost your trust in me and there wasn't any point in telling you then. Anyway, you are Aaron's biological father."

I took my wife's face between my hands and kissed her soundly on the lips. "You should probably kill me. We went through all that for nothing."

"I disagree. It taught us a lot about each other. You learned not to be so self-centered and I learned my assumption about you being an ass was true." She laughed. "But ... you came around eventually."

We laughed for a moment, but then I became serious. I slid my hands into her hair. "All the heartache. I am tremendously sorry. I never told you, but Susannah wasn't a warm person, nothing like you are. All those years we were together, I thought we were fine. I asked Hudson not too long ago if he thought she was a pompous bitch. He did but never said a word to me about it. I was a fool. God knows what she did to me behind my back and I was determined not to be made a fool again. So, when I thought you did that, it struck below the belt. Betrayal is a difficult thing to bear, you know? But I was so closed off, I didn't give you a chance."

"It is difficult. Especially when it comes from the people you put the utmost trust in. But I promise you, Grey, I won't ever betray you or your trust in me."

"I know that."

I grabbed her hand and said, "You are the solitary person I would trust with my life, with my children's lives. You are the love of my life … the one who took my life from ashes to flames. I was nothing but a charred-up wreck of a man when I met you, but you put the fire back into my heart. You're forever mine, Marin West."

The End

Epilogue

For The Secret Epilogue copy and paste this link into your browser: https://www.subscribepage.com/f0r1i5

Stalk A. M. Hargrove

If you would like to hear more about what's going on in my world, please subscribe to my mailing list on my website at http://bit.ly/29j74CX
You can also join my private group—Hargrove's Hangout — on Facebook if you're up to some crazy shenanigans! Please stalk me. I'll love you forever if you do. Seriously.

www.amhargrove.com
Twitter @amhargrove1
www.facebook.com/amhargroveauthor
www.facebook.com/anne.m.hargrove
www.goodreads.com/amhargrove1
Instagram: amhargroveauthor
Pinterest: amhargrove1
annie@amhargrove.com

For Other Books by A.M. Hargrove visit
www.amhargrove.com

From Ashes To Flames—

For The Love of English
For The Love of My Sexy Geek (The Vault)
A Special Obsession
Chasing Vivi
Craving Midnight
I'll Be Waiting (The Vault)
From Ashes to Flames
From Ice to Flames (Late July 2018)
From Smoke to Flames (October 2018)

Cruel and Beautiful
A Mess of a Man
One Wrong Choice
A Beautiful Sin

The Wilde Players Dirty Romance Series:
Sidelined
Fastball
Hooked

Worth Every Risk

The Edge Series:
Edge of Disaster
Shattered Edge
Kissing Fire

The Tragic Duet:
Tragically Flawed, Tragic 1
Tragic Desires, Tragic 2

The Hart Brothers Series:
Freeing Her, Book 1

Freeing Him, Book 2
Kestrel, Book 3
The Fall and Rise of Kade Hart

Sabin, A Seven Novel
The Guardians of Vesturon Series

Acknowledgments

I start with the readers because you make it all happen. Without you, there wouldn't be a book world. End. Of. Story. So THANK YOU with everything in my heart. I hope you loved Grey and Marnie! Grey was in bad shape but Marin had the fortitude to straighten him out. That's what women do, right? Look out for Hudson's story coming next—From Ice To Flames. I think you'll love this one. Thanks again for taking a chance on me—I love you all.

Terri E. Laine—my book wifey—there aren't enough words. Even though we act like an old married couple, I love you to the stars and back and you're vanilla to my chocolate. A day without you is a day without the sun.

Ashley, Heather, and Kristie. Oh, man, you guys killed it. Grey was an ass and you helped make him a much better ass, if there is such a thing. I love you ladies and wouldn't know what to do without your brutal honesty, your awesome critiquing, and your amazing help. THANK YOU!

Amy Jennings—you have brightened up my world and

enhanced my travel life. With or without RARE, I love you to pieces. Italy, here we come!

Harloe Rae—thank you for all your help and I know my questions were enough to drive you crazy but your patience was greatly appreciated. I hope to meet you someday and share some adult beverages.

Also, a HUGE thank you to Sejla and Selma Ibrahimpasic my amazing tour guides who showed our group around Vienna. They were the ones who introduced us to the catacombs beneath St. Stephen's cathedral, which was the inspiration for this story. And if you're wondering, they are definitely creepy.

Ellie McLove and Petra Gleason—thank you ladies for your mad editing skills. You make a fabulous team and I totally appreciate you!

Letitia Hasser at Romantic Book Affairs for the amazing cover. Every time I send you a photo, I'm always giddy when I get the cover back. Your talent is beyond words.

To all the bloggers and reviewers who made it happen with this book—you guys rock! Thank you so much for all your help!

One last word—I am so thrilled to be a part of the romance world. This amazingly talented group of writers, who lift each other up and offer each other assistance, are such a blessing. I cannot express this enough. It is simply overwhelming to be a part of this great group of women. Thank you to everyone!

About the Author

One day, on her way home from work as a sales manager, USA Today bestselling author, A. M. Hargrove, realized her life was on fast forward and if she didn't do something soon, it would be too late to write that work of fiction she had been dreaming of her whole life. So she made a quick decision to quit her job and reinvented herself as a Naughty and Nice Romance Author.

Annie fancies herself all of the following: Reader, Writer, Dark Chocolate Lover, Ice Cream Worshipper, Coffee Drinker (swears the coffee, chocolate, and ice cream should be added as part of the USDA food groups), Lover of Grey Goose (and an extra dirty martini), #WalterThePuppy Lover, and if you're ever around her for more than five minutes, you'll find out she's a non-stop talker. Other than loving writing about romance, she loves hanging out with her family and binge watching TV with her husband. You can find out more about her books www.amhargrove.com.

To keep up to date with my new releases subscribe to my newsletter here: http://amhargrove.com/mailing-list/

Made in the USA
Middletown, DE
21 November 2023

43213079R00229